APOCALYPSE Z THE WRATH OF THE JUST

APOCALYPSE Z SERIES

THE BEGINNING OF THE END

DARK DAYS

THE WRATH OF THE JUST

APOCALYPSE Z
THE WRATH OF THE JUST

MANEL LOUREIRO
TRANSLATED BY PAMELA CARMELL

amazon crossing

Apocalypse Z: The Wrath of the Just was first published in Spain by Dolmen as *La ira de los justos*. Translated from Spanish by Pamela Carmell. Published in English by AmazonCrossing in 2014.

Published by AmazonCrossing, Seattle

www.apub.com

Amazon, the Amazon logo, and AmazonCrossing are trademarks of Amazon.com, Inc., or its affiliates.

ISBN-13: 9781477818442
ISBN-10: 1477818448
Library of Congress Control Number: 2013919470

Cover design by Cyanotype Book Architects

1

When you set sail for Ithaca,
wish for your road to be long,
full of adventures, full of knowledge.
                           —Constantine Cavafy, "Ithaca"

Like so many things in life, that leg of the journey started by chance.

For a year and a half, nothing unusual happened on the Atlantic Ocean midway between America and Europe. A few whales and some trash floated by, but not a single ship or sailboat or column of smoke loomed on the horizon. Nothing. It had never been part of a major trade route, but the absence of humans was even more pronounced now. It was as if every human had disappeared off the face of the earth, leaving no one to give a thought to the unusual things happening there.

Over several days, the August sun heated up the water's surface by four or five degrees. Tons of water evaporated, then cooled and formed a dense layer of clouds. At the same time, the atmospheric pressure plummeted, causing the wind to move in giant, lazy circles and pick up speed.

Had a meteorologist been there (only about forty were still alive around the world, and they were too busy trying to survive to worry about isobars), he'd have said that a convective storm cell—a supercell—was brewing. But no one was monitoring the storm, so no one posted a warning. Meteorological satellites had gone dark or crashed into the atmosphere. Thirty hours later, no one witnessed the moment the supercell became a Category 5 hurricane headed for the coast of Africa.

And no one alerted the crew of a small sailboat, four hundred miles to the east, that all hell was about to break loose.

2

"What's for dinner?" Prit demanded to know as he stuck his head into the *Corinth II*'s cabin.

"Guess," I said with a wry smile and turned toward the voice.

My old comrade Viktor Pritchenko was short, wiry, and in good shape for a guy nearly forty. His piercing blue eyes watched me from the cabin door as the wind tore through his long blond hair. The sun had tanned the Ukrainian a deep copper and bleached his mustache the color of straw.

"Let me guess—fish. Again." Prit groaned. "I'm sick of fish!"

"Me too, but we're sailing through a good fishing area and we have to take advantage of it. Who knows when we'll we reach land or what we'll find to eat when we get there. Besides, our supplies are for emergencies."

I could tell my old pal was mentally licking clean the cans of food stored in the cabin there. He groaned again and let out a string of Ukrainian curse words. As he started back up the steps, a large ball of orange fur bounded over him and sent him reeling backward. He cursed louder and grabbed for my cat, who by then was watching him from the top bunk, his tail twitching. But it took a lot more than that to make Prit lose his cool.

"Control your damn cat or, I swear to God, I'll throw him overboard!" he said with a half smile.

"I don't believe you." I didn't look up from the mackerel I was cleaning. "Deep down, you're really fond of him. Besides, he's not my cat; Lucullus thinks we belong to him."

As if agreeing with me, Lucullus let out a long, loud meow and then jumped off the bunk and swaggered toward me in his feline way, waiting for some fish guts to land in his bowl. Pritchenko shook his head and went back on deck, leaving me alone with my thoughts.

I looked at my calloused hands covered in fish scales and laughed bitterly. A year and a half ago, my life was completely different. I was a respected lawyer living in Pontevedra, in northwest Spain. I had a family, friends, and a cushy, very middle-class life. I was tall, thin, and handsome (some said), with a great future ahead of me. The shining offspring of baby boomers. Born with a flower up my ass, as my family used to say.

But my little world had had its downsides too. Not long before the pandemic, my wife died in a traffic accident. I slid into a black hole of depression and almost didn't climb out. Despair and guilt had me in a choke hold. *Why'd I let her drive on such a stormy night?* I almost turned my back on my job, my friends, and my family. Those months were an alcohol-soaked blur. Looking down the barrel of a shotgun sounded like a good idea. It'd be easy, fast, and, if I did it right, painless.

Then Lucullus came along. Worried about my descent into a personal hell, my sister gave me an orange Persian kitten. *What the hell happened to my sister? Where the hell could she be?* Surprisingly, her gift did the trick. Taking care of that kitten helped me get over my self-pity and move on.

Then at Christmastime a year and a half ago, the hell unleashed in Dagestan dwarfed everyone's petty problems. Like most people in the West, I'd never heard of the former Soviet republic deep in the Caucasus Mountains in central Asia. The tiny country's ministry of tourism should get a fucking prize—posthumously, of course. For two weeks, while the planet still had media, that little republic was all anyone talked about.

Anyone still alive knows the story all too well. A group of extremist lunatics from neighboring Chechnya got it into their heads to steal some Soviet-era weapons for their jihad. They successfully broke into a munitions compound, but all they got was worthless shit. Instead of AK-47s, grenades, RPGs, and ammunition, they found a nearly forgotten Cold War–vintage laboratory, guarded by a dozen soldiers. All it contained were test tubes, flasks, and some high-security freezers plastered with warning labels in Cyrillic. In frustration, the pissed-off Chechen leader ordered his men to trash the place, including the freezers.

That was the stupidest—and the last—order he gave. Less than fifteen minutes later, he and his men were infected with the TSJ virus that had been waiting quietly for over twenty years in a flask inside that freezer. Just forty-eight hours later, the virus had spread throughout Dagestan; in just two weeks, it was racing out of control across the globe. By then the guerrilla leader was dead—or rather undead—unaware that he'd unleashed the Apocalypse. Humanity was wiped off the map all because a band of wannabe jihadists couldn't read the warning labels on a freezer.

As the TSJ virus swept throughout the world, things happened fast. The little virus proved to be the worst kind of bastard. It was extremely contagious and lethal, plus it was genetically programmed to keep spreading even after it destroyed its host.

TSJ's creator was one of the top virologists in the Soviet Union, but he'd been dead and forgotten for a couple of decades. He'd had a brilliant career as a bioengineer; the TSJ virus was the apex of his scientific legacy. After he died fleeing to the West through West Berlin, the project was purged and all his experiments were stored away in freezers, pending a reevaluation. Because of the heavy-handed Soviet bureaucracy and, later, the fall of the USSR, his work was forgotten. Until that fatal day.

Dying of the TSJ virus was a hard way to go. First its victims languished in terrible pain, with violent convulsions similar to Ebola; hours later, they arose like murderous sleepwalkers. After they were clinically dead, they attacked every living thing that crossed their path. The Undead, the press started to call them . . . until the press ceased to exist. Most of the journalists succumbed to the infection too.

It all seemed like a nightmare. Before I could process it all, my country was swept up in the evacuation efforts taking place worldwide. Social structures fractured and chaos spread like wildfire. Telecommunications shut down, then the government. Three weeks after the infection reached Spain, the world order disintegrated. Of the billions of people who'd inhabited the planet a month earlier, only a few thousand had survived and they were dashing helter-skelter, trying to stay alive, surrounded by a sea of Undead. The creatures weren't smart, but they were unrelenting and their numbers were overwhelming. We survivors had only one choice. Run.

I dropped the gutted fish into a bucket of saltwater and set its guts in Lucullus's bowl. He watched me with feline intensity, as if to ask what the hell was taking so long.

"Here you go, your majesty." I stroked his back as he pounced on the fish guts. "It's not Whiskas, but at least you won't starve, buddy."

Lucullus chewed noisily, smacking and purring, and a wave of nausea washed over me. I leaned against a doorframe until the feeling passed. I'd seen too many people die terrible deaths over the last year and a half. Sometimes ordinary things, like watching a cat eat fish guts, turned my stomach. Before the Apocalypse, the closest I'd gotten to death was buying steaks at the supermarket.

Lucullus looked up from his bowl and stared at me, apparently surprised to see me slumped against the wall. He made a typical cat comment and went back to eating.

I picked my way through the small cabin and into the head, where I splashed my face several times. We hadn't had time to stock up on fresh water before we sailed, so we had to severely ration what little we had. We stored water right out of the ocean in the tank in the head, and used it for bathing. Washing with saltwater made our hair frizzy and our clothes stiff, and the salt would corrode the boat's pipes in a few months, but I didn't expect to be on the boat that long.

I studied myself in the chipped mirror above the sink. A sharp-featured, deeply tanned man with a thick mop of black hair looked back at me. His eyes were sunken and bloodshot from stress and lack of sleep.

My life had been an odyssey from the moment the pandemic forced me out of my home. First I'd sailed to the nearby city of Vigo, headed for the largest Safe Haven in Galicia, only to discover that the city was devastated. After a series of adventures among the charred ruins of the city, I became fast friends with Viktor Pritchenko, a Ukrainian helicopter pilot who'd fought forest fires in that part of Spain. The catastrophe had stranded him there, thousands of miles from his family and home.

Prit and I had been inseparable ever since and had saved each other's lives many times. We first teamed up to flee from Vigo and the hordes of Undead there. Then we made a nerve-racking flight in his helicopter to Tenerife in the Canary Islands.

But our hopes for restarting our lives there were dashed when we discovered that the islands had become a huge refugee camp for survivors from around the world. Everything was strictly rationed and a repressive military ruled. When civil war broke out, our lives were in danger, so we set sail down the African coast headed for the Cape Verde Islands, not too far away. Before the Apocalypse, they'd been sparsely populated and isolated. We were hopeful that the virus hadn't spread there.

And then there was Lucia.

I walked out of the head and inched between the central table and the base of the mast. The cabin door was standing ajar. I stuck my head in, trying not to make any noise. Lucia was lying on the bed, fast asleep and wearing a pink-flowered bikini she'd found stuffed in a drawer on the boat. One arm hung limply over the side of the bed. She clutched an old issue of a fashion magazine; it, along with a navigation manual and a sports magazine, comprised the entire onboard library.

Lucia joined our little group several days after Prit and I met. She was only sixteen when she got separated from her family during the chaotic evacuation of her hometown. Lost and scared, she and Sister Cecilia, a nun and trained nurse, took refuge for a year in the basement of a hospital—all alone—until Prit and I stumbled upon them. Before Lucia and I could stop it, we were deeply in love, despite the ten-year difference in our ages.

The world had changed drastically. Most of those changes added up to a pile of shit the size of an aircraft carrier, but I was grateful I'd met Lucia, I thought with a half smile.

With all the chaos, death, and devastation in the world, some things hadn't changed. People were still violent, selfish, and dangerous. Some became murderers if the situation called for it. But people still laughed, sang, dreamed, and cried—and even fell in love. How could they help it if they met a woman like Lucia?

Eighteen now, Lucia was tall and slender with legs that went on forever, black hair, high cheekbones, and bright-green eyes. She had a sensual beauty that could stop traffic. I'm sure that before the Apocalypse, every man who saw her did a double take. She reminded me of a panther, especially when she stretched lazily, like she was doing just then.

I didn't want to startle her, so I gently kissed her hair. Lucia moaned in her sleep and turned, opening her eyes just a slit.

She asked in a sleepy voice, "Is it my turn to take the watch already?"

"No, honey," I whispered as I ran my hands along her long legs.

Lucia had slept only four hours since she'd taken the night watch. We'd all agreed to stand watch the same number of hours, but Prit and I knew that Lucia was at the limit of her endurance, so we tried to spare her a couple of hours when we could. She wasn't stupid; she knew what we were doing. Exhaustion was taking its toll on everyone, but Prit and I had more stamina. For the moment, anyway.

"Go back to sleep. It's still three hours before it's your turn again."

"Why do you smell so fishy?" She wrinkled her nose.

"Guess what's on today's menu." I'd washed my hands, but they still smelled, so I stuck them under the quilt.

"Yuck!" Lucia covered her head with the pillow.

Just then a wave struck the hull and the boat lurched. If the sea was getting rough, I needed to finish fixing dinner and then go help Prit tie down loose lines.

"Well," I continued, faking nonchalance, "I was torn between beef Wellington with a port wine reduction and roasted potatoes or a plain mackerel with no sides. I know deep down, you and Prit have simple tastes, so I decided on the lighter menu."

"Shut up or I'll shut you up!" she said as she linked her hands behind my neck and stared at me with her big green eyes.

When the boat lurched again, I lost my balance and fell on top of her. Her breasts pressed against my bare chest and her kiss seemed to go on forever. The temperature in the cabin shot up several degrees.

"Maybe we should have dessert first," I whispered in her ear, as I slid my hand toward the knot in her bikini top.

She arched her back as I nibbled her neck. The sea surged again, shaking the *Corinth II* so violently that we rolled against the bulkhead. My back hit a sharp corner and knocked the wind out of me, proving the old maritime adage that you always hit the part of your body that will hurt the most.

"You OK?" Lucia asked, trying to stifle her laughter.

"What the hell's Prit doing up there?" I grumbled as I rubbed my back. It felt like someone had hit me with an ax.

The Ukrainian's urgent voice broke in. "Get up here! Now! You gotta see this!"

I jumped off the bed and shot through the hatch. As I crossed the galley, I noticed that the bucket of fish had fallen. Lucullus was stalking the gutted mackerel that skidded across the floor each time the boat pitched and rolled. I decided I'd rescue our dinner later and rushed up the stairs onto the deck.

What I saw left me speechless. When I'd caught the mackerel two hours before, the sky had been crystal clear, as it had been every day since we left Tenerife. Now it was an eerily white mosaic.

Clouds shredded apart, clumped together, then wildly broke apart again. The sea had been calm, but now whitecaps the size of rams broke against the sides of the boat.

When I faced the other direction, into the wind, the blood drained from my face. Across the horizon as far as I could see stretched a black wall; flashes of lightning lit up the dark sky every few seconds. It was a monster storm.

I slid across the cockpit past the wheel and looked at the barometer. The mercury was incredibly low, and it kept falling as I watched.

I gulped, wishing it were a nightmare. I never thought I'd witness a barometric crash—especially hundreds of miles from the nearest port, in an old sailboat with beaten-up rigging.

"What the hell is that, Cap'n?"

My Master's certificate made me a seasoned sailor in Prit's eyes. He didn't care that the license only authorized me to pilot small vessels, or that I'd never been more than a few miles from shore.

"Not sure, Prit," I said as I turned and hastily started furling the jib. "If it's what I think it is, we have a big problem on our hands."

"How big?" the Ukrainian asked as he helped me shorten sail.

"Prit, this is serious."

Lucia peered out through the hatch wide-eyed, watching the wall of clouds race toward us.

"We could be dead in a couple of hours," I said quietly.

3

Had that supercell blown in when the world was still inhabited, the Hurricane Center would've tracked every moment of it. Someone would have consulted the Center's list of names and baptized it. Having a name made it easier to track and allowed news reporters to add drama when the hurricane made landfall, as if it were an erratic, destructive, evil person rather than a low-pressure center. But no one was around to do any of that. So let's call it Edna. Not a bad name.

When Edna finally touched down at Casablanca, nobody witnessed the devastation of that city or how Edna leveled what little was still standing and buried thousands of Undead in the ruins. And no one witnessed the fury she unleashed two hundred miles offshore. No one but three people.

4

"Watch out, Prit!" I shouted as a wave the size of a two-story building crashed into the *Corinth II*'s battered hull. The rigging moaned and the mast bent dangerously to starboard. The cabin was completely submerged. I was sure the boat would capsize.

I wiped the saltwater out of my eyes and tried to make out the bow. Two seconds before, the Ukrainian had been there, struggling with the foresail as it flogged in the wind. As blasts of water sprayed in all directions, I finally spotted Pritchenko. He was wrapped in a rain slicker, clinging to a lifeline, coughing and gasping like a drowning dog. He'd been hurled against the mast, but his life jacket had cushioned the blow. If the water had dragged him a foot on either side of the mast, he'd have been tossed overboard.

"You OK, Prit? Answer me, dammit!" I cupped my hands to project my voice, but although he was just ten feet away, the wind was howling so loud he couldn't hear me. He must've guessed my question, and he gave me a thumbs-up.

The hurricane whipped us around mercilessly. We nearly drowned a dozen times. Even brand-new right out of the shipyard, the sailboat wasn't built to withstand wind gusts that strong, but the *Corinth II* rode the monster waves admirably.

Two hours into the storm, the halyard that held up the jib broke with a shriek and flew off like a flapping witch's cape. After that, we battled the storm with just a ragged piece of mainsail left, trying to stay ahead of waves that threatened to swallow us. My arms were stiff from gripping the wheel for so long. Our only chance for survival was to steer with the wind and waves directly astern.

Each time one of those monsters broke over the deck, the boat slowly climbed the curved surface of that wave, topped by swirling, dirty foam. There, the wind pounded the entire hull, sending the boat racing to the crest. Then thousands of tons of water, moving at top speed, thundered as the boat rushed down the other side, its bow pointing into the hollow between two giant waves. When it reached the bottom, it was held tight between two giant waves, and, for a few seconds, the wind stopped blowing. Then the next wave lifted the *Corinth II*, and the cycle started all over again. It lasted for hours.

I could see only one way this could end—a treacherous wave would turn the boat a few degrees to port or starboard and point the boat straight down into the hollow. When the next wave struck, the boat would capsize.

An ominous creaking shook me out of my gloomy thoughts. A small crack the width of a pencil appeared along the mast. It hadn't been there a second before. Every time the boat reached the top of a wave, the crack got longer and wider. The mast could last only a couple minutes before it broke completely.

"Prit! Prit!" I yelled, flapping my arms and pointing to the mast. "Cut all lines and rigging!"

At first the Ukrainian looked confused; then the gravity of the situation hit him. If the mast was still tied to the boat by the braided steel shrouds when it broke and fell overboard, it would drag all the rigging with it and form a giant sea anchor. The *Corinth II* would lose all maneuverability, and we'd drown in seconds.

Prit wasn't a born sailor, but he was a fast learner. His quick reflexes had kept him alive through all the madness while billions of people died. He grabbed the nearest sail and, with his rigging knife, attacked the sheets and halyards that attached the sail to the spar, then struggled to release the steel cables. The veins in his neck bulged as he levered the knife blade. Even in the gusting wind, I could hear the growl he let out when the end of his knife broke off.

"It's no use!" he shouted, waving his broken knife. "I can't get the damn thing loose!"

I froze. We were dead. Totally fucking dead.

A fist hit me in the back. Still gripping the wheel, I turned and saw Lucia. She'd come on deck, wearing a life jacket, like we were, but no rain slicker. Rain and waves had drenched her in seconds, but that hadn't fazed her. Her eyes glowed with a fierce determination to stay alive.

"Try this!" she shouted in my ear as she held out a long heavy object.

I grabbed hold of it as best I could. It was one of the HK assault rifles on board. It would be hard to pull this off, but I didn't have any better ideas.

"You'll have to do it! I have to keep us on course! You shoot out the backstay, then pass the rifle to Prit so he can do the same at the bow!" I coughed as I swallowed mouthful after mouthful of saltwater as the boat's cockpit flooded.

Lucia nodded and steadied her right arm on the rail, above the wheel. The wind whipped straight into her face, driving rain and saltwater into her eyes.

"Stay calm, honey, stay calm," I muttered, more to myself than to her.

We were at the top of a huge wave when alarming sounds came from the mast. Pieces of carbon fiber peeled off lengthwise, leaving a hole in the mast as wide as my finger. The rigging howled and threatened to collapse. The sailboat heeled sharply as it rode the crest of the wave. With a roar, it rushed down the slope in a waterfall of foam.

For a couple of seconds, the wind stopped. The *Corinth II* was protected in the thirty-foot-high gap between two huge waves. All was surreally calm. I could plainly hear the raindrops falling onto the deck. That lull was what Lucia had been waiting for. She calmly slung the HK over her shoulder, aimed at the mount holding the backstay to the hull, and pulled the trigger.

The HK sprang to life in Lucia's hands, though she could hardly control its powerful recoil. A string of holes appeared in the rear deck and pieces of teak, fiberglass, and hot metal rained down on us. Two of the bullets hit the spot where the stay was attached to the hull. When the bullets tore into the steel cable, drawn taut by the enormous power of the wind in the sail, it snapped like a twig and unraveled before our eyes.

"Look out!" I let go of the wheel and shoved Lucia to the ground. I fell on her as the cable split apart over my back with a snap and the pieces lashed out like whips.

The torn end of the backstay flew past the spot where Lucia's head had been seconds before and crashed against the porthole, sending huge teak splinters and broken glass flying, and breaking the cabin door. The cable rose in the air, shaking like an angry cobra, and crossed to the other side of the mast, where it tore off part of the storm sail we'd hoisted up. Then I realized Pritchenko wouldn't need to cut the forestay. The hurricane had solved that problem for us.

As the boat perched sideways on the crest of a wave, an enormous gust hit us and we witnessed a sight few sailors have seen and lived to tell about. The mast of the *Corinth II*, weakened after hours in the storm, finally surrendered. With a crunch that set my teeth on edge, the crack gaped wide like a dark mouth and burst, splattering the deck with carbon-fiber pieces. The mast rose into the air, sucked up by the hurricane. The bow mast hung in the air for a few seconds, tied to it by the other shroud, like a strange X made by a crazed carpenter. With a jolt, the other shroud ripped, amid the swirling rain, and the mast fell into two gigantic waves that passed us on the right. We were safe by a hair. But the situation was still grim.

"Better get inside!" I howled over the wind. "There's nothing more we can do up here!"

"Like hell!" Pritchenko snapped as he helped me to my feet. "If I'm gonna drown, I wanna be outside—not entombed in this tub."

"Prit . . ." I clenched my fists. The Ukrainian could be very stubborn. "Get the hell down there. It's too dangerous to be on deck!"

"I'm not moving from this spot!"

"Get   down   there,   you   stubborn   Russky!"

"I said no! And I'm Ukrainian, not Russian!"

Lucia, who had retreated below, poked her head through the shattered cabin door. The look on her face told us something was wrong.

"There's two inches of water in the cabin," she said, trying to control the fear in her voice. "We're sinking."

That's just what we need, I thought. The old hull must've developed a hairline crack after years of neglect and exposure to the sun. And a little bubble of air hidden in the hull must've broken through the fiberglass. During the storm, that crack had grown without warning. Water was leaking in below the water-line. I didn't know how fast, but in minutes, hours, or days—*if you were a real sailor, you could figure that out, asshole*—the boat was done for.

A sailboat with no mast and a leak who-knew-how-big in the worst storm I'd ever seen. Fabulous. Fucking great. I didn't need the Undead to drag me to my death. I could do it without their help. And take everyone with me.

"Is it true?" Prit asked, with a chill in his voice. "We're sinking?"

"No," I lied. "Water must've leaked in through a broken porthole. Just to be safe, get the extra bilge pump."

"I'll get it," Lucia said.

I grabbed my girl's hands for a second. I saw fear in her eyes, but also a deep serenity born out of so much suffering over all those months. If we were going to die, Lucia would calmly stare Death in the eye—and spit in its face too.

I knew I had to tell Prit the truth. The Ukrainian needed to know that the boat could sink at any minute. But my old pal had figured it out from the look in my eyes.

"We're screwed, right?"

I didn't answer. My gaze was glued to the horizon, at the ter-rifying spot where water and sky indistinguishably meshed. I'd lost track of time, but it must've been almost midnight. Bursts of foam and black waves made it hard to see anything. The boat was bouncing around so much that I couldn't fix my eyes on one point. But, for one moment, I thought I saw something not too far away. I rubbed my eyes and tried to spot it again. After a moment, as the *Corinth II* rode another wave to towering heights, I saw it again. I had no doubt.

Less than half a nautical mile downwind, I saw a green light.

5

I took a few deep breaths to calm my wildly beating heart. That green light could mean just one thing.

"What is it?" Prit asked. "You look like you've seen a ghost!"

"What do you see out there?" I pointed to the spot on the horizon. "Do you see a flashing green light?"

"What the hell are you talking about?

"Wait . . . There! See it?"

"I'll be damned! It *is* a light! Where the hell's it coming from?"

"It's gotta be the signal from a ship!" I said. I could barely contain my excitement. "And judging from how high up it is, the ship's huge."

"How huge?"

"Can't say for sure, but a lot bigger than our puny sailboat." I tried to turn the wheel, but it barely moved.

"What do we do?" Lucia blurted out. I sensed hope in her voice. She'd come back on deck with a wet and angry Lucullus in her arms.

"For now, hope our boat keeps moving toward the light. When we get closer, we'll send up a flare. Then we have to find a way to get off this wreck and onto the ship without drowning."

"We don't know who's on it," Pritchenko observed grimly. "Could be a patrol from Tenerife sent to arrest us. Or a boat full of Undead, adrift for months."

"A boat full of Undead would've run aground a long time ago," I replied as I tried to steer the *Corinth II* toward the light. "At this point, I'd climb back aboard that Russian tub, the *Zaren Kibish*, even with its crew of armed lunatics."

The Ukrainian nodded with a wry smile. He knew our situation was desperate. Reaching the mysterious ship was our only hope.

The next five minutes seemed like an eternity. Each time we crested a wave, our eyes scanned the horizon for the light, but in that short time we'd lost track of it.

I briefly toyed with the idea that we'd been hallucinating. Then a more chilling thought popped into my head. If that gale had blown us just thirty feet from the mystery ship, we'd never see it. If we saw the red light on the ship's port side, we'd know we'd passed right by. In that wind and with no mast, turning around was out of the question.

Suddenly, a huge wave struck the side of the boat, sending freezing black water over the deck. The boat lingered a moment at the top of the next wave, but when it started down the other side, it spun sharply. We were going to capsize.

"Get ready to jump!" I shouted, my throat raw from saltwater and yelling.

Suddenly, the spinning stopped. The boat was at the bottom of the trough between two waves. The huge crest had swept us farther away, across the horizon. The next giant wave came roaring toward us. The wheel spun wildly and the boat rocked from side to side. Then the wind died down as if by magic.

"What the hell?" Prit asked.

"Not sure, but I think we're in the eye of the hurricane."

"Look!" The fear in Lucia's voice made my heart clench. When I looked where she was pointing, I was stunned.

Fifty feet away, the huge bow of a tanker blocked out the black sky. It was headed full speed right for the *Corinth II*'s fragile hull.

"They'll roll right over us!"

There was nothing we could do. Our boat was adrift. The rudder was probably gone, the auxiliary engine was out of fuel, and we had no time to maneuver. The behemoth tanker couldn't see its bow from its bridge, much less a little sailboat in its path. They'd never spot us; in the storm, we were invisible to radar.

The giant's keel parted the sea in crests like foam-covered murky-green mountains. One of them rolled into the *Corinth II*'s battered hull and shook her like a twig in a stream. We were so close to the tanker that we could see the rivets, dents, and weld marks on its hull. As the tanker bore down on us, the wall of water the tanker pushed forward, along with a gust of wind, turned our boat with excruciating slowness and saved us from being crushed.

We still had a chance, but we had to act fast. I turned to Prit, who stared, slack-jawed, as the massive vessel passed no more than five feet from us.

"Prit, find the flare gun and send up a flare!"

The Ukrainian snapped out of his stupor and held up the gun he'd brought with him from the cabin. He raised it over his head and pulled the trigger. The flare shot out with a hiss and exploded, bathing the entire scene in bright red light.

As the flare drifted down, tied to its parachute, I leapt into the cabin. The once-cozy cabin was now in shambles, flooded with cold, ankle-deep water. Oil, food, navigational charts, and papers sloshed around. I was pretty sure I knew where the leak was, but there was no way to fix it. In one corner of the room, Lucia clutched the cat, looking at me expectantly.

"How do you propose we get on that thing?" she asked in an astonishingly calm voice.

"Don't know yet, but first we have to keep them from leaving without us."

I grabbed one of our two spearguns and slung it across my back. Ignoring Lucia's incredulous look, I dug around in the locker for the strongest sail. After I'd found it, I looked for its line and tied it to the end of the spear. It was crude, but it might work.

"What's that?"

"A guide wire, or something like it," I yelled as I rushed back on deck.

By then the tanker had advanced nearly half its length. Rising as high as an eight-story building, it sheltered the sailboat from the wind and waves that pounded its other side. I watched stunned as the *Corinth II* bobbed gently in that small oasis of calm, still lit by the red flare. A few feet away, at the edge of the flare's light, the protective barrier created by the tanker ended and the sea rose up furiously.

We only had one chance. I aimed the speargun up toward the deck of the tanker, nearly invisible in the black night. I did some quick calculations. It was the most powerful speargun available, but it had to travel a very long, very steep distance. Add to that the weight of the rope and . . .

Fuck it! Take a deep breath, and shoot! The annoying voice in my head nagged me. *If you don't hook this tanker, you're dead.*

Their propellers will suck you under and make mincemeat out of you. If not, the storm will finish you off. This is your only chance.

"Shut the fuck up, smart-ass!" I muttered, clenching my jaw.

I shook off my doubts and fired. The spear flew out with a snap. The cable tied to it uncoiled at full speed. I counted in my head—fifteen feet, thirty, fifty . . . At seventy-five feet, it stopped dead. Trembling, I grabbed one end and tugged gently. Then I tugged harder, but the cable still didn't give. We'd hooked onto the tanker.

The sailboat's winch, where the line was attached, groaned as we were dragged forward—but it held. The *Corinth II* had latched on like a remora to a whale and was moving alongside the huge ship. Inertia propelled our boat against the tanker's hull, each blow tearing off sheets of carbon fiber and jarring us all to our bones.

Sudden beams of light danced on the sailboat's deck as several flashlights found us. At that distance, we couldn't hear what the crew was saying, but they had to be asking themselves who the hell we were and how the hell we'd gotten there. After a few long minutes, they unwound a boarding net down the side of the tanker. It must've taken a titanic effort to haul that heavy net across their deck as the storm whipped around at full force. Whoever they were, they were determined to help us climb aboard.

"Come on, before they change their minds!" Prit shouted.

The Ukrainian grabbed hold of the net and scrambled up as agile as a monkey. Lucia settled Lucullus into my arms, gave me an excited kiss, and followed Pritchenko up the net. I stood on the deck of the sailboat with a knot in my stomach. The last time I'd boarded an unknown ship was in Vigo. That experience had not gone well. I hoped that, this time, there wouldn't be anyone pointing a gun at me when I reached the deck. I tucked Lucullus into my slicker and cinched it tight. He squirmed around inside the improvised bag, then stuck his head out the neck hole.

With a last backward glance, I started up the net, wrapped in the smell of wet fur. I realized we'd left all our gear on the sailboat. Of course, scaling the net like Spider-Man, I couldn't have carried much anyway.

When I reached the tanker's deck, several things happened. First, the wind hit me so hard that I nearly pirouetted backward in a fall that would've been fatal. Second, a pair of strong arms grabbed me and pulled me on board, while others threw a blanket over my shoulders. Third, and most surprising, an elegantly dressed, Nordic-looking officer with a dazzling smile and pearly white teeth walked up to me and held out his hand.

"You are the strangest fish we've ever caught, I can assure you," he said in very proper English, with an accent I couldn't place. "Allow me to welcome you aboard."

"What's the name of this ship? Where are we?"

The officer's gesture swept the entire tanker as the curtain of rain soaked us. "Welcome to the *Ithaca*."

6

Edna made landfall south of Morocco, then quickly weakened. Twenty-four hours later, her violent winds were gentle breezes. After dumping gallons and gallons of rain on the ocean, the clouds were wispy and no longer menacing. The August sun beat down on the African coast once again. By the time Edna passed through the Strait of Gibraltar and drifted onward to the Mediterranean Sea, she was just a harmless rainstorm. But we saw none of that.

The moment I woke up, I instinctively felt around for my HK. When it wasn't next to my bed where I always kept it, I panicked. Then the fog in my head cleared, and I remembered it was back on the sailboat—probably at the bottom of the ocean.

I realized that I was in an unfamiliar cabin. Sunshine streamed in through an open porthole and glinted off the light-blue walls. I bolted upright and regretted it instantly, as every muscle in my arms and back exploded in pain. Even the muscles in my neck cramped. I was so stiff I struggled just to reach the bottle of water on the nightstand.

I gulped down the entire bottle in seconds, belched, and then took a better look at the cabin. It was a simple room, about ten feet square, with a small closet next to the door. Another bed stretched along the wall across from mine. The warm sunlight coming through the porthole meant the storm must have passed. That answered my first question.

Judging by what I could see of the sky, I must've slept for over twelve hours. That was no surprise, considering how exhausted we were when we boarded the tanker. I vaguely remembered two burly sailors in jumpsuits whisking me off to this room and Lucia helping me get undressed and into bed before she collapsed onto a mattress on the floor. That answered my other question. Lucia was still right there, sleeping peacefully; next to her was Lucullus, sprawled on a pillow, dead to the world.

I didn't have to wonder where Prit was. The Ukrainian was snoring loudly on the bed across the room. I had a hazy memory of him, exhausted like the rest of us, refusing to go to bed until he was sure Lucia and I were warm, dry, and in no danger. Our blond guardian angel.

I winced as I stood up and stepped over Lucia, trying not to wake her. The throbbing pain was almost more than I could bear, but my curiosity prevailed. Hanging in the closet were three yellow jumpsuits like those the crew wore. I saw no sign of my clothes, so I put one of them on; it fit perfectly. I also found three pairs of boots in roughly our sizes. In clean clothes and dry boots, I tiptoed to the door. Lucullus opened his eyes and watched me for a moment. He must've decided that following me wasn't worth interrupting his peaceful sleep, so he curled up again.

When I reached the door, I cursed under my breath. We were probably locked in. If they were smart, they'd keep us under quarantine until they were sure we weren't carriers of that demon virus. These people looked like they knew what they were doing, and they had to be prudent to have survived this long. But I gave the knob a turn anyway. The latch clicked softly and the door swung open.

I stuck my head out and was surprised to see a well-lit, immaculate hallway stretching out before me. Pipes of all colors, shapes, and sizes snaked along the ceiling as far as I could see. Every few feet, there were doors like ours, presumably to other cabins. The only sound was a low hum coming from air-conditioning vents. Except for the reinforced metal doors and bare floors, it could've been a hotel.

As I crept down the corridor, an uneasy feeling gripped me. Something wasn't right. There were no locks or short-tempered guards brandishing rifles. This was too good to be true. I was on alert, braced for anything. Just then a door flew open and out came a waiter pushing a cart. I yelled so loud we both nearly had a heart attack.

"Who are you? Where is everyone?" I stammered. My heart felt like it would jump out my mouth.

"*Signore, Signore, non passa niente. Sei sicuro.*" A little, balding, middle-aged man with a big black mustache tried to catch his breath. "*È dell'Ithaca aboard, ricorda?*"

He seemed to be speaking Italian, so I tried to dredge up what little Italian I learned during a wonderful, wine-soaked year at the University of Bologna. Either my accent was wrong or my vocabulary was rusty, but I couldn't get the guy to understand me. I tried Spanish, Portuguese, and English, but none of those languages helped. I was about to try my broken German or my even worse Russian (thanks to Prit, I could curse and talk about sex and liquor in that language) when someone came up behind me.

"I see you've met Enzo," he said in English, with that same unfamiliar accent.

I whipped around and came face to face with the same tall, blond officer who'd welcomed us during the hurricane. His spotless navy uniform fit him like a glove. I half expected him to invite me to a fancy dress ball.

"My name is Strangärd, Gunnar Strangärd. I am the first mate on this ship. I hope you won't mind my saying so, but it's considerably larger than the one that brought you."

As we shook hands, I felt embarrassed at the contrast between the officer's well-manicured hands and my own, which were covered with motor oil, fish, and God knows what else. My nails were broken and black.

"Enzo is bringing breakfast to you and your friends." He pointed to the waiter's cart. "The doctor said that eighteen hours of sleep should be enough, so we thought we'd wake you. If you prefer to return to your cabin to have breakfast with your friends, that's perfectly fine. However, the captain asked me to invite you to join us for breakfast in the officers' quarters." He was silent for a moment, taking in my shocked face. "That is, if you don't mind."

"Not at all, not at all," I stammered. After months of violence, danger, hunger, and hardship, I felt like I was dreaming. The more polite and educated these people were, the more astonished I was. "It'd be a pleasure, believe me."

After saying good-bye to Enzo and his cart loaded with wonderful-smelling food, I followed Officer Strangärd through the labyrinthine hallways.

"Who are you? Where are you headed? Where's this ship from?" The questions flew out my mouth as we climbed a flight of stairs and headed down another long corridor.

"I'll let the captain explain in depth, if you don't mind." Judging by the officer's name and accent, he had to be Swedish or Norwegian. "You are on the supertanker *Ithaca*. Before the

Apocalypse, it belonged to a Greek shipping company. Now," he added with a bright smile, "it belongs to the AC."

I was about to ask what the hell the AC was when Officer Strangärd opened a door into a bright, airy room. Half a dozen officers sat at a long table, drinking coffee in silence. My gaze was instantly drawn to the view out the large window behind them. I finally got a good look at the entire length of the tanker. The giant was easily fifteen hundred feet long. Its bow shimmered in a wispy fog. A sailor leisurely pedaled a bicycle along the deck, dodging huge hoses.

"Breathtaking, isn't it?" The voice behind me belonged to a man of about fifty, average height, with a wind-beaten complexion. A trim white beard framed his round face and set off slightly puffy light-blue eyes. "I'm Captain Birley. I'm glad you decided to join us for breakfast."

I mumbled something unintelligible as I took a seat at the captain's personal table. Out of the corner of my eye, I saw a sailor enter the room. A large pistol hung at his waist and bounced against his thigh as he walked briskly in my direction. He was carrying a strip of paper and a vial of amber liquid.

"There's one small procedure we have to carry out first. I hope you don't mind," continued the captain, sitting down again. "Please spit on that strip of paper."

I froze, thinking I hadn't heard him right. The sailor with the pistol set the strip of paper on the table in front of me. I didn't want to offend my hosts. Plus, I felt sure that pistol wasn't for show, and if I didn't spit, the courtesy I'd enjoyed would evaporate. Feeling a bit ridiculous, I gently spit on the paper. The sailor poured a few drops from the vial onto the glob. Nothing happened that I could see, but I must've passed the test since the sailor nodded and everyone in the room visibly relaxed.

"Mystery man, you're clean. Now, I'd love to hear your story. Coffee or tea?"

I pinched myself under the table. I had to be fucking dreaming.

Over cup after cup of coffee, I filled the captain in on our travels while the other officers carried on lively conversations at the next table. I told him how I'd fled Spain through a sea of Undead, and about my little group's helicopter flight to the Canaries, and the overcrowding and poor living conditions there, which led to our decision to head for Cape Verde. It was a watered-down version, only half-true, but I figured he didn't need to know all the details. Plus, I was always guarded until I knew a person better.

"Now, it's my turn to ask." I smiled, trying to sound more confident than I was. "Who do I have to thank for saving our lives?"

"Our Lord Jesus Christ, of course," Captain Birley answered, straight-faced, as we stood and walked over to the table of junior officers. "He set you on your path. Everything on earth is His doing. It's a sign from God that our paths crossed in that terrible storm. His name be praised forever, amen."

A chorus of "amen" echoed around the table. Even Strangärd chimed in, serious and thoughtful. I was a little taken aback. I hadn't expected such a show of religious fervor.

"Um . . . Yes, yes, of course. And who did God place in my path? I mean, who are you?"

"We're part of the AC. We're from the Christian Republic of Gulfport, Mississippi, crossing the Atlantic on a mission from God."

"The AC? The Republic of what? What mission?" To say I was amazed would be an understatement. "I don't mean to sound rude, but I don't understand any of this, sir."

"The AC is the Army of Christ," replied a redheaded officer at one end of the table.

Army of Christ? What the hell was that?

"When Our Lord decided to punish the iniquities of the human race," the officer continued, caught up by what he was saying, "all the sinners—those with impure hearts, hedonists, pagans—were punished by the Lord's wrath. Only those of us who were pure in the Almighty's eyes were saved. For a while, we wandered, lost and alone, surrounded by His divine punishment and the fruits of evil, but then we heard the call." The sailor's eyes glowed with a strange light. The kid believed every word he was saying.

"The call?"

"The call of Reverend Greene," broke in another officer, a pimply-faced kid no more than eighteen. "He who brought us together in Gulfport and created the Refuge. There, we—the Lord's Chosen—will witness the Second Coming of Christ."

A new chorus of "amen" and "hallelujah" rang out. I didn't know if these guys were pulling my leg or if the Christian Republic of Gulfport was real. I decided to play along. I didn't want to be saved from drowning only to be burned at the stake for making a joke about Jesus.

"And is Reverend Greene here now?" I asked, casually.

"Of course not!" Strangärd replied with a chuckle. "He's in Gulfport, keeping things running smoothly. He's a busy man. In addition to saving our souls, he also governs that town of ten thousand inhabitants. Not counting the helots, of course."

I nodded like I understood all the religious mumbo jumbo. I assumed that the "helots" were the Undead and survivors like me who wandered through the world outside of the Gulfport Refuge, but I couldn't help asking. "So, am I a helot?"

"No, of course not," said the captain. "We're quite sure of that. By the way, what religion do you and your friends practice?"

The sudden shift in the conversation threw me for a loop. I was silent for a few seconds, thinking at full speed. Sister Cecilia would've been a big help right then.

"Let's see, Lucia and I are Christians. Catholics to be exact. Prit is Ukrainian, so he's Russian Orthodox." The truth is, Lucia and I had never discussed religion and Viktor Pritchenko had no faith in anything but himself, but this was not the time to expose our religious failings, so I tossed in an outrageous lie. "We pray together several times a day and give thanks to God for saving us from damnation."

"That's good, very good." Captain Birley slapped me on the back and everyone seemed satisfied. "Reverend Greene will rejoice to meet you when we reach Gulfport. You are the prodigal son, lost in the dark, far from the Light, amid the squalor and wickedness of the Undead. But the Lord has set you on the path to salvation. Today is a day for rejoicing!"

Another round of "hallelujahs" exploded around the table. Many of the officers hugged me or shook my hand. I smiled and wondered what the hell we'd gotten ourselves into.

"So," I asked, "are we sailing to Gulfport?"

"Not yet," Birley said as he poured me a fresh cup of coffee. "As I said, we're on a divine mission that the Lord revealed to the reverend."

"And what is that destination?" I asked, not really wanting to know the answer.

"A place you should be familiar with since it was once a Spanish colony—the city of Luba, in Equatorial Guinea, on the west coast of Africa," Captain Birley said with a knowing smile. "It is God's will."

7

About two thousand feet away, the port of Luba shimmered beneath the scorching African sun. After a slow, cautious approach, the *Ithaca* finally dropped anchor. Captain Birley and his crew had taken two full days to sail fifteen miles into port and then another day to ease the boat in those last few feet. They were serious professionals with a lot of experience. The *Ithaca* was too big to simply sail into port, especially since its pilot wasn't familiar with the waters. Up on the bridge, they pored over digital navigational charts. They'd lucked out and the GPS was working, even though lots of satellites had dropped out of the sky. Still, this crew left nothing to chance.

That same day, they lowered a small Zodiac equipped with a probe. The inflatable boat made its way three miles ahead of the tanker, probing every inch of the planned route. Officer Strangärd told me they were trying to avoid rock shelves and coral reefs, as well as sunken ships that might block our way. Given the tanker's size, an impact could be catastrophic.

"But why sail that little boat so far ahead? Why not use the ship's sonar?" Pritchenko asked, leaning on the railing next to me.

"Simple," said the red-haired officer standing next to us, scanning the water through binoculars. I suspected he was also keeping us under surveillance. "The *Ithaca* has a carrying capacity of nearly a million tons. We're sailing at a speed of twelve knots, generating an enormous amount of inertia. If the captain gave the order to reverse the engines, it would take about twenty minutes to come to a complete stop. In that time, we'd cover several miles. It's not like stopping a car. Even after we cut the engines, this beast drifts for a while, almost as if she had a mind of her own."

Pritchenko grunted and peered through his own pair of binoculars. My pal was a suspicious grouch by nature. He didn't like these people and didn't really hide it. In spite of that, he took my advice and attended the three daily church services like a true believer. Prit prayed more on that ship than he had in his whole life. Lucia and I did the same. Everyone seemed pleased that we joined in their routine. Their polite but firm invitation made it clear they wouldn't take "no" for an answer.

Prit and Lucia had also spit on the strip of paper. The results must have been acceptable since the crew gave them the same jovial welcome they'd given me.

My friends were as bewildered as I was by the crew's religious fervor. Our best guess was that most of them came from the southern United States, where deeply felt Baptist beliefs prevailed and preachers abounded. But I wasn't convinced that was the whole story.

Our questions about the mysterious Reverend Greene went unanswered. All they said was, "You'll meet him when we get to Gulfport. You'll see what a wonderful man he is."

The *Ithaca*'s propellers stopped and we drifted for the last few miles. When we were right alongside a massive steel structure with three towers, the captain gave the order to drop anchor.

With a splash, the ship's giant anchors sank into the sea. A couple of minutes later, the chains tensed. The ship crept forward a bit, then came to a stop.

Strangärd turned to Captain Birley and saluted. "Anchoring maneuver completed without incident, sir. Ready to secure the ship."

"Well done, Gunnar," Birley said. His eyes didn't miss a single detail on board his ship. "Proceed with security checks, and prepare to load the cargo."

The Swedish officer saluted again and left the bridge to carry out his orders. The entire crew worked with the precision of a Swiss clock.

The "divine mission" that Reverend Greene had sent them on turned out to be more worldly than I'd imagined. They weren't bringing the word of God to Africa, distributing food to survivors stranded on the coast, or anything usually associated with a divine message wrapped in light and accompanied by blaring trumpets with angels and cherubs fluttering around as a voice thundered down from heaven. The mission was much simpler: fill the *Ithaca*'s holds with crude oil.

When Captain Birley told me their mission, I asked what seemed like a logical question. "Why Africa? Why not Texas or the Gulf of Mexico? They're a lot closer to Gulfport."

"The land route to the Texas oil fields is impractical," the captain explained. "Those oil fields are infested by millions of Satan's children and the roads are impassable. We'd need a fleet of trucks just to reach the wells. On top of that, the trucks wouldn't provide us with enough protection once we got there, let alone transport all the oil we need. The drilling platforms in the Gulf of Mexico are out of commission due to hurricanes and lack of maintenance. This is the nearest reliable oil supply.

Besides, Reverend Greene said that this is the Lord's will, so it must be." He shrugged as if that explained everything.

Prit and I exchanged a knowing look, but kept our mouths shut. I discreetly stepped on his foot just as a smart remark was about to pop out of his mouth.

Let it go, I mouthed.

So there we were in Luba—population about seven thousand—on Bioko Island, part of Equatorial Guinea. The island would have been just another forgotten corner of Africa if the country's dictator, Theodor Obiang, hadn't had it surveyed in the eighties. The survey revealed that Bioko was floating on a sea of oil. Eager to get their hands on the wealth lying beneath them, the Guineans started drilling almost immediately. The port in Malabo, the country's capital, proved too shallow, so the multi-national companies doing the drilling created a deepwater port in the nearby town of San Carlos de Luba.

I had to admit that Reverend Greene's choice was a good one. We were anchored near a charming tropical city whose port looked to be in pretty good condition; its deep waters allowed our ship to sail right up to the oil rigs. With only seven thousand inhabitants before the Apocalypse, the number of Undead was much lower than in other ports with oil rigs. But seven thousand were still way too many.

The small, sonar-equipped Zodiac pulled alongside the ship, but didn't stop to be raised up by the crane. Instead, it motored along parallel to the *Ithaca*'s bow, almost on the other side of the ship, about three hundred feet away.

Prit elbowed me. "Look at that," he murmured, pointing to a covered area on the ship's deck about two hundred feet from the bow.

I trained my binoculars on a spot where the tangle of pipes and hoses was sectioned off by a metal barrier about four feet high. It ran from one side of the ship to the other and was topped by barbed wire. No door seemed to connect it to the rest of the ship.

"Whaddya you think that's for?" I asked.

"Not a clue. You?" Pritchenko replied.

"I have no idea. It could be a line of defense in case some Undead get on board, or maybe it's to ward off a pirate attack on the high seas. These people have traveled thousands of miles. Who knows what's going on in other parts of the world."

"Well, my gut tells me it has something to do with those guys."

The Ukrainian pointed at the bow again. About three dozen people emerged from a hatch on the far side of the barrier. Through our binoculars, we watched them file out in orderly fashion. They wore US Army fatigues and were heavily armed. A tall, muscular black guy with a shaved head and tattoos covering one arm quickly organized the men and women into five-person squadrons. Then they unrolled a net like the one we'd climbed up on and scrambled down to the Zodiac as it swayed rhythmically against the tanker. Three other Zodiacs appeared from around the other side of the tanker. When all the boats were full, Captain Birley radioed his orders and the boats approached the dock, which was filled with Undead.

"See that?" Prit asked, glued to his binoculars.

"Yeah. That dock is crowded with Undead. They'll have a helluva time getting through."

"I don't think they'll have much trouble," Prit replied. "But did you notice there's not a single white person on those teams?"

I looked closer. Most of the soldiers were black, Native American, or Latino, and a couple were Asian. The rest of the soldiers looked puny next to the tattooed giant running the operation.

"What's so unusual about that? Even before the Apocalypse, the American army was full of Latinos and blacks."

"Yeah. And a lot of white country boys who enlisted when their farms failed. I don't see a single one down there. If any of those soldiers are white, I'll shave off my mustache."

Prit was ex-military; his trained eyes picked up on things like that. Once he pointed it out, it did seem strange that there were no white soldiers.

Just as I was about to ask Strangärd about the soldiers, the boats reached the dock and they started to disembark. From the deck of the ship, we had a clear view of the harbor. I grabbed my binoculars—I didn't want to miss a single thing. For once, I was watching all that shit from a safe distance instead of being in the thick of it.

As if he'd read my mind, Prit whispered, "Too bad we don't have any popcorn."

I didn't answer him because the action was starting.

The first boat landed at the dock alongside the oil deposits. About thirty Undead were wandering around. They were all black except for one white guy wearing a torn REPSOL oil company uniform—he must've been a technician. Four of the Undead had on army fatigues. The strap of an assault rifle was wrapped around one guy's leg. His calf was in shreds and the bone was sticking out. The rifle was in pieces. The poor devil must've been dragging it around for months, the way a prisoner drags his chain.

The other two boats landed nearby and the soldiers climbed onto the dock, but one of them slipped on the ladder. He comically waved his arms in the air trying to get his balance, then hit the water with a loud splash.

The sound set the Undead in motion. Hundreds of rotting heads whipped around in unison and headed for the end of the dock. The other soldiers were busy dragging their comrade out of the water and didn't notice the tide of Undead until the monsters were nearly on top of them. The scene gave me chills.

"Those filthy beasts amaze me," commented one of the officers as he leaned on the rail. "It's like those sons of bitches have fucking telekinesis or something."

"You mean telepathy, dummy," another voice said. "And you better watch your language. If the captain hears you blaspheme like that, you'll get a look at those Undead up close."

As the two officers chatted away, the soldiers on shore were running down the dock. One group opened fire on the Undead. The gunfire broke the town's silence.

"According to our calculations, they have twenty minutes," said Captain Birley, who had silently appeared beside me.

"Calculations?"

"Yes. Based on the soldiers' speed, the estimated number of Undead, and the size of the town, we calculate that, in twenty minutes, there'll be so many of those evil creatures that our helots won't be able to get out of there. So they'd better hurry."

The first row of Undead had fallen like bowling pins, but more kept coming. One group of soldiers was out in front and about to be surrounded. The group's leader realized the danger they were in and ordered his team to retreat, but it was too late. About thirty or forty Undead had already gathered and were almost within arm's reach. One of the Undead lashed out at the nearest soldier and grabbed his rifle. The soldier pulled away and tried to recover his rifle, but another Undead pounced on him. Before anyone could do anything, the Undead sank his teeth into the soldier's neck. He let out a gut-wrenching howl you could hear all the way up to the Ithaca's deck. With a twist of his head, the Undead ripped off a piece of the guy's neck just before another soldier shot him in the head. But it was too late. The man lay sprawled on the ground, blood shooting from his carotid artery as his heart kept pumping. The group continued their panicked retreat as the poor guy bled to death on the boiling pavement.

By then the shooting was everywhere. Two-thirds of the soldiers were climbing over a retaining fence as the remaining third struggled to connect long hoses to the rusty pump spouts that stuck out of the huge reservoirs. Someone inside the fence had started up a small portable generator, presumably to run the pump. The gunfire and the pump's piercing screech were deafening. I looked in horror at the other end of the dock. Drawn by the noise, hundreds of Undead were lumbering down every street toward the soldiers who were distracted by their work.

"They'll be slaughtered!" I couldn't contain myself. "Captain Birley, you've got to get them out of there! Order them back!"

Birley shrugged with a dismissive wave of his hand. "Don't worry about them," he said impassively. "They're just helots doing their job. But maybe we can help them out. It'll be fun. Culling!"

"Sir?" One of the young officers snapped to attention next to the captain.

"Bring up the M24s. Let's have a little target practice."

A murmur of excitement spread across the deck. I wondered what he meant by fun. Another six or seven men in the landing party had fallen, and the circle of Undead was slowly but surely closing. Three other soldiers had bites on their arms and legs. Considering how contagious the virus was, the bites were fatal, but they gripped their weapons and fought on admirably.

An officer dragged several heavy metal boxes across the *Ithaca*'s deck and started handing out rifles with telescopic sights. There was pushing and shoving and some sneaky elbow-ing to get one of the guns. Some walked away empty-handed, grumbling, while other hopefuls tried to bribe those with rifles into sharing them for a while. Pritchenko snagged one of the rifles without much effort.

"A Remington M24," he muttered as he examined the rifle with an expert eye. "Snipers' weapon. I wonder where our friends got them."

Suddenly, all hell broke loose on deck. A dozen rifles fired on the crowd of moaning Undead as they advanced toward the dock. With a continuous staccato, the shooters cocked their weapons, aimed carefully through the scopes, fired, then started all over again. The audience cheered each bull's-eye. Some guys were even placing bets on their aim.

I focused my binoculars on the port. At such short range, the shooters couldn't miss the Undead teetering on the dock. In the blink of an eye, three of the monsters went down. Exploding bul-lets hit two of them in the head, spraying flesh, bone, and gore everywhere. Another bullet hit the third Undead in the chest and threw him back ten feet. The creature lay on the ground, with a puzzled look on his face as if he wondered what the fuck happened and why he was lying on the ground with a tunnel-size hole in his gut.

It would've been fun, but I couldn't stop thinking that those monsters had been people once. When the head of a little girl in pigtails went flying and the shooters cheered, I stopped watch-ing. For God's sake! She couldn't have been more than seven! I could handle killing Undead in self-defense, but here they were sitting ducks.

The team that had scrambled up the reservoir fired a flare, filling the air with thick red smoke. Several other soldiers pulled a guide wire that dragged a thick hose connected to the reservoir to the nearest Zodiac. With a slow purr, the boat pulled up to the tanker.

What was left of the ground team realized that the hose was secure and retreated to the shore. From the safety of the ship, I watched in fascination as twenty men and women slowly walked backward in a strange choreographed motion, dragging their wounded comrades. The muscular black guy towered over them and covered their retreat. He was one brave fucker. The guy rhythmically fired his M16 until he ran out of ammunition. He was too close to the Undead to reload, so he grabbed the gun by the barrel (it must've been red hot) and swung it like a club.

The officers on the *Ithaca* cheered as if they were watching a football game. The giant man with all the tattoos was cut off some fifty feet from the shore. The Zodiacs had pulled back a little to keep the Undead from hurling themselves on board, but one of them stayed in close so the guy could jump on. The soldiers on the boats yelled for him to get on, but he was too busy fending off Undead to hear.

The M16 whirled over his head with a shrill whistle, striking the head of an Undead with a brittle crunch. The blows probably weren't fatal, but they were enough to help him break through the line as the Undead fell like sacks of potatoes. Seconds later, though, three new Undead closed in. The soldier split open the heads of the two closest to him with the butt of his rifle, then gave the third a kick to the solar plexus that must've broken some ribs.

The officers stopped shooting and cheered like crazy as the guy fought for his life.

I whipped around to Prit. "What the hell's going on? Why aren't they shooting?"

THE WRATH OF THE JUST

"Clearly they don't want to shoot. If we don't want any trouble, we shouldn't either," the Ukrainian muttered as he cast a furtive look at the officers.

I couldn't read his mind right then. I was too upset.

"That's murder!" I protested.

No one paid any attention to me. The soldier continued swinging his rifle, fighting his way to shore, and for a second I thought he'd make it. He was just a few feet from the dock with only two Undead between him and salvation. He tackled one of them like a defensive linebacker. The Undead flew into the water and sank with a splash. He grabbed the other beast by the arm and swung him around, letting him fly into a nearby group. The monsters fell in a tangle of arms, legs, and heads.

I got carried away and started to yell too, then suddenly the cry died in my throat. The soldier took a step back to make a running leap onto the Zodiac. Just as he started to jump, one of the Undead lying in the dirt a few feet away reached out and with his rotting fingernails snagged the man by his bootlaces. The soldier fell hard onto the dock and two Undead pounced on him. One of them sank his teeth into the guy's bicep, leaving a deep, jagged wound. The other ripped into one of his calves. With a grunt, the soldier used his free foot to lash out at the head biting his leg and landed a kick that would have broken an elephant's neck. He crawled to the edge of the dock and let himself fall into the water. After a second, his head popped up alongside the Zodiac. The soldiers dragged him on board, leaving a trail of blood across the boat's canvas hull. Then they tacked and started their slow return to the *Ithaca*.

It was a monstrous crime. The guy was a dead man. Millions of TSJ virions had entered his body through those two bites and were reproducing wildly. In a few hours, that giant of a man would be a very large, very dangerous Undead. All because the men laughing and cheering beside me didn't feel like helping him.

"Come on, Prit. I can't take another minute of this. I'm just glad Lucia's not on deck."

"That was very strange," Prit replied. "A landing party made up entirely of black, Latino, Asian, and Native American soldiers, but not a single white one. And they let their own people die like flies. Doesn't make sense."

"Nothing has made sense for a long time."

"Yeah, but that was really strange," the Ukrainian insisted.

The battered landing party finally reached the ship. Sailors connected the hoses to the tanks as the battle-weary soldiers climbed the net back onto the tanker. They lowered stretchers to the boats to bring up the most gravely injured.

Although it was heartwarming that they hadn't left any wounded behind, their efforts were futile. The virus would transform the injured soldiers into Undead in minutes. In fact, some of the officers were firing down at the dock, targeting the fallen soldiers who'd already risen as Undead.

Prit, the officers, and I left the deck, which shimmered in the tropical midday heat, and headed down to the dining room, where Enzo directed waiters in white uniforms laying out a fabulous lunch. The contrast was deeply disturbing. Looking through a window, I could see the exhausted survivors sprawled on the deck, shedding their heavy equipment and greedily gulping down bottles of some liquid. Inside the dining room, the officers chatted, smoked cigarettes, drank gin and tonics, and bowed politely as Lucia passed among them. Only minutes before, they'd fired on the multitude of Undead on the dock, then allowed several of their own men to die without lifting a finger. The dock was still packed with Undead, rocking back and forth. Their monotonous moans could be heard above the hum of the air-conditioning. It was like being in the cocktail lounge of an exclusive country club, looking out a window onto hell.

The captain made his way through the officers, courteous and smiling, and walked over to us. He kissed Lucia's hand politely.

"Miss, it is a pleasure to have you share this simple repast with us," he said. "I think I speak for all my officers when I say that your presence on board is wonderfully refreshing. A lady as beautiful as you is a joy to behold."

"Unlike that spectacle of your men out there," I said curtly.

Lucia and Prit shot me a warning look.

"It's obviously not pleasant, sir," said Captain Birley, unfazed. "Keep in mind we're immersed in a struggle between the powers of God and Satan, between Light and Darkness. We must set aside social conventions, such as compassion."

"But they're your men!" I protested.

"The landing party?" Birley shrugged. "They're helots, an inferior class of people, sinners all of them. They fight and give their lives to atone for their sins and earn a place at the Lord's Table. Right now, those fallen soldiers are seated with our Lord Jesus Christ, at a banquet much bigger and better than this simple meal. I hope you don't have a problem with that . . . sir."

I picked up on the elegant pause the captain had tacked on and backed down. "Um, no, of course not, Captain Birley. We're eternally grateful for your hospitality and we fully understand your methods."

"It would be a shame to discover that you don't deserve this status," Birley said. An implied threat hung in the air. "Now, if you'll excuse me, I need to radio Gulfport and report the success of our operation."

Captain Birley walked to the radio room, stopping to chat with a group of officers along the way. The hum of conversation and soft classical music mingled with the groans of the Undead still lingering on the dock. It was truly surreal.

"What do you make of all this?" Prit asked, taking a sip of his drink.

"I don't know, but I don't like it," said Lucia. "These people are so formal, so polite, and yet they give me the creeps. Something doesn't fit."

Just then Strangärd casually walked up to us. Keeping his eyes on the crowd of Undead on the dock, he stood so the other officers in the room couldn't see his face. Anyone would think he was lost in thought, distracted by the scene on the dock.

"Be careful," he muttered through clenched teeth. "Birley is watching you closely. The captain is very suspicious and will write a report about you for the reverend as soon as we get back. You're treading on thin ice, friends."

"What's going on? Who're the helots? What's this all about?" I asked, keeping my eyes on Lucia and flashing her a bright smile, as if she and I were having a lighthearted conversation.

"We can't talk here. The walls have ears. Just know that there are other people who think this is an aberration. When we get to Gulfport, I'll explain everything."

Strangärd moved on and joined another group. I heard him laugh at a joke. That Swede certainly knew how to cover his tracks. *How many more like him were there? In Gulfport, someone better give us an explanation. And it better be good.*

8

Forty-eight hours later, the *Ithaca*'s holds were nearly overflowing with a half million tons of high-grade petroleum. I stood on the deck, watching as sailors disconnected the hoses, sealed them with layers of rubber tar, tied them to buoys, and then tossed them into the ocean. If they returned to Luba, they'd just have to fish those hoses off the buoys and reconnect them.

A slight tremor signaled that the *Ithaca*'s engines had started. The tanker's slime-covered anchors were raised, and the behemoth started slowly out to sea. Before we left the harbor, several helots on the other side of the fence brought four flag-draped coffins on deck, fired a salute, and cast them into the ocean. The TSJ virus had taken its toll among the wounded, as I'd predicted.

The *Ithaca* picked up speed and headed for the open water. The wind began to blow hard across the deck. As I turned to head back inside, I stopped in my tracks and stared in disbelief. Among the soldiers saluting the sinking coffins was the giant black man who'd led the landing party. He'd been bitten twice, yet he looked to be in excellent health. He certainly wasn't an Undead.

9

Kill them, kill them all! Even in their mothers' womb!
—Ilya Ehrenburg, "Kill"

HANGEUL 9 LONG-RANGE LISTENING STATION WONSAN, NORTH KOREA

Lieutenant Jung Moon-Koh was bored. He'd been at his post for seven hours. And just like every day for over a year now, his screen displayed the same thing: nothing.

The Hangeul 9 Long-Range Listening Station was one of more than a hundred stations strung across North Korea, built to monitor South Korean radio transmissions. Back in the sixties, someone convinced Dear Leader Kim Il-Sung that listening in on those ruthless capitalists in the south was the best way to uncover and foil an attack.

The bold promoter of the plan didn't realize that radio transmissions numbered in the millions at the height of South Korea's "Asian Tiger" economic boom. There were far more transmissions

than in North Korea—where Juche, an extremely xenophobic, par-
anoid version of Marxism, was practiced, and where owning a
radio was against the law. Sorting through all the transmissions
was an impossible task for an impoverished country with limited
technological capabilities. After a two-year investment of time and
money, the idea was quietly shelved. A bullet cut short the brilliant
career of the plan's author—the usual reward for failure in the
Workers' Paradise.

For over forty years, almost all the stations sat shuttered. A
few monitored transmissions from the US fleet as it patrolled the
Sea of Japan, but since most naval communications were
encoded, that didn't prove very useful. No one had suggested
changes to the system for decades—initiating a task without
Dear Leader's request was unthinkable.

Then came the Apocalypse.

At first, the news filtering in from North Korea's embassies
around the world was confusing. They reported that a disease
had broken out in Dagestan and was spreading like wildfire
throughout the world, but the details were sketchy. Government
officials and military leaders in Pyongyang concluded that the
news must be a smoke screen to hide the South's imminent
attack on the North. In response, the ever-paranoid North
Korean regime activated all its defenses. The People's Army was
put on high alert and the country's borders were sealed tighter
than ever. That paranoia saved the country.

As the pandemic raged out of control, North Korea dug in
the way it had since the 1950s. At first its embassies were the only
source of news, but they soon fell silent as the pandemic swept
through one country after another. Embassy staff pleaded to be
evacuated, but the government turned a deaf ear. By then the
country's leaders knew that the TSJ virus was highly contagious
and that its consequences were devastating.

When TSJ finally reached South Korea, chaos swept that country for three weeks. In just five days, Seoul became a city of the damned, and other cities fared no better.

The soldiers and sailors stationed on US bases tried to blast their way to the sea, but their massive convoy of tanks disappeared, as if the earth had swallowed it up somewhere between Seoul and the port of Ulsan, where more than a million people were waiting to be evacuated. Not one of the fifty thousand American military personnel stationed in South Korea survived.

Wave after wave of desperate refugees tried to flee across the border into North Korea. The Politburo met briefly and ruled that citizens from the South had no right to safety in the North. The borders remained closed.

Even before the Apocalypse, the border separating the two Koreas was one of the most tightly sealed and well defended in the world. The Korean War ended in a cease-fire in 1953, but because no peace accord was signed, the two countries remained officially at war. The Demilitarized Zone (DMZ)—a strip of land 148 miles long and two and a half miles wide along the 38th parallel—divided the Korean Peninsula in two. Thousands of miles of walls, fences, minefields, and bunkers made it impassable.

Hundreds of thousands of terrified civilians dug in at the border, but they found it locked up tight. What took place at the Joint Security Area at Panmunjom—one of the most photographed sites in the DMZ—was a tragic example of that deadlock. In just twenty-four hours, ninety thousand people fled there. They tried to negotiate their way in, but were met with silence. The crowd rioted, but unarmed and frightened civilians were no match for North Korea's well-trained, well-armed soldiers. As the hours passed, the crowd's threats changed to pleading. Once again all they got was silence.

North Korean soldiers held their positions and waited. Even the loudspeakers that had been broadcasting propaganda non-stop for decades fell silent.

One night, the first Undead finally showed up. Chaos broke out as the crowd surged against the border in the dark, fleeing the bloody shadows that pulled entire families out of the cars where they'd taken shelter against the cold.

Then the soldiers started shooting.

The next morning, thousands of bodies lay piled up in the ruins of the Joint Security Area. A bullet to the head was all that distinguished the Undead from civilian corpses. In the background, out of reach of the machine guns, tens of thousands of Undead swayed, taking the first steps of their new "life."

Not one person, living or dead, managed to cross the DMZ. As the weeks went on, North Korea's powerful defenses held off the tide of Undead. The creatures shambled toward the line, but they fell into minefields, got tangled in the barbed wire, or were gunned down.

No one crossed the border by air or sea either. Boatloads of refugees set sail from fishing villages in South Korea, but North Korean soldiers shelled them before they could land. In one town, the mayor couldn't bring himself to murder a boatload of six hundred children, so he allowed them to land. Three hours later, an army battalion was dispatched to correct that error. To be on the safe side, they killed the town's six thousand inhabitants too. The People's Army carried out their Dear Leader's orders without question.

Other people who set out on sailboats, alone or in small groups, did manage to land north of the DMZ. But because the country had been closed off for over fifty years, they stood out like fleas on a white sheet and were immediately arrested and executed—along with those who captured them. Patriotic

Squadrons for Containment, as the groups guarding the border were called, fired thousands of rounds during those tumultuous weeks.

Finally, the situation stabilized. The Undead who approached the border were few and far between. Over a million Undead roamed South Korea, but they were kept busy chasing the few survivors left there, far from the border.

So, thanks to Kim Jong-Un's paranoia and a twist of fate, North Korea was the only country with no Undead inside its borders. A backward Communist regime became not only the only surviving nation but also the most advanced one on Earth.

The country's leaders suspected that there were more people out there. Other countries, or at least parts of them, must have survived. They became obsessed with finding out who and where they were.

Although North Koreans were safe behind their walls, they were prisoners within their own borders, just as they'd been for half a century. Most of the population went about their daily lives, with no knowledge of the Undead or the fall of civilization. But the Politburo needed to know what was going on.

That's when someone remembered that the abandoned Hangeul network could pick up radio transmissions from any-where in the world. The system mothballed so long ago now seemed like the perfect tool. Survivors would have to communi-cate somehow.

Young Lieutenant Jung Moon-Koh knew nothing of this. A year and a half before, he was transported in the dead of night from his barracks near the Chinese border to a telecommunica-tions school. After a three-month crash course, he ended up at Station 9. Every day, Jung asked himself if he was being punished for some mistake he'd made.

His job at Station 9 was anything but fun. Operators wore headphones and stared at their computer screens for ten-hour shifts, trying to detect signals. Mostly they picked up static.

They located 1156 steady radio signals worldwide. Most stations were operating on automatic mode, broadcasting a prerecorded message over and over. Some were weather stations that sent out automatic daily forecasts. Others—such as the broadcasts from Los Rodeos Airport in Tenerife on the Canary Islands or the National Gallery in Copenhagen—had been set up by survivors, but no living person was running them anymore. The operators even located a country music station with a powerful generator somewhere in Tennessee that still played music almost two years after its last employee died.

What they were really interested in were signals from the few remaining human settlements. Most were small, wretched groups, clinging to isolated islands, on the verge of chaos and famine. The Politburo wasn't interested in them. It was convinced that a stronger settlement existed out there but that their broadcasts were too weak for the Hangeul network's enormous ears to detect.

Jung pulled off his headphones, stretched, ran his hands through his crew cut, and glanced furtively around the room. The captain had been gone for a while, leaving him and the other lieutenant alone in that cavernous room. Jung guessed he was sneaking a drink.

"Hey! Park! Park!" Jung tugged on the other lieutenant's sleeve.

"What do you want? If Captain Kim catches us looking away from the screens, our heads are gonna roll!"

"Don't worry. The captain is having his usual afternoon break." The young man laughed. "He won't be back for half an hour. Let's have a smoke."

"What about listening?" Park reluctantly looked back at his equipment. Then his eyes zeroed in on the pack of Chinese cigarettes in Jung's hand.

"We can listen through the loudspeakers, you numbskull," Jung replied with a sly grin.

Jung threw a switch on the Soviet-era relic. The room filled with the same static the two young soldiers had been monitoring for hours.

"See?" Jung said, lighting two cigarettes. "We can smoke and talk and still do our job. We just have to be organized."

"The captain'll have our heads . . ." Park wavered. It was hard to say no to a cigarette. Tobacco had gotten harder and harder to find, but nobody knew why. The only cigarettes available were the foul-smelling national brands that burned your throat. Chinese cigarettes were much better, but they cost a fortune on the black market. That wasn't a problem for Jung, whose father was some high-ranking official.

"Where'd you get those?" Park asked, his eyes shining.

"My old man gave them to me, but he's lately gotten tight-fisted. He said he doesn't know when he'll get more, so I better make them last." He shrugged and exhaled a cloud of smoke. "Like it's so hard for him to go to China and bring back a few cartons!"

Park stared at the pack, breathing in the smoke. He wondered what he could get on the black market for that pack of cigarettes. Enough to send for his poor parents? But Jung would never give it to him. His comrade was a good guy, but his father was a big shot in the party. He didn't understand how hard life was for peasants.

"When was the last time your father went to China?"

"He used to go every three or four months. Geez, now that you mention it, it's been a long time! That's strange."

"Not that strange. Ever wonder why we're listening to nothing for hours on end?"

"We're doing what we're told," Jung replied, with a wave of his hand. "We pick up the imperialists' signals so we can strike the moment—"

"What signals? We got here months ago and all we've picked up are broadcasts on automatic pilot in languages we don't understand and a stupid country music station. That's it. Call me crazy, but I don't think anyone's alive out there."

"You're just saying that to scare me." Jung took a deep drag on his cigarette.

"I'm serious, Jung. I think we're alone. I think everyone's dead and we're the only ones left."

Jung thought, *This is the last time I share a cigarette with Park. He's bad news. What he's saying is really weird. And scary . . . He needs more lessons in Juche.*

"Know what's wrong with you, Park—"

"This is the *Ithaca*," the speakers suddenly blared. "Calling Gulfport. Gulfport, come in. This is the *Ithaca*, the operation was a success. We're returning home . . . (static) . . . half a million tons of oil. Gulfport, come in . . ."

The door flew open and Captain Kim rushed in, wide-eyed. He was so shocked by the radio signal he didn't notice that his subordinates were disobeying orders, standing next to their computers, cigarettes in hand. Kim was in charge because of his rudimentary knowledge of English, the language of those damned imperialists. Through the static, he clearly made out the word "oil." He knew what to do.

"Record that signal," he snapped at his men. "My superiors need to hear that."

1 0

Two hours later, a government car sped along the deserted streets of Pyongyang, North Korea's capital. In the backseat, Colonel Hong Jae-Chol stared blankly out the window as the car headed for the Ministry of Defense.

All around him stretched Pyongyang, grandiose, beautiful—and sad. His car crossed one of the bridges over the Taedong River in the lane reserved for Communist Party vehicles. They had passed only about a dozen cars and trucks along the way; there were no private cars in North Korea.

As the car passed through the shadow of the nearly empty 105-story pyramid-shaped Ryugyong Hotel, he noticed that people on the street looked more downtrodden than usual. Hong spotted two people rummaging through a garbage can in an alley. He knew that his country had endured a punishing famine since the nineties, but he'd never seen such deprivation in the capital, whose residents were mostly party officials.

Colonel Hong was about forty-five, above average height, lean, with streaks of gray in his black hair. Few could say with certainty what the colonel was like since almost no one knew him well. His fellow students at officer candidate school would say that Hong was battle-tested, a manic overachiever, but reserved and quiet. Those who served under his command called him a heartless tyrant capable of pushing you until you dropped. The enemies he'd fought against had nothing to say; they were all dead. Everyone agreed that Hong was a disciplined soldier. If they ordered him to jump out a window at the Ministry of Defense, they wouldn't have to tell him twice. He'd jump with an impassive look on his face. His fervent adherence to the Juche ideology influenced everything he did—especially its motto: Duty first.

Colonel Hong belonged to the small, elite group of officers who were aware of the horrors of the Apocalypse. He'd taken part in the airborne mission that wiped out anyone who dared to cross the DMZ or North Korea's border with China.

His car stopped at the ministry front steps; a young soldier hurried to open the car door. Hong got out and stretched. It wasn't too cold yet, but winter snows would start soon. In about five weeks, he'd exchange his light summer cloak for his winter coat. He wondered how the extreme cold would affect the Undead on the other side of the border. Last year it didn't seem to have much effect on them.

"Colonel Hong?" A captain in dress uniform saluted him.

"That's me," muttered Hong. He was a man of few words. He stared, unblinking, straight into the man's eyes. Some swore he had eyes in the back of his head. His emotionless gaze made people very nervous. The captain was no exception.

"Please . . . follow me . . . sir," the captain stammered. "They're waiting for you in the minister's office."

The minister himself. This was new. Hong took off his hat and cloak as he entered the building, wondering why he'd been summoned. He hadn't been to the capital since his team carried out that cleanup in the Sea of Japan. A messy job, but necessary.

The worst part was the six hundred children, but what choice did he have?

He had no illusions. He knew leading that operation had made him a marked man. Even given all the horrors of the Apocalypse, if the details of what he'd done ever leaked out, people would look at him with terror. He made his superiors doubly uncomfortable since he knew exactly who had ordered the massacres and why. When they'd summoned him that morning from the remote base where he'd spent the last several months, he suspected something big was about to happen. Hong wasn't very imaginative, but he guessed he'd end the day either with a medal on his chest or a bullet in his head. He was surprised to realize he didn't care which.

"Wait here, please. I'll be right back." The captain rushed off to the minister's office.

Hong let his mind wander as he looked out the window. The gray, half-empty city, dominated by Eastern Bloc architecture, stretched all the way to the horizon. He tried to picture Pyongyang filled with Undead but found he couldn't.

The captain reappeared. "Please follow me."

Hong checked to be sure his uniform was spotless, then entered the room.

Vice Marshal Kim Yong-Chun, Minister of Defense of the People's Republic of Korea, awaited him at the head of a long conference table. Sitting beside him were three uniformed men Hong didn't know. With a vague uneasiness, he realized that he was the lowest-ranking soldier in the room.

"Colonel, please have a seat," the minister said in a friendly voice as an assistant brought him a thick folder. "Allow me to introduce Generals Kim, Chong, and Li. They are part of our Dear Leader Kim Jong-Un's advisory team for this . . . special mission."

Hong sat down, not paying attention to the names. He surmised that those men were just there to witness what was said. In the end, they didn't matter, despite their rank. He just nodded and fixed his unblinking gaze on the minister.

"Allow me to introduce Colonel Hong," the minister began. "He is an experienced member of our special forces, with a lengthy resume. He took part in three raids south of the DMZ and another off the coast of Japan. He carried out each mission with true revolutionary spirit. I am convinced he's the right man for this sensitive matter."

Hong was lost in thought. As they sat around a table in the minister's plush office, his past missions sounded so honorable. The truth was that each of them had been a hell awash with blood. The three forays into South Korean were spy missions. On the last one, he'd been shot in the hand and lost half of two fingers. The wound still ached from time to time. The mission into Japan was dirtier and darker. The goal had been to kidnap Japanese citizens and bring them to North Korea as language instructors in schools for spies. That mission almost ended in failure. Of the three men and three women he captured, he'd only brought back the men. One of the women had cried out when a Japanese patrol passed by; he'd strangled her with his bare hands. It upset the other two women so much he'd had to cut their throats to shut them up. He hadn't blinked once. Duty first.

"Now to the situation that brought us here today," the minister said as he opened the file in front of him.

Brace yourself, thought Hong.

"This afternoon at half past three local time, the Hangeul 9 Long-Range Listening Station picked up a radio transmission two minutes and twenty seconds long. The message was broadcast in English and repeated several times. You have a transcript of it in your file."

For a few moments, there was just the sound of shuffling papers. Then the minister continued. "The signal came from a few miles off the African coast and was transmitted by an American ship."

"Military?" asked one of the generals in alarm.

"No, a civilian tanker, judging by the message."

"Does it have a military escort?" asked another general, who looked old enough to have fought during the Dark Ages.

"We don't know, but that's not important," said the minister. "It's too far away for any ship in the People's Navy to intercept it."

"Why would we want to intercept it?" Hong asked cautiously. All eyes turned to him, then quickly looked away. No one could stare into the Colonel's lifeless eyes for long.

The minister cleared his throat and glanced at the generals. The oldest one nodded slightly. Minister Kim mustered up his courage and looked straight into Hong's eyes.

"Colonel, the situation is complicated. In spite of our Dear Leader's wise, shrewd counsel, we've reached a critical juncture. The Apocalypse has affected us much less than it has the decadent imperialists, including our southern neighbors. Thanks to Kim Jong-Un's sensible tactics, not one of those monsters has crossed our borders, so the disease hasn't spread into North Korea. In that sense, we're safe."

The same gibberish, but not a word about the real problem. *He's a typical bureaucrat covering his ass,* thought Hong. He decided to take the direct approach. "What is the problem then?"

"That, regrettably, we aren't entirely on our own in the world. Our policy has always been that we manufacture all our consumer goods and try to depend on only our own resources.

Despite all our efforts, though, some things keep us from being completely self-sufficient."

Hong slowly folded his hands on the table. It was an open secret that their system had failed. North Korea had been a rural country for decades. After years of poor harvests, the famines were devastating. Years ago, they'd been humiliated when they had to accept US grain and medicine to rescue entire regions from starvation. Millions of lives were saved, but the shameful insult was hard to bear. The colonel firmly believed that North Korea must sustain itself, wholly apart from imperialist influences.

"I fail to see the problem, Comrade Minister. We can certainly live without Chinese cigarettes or contraband Japanese beer." The look on his face remained passive.

"No doubt, Colonel. But without oil, we'll be on our knees in three months."

The damn oil, of course. "I understand. How bad is the situation?" he asked slowly.

The minister looked nervously at the elderly, bald general, who again nodded almost imperceptibly. He reminded Hong of a very old, very ugly turtle.

"Catastrophic. Our Chinese comrades used to supply the People's Republic of Korea with all its oil, but since the Apocalypse, we haven't received a drop."

"Did the Chinese cut us off?"

"Not exactly." The minister's voice trembled.

"What is the problem then?"

"We believe there's no one left in China, except for a few scattered groups. And the Undead, of course. What's more, the oil refineries were destroyed when Beijing detonated nuclear bombs in an attempt to contain the plague."

"How long do we have?"

"Heavy industry is practically at a standstill and light industry is operating at only a quarter of its capacity. Gasoline is severely rationed, even in the People's Army. We are stockpiling for winter, but there still won't be enough. In three months—at most—our reserves will be completely depleted. This winter, many people will freeze to death."

"Our top priority is capturing that ship and its crew, Colonel," said General Turtle in a brittle voice. "We have to find out where the oil came from and get that area under the control of the People's Army right away."

"If we could get a reliable source of oil, Colonel," the minister chimed in, "our situation would change radically. It would guarantee the viability of the People's Republic of Korea and further our Dear Leader's master plan. We'd be invincible."

"Invincible?"

"Think about it, Colonel. North Korea is the only country in the world that survived the Apocalypse." Here the minister got choked up, and his face grew increasingly red. "Once we have a fuel source, we can move our ships, tanks, and planes wherever we want. Conquering the world will be child's play. Those bands of frightened survivors scattered here and there, clinging to their ragged flags, will be no match for our glorious forces. Our Dear Leader, Comrade Kim Jong-Un, will realize his Manifest Destiny: to be the first to rule a world united under the Juche ideology. We Koreans will be the driving force in that world!"

The three generals pounded on the table and applauded, their eyes shining with excitement. Their plan was ambitious, but if they pulled it off, the result would be staggering. For the first time in history, there would be only one true superpower: North Korea. Kim Jong-Un would achieve what Alexander the Great, Genghis Khan, Caesar, Napoleon, and Hitler only dreamed of—he would rule the world.

"Colonel, you will spearhead the mission. From the radio transmission, we learned that the ship is headed for Gulfport, a town in the southern United States. You and three hundred men will fly there, capture that ship and its crew, and find out where their oil is from. After that, nothing will stand between us and our heroic destiny."

"I will carry out my orders, Comrade Minister, but there is one thing I don't understand." The Colonel chose his words very carefully. "The Undead. They're everywhere. Billions of them. The People's Army is unquestionably the most glorious army, but even we can't kill all the monsters. What is our Peerless Leader's plan for conquering the world with all those things roaming around?"

The elderly general looked at the minister and nodded again.

"The truth is, Colonel," Minister Kim said as a satisfied smile spread slowly across his face, "those things—those Undead— aren't long for this world."

"What do you mean?" Hong, stupefied, blinked for the first time in the whole meeting.

"The Undead are dying. All of them."

"Lucullus! Come here right now! Damn cat!" Lucia was furious as she tried for the umpteenth time to grab the big Persian cat, who studied her with a gleam in his eyes. During the first week on the *Ithaca*, Lucullus became very popular, since few cats had survived the Apocalypse. Officers and sailors alike were immediately won over by that mischievous orange fur ball. No place was off-limits to him, except for the front of the ship where the helots were housed. At least, that was the case until three days ago, when Enzo caught him lying on the captain's bed, sprawled across Birley's dress uniform. After a stroll through the engine room, he'd left a large swath of motor oil all across the jacket, which upset Enzo and, of course, Captain Birley. After that, Birley ordered that Lucullus's movements be "restricted." Lucia was delegated to rein him in.

"Come on, Lucullus," Lucia said sweetly as she waved a little piece of meat in front of the cat. "Come here, handsome, come on . . ."

Lucullus did what any cat would do in that situation. He turned, scampered a few feet across the deck, and then jumped up on a porthole, just out of reach. He was having a great time.

Lucia sighed. The afternoon sky was overcast. It could rain any minute. The last thing she wanted was to chase after the cat in a downpour.

"Come on, Lucullus. Be a good boy . . ."

Lucia slowly inched up to the orange cat, but each time she got close, Lucullus skittered a few feet away and waited, swishing his tail. Lucia had never owned a cat, so she didn't understand that, sometimes, a cat doesn't want to be caught. Lucia didn't know that if she just feigned disinterest and walked away, Lucullus would come trotting behind her. Instead, she slowly inched across the length of the ship behind the little orange beast until he reached the fence that divided the ship's two groups.

"I've got you now, you little bugger," Lucia muttered, cornering him. The cat realized the game had changed and looked around for a way out. He spotted a gap the size of his pudgy body in the tightly strung barbed wire and shot through it, leaving orange fur behind.

Lucia lunged in a desperate attempt to catch him, but came up empty-handed. She kicked a pipe in frustration, cursing like a truck driver.

"Damn cat! Your owner's going to have to take care of you from now on—"

Lucia stopped midsentence. On the other side of the fence, a man in his thirties, wearing US army fatigues, materialized out of the shadows. He calmly lit a cigarette, stuck his hands in his pockets, and, limping slightly, walked over to the cat. He bent down and ran his hand along the cat's back. Lucullus purred and stretched every muscle.

The soldier gathered Lucullus in his arms and walked over to the fence, still scratching the cat behind his ears. He carefully passed the cat through the hole in the wire and placed him in Lucia's arms.

Lucia stared at him. He was tall and swarthy, with black hair and dark-brown eyes. He looked part Native American, so Lucia was surprised to read "Dobzhansky" on his nametag. "Thank you . . . uh . . . Mr. Dobzhansky. If weren't for you, I'd never have caught this troublemaker."

The man froze for a moment, then burst out in hearty laughter. He gave Lucia an amused look and threw his cigarette on the ground.

"My name's Carlos, Carlos Mendoza," he said in Spanish with a Mexican accent. "I don't know who Dobzhansky was. They gave me this uniform when I got to Gulfport. Either that damn *güero* has been dead for a while, or he's one of those fucked-up lost souls wandering around out there. Pardon my French. Who are you, señorita?"

"Lucia. I'm from Spain," the girl muttered, mesmerized by the soldier's eyes. "Our boat sank in the storm and the *Ithaca* rescued us. I was chasing Lucullus, but he got away and wouldn't mind me and then—" Lucia realized she was babbling. She always did that when she was nervous. She cursed inwardly. "What happened to your leg? You're limping."

"This?" the Mexican man replied nonchalantly. "It happened the other day, when we went ashore to connect those damn hoses. Nothing serious."

"An Undead attacked you?" Lucia took a step back.

"Yeah, but it's OK, señorita. It'll heal in a couple of weeks. It wasn't a very deep bite. The bastard jumped me from behind while I was shooting. Never saw him coming. Luckily he was missing half his jaw."

Lucia stared at him. Was she hallucinating? She knew that the TSJ virus was terribly infectious. She'd seen infected people turn into Undead in minutes. Yet the man in front of her was alive and well, casually telling her an Undead had bitten him.

"Are you immune? The TSJ virus didn't infect you? I don't believe it!"

The soldier laughed again, this time bitterly. His deep voice reminded Lucia of Benicio del Toro.

"Of course not, señorita. Don't I wish? The fucking truth is nobody's immune. That virus is the worst kind of bastard. You know that. Once it infects you, you're fucked."

"So, how the hell—?" Lucia started to ask, but then she heard a voice behind her.

"Miss, please step away from the barricade. And you, you fucking helot—more than six feet from the fence. You know that. Don't make me tell you twice, or I'll blow your brains out. Now get moving."

Lucia turned. Behind her stood two sailors and an officer in a pristine navy-blue uniform, all three wrapped in raincoats, armed with M16s. Lucia noticed that, although they weren't pointing their rifles at the man, their fingers were resting on the triggers.

Carlos Mendoza slowly raised his arms and backed away, never taking his eyes off the sailors. His expression was a mixture of pride, contempt, and anguish.

"Don't get all bent out of shape. I didn't touch her or her fucking cat. We were just talking."

"Is that true?" The officer looked at the Mexican soldier, whose face was unreadable. "He didn't touch either of you?"

"No." Lucia wasn't sure why she lied. "He didn't touch us."

"OK, but please don't approach this area without telling us first. Those men are dangerous criminals, the worst kind."

"Good-bye, Lucia." Mendoza waved and took a swig from a flask. "Don't forget Carlos Mendoza. If you need me, say you're one of the Just. You never know when our paths'll cross."

"The Just? What're you talking about?"

But Mendoza had turned and was headed back into the bowels of the ship.

Lucia walked slowly back to the stern, petting Lucullus as the first drops of rain splashed onto the hot metal deck. She felt light-headed, and her thoughts were racing. That man wasn't immune, and yet the virus didn't affect him. It made no sense. She'd seen the crew cast several soldiers into the ocean. TSJ had killed them. But Carlos and the giant black soldier with the tattooed arm were still walking around as if nothing had happened, even though they were infected.

She couldn't get the man's bold smile and his bright, defiant eyes out of her mind. The more she thought about him, the better-looking he got.

Reverend Greene had never been good-looking, but the sour expression on his face that morning didn't help. He was short, skinny, and in his seventies. Age spots dotted his leathery skin. He was dressed the same way he'd dressed for over forty years: gray suit, a bolo string tie with a silver slide, and a Stetson hat. Even though his sermon at the morning prayer service had been particularly inspired (*Praise the Lord Jesus Christ forever, amen, hallelujah!*), the reverend wasn't happy. He sensed something was wrong. Rather, his knee sensed something was wrong. And his knee was always right.

Back in 1974, in Waynesboro, Virginia, some drunks had broken that knee because they didn't like his looks. The fracture wasn't serious. It was common among athletes, dancers, climbers—and victims of angry drunks. Most people were good as new in a few weeks. (*Praise the Lord, amen, hallelujah!*) However, a few found that their broken knee reliably predicted changes in the weather. They could forecast that a lovely spring day would turn into a stormy night.

Reverend Greene's case was slightly different. After five long weeks in the county hospital, he was finally discharged. Back out on the street, his knee started to throb. The pain was mild at first, but it got worse as the time went by until he thought it was going to explode. He wondered if he should go back to the hospital.

And then all hell broke loose.

One day, he was walking down the street when two masked men ran out of a jewelry store, firing shots left and right. The store's earsplitting alarm was going off, drowning out any other sound. An old man chased after them, clutching a shotgun big enough to hunt large game in Africa. *Probably the owner,* Greene thought. The robbers had held him at gunpoint during the robbery, but the guy had found a way to activate the alarm.

"Get back here, you sons of bitches!" The man planted himself in the middle of the street and shouted at the top of his lungs. He jerked the rifle up to his shoulder and aimed at the fleeing robbers. "No one fucks with me!"

The shotgun's recoil threw the old man back several feet, but he raised it and fired again. Bright-red blood bloomed like a flower across the back of one of the robbers, and he collapsed on the ground. The other robber turned and took aim at the old man. His .38 looked like a toy compared to the jeweler's shotgun, but at that range, size didn't matter. The first bullet pierced the old man's side; the second bullet went through his right eye, killing him instantly. In a final reflexive gesture, the jeweler's index finger pulled the trigger even though its owner was dead. The shot sent the old man's limp body flying backward as the robber's head turned to jelly and splattered in every direction.

The whole thing only lasted ten or twelve seconds. The street got very still, except for the wailing alarm. The smell of gunpowder, blood, and shit hung in the air. Greene had flattened himself against a wall during the shooting. As he backed away from the bodies, he heard police sirens in the distance.

Then it dawned on him: his knee had stopped hurting. It felt good as new.

Greene didn't give it much thought until the next week. His knee was throbbing again as he sat in a coffee shop, pondering what to do with the last twenty-seven dollars in his pocket. Just then a dump truck ran a red light right in front of him, crushing a Chevrolet and the family of five inside it. Everyone was killed, including the truck driver.

And just like that, his damn knee stopped throbbing. The deaths he witnessed seemed to soothe it.

At first he told himself it was just a grim coincidence. But the same thing happened again and again, no matter where he was or what he was doing. The pain started out dull and pulsating, then grew until it was searing. Sometimes the pain went away when he left the place where it had started. When he consulted the newspapers or watched TV the next day, he'd learn that the place had been the scene of a bloody accident or crime after he left.

Other times, morbid curiosity got the better of him. When the throbbing started, he'd follow his macabre knee, guided by the pain the way sonar guides a bat. When he reached a spot where the pain got really bad, he'd hide and wait. Something always happened.

Over the next thirty-five years, he witnessed fifteen car wrecks, nineteen murders, an accidental decapitation, and two rapes that ended in death. To his surprise, he enjoyed every one of those tragedies, though he never admitted it—not even to God.

As the years went by, Reverend Greene developed a strange image of himself. He came to believe that his visions were a gift from the Lord (*Praise His name forever, amen, hallelujah*).

He could sense the presence of evil. More importantly, he could anticipate evil. In his mind, that qualified him as a prophet, one of the Lord's chosen few. If he could prophesy the coming of evil, didn't that make him the Lord's mouthpiece, announcing the inevitable arrival of the Antichrist?

Greene had been an itinerant preacher in the South since he was a teenager. The seventh son of barely literate farmers from Alabama, Greene never went to college. He set out to preach the word of God because he thought he felt the call. More likely he was fleeing his alcoholic father, who beat him, and his mother, who was schizophrenic. His words were stirring, but his knowledge of Scripture left a lot to be desired. That was a drawback for an itinerant preacher in the Bible Belt, where evangelical Christianity had deep roots and influenced every aspect of daily life.

But after the injury to his knee and the tragedies that the pain foretold, his sermons changed radically. Now he saw himself as the harbinger of the Apocalypse—and that changed everything. His obsessive message reached a fever pitch. The Lord would punish the sins of His wayward children. Those who lacked piety or were sodomists, Democrats, blacks, Jews, Mexicans, Muslims, Communists, or anyone who listened to rap music all fit into the huge cauldron where Greene cooked up his sermons. In the eyes of the Lord, anything that deviated from the tried and true principles of the old South was offensive. The Lord (*Praise His name forever, hallelujah, amen!*) was enraged and would soon unleash His righteous anger.

One day, the pain in Greene's knee became rhythmic and intense in a way he'd never experienced. He assumed an especially awful crime was about to take place. He waited for a few days, but nothing happened. Yet the throbbing got stronger. He downed Vicodin like candy, but the pain didn't stop. When he couldn't take it anymore, he decided he didn't want to witness whatever horror that throbbing foretold. In the middle of the night, he took down the tent where he preached his sermons, loaded it in his camper, and fled farther south.

Even then, the pain followed him like a faithful dog. For fifteen days, no matter where he went, the pain stuck to him the way dog shit sticks to a shoe. Disoriented, almost delirious, Greene instinctively drove on. If he'd listened to something other than Christian radio stations, he'd have learned that a pandemic was spreading around the world and that it had landed in America. When Reverend Greene reached Gulfport, Mississippi, he had no clue that the Apocalypse he thought he was destined to proclaim had already started two weeks earlier. What he did learn was something else again.

His knee stopped throbbing. The pain disappeared completely.

That had to mean something, but so much was going on in Gulfport, he couldn't figure out what. The National Guard was evacuating all residents to a Safe Zone in nearby Biloxi. Two-thirds of Gulfport's inhabitants had already fled; the rest were rushing around, packing up their belongings. When Greene drove his old camper down Main Street, hardly anyone noticed him. But Greene saw it all very clearly. That was what he was destined for, what he'd been waiting for all those years. The End of Days was upon them, but he knew where the Righteous could take shelter. He knew where they'd be safe from the wrath of the Lord—where the pain couldn't reach him.

Greene immediately set up his tent on the road between Gulfport and Biloxi, and as he mounted his pulpit, a current of energy shook his body like an electric shock. For the first time in all those years, he felt the call of the Lord burning inside him. Not even the muscles he'd used to set up the tent were sore.

"Listen to me, good people of Gulfport! Don't run away. You have nothing to fear! The Lord has sanctified this place and the plague *will not come here!*"

He ranted and raved at the top of his lungs for hours, but only a few curious onlookers or people too exhausted to go on stopped to hear his sermon. Then the Lord decided to help him, and Stanley Morgan crossed his path.

Stanley Morgan, known to his neighbors as Old Stan, had been mayor of Gulfport for nearly twenty years. White, Southern Baptist—and Republican to the core—Stan thought there was only one right way to do things: his way.

So when a spit-and-polish marine colonel with a Yankee accent planted himself in front of Stan's desk and ordered him to evacuate the entire town of Gulfport to the Biloxi Safe Zone in forty-eight hours, Stan had to muster every ounce of self-control not to punch out the guy's pearly white teeth.

Nobody told Stan Morgan what to do, and certainly not a cocky East Coast marine colonel. *Evacuate my city, my ass!* Gulfport had weathered thousands of emergencies. In 2005, Hurricane Katrina leveled the city, but even then, it was never completely evacuated. *They should name a library or a park after me. I deserve it, damn it!* But Stan was sure that would never happen if he were known as the mayor who evacuated his beloved city.

So he did everything he could to look like he was complying with evacuation orders, without actually lifting a finger. He kept one eye on the soldiers and the other on the TV, which showed the entire world crumbling.

Everyone in his town also tuned in to CNN and saw the Undead spreading unchecked across the country. When the media informed them that the nearest Safe Zone was in Biloxi, they all panicked. Families shoved their belongings into their cars and took off. But with no organized evacuation, all they managed to do was shut down the interstate between the two cities, trapping tens of thousands of people in a massive traffic jam. In just a few hours, when the Undead closed in, it would be the scene of an unimaginable massacre.

Stan did all he could to stop the people of Gulfport from leaving, but that proved harder than directing the floats at the homecoming parade. Panic kept everyone from thinking rationally. He argued, reasoned, pleaded, and cursed, but the imminent arrival of the Undead scared most people shitless. They said, "Sorry, Stan, really sorry, but . . ." then climbed into their cars and didn't look back.

That was until fate brought his town a half-crazy preacher yelling himself hoarse under a tent by the side of the road. Of course, the woods were full of guys like him: an itinerant preacher, living on charity, donations, and, Stan suspected, false miracles. He was yelling about the End of Days (a common theme in the Preacher's Manual). The really interesting part was what this particular preacher added: Gulfport was the only safe place for thousands of miles. Gulfport. His city. That gave Stan an idea.

Not pausing to ponder the situation, Stan climbed up on the preacher's rickety stage and stuck out his hand, flashing the same fake smile he used to seal a real estate deal.

"Good afternoon, Reverend. I'm Stan Morgan, mayor of Gulfport. I believe God has placed you in my path."

Two hours later, Reverend Greene's little tent was gone. In its place stood a tent as large as a circus big top that held over four hundred people and had a sound system that could rival the one in the Gulfport Marlins' stadium. No one on the interstate could miss Reverend Greene with Stan Morgan by his side.

People were drawn by the combination of Reverend Greene's magnetic preaching and the impressive figure of Stan Morgan, a man known to everyone in Gulfport. First, a couple of cars stopped, then three or four trucks. In less than half an hour, a small crowd had gathered under the tent, where Greene was declaring, in a raspy voice, that Gulfport was the only safe place in Mississippi. Stan knew that human beings were gregarious and would do what other people were doing, and soon, one after another, they followed their neighbors to the tent by the side of the road.

Stan circulated among the crowd. Greene's words were like a gentle hand stroking the back of a terrified dog. Suddenly, the mass hysteria was soothed. Before, their only plan had been to flee to the Biloxi Safe Zone. Now they were willing to listen to Stan.

"He's a holy man," Stan whispered, as he clutched hands and slapped backs. "He traveled across three states in that beat-up camper, surrounded by millions of the monsters, without getting a scratch on him. The Lord has surely blessed this man."

The frightened people looked at the reverend with changed eyes as they drank in his words. For weeks they'd lived in terror; the only news they heard was of death, devastation, and the mysterious plague of Undead headed their way. Greene's rousing talk of salvation and safety in their own home was music to their ears.

Thanks to the Apocalypse, for the first time in nearly forty years, the Reverend Josiah Greene addressed a congregation willing to listen to him. He was happy until months later, when the *Ithaca* sailed back into port, and his knee resumed its throbbing. The pain was slight, but unmistakable. Suddenly, Reverend Greene was afraid.

"Lucia! Prit! You gotta see this! I can't believe it!" I gasped as the *Ithaca* entered the Port of Gulfport. A pair of tugboats, exhaling huge puffs of smoke, slowly guided the colossal ship through the channel and into its berth. Enormous jets of water shot up along the tugboats' sides. People ran along the shore, cheering and waving their arms. Cars sped down the wide street along the waterfront as people leaned out the windows and honked their horns. The quiet town had gone a bit crazy.

No wonder. All that oil in the *Ithaca's* holds meant they'd have fuel for at least a year. Less than that if they continued to drive the six gas-guzzling Humvees that rushed toward the ship, a police car leading the way through the jubilant throng. I got worried when I got a closer look at them—they were the doorless version used in combat. A yellow school bus followed close behind. Crammed inside each Hummer were several men armed with assault rifles, each wearing a green band around his right forearm.

"Mission accomplished," Captain Birley said, lighting his pipe and surveying the harbor with a satisfied gaze. "With the Lord God Almighty's blessing, we went halfway around the world and returned home in one piece. Blessed is the Reverend Greene and blessed is this ship, wouldn't you agree?"

I almost pointed out that the half-dozen men who died back at Luba and the other four who were dumped into the ocean as fish food wouldn't agree. But I bit my tongue. Being cautious had kept us alive up till now.

"Is the Reverend Greene in that convoy?" Lucia asked as it came to a stop.

"Oh, no," Birley chuckled. "That's the reverend's Green Guard. They keep the peace in the Lord's city. They're here to collect that rabble in the bow. I'll feel a whole lot better when every one of those stinking lowlifes is off my boat."

"Hey, that's a terrible way to talk about those people!" The anger in Lucia's voice took me by surprise. "They risked their lives to fill your damn ship with oil. Without them, the trip would've been a complete failure."

Captain Birley stared at Lucia for a long moment with a menacing look in his eyes. He studied her as if he'd never seen her before, as if she'd magically materialized on his ship. He replied in an icy voice, drawing out his words.

"Watch what you say, young lady. It'd be a shame to have to spank a girl as lovely as you. You're a woman, so of course you don't know what you're talking about, but your menfolk need to teach you some manners."

"Who do you think you are, you piece of shit?" Lucia hurled insults at him in Spanish, which, fortunately, Birley didn't know. "Racist asshole! Prick! Macho pig!"

"Lucia, get ahold of yourself," I whispered and held on to her so she couldn't scratch Birley's eyes out.

"Did you hear what he said about those people? He's fucking sick!" Lucia struggled in my arms.

"I agree with you one hundred percent, but hear me out. I don't know what the hell's up with these people. One thing's clear—if your skin isn't white, you end up as cannon fodder," I said, forcing her to look me in the eyes. "And these people saved us, we're far from any place we can call home, and our lives depend on their goodwill. So, please, tone it down and apologize to the captain."

Lucia snorted in fury and shook me off. She stomped off to the other end of the bridge, brushing past Pritchenko, who watched her, stunned.

"What was that all about? She looked like a pissed-off Siberian tiger."

"Believe me, Prit, a Siberian tiger is a pussycat compared to Lucia."

I turned to Birley, who had witnessed the whole scene in silence. "Please excuse Lucia, Captain Birley. She's young and impulsive, plus I don't think she's feeling very well."

"Oh, don't worry, young man," Birley said, with a dismissive wave of his hand. "She's just a woman, so her opinion doesn't matter. Besides everyone knows that the female is a very fickle creature, especially if it's one of 'those days,' right? Trust me, you should keep her on a short leash, my friend."

Birley laughed and patted me on the back. I smiled, relieved that a confrontation had been averted; we'd live to see another day. Still, I felt miserable, like a damn traitor.

By then the *Ithaca* had docked. Lines as thick as a man's waist held it fast. Dockworkers secured two gangways to the ship, one forward and one aft. The school bus and the Humvees stopped in front of the aft gangway. Some of the men in the Humvees got out and stationed themselves around the vehicles; another group boarded the *Ithaca*. With shouts, curses, and kicks, they forced the soldiers on the bow into a compact cluster.

Those men who'd fought so bravely at Luba acted like frightened sheep . . . or like sheep resigned to their fate.

I studied the muscle-bound black soldier who'd led the troops. Even from where I stood, I could see the anger in his eyes. If looks could kill, half a dozen guys in green armbands would've died on the spot. But even he hung his head and got in line as the guards herded him and the other soldiers to the gangway.

Once on the ground, the guards ran a metal detector over their bodies, looking for weapons stashed in their clothes. Another guard passed out bottles of water, and a third checked them off a list as they boarded the bus.

"What do you make of that, Prit?"

"I have no idea. I'm sure those guys could make mincemeat of the guards in a heartbeat. And yet, there they go, like lambs to the slaughter."

"Amazing, isn't it?" Strangärd's voice behind us made me jump, but Prit didn't seem surprised. I was sure the Ukrainian had eyes in the back of his head.

"Who are those people?" Prit asked, curtly, pointing to the guards.

Strangärd looked from side to side to be sure no one was listening. "Those guards are ex-cons. The scum of the earth. The dregs of society. Evil incarnate. Don't cross their path and don't piss them off. They shoot first and ask questions later. But they're the law here, the reverend's private army. They carry out his orders to the letter. On top of that, most people in Gulfport adore them. They're convinced that those thugs make it possible for them to live in peace and safety."

I nodded, but what he said didn't make any sense. I studied the men carefully. They had bulging muscles from hours and hours of lifting weights. Most wore khaki pants, white shirts, and a green armband around their right bicep. Their heads were shaved; a few sported unruly beards.

"Some tattoo artist made a killing with that group," Pritchenko joked, cutting his eyes toward the guys nearest us. They were covered in tattoos of swastikas, cobwebs, skulls, and slogans spelled out in Gothic letters. One had "White Pride" tattooed on the back of his head.

White Pride. I realized with a chill that those rifle-toting guys were wearing the Aryan Nations armband. Those white supremacists made the Ku Klux Klan look tolerant. Before the Apocalypse, the organization had been implicated in extortion, drug running, murder, and arms trafficking. Every US federal prison had housed Aryan Nations members. Now they were the law in Gulfport.

Three of them walked up the aft gangway and headed in our direction. In the lead was a blond giant of about forty with ghostly blue eyes. A silver eagle was pinned to his armband and his white shirt strained over his beer belly. A black swastika peeked out at his collar. Tattoos on each knuckle spelled HATE JEWS. He planted himself in front of us and looked us up and down, letting his eyes linger on Lucia. She crossed her arms and looked down.

"So, these're the fish Birley reeled in on the high seas," he said to no one in particular. "When they told me you spoke Spanish, I thought you'd be one of those little Mexican shits. But you don't look like Mexicans. You, with the mustache, you look Aryan, even though you're a runt. Why do you speak that spic language, amigos?"

"We're Europeans." I stepped forward before any of my pals could speak. "He's Ukrainian and we're from northern Spain. We speak Spanish there too."

I doubted that tattooed giant could find Ukraine on a map, maybe not even Spain, but that explanation seemed to suffice.

He shrugged. "I don't give a rat's ass where you're from so long as you're white, Christian, and you don't fuck with Reverend Greene. I'm Malachi Grapes, head of the Green Guard. We make sure the white people of Gulfport live in peace. Do what the reverend says and you'll enjoy all the comforts of home. Buck the rules and we got a problem."

I didn't ask what kind of problem, but I could guess. Grapes then fixed his gaze on Pritchenko, who stared back calmly, not flinching. The Ukrainian didn't blink when the big man brought his face close to his, almost nose to nose.

"Fellas, we got a little rooster here," Malachi Grapes growled. "You got a problem, dwarf?" A chorus of laughter rose from the other two skinheads.

Prit took a deep breath, dragging phlegm from the back of his throat. For one tense second, I thought he was going to spit in the guy's face, but he just belched.

"You know, those black guys and Latinos you despise so much fought admirably," the Ukrainian replied casually, as if he were talking about the weather. "If a couple of them on that bus ever caught you without your backup, your white ass would look like the flag of Japan. You'd better not insult them like that when they're in earshot. And no, I don't have a problem with you, amigo. For now."

Time seemed to stand still. Grapes's face turned several colors. Finally he laughed and walked away. "Gotta hand it to you, shrimp, you got balls. But don't fuck with me or my men. Today's your first day, so I'll let that comment slide, but I won't always be so nice. Now let's go. The reverend's waiting."

We followed the guards down the gangplank. We had no luggage, except for Lucullus, who fidgeted, happy to be back on land. Strangärd climbed into a Humvee. He'd act as what he called our "liaison." The reverend wanted to hear about our rescue from a crewmember. With Captain Birley's hands full unloading the cargo, the task fell to Strangärd as first mate. As we roared off in the Humvees, I was relieved he was coming along. He was the closest thing to a friend we had, and something told me we were going to need all the help we could get.

1 4

Gulfport, Mississippi (The Magnolia State), was never a large city, and before the Apocalypse, it rarely appeared in national news. But its residents were proud of their town for three things: the Gulfport Marlins football team, the St. James Fall Festival with its pumpkin patches and hayrides, and for the Naval Construction Battalion Center—home of the Atlantic Fleet Seabees.

The Seabees had been part of the Civil Engineer Corps since the forties. They'd earned the nickname on account of the massive work they did during World War II. They contributed to Japan's defeat by constructing bases and airstrips on atolls in the Pacific Ocean. After the war, the Seabees expanded. Although its men would never win a shooting contest (most never held a rifle), they could erect infrastructure anywhere in the world.

When the plague broke out, half the base's personnel were in Afghanistan setting up a supply route to Kabul. A rescue was planned, but with the whole world plunged into chaos, combat units had priority on all flights. The planes that should have rescued them never got off the ground. If any of the corps survived, they were probably lost in the Afghan mountains, dodging the

Taliban, the Undead, or both. The other half of the corps was rushed to major US cities to build the Safe Zones. It's not hard to imagine their sad fate.

When Stan Morgan teamed up with that sleazy preacher on the outskirts of town, only about two dozen soldiers were left on the base in Gulfport, but they had mountains of supplies that had been stockpiled for decades.

Mayor Morgan was stubborn, ambitious, and unfaithful to his wife of twenty years, but he was also sharp as a tack and resourceful. When he returned from the Vietnam War, poor as a church mouse, he saw an opportunity in the emerging real estate market. He founded Morgan Real Estate and within two years became one of Gulfport's richest citizens.

Like the rest of the country, Stan watched the Undead attack the Safe Zones on CNN. Unlike everyone else, he decided that the best way to protect his town was not to defend it with weapons, but to build a wall around it so high and so strong that no Undead could scale it.

He knew the Seabees had warehouses with thousands of tons of steel and cement just waiting for someone to use them. After Hurricane Katrina, the Seabees' engineers came up with an ingenious system for building dams with metal rods and modified Portland cement that would keep the rivers from overflowing their banks and flooding fields and towns again. It was called the Mobile Containment Dike Fabrication Unit, but the soldiers baptized it "the Wallshitter."

The Wallshitter was a monster vehicle that looked like the love child of a dump truck and a locomotive. It could extrude a concrete module ten feet high by eight feet long in fifteen minutes. The best part was that the module came out half-set. In less than twenty-four hours, it dried rock hard, as sturdy as if it'd been there for years. The Gulfport Seabees base had twenty Wallshitters.

Stan's construction crew had years of experience, so with the help of manuals and the one tech left on the base, they learned how to run those monsters in under six hours. In another six hours, those twenty Wallshitters were at work setting up a steel and concrete perimeter around the entire town. In just seventy-two hours, Gulfport was completely surrounded by an impenetrable concrete wall, ten feet high. It was crude, ugly, and looked like the Berlin Wall's bastard sister, but it fulfilled Stan Morgan's objective: to keep the living in and the Undead out.

Besides the Wall, other factors saved Gulfport. For one thing, southern Mississippi was not heavily populated. And although the area was flat, there were swamps so dense even the most determined Undead couldn't get across them.

Strangärd explained all this to us as the Humvees raced through town. The green flag waving on the hood of the lead vehicle allowed them to ignore traffic lights and speed through crowded intersections. We could hardly believe how quiet and prosperous the town looked. People walked along clean, well-swept streets, stopping to talk, laugh, and joke as if hell had never been unleashed on earth. Shops were open, gardens were well tended, and cafes and restaurants operated normally. Everything was beautiful and perfect. Except for one flaw: there were only white people.

"This is . . . It looks like . . ." I stammered, trying to digest the scene.

"Like the set of a TV show? Amazing, isn't it?" Strangärd said with a half smile. "This was a middle-class town even before the Apocalypse. Most people are retirees, professionals, divorced, or here with their families—and rich. They moved here to escape their stressful lives back in larger cities and were lucky enough to watch the fall of civilization from this side of the Wall." His grin twisted into a sneer. "In the future, civilization will spring from them. Funny, isn't it?"

I didn't see anything funny about it. Kids, adults, and old people alike looked prosperous, healthy, and well fed, light-years from the skinny, impoverished survivors on Tenerife. There were only about thirty thousand people in Gulfport, whereas Tenerife was packed with several million refugees, straining the island's resources to the limit. Everyone looked relaxed and contented, a far cry from the fatalistic fear we couldn't shake after months of confronting hunger, destruction, and the Undead. These fine, upstanding people had barricaded themselves inside their Arcadia—the remote refuge Homer describes in the *Iliad*—while the rest of the planet slid down Satan's sewer.

"There's one thing I don't get. How can such classy people put up with those thugs? They look like ex-cons," I said, looking over at Malachi Grapes and one of his henchmen sitting in the front seat, enveloped in a cloud of cigar smoke.

"They *are* ex-cons." Strangärd lowered his voice. "Former inmates at Parchman Farm, maximum security prison for men—Mississippi's oldest and most notorious prison."

"How the hell'd they end up here?" Lucia demanded. She was still angry with me, and hadn't spoken since we got off the ship.

"They were on their way to Biloxi to build housing for the refugees. Due to a clerical error, four buses packed with prisoners ended up in Gulfport. No one knew what to do with them. The bus drivers didn't give a fuck what happened to them. They just wanted to unload their cargo and get back to the Safe Zone in Biloxi. They locked up the vans, gave the police chief the keys, and ran. The prisoners were closed up in there for twenty-four hours, parked at the port's loading dock in the hot sun. The

Aryan Nations gang outnumbered the other prisoners and were well organized. When the doors opened, they were the only ones left standing."

"They killed them?" Lucia asked.

Strangärd didn't answer; he just stared out the window, disgusted.

"That explains how they got here, but not how they became Greene's soldiers."

Riding in the lead Humvee, Malachi Grapes puffed on his cigar and a big smile spread across his face. He remembered every little detail of that day.

1 5

GULFPORT, TWO YEARS EARLIER

"Guards! Guards! Where the hell are you! It's a fucking oven in here!"

The prisoners beat on the barrier between the driver's seat and the rear of the bus. All forty guys shouted, banged on the windows, and cursed a blue streak. They'd been parked in the lot for an entire day. The heat was addling their brains.

For the first few hours, the guards had brought them water and some food, but as the day wore on the situation was growing more and more explosive. One fat, red-faced prisoner had died of a heart attack a few hours before. They'd tossed his body in the rear of the van. The black gangbanger chained to him wasn't acting so tough anymore. He whined and tugged on the chain that tethered him to the body that was starting to bloat.

"Help! Get me loose. I'm fuckin' beggin' ya. Help me, please. This guy's about to explode. I don't wanna die! Please help me!"

From his seat several rows up, Malachi Grapes shrugged. He could've easily freed the guy if he wanted to. He could've cut off the fat guy's hand with the knife he had in his orange prison jumpsuit, but he didn't move an inch. For one thing, he despised the gangbanger because he was black. Plus, he was keeping the knife hidden. The Day of the Pig was about to begin.

The previous day, the guards had hauled the prisoners out of Parchman, driven for several hours, and then abandoned them in the parking lot. Grapes knew it wasn't a transfer. A guy with connections could find out anything, especially if you were the head of the local Aryan Nations. Plus, he'd never heard of transferring every inmate in the prison.

Fifteen Aryan Nations members were on that van. The rest of the inmates were Crips or Bloods or members of Mexican or Asian gangs, including the Filipino guy rotting at the back of the bus. Grapes felt sure the situation was the same in the other three vans.

In prison, the guards had blocked communication between gang members, so they'd come up with many ways to send messages. With no one standing guard over them, sending messages from one bus to another was a breeze—they just shouted a little louder. Over the last few hours, they'd concocted a plan. Grapes's instructions raced through the other buses.

"When do we start, Malachi?" Seth Fretzen leaned across the aisle with eager eyes.

"Any minute now, Seth," Grapes muttered under his breath.

A white liquid seeped out the corner of the dead guy's mouth. When it dripped on the prisoner chained to him, he became hysterical.

"This motherfucker's gonna explode! Get me loose! Get me the hell loose!"

A prisoner stood up to lend a hand, but he was chained to an Aryan Nations gang member, who yanked the chain that bound them. The prisoner fell to the ground, and a fight broke out in the back of the bus.

"Now," Malachi Grapes said. "Let's go."

Seth Fretzen lit a piece of paper with a match he'd hidden and waved the flame in front of the barred window. Someone in the next bus spotted the signal and passed it along to the other buses.

Grapes didn't wait for the flame to go out. Lightning fast, he drew the knife out of his sleeve and plunged it into the neck of the Puerto Rican guy next to him. The guy's eyes flew open wide, blood bubbled up on his lips, and he drowned.

Seth Fretzen used his chain to strangle the guy next to him, a black guy from the West Coast. The man struggled for a few seconds, but he didn't stand a chance. When Seth let go, the guy's arms fell down at his sides as if they were filled with sawdust.

Malachi headed to the back of the bus to help out, but his boys had the situation under control. Since they were in the majority, were well armed, and had the element of surprise, they'd taken out the other prisoners in short order. Only one of his guys was injured. He'd cut his own arm as he hacked through another prisoner's neck.

Adrenaline rushed through their bodies. They roared, high-fived, beat their chests, and spat on the bodies. Then they sat down to wait.

Two hours later, it occurred to Malachi Grapes that maybe offing those losers wasn't such a good idea. In prison, you barely had time to get rid of your weapon before the guards arrived. But here, no one came. And the bodies were starting to stink.

With one swat, Grapes crushed a greedy fly that had landed on his neck. His mind was racing, devising an alternate plan. Then suddenly someone opened the door of the bus. Fifteen skinheads shouted insults at the guards, but then a heavy silence fell over the crowd.

Instead of guards in riot gear on the other side of the barrier, there stood a man of about sixty, wearing a suit and a huge Stetson hat, holding a Bible. His face gave nothing away as he stared at the carnage.

That asshole's praying, Grapes thought, as the old man's lips moved soundlessly. The man absentmindedly rubbed his right knee, pulled some keys out of his pocket, and headed for the door. But then he stopped, as if he'd suddenly remembered something.

"Do you men fear of the wrath of the Lord?" he asked.

Grapes shook his head, wondering if he'd heard correctly. *I must be hallucinating in this heat.* "What'd you say, Reverend?"

"I asked if you men fear of the wrath of the Lord," Greene said patiently.

When Grapes got to his feet, the corpse of the Puerto Rican man fell to the floor with a thud. His sweeping gesture encompassed the entire bus as he turned back to the man behind the barrier. "Look around, Reverend. We are the fucking wrath of the Lord."

The old man seemed pleased by that answer and nodded in satisfaction. "I see you've cleaned up the scum and sin on this bus. Those bastard races have no place in New Jerusalem." His hypnotic voice silenced even the most disrespectful Aryans. "But the real evil is out there, ready to pounce on this corner of the world that God is protecting. So I ask you, if I free you, will you be the instrument of the Lord's wrath?"

"We'll be whatever you want, Reverend, just get us off this fucking bus."

"Alright." Greene's face lit up as if he had found the solution to a particularly difficult puzzle. "But first, let us pray to enlighten your souls. Please kneel."

"What the hell's this lunatic saying?" Seth snarled.

"Shut the fuck up," Grapes growled. He couldn't take his eyes off the preacher. "Do what he says. Kneel and pray. If you don't, I'll kick your teeth out your ass."

The Aryan Nations members knelt and prayed along with Greene, who whispered, eyes closed, arms raised toward the sky, his face contorted in ecstasy.

At the end of the prayer, Greene unlocked the door with the ring of keys he'd found in the police station. Then he walked down the aisle, unlocking the prisoners' shackles, stepping over the bodies of the murdered prisoners as if they were piles of garbage. He held out his Bible for every Aryan to kiss and laid his hands on their heads.

Grapes had to bend over so the reverend could lay his hands on his bald head. The moment Greene touched him, Grapes felt an electric current run through his body from head to toe. He gasped in surprise and stared at Greene. He had to lean against the seat to keep from falling. The reverend's eyes were fiery black pools. Grapes thought he saw sparks of madness in the midst of those flames, shrouded in a suffocating evil darkness so thick he could almost touch it.

The preacher terrified him, but at the same time, the dark force in the strange man filled Grapes with the most forceful feeling he'd ever experienced. In prison he'd met some of the craziest, most evil men imaginable, but they couldn't hold a candle to the menacing energy radiating from the reverend's eyes. Grapes understood the man and feared him. He fell completely under the preacher's spell. Whatever it was, he loved the guy.

"Who do you want knocked off, Reverend?" he asked respectfully.

"Follow me and I'll show you," said Greene as he climbed off the bus. Grapes was surprised to see that the preacher dragged his right leg. He was sure the man hadn't been limping when he climbed on the bus.

Outside, Grapes saw that the rest of his men were being released too. Forty-four Aryans stood on the parking lot, squinting, looking around as if they couldn't believe they were outside with no chains, no walls, and no guards.

A van was parked in front of them. The sign on its side read:

MUNICIPAL SERVICES OF GULFPORT
—WHERE YOUR SHIP COMES IN

Two people stood beside the van: a tall, burly guy who looked like he was used to being obeyed and a short, bald, potbellied sheriff in his fifties who looked extremely nervous. *Can't blame him*, thought Grapes. *I'll bet he's wondering what the fuck he'll do if we suddenly go apeshit.* But nobody was going to do that. The reverend said he needed someone killed, and Grapes would've killed his own mother just to see the black force in that man's eyes.

"Maybe this wasn't such a good idea, Reverend Greene . . ." said the tall guy, trying to act important.

His name is Greene, Grapes thought.

"Arming these guys might've been a bad idea . . ." The sheriff's whiny voice chimed in as he wrung his hands.

"It's a revelation from the Lord Himself. God told me Gulfport would be a safe place, a New Jerusalem. He told me these sinners are part of His divine plan." The reverend was on a roll. He took Grapes by the shoulder. "This man's name is—"

"Malachi Grapes," the ex-con heard himself say.

"Malachi." Greene mulled over the biblical name with delight. "He's a soldier of Christ and he won't have any trouble getting rid of those things."

Gulfport had always been a quiet place. The worst problem the police had to deal with was the occasional wayward teenager or obnoxious drunk. The idea of having forty gang members armed with assault rifles around town didn't inspire confidence. It dawned on the sheriff that he and his one deputy would have to confront them if things took a bad turn. But the reverend seemed so sure. Since he'd turned up, life in Gulfport had gone extremely well—even while the rest of the world went to hell. Until that morning, when those Undead monsters invaded the Bluefont subdivision, south of town.

The reverend seemed to cast the same spell on Mayor Morgan, who stared at the huge Aryan gang member for a few seconds, then made a decision. "In this truck are assault rifles and ammunition. Five minutes from here is a neighborhood in trouble. At least fifteen of those things showed up. We don't know what shape the residents are in. You need to go in there, wipe out the monsters, and rescue my people. Can you do that?"

As an answer, Grape opened the truck's tailgate, grabbed an M16 and a magazine, and with the expertise that comes from lots of practice, loaded it in the blink of an eye.

"I don't know who you're talking about, but you have my word that tonight they'll be dining with Satan."

Grapes passed around the weapons. Bunched up at the back of the van was a green tarp some worker had left there. In a flash of inspiration, Grapes tore it into strips, tied one around his bicep, and handed the rest to his boys.

"Since we are Reverend Greene's soldiers of God, shouldn't we wear a green armband?" He flashed a wolfish grin at his men.

Greene nodded, pleased, but that idea was a bitter pill Stan Morgan had to swallow. He liked to have the upper hand, and he had the feeling they were leaving him out. "I don't want any complaints from the neighbors," Stan said. "No theft, looting, or destruction of property. Finish off those monsters and come straight back. Got it?"

"Whatever you say, boss. Come on, boys! Let's kick some ass!"

Ten minutes later, they were at the entrance to Bluefont, a subdivision of about three hundred houses. A deep river, crossed by two bridges, ran in front of it and emptied into a marsh nearby. The south side of the river was being guarded by a kid right out of high school and a handful of men in their fifties armed with hunting rifles, all about to shit their pants.

"The Undead entered by the north bridge," one of them said. "The Wall isn't closed on that side yet. Ted Krumble and his boys were supposed to be watching the bridge. We heard shots and an explosion an hour ago. I don't know what the devil happened to them. We've been calling them on the radio ever since, but they don't answer. That's all we know."

Grapes nodded, guardedly. "Who are these . . . what'd you call 'em . . . Undead?"

The guards looked at him with amazement. Annoyed, Malachi explained they didn't get any newspapers in prison, so they had no idea what was going on. The men quickly brought him up to speed. The gang quietly absorbed the information. It wasn't that they didn't believe those frightened old men, but surely the situation wasn't as serious as they made it sound. Probably just some guys on a rampage. A few ounces of lead would fix that problem.

"On the radio, they said you gotta shoot 'em in the head," a resident said in a frightened voice.

"I'll keep that in mind." Grapes strode quickly across the bridge, followed closely by his men.

Once on the other side, he noticed that something wasn't right. Bluefont was a typical American suburb with big houses and gardens, the kind of place rich white people moved to as soon as they got the chance. But they didn't see anyone on the street. A lawn mower was lying on its side, still running. Its bag had come off and grass clippings floated down the sidewalk on a gentle breeze. A Subaru sat in the middle of the street, its engine running, all its doors standing wide open. Grapes carefully reached in and turned off the engine. The silence was unsettling. Then they heard the groans coming from the north end of the subdivision.

"Trent, take Bonder, Ken, and three other guys. Cover those houses. The rest of you, go house to house in groups of three. Make sure they're empty. If you steal so much as a pen, I'll personally rip your guts out. Got that?"

The men nodded and split into groups. Grapes continued down the center of the street, on high alert, followed by three guys—Seth Fretzen, a small, quiet guy named Crupps, and a fat, bearded guy they called Sweet Pussy, God knows why.

They came to an abrupt stop at one house. The door was ajar and there was a puddle of fresh blood on the ground. Someone had leaned against the doorframe and left a bloody handprint. A drop of blood trickled slowly down the white wood.

Something shattered inside the house. Grapes signaled for his men to stay close as they headed for the porch. He climbed the staircase slowly, trying not to make any noise, but the stairs creaked with each step.

When he reached the door, he thrust the barrel of his M16 inside. The interior was dark and cool. A hallway led to a living room in the back. On the right was a staircase to the upstairs;

blood was splashed on several steps. Someone had dragged himself along the wall. All the pictures that once hung there now lay shattered on the ground.

He gestured to Seth and Crupps to head upstairs. With Sweet Pussy at his heels, he walked down the hall to the living room.

The room screamed, *My owner is fucking rich.* The furniture was high-end. A dozen people would fit on the sofa. A monstrous TV hung on the wall. The carpet was so thick, if a coin fell onto it, no one would ever find it.

Sweet Pussy tugged on his sleeve and pointed to the ground. In one corner, next to a huge china cabinet, lay a broken vase. That must be what they had heard crash.

A dragging sound came from the kitchen. They stepped over the broken vase and eased up to the door. Grapes stopped in his tracks, stunned.

A girl in her early twenties swayed in the middle of the room, a blank look in her eyes. She was tall, slim, with a great body. She was wearing nothing but a tiny thong.

She must be stoned out of her mind, Grapes thought. It was hard to tear his eyes away from the girl's perky boobs. Straight blond hair hid half of her face. She hadn't noticed the two men enter the room.

Something's wrong with this picture. His brain was shouting warnings, but he couldn't fit the pieces together. Sweet Pussy came up behind him. When he saw the naked girl, his eyes opened wide.

"Fuck! Hello, gorgeous!" he exclaimed and walked up to the girl. "You see this, Grapes? What a rack—"

With a lustful leer, Sweet Pussy reached for the girl's breasts, which were covered with burst veins. The girl looked at him with dead eyes and, before he could react, sank her teeth into his neck.

The Aryan let out a surprised shout and shoved the girl away. With the butt of his rifle, he struck her face and shattered her front teeth. Grapes stared in amazement. Instead of collapsing, the girl threw herself on Sweet Pussy again, as if nothing had happened.

Things got crazy fast. Sweet Pussy tried to hit the girl again, but her bite had severed his carotid. He didn't know it, but his brain was already dying. He swung wide, but couldn't stop the girl from pouncing on him. They rolled on the ground as a mountain of dishes crashed around them. With a shove, he was able to back up a few feet and fire his M16 at the girl.

The hollow-point bullets opened a huge hole in the girl's abdomen and sent her flying backward. Her body slid slowly down the wall as her guts spilled out.

"Grapes . . ." Sweet Pussy stuttered, lying on the floor, as he put his hand on his neck. "Grapes . . . help . . . me."

Grapes knew the guy was done for. Blood streamed out of his neck as his heart kept pumping, trying to feed his dying brain. The light went out in Sweet Pussy's eyes, but Grapes wasn't paying any attention to that. The naked girl had risen again.

With an unintelligible moan, she stumbled toward him, stepping on broken dishes, her feet tangled up in the intestines spilling out of her abdomen.

Grapes raised his rifle and blew the top of the girl's head off. Her forehead split open like a rotten orange, splattering blood and bone graffiti on the wall behind her. Only then did the girl fall to the ground, dead as a doornail.

"Let's see you get up now, bitch." Grapes kicked the girl's buttocks. Then he heard a noise behind him.

Sweet Pussy was struggling to his feet, skidding and flailing around like a drunk. Grapes turned and almost fell backward at the sight. The guy's neck was torn and his prison jumpsuit was drenched with his blood. The worst part was that Sweet Pussy's skin was covered with thousands of small veins.

"Hey, Sweet Pussy," Grapes said, with a strange tremor in his voice. "You look really bad, buddy. Someone should take a look at that wound . . ."

Sweet Pussy didn't answer. He raised his head and looked at Grapes with the same lifeless expression as the girl. With a low growl, he lunged at Grapes but stumbled on the girl's leg and fell to the ground, smashing the rest of the dishes.

He's like her. Vampires or something. Grapes's mind was racing as he raised his rifle. Three feet away, he couldn't miss. He fired three shots into Sweet Pussy's heart and chest. What was left of the Aryan got up, as if Grapes had blown him kisses.

"You gotta be dead!" Malachi yelled, terrified for the first time since he was sixteen and in reform school. With the bitter taste of panic in his mouth, he held the barrel eight inches from Sweet Pussy's face and opened fire. Sweet Pussy's face disappeared in a mass of red jelly. He collapsed onto the girl's body and finally stopped moving.

The room smelled of blood and gunpowder. Grapes leaned against the china cabinet, shaking. *That's not possible; it's just not possible,* he thought over and over. Then he heard gunshots coming from the top floor and an explosion a few blocks away. It dawned on him that kicking these things' asses would be a lot harder than he'd thought.

Six hours later, thirty-three exhausted Aryans, trembling and covered in blood, regrouped at the south entrance to the bridge. They'd cleaned out Bluefont, but it had taken a terrifying toll. Reverend Greene was waiting for them with a radiant smile. The neighbors gazed at them with reverence. Those fellas had saved Bluefont. Greene's boys had saved Gulfport. The reverend must truly be blessed by God.

Grapes walked up to the reverend, asking himself, *Is this really the right place for him and his men? It must be even worse outside of that town.* Then Greene gave him that look. Grapes gasped as the black force hit him, and he struggled to catch his breath.

Malachi Grapes realized he'd found his place in the world. A fucking great place.

"Sir, they're here." Susan Compton, the reverend's private secretary, waddled around on her short legs. She was in her late fifties, heavyset, myopic, and uglier than sin, but she was extremely efficient and ran the mayor's office with an iron fist.

"Show them in, Susan." Reverend Greene walked behind his desk and sat down in the big chair that had belonged to Stan Morgan (*God rest his soul, amen, hallelujah*). The mayor of Gulfport had conveniently died of a heart attack the week after he appointed Greene his chief advisor, handing the city to the reverend on a silver platter.

Reverend Greene's knee had been throbbing off and on all day, but just then the pain went up a notch.

Five people followed Mrs. Compton through the door. Malachi Grapes led the way, followed by Officer Strangärd. Greene was more interested in the three people behind him.

First came a tall, thin man around thirty, with tangled black hair and a wary look on his face. Close behind him strode a blond guy with strange blue eyes and a bushy mustache. The third member of the group was a tall, very pretty young girl, with a huge orange cat asleep in her arms. Most importantly, all three were white.

"Welcome to New Jerusalem, my children! Welcome to Gulfport, the Lord's fortress, home of the Righteous and the Second Coming of Christ!" The reverend walked over and laid hands on each of them.

"It was a long trip here," replied the tall guy, confused by the reverend's gesture.

"I'm anxious to hear the story from your own lips, but first I would like Officer Strangärd to tell me how God put you on the path to salvation." The reverend waved Grapes out of the room, thinking, *Let not your right hand know what your left is doing, saith the Lord.*

The officer related how the trio had sent up flares and described their rescue in the middle of the storm. Strangärd narrated the story in a methodical, professional way. When he'd finished, he relaxed slightly and waited patiently for the reverend to ask questions.

Reverend Greene nodded. He was sure Captain Birley's report would corroborate the first mate's version. *Have eyes and ears everywhere,* he thought. That wasn't from the Bible. His father said that—one of the few things he'd learned from the crazy drunk.

"That will be all, Strangärd." Greene ushered him to the door. "I don't want to take up your valuable time. I'm sure Captain Birley needs your help unloading the *Ithaca.*"

The Swede started to protest, but Greene stood firm. Once they were alone in the office, he invited the three shipwrecked people to take a seat.

"Alright, now. Please begin," he said and leaned back in his chair.

Their spokesman was the tall man, who he said he'd been a lawyer before the Apocalypse. Occasionally the blond guy added something. The girl just nodded, stroking the cat absentmindedly.

" . . . when we reached Tenerife," the lawyer said, "we were surprised to discover that the island was full of refugees from all over Europe."

"Full of refugees?" Greene sprang out of his chair. "Weren't there any Undead?"

"No, the island was safe, like Gulfport, but living conditions were harder. All those people consumed huge amounts of resources. Life was hard, but people had dignity."

"And there were no Hitler-style racial-purity laws," the girl grumbled, scowling.

The lawyer shot the girl a warning look, but Greene wasn't listening. His mind was racing. *An island full of refugees! Someplace besides Gulfport where people had survived the Apocalypse!* Cold sweat ran down his back. *Did that mean that Gulfport wasn't the New Jerusalem, that they weren't the only lambs saved by the Lord? If they weren't the only ones . . . No, that was impossible.*

Reverend Greene knew he was the Prophet. The savior of the Righteous. Everyone in Gulfport believed that, and he drove home the idea in his daily sermons. The community never questioned his leadership. If the people of Gulfport found out there were other refuges, they might decide they didn't have to rely on the reverend for their salvation, that his ideas weren't the Lord's revelations. *I can't let that happen.*

The lawyer finished his story. Greene studied them in silence, then leaned forward with a huge smile on his face. "Dear brothers and sister! You're like the prodigal son. You have walked through the valley of the shadows to the land of milk and honey, where the lamb and the lion lie down together. Henceforth the Christian Republic of Gulfport shall be your home."

"We greatly appreciate that, Reverend," said the lawyer, relieved. "Of course, we're willing to help out in any way we can. If there's anything we can do . . ."

"Yes, my son, I do have a huge favor to ask of you."

"What is that?"

"I must ask you to not tell your story to anyone. Not a soul. Have you told anyone?"

"Captain Birley knows." The lawyer thought for a moment, then continued. "Now that you mention it, none of the other officers asked any questions."

Well done, Birley, Reverend Greene thought. *You certainly know how to keep your men in line. Now I see why that damn Swede was so anxious to stick around.*

"Well," Greene continued, taking a moment to think up an excuse. "That's good. I need you to keep the secret for one simple reason. If the good and pious people of Gulfport found out that there are needy people on the other side of the world, they'd insist on undertaking an expedition to rescue everyone from darkness and sin."

"I understand," said the lawyer. A warning bell went off in his head.

Experienced in detecting lies and half-truths, Greene noticed the nervous glances the three exchanged. They were hiding something. *I don't want to know a thing about Tanereefay or whatever the hell that place is called. They were on the run when they met up with the* Ithaca. *Something had spooked them.*

"The good people of Gulfport would gladly risk their lives to undertake such a trip. That's the kind of faithful followers of Christ they are." The reverend opened his arms, as if embracing that multitude. "But I must watch over my flock. I can't allow them to launch a suicide mission to bring all those people to the safety of Gulfport. So I ask for your silence. You understand, don't you?"

"Of course, Reverend," the lawyer quickly assured him. "Our lips are sealed."

"But people have the right to know there are other survivors around the world!" the girl protested. "If they don't know, they're like prisoners in this city! All those people, those 'helots,' are entitled to decide if they want to live elsewhere, someplace they're not treated like criminals!"

"Lucia, this isn't the time for that," the lawyer cut her off. "The reverend asked us a favor, just one favor in return for his hospitality. I think we owe him that."

Lucia opened her mouth to add something. Seeing the lawyer's stern look, she stopped, pressed her lips in a tense line, and stroked the cat so hard he yowled in protest.

"My dear child," interrupted Greene, in a pious voice. "Let me tell you a story. Long ago, there was a Greek city named Sparta. Certainly they were wicked idolaters who worshiped false gods of clay, far from the Light of our Lord, yet it was an admirable society in many ways. The Spartans were surrounded by enemies who wanted them dead at any cost, as it is with us today. To survive, they created a caste called 'helots' who cultivated their fields, tended their cattle, and provided all material goods, thus allowing the Spartans to devote their time to defending their walls. And so it is here. That is precisely why we have our helots."

"Who decides if a person is a helot or not?" Lucia asked in a small voice.

"The Lord God, of course," Greene said, genuinely surprised. "Adam and Eve were white. So were the Apostles, Moses, and all the prophets in the Bible. God decided that. The other races are either mongrels, like those Mexicans, or the fruits of sin, like the Negros who bear the mark of that sin on their skin. They live under our holy protection so they can atone for their wicked ways."

Lucia made a colossal effort to bite her tongue as Prit shifted uncomfortably in his chair. Only the lawyer kept a passive look on his face, not betraying the slightest emotion.

"Reverend," the lawyer said in an even voice. "Where we come from, that way of thinking would be frowned upon. Please understand—"

"No!" Greene cut in, slapping his hand on the table. "There's nothing to understand! Because of mankind's negligence, toler- ance, and hedonism, God has punished the human race! For years I warned that this would happen, but no one listened! Everyone ignored me! Do you understand? Then it was too late! I was right! I am the Prophet!" Greene was on his feet and waving his arms wildly as he spoke, his eyes feverish. His tie had come loose and he spewed tiny flecks of spit. "God has unleashed His fury because we've lived side by side with queers, Communists, blacks, Indians, and Latinos! Until we get back on the righteous path, there will be no Second Coming! If you don't accept this truth, there's no room in Gulfport for you!"

Greene slumped in his chair, panting. He poured a glass of water with a trembling hand. Drops of water spilled on his chest as he drank.

"Well? What's your answer? What side of the Wall are you on?

"We . . ." the Ukrainian began.

"We accept your hospitality and your rules, Reverend Greene," the lawyer broke in. "We promise to be good citizens of Gulfport."

"But this is—" Lucia started to say. The lawyer's eyes told her to shut up.

"Is she your wife?" asked the reverend.

"She's my girlfriend, but I don't see what—"

"Keep her on a tight leash, my friend. 'Let the woman learn in silence with all subjection. Suffer not a woman to teach, nor to usurp authority over the man, but to be in silence.' Timothy 2, 11–12." Reverend Greene recited from memory, caressing his Bible. "The Lord tells us where a women's place is. They are mothers and wives, but their brains are clearly not made for thinking."

"Don't worry, Reverend. She'll learn to control her tongue," said the lawyer, giving Lucia another look. Red-faced with anger and humiliation, the girl looked down and stroked the cat.

"In that case, I think we're done. Mrs. Compton will tell you where your new home is. There's plenty of space in Gulfport. When you see where you're living, you'll be—"

The door flew open. *What now? This meeting isn't going the way I'd hoped.*

Malachi Grapes stood in the doorway, looking nervous and shifting uneasily from side to side as if he needed to take a piss.

"What's the matter, Malachi?" Greene asked, extremely annoyed. Everyone knew not to interrupt the reverend except in an extreme emergency.

"There's problems with the helots from the *Ithaca*, Reverend. A Mexican group refuses to accept their payment. They're arguing about something, but I have no idea what they're saying. They don't speak English, just that Spanish shit." Grapes put his hand over his mouth.

"Excuse my language, Reverend."

"How dare they!" The reverend sprang to his feet and pointed his calloused finger at Grapes. "Teach them a lesson! Kill half of them! That'll put them in their place!"

"No!" Lucia blurted out. The Ukrainian and the lawyer turned to her, shocked by the passion in her trembling voice. "Don't kill them, Reverend! I beg you!"

"Shut up, girl!" the reverend snapped. "Grapes, you know what to do."

"Right away, Reverend."

The Aryan turned and started out the door. The lawyer jumped to his feet.

Now what? thought Greene.

"Just a minute, Reverend. Spanish is my native language. Let me talk to them. Maybe I can find out what their demands are and avoid bloodshed."

Greene sat back down and mulled over the lawyer's words. There were hundreds of helots. They could always be replaced, but the situation was still explosive, and a purge wouldn't calm that down. He couldn't risk an all-out rebellion.

"Alright," he said, as he grabbed his hat. "Come with me. Your wife and your friend can go to their new home. Mrs. Compton will escort them."

Without another word, he strode out of the room. The lawyer exchanged a few rushed, angry words with his friends, but Greene was too enraged to care. *You fix the problems in your home. I have to fix my problem. Now.*

Grapes waited behind the wheel of the Humvee with the engine running. The reverend climbed in the back and the lawyer sat up front. They drove north for a few minutes in total silence, each lost in thought. When they arrived, the Humvee stopped at a bridge that crossed a wide river channel. A high, reinforced concrete wall, topped with barbed wire, ran along both shores. On the bridge was a rusted sign, riddled with bullet holes, that read, "Welcome to Bluefont!" Next to it stood a massive fortified tower that resembled something you'd expect to see on a castle from the Middle Ages, with searchlights on the top. Two Aryans were stationed up there behind M60 machine guns, aimed at the heavy steel gate that sealed off the bridge. On the other side of that gate was a group of about fifty helots shouting, shaking their fists, and throwing rocks and bottles at the tower. None of them was armed. The helots weren't allowed to have weapons inside Gulfport's borders.

"Well, my son," Greene said, getting out of the vehicle. "Here's your chance. Show me what you got."

The lawyer got out of the Humvee and walked up to the steel door. An Aryan opened a side door and let him pass, slamming the door behind him.

The helots fell silent when they saw the nervous lawyer. He took a deep breath and walked toward them, trying to look more confident than he felt.

"Hello everyone," he said in Spanish. "I'm here on behalf of Reverend Greene. What's going on?"

A tall, dark guy in a military uniform with the name tag "Dobzhansky" on the pocket stepped forward. "I'm Carlos Mendoza. Who're you? Whaddaya want?"

"I'm the guy who can stop those thugs from you wiping you out." He pointed to the two Aryans with machine guns. "Tell me what the hell you want or Greene'll order them to open fire. He's right on the edge. So I'll ask again, what's going on?"

"They tricked us!" bellowed a voice from the crowd. "They promised us ten liters per person, and we only got three!"

A chorus of voices joined in. Carlos Mendoza raised his hand for silence and turned back to the lawyer.

"You heard 'em. They owe each person who was on the *Ithaca* seven more liters of Cladoxpan. Tell your reverend we're not moving till he gives us what he owes us."

"Cladoxpan? What's that? Some kind of alcohol?"

Mendoza sighed. "You're kidding, right? You don't know what Cladoxpan is? Where'd you come from? Wait a minute. You're one of the shipwrecked people the *Ithaca* rescued, aren't you?"

The lawyer nodded uneasily. Mendoza laughed mirthlessly.

"You gotta be fucking kidding me, man. Those assholes don't have the balls to come to this side of the fence. They send some poor fool who doesn't know shit."

"Tell me what you're talking about and maybe I can help," the lawyer replied calmly.

"Cladoxpan's a drug," Mendoza explained as if he were talking to a child. "It keeps TSJ at very low levels so we can live as humans. We're all infected with that fucking virus. If we don't drink at least a pint of that stuff a day, we're screwed. Got it, white boy?"

The lawyer took a breath, thinking over what he'd heard. "So, it's a palliative. Cladoxpan doesn't cure TSJ. It just weakens it so it can't take effect."

"Very good, Einstein," Mendoza said bitterly. "It's like insulin for diabetics. If we keep taking it, we're fine. If we stop . . . it's over. That asshole promised us ten liters if we got on that fucking ship, so he owes us seven more. We held up our end of the deal!"

"How'd you get infected?" the lawyer asked, ignoring Mendoza's demands.

"How do you think, asshole?" Mendoza rolled up his sleeve. He had a huge scar on his shoulder from what was clearly a human bite. Part of the muscle was missing too.

"Tell your fucking reverend to cough up what he owes us. We're not moving till he does. Got that?"

The lawyer nodded and slowly walked back to the steel door. On the other side, Greene was pacing beside the vehicle while Malachi Grapes barked orders to the heavily armed Aryans perched in the tower.

"Well? What do they want?"

"They say you owe them seven liters per person of something called Cladoxpan. They say you promised it to them in exchange for participating in the operation at Luba. They say they're not moving till you give it to them."

The reverend turned bright red, and his lower lip trembled with rage. "Who do they think they are? Filthy, stinking wetbacks! I'll kill 'em all! And good riddance! The wrath of the Lord will rain down on them! I won't tolerate such insolence!"

"Wait, Reverend," interrupted the lawyer. "I don't think that's such a good idea. Killing them won't solve the problem, and Gulfport will lose a lot of brave men. I saw how they fought in Luba. They're real tough guys. If you kill them, it'll take a lot of time to train other men to be that good, and the city will be vulnerable without well-trained helots."

Then, in a moment of inspiration, he blurted out, "On top of that, it would be an affront to God to wantonly destroy the useful tool He has placed in your hands."

Don't lecture me, boy, thought Reverend Greene. But after he reflected for a few moments, he saw some truth in what the man was saying.

"Fine. But I'll only give them five liters each. Not one drop more. They can accept that or I'll order my Green Guard to exterminate them—like a gardener weeding his garden." Without another word, he got back in the Humvee, his gaze straight ahead.

The lawyer ran back to the other side of the Wall, where the helots waited restlessly. They debated Reverend Greene's offer and then agreed.

Mendoza scowled. "Tell your Reverend Greene we accept. But this isn't over."

The lawyer nodded, relieved.

As he walked away, Mendoza called to him. "Oh, hey." The Mexican had a bold smile on his face. "Say hello to Lucia for me. Tell her I was glad we got a chance to talk and get acquainted. Tell her she can visit any time." Then he turned and walked away, leaving the lawyer confused. Uneasy feelings swirled around in his heart.

It was almost dark when Grapes's men dropped me off in front of the house we'd been assigned. A gentle rain was falling and light from the streetlights was pooling in strange shapes. It felt like the rain was seeping into my bones as a strange cold flooded over me.

I was dirty, tired, and emotionally drained, but I lingered outside, delaying the inevitable. I didn't have the energy to face what awaited me. Finally I climbed the front steps and entered my new home.

It was a typical two-story suburban home with a lawn, a wooden porch, and a garage. The interior was welcoming and spacious, with expensive furniture that was too ornate for my tastes. On one wall hung an autographed photograph of Charlton Heston addressing the National Rifle Association, a gun raised over his head.

"You're finally here," Pritchenko said, sticking his head out of the kitchen door. "We were worried. What happened?"

"Long story short, Prit: this afternoon I saved fifty people from dying at the hands of religious fanatics."

"Well, at least you did something good," the Ukrainian said sadly. "You'd better talk to Lucia. She's really angry at you."

I sighed, downhearted. I couldn't put off that conversation until the next day.

"I'll talk to her." I patted my buddy on the shoulder. "Don't worry, old friend."

I went into the living room. Lucia was sitting on an over-stuffed couch. The cat was playing with a sock at her feet. She had a book in her lap, but hadn't read past the first few pages. She scowled and said in an icy voice, "You're home."

I dropped into one of the chairs. "I was at city hall with Greene until a half an hour ago." *The sooner you tell her, the better.* "He offered me a job."

"What'd you say?" Lucia stared at me, stunned.

"He needs an intermediary with the helots who live in the suburb of Bluefont. It's across the river, inside the Wall, but surrounded by barbed wire. Over half of those people are Hispanic, but no one in Gulfport speaks Spanish."

"You said no, of course."

I took a deep breath. *Here goes.* "Actually, I accepted his offer. I start tomorrow."

"What the fuck are you doing?"

"Lucia, I saved a lot of lives today." *Although,* I thought bitterly of Mendoza's comment about Lucia, *if it were up to me, they could've shot one of them.* "If I take the job, I can at least look after the helots' interests and improve their living conditions."

"Look after their interests? Improve their living conditions? Are you going to get that loony preacher to stop treating them like second-class citizens so they don't have to risk their lives anymore?"

"I don't know yet. I'll figure something out." I tried to stand my ground. How could I tell her that, as I'd headed off the slaughter in the Bluefont ghetto that afternoon, the old euphoria I'd felt for years as a lawyer rushed back over me.

Before the Apocalypse, I'd had a real talent for closing deals and negotiating impossible terms. I'd felt invincible. Settling a dispute was like a powerful drug that had driven me for years. When the Undead arrived, all of that ended. I'd dragged myself halfway around the world, surviving by some miracle. It was quite a blow to discover that all my knowledge and skills were worthless in a society in ruins. But that afternoon, the old magic came rushing back. I'd done it again. For the first time in a very long time, I felt useful.

I knew Lucia wouldn't understand that. At least not right then. But I had to make her see that I was also revolted by Reverend Greene and the hate-filled racist society in Gulfport. And I was furious with myself too. I felt dirty for pandering to Reverend Greene.

"Lucia, for better or worse, we're here. We have to try to fit in."

"Why?

"Gulfport may not be our permanent home, but we'll probably be here for a while. If we leave, we'll have a really hard time out there."

"Maybe." Lucia took my hands and looked me in the eye, pleading. "But we'd land on our feet, like we always do. This place is sick—these people are sick—and you know it. Gulfport isn't for us. We're not like them. Let's leave. Today. All three of us."

"Where would we go? We can't just start walking. This is America, damn it. It's huge. There're millions of Undead out there. We have no choice. We have to stay."

"Well, if we stay, let's confront Greene about the prophesies he rants on and on about!"

"How do you propose we do that? He offered us his hospitality! He saved our lives! We owe him!"

"We don't owe him a thing! Are you blind? Do you see the way they treat those people?"

"Lucia, you've seen the world out there! Haven't you had enough of blood, death, and destruction? Aren't you tired of sleeping with one eye open, always cold, afraid, and hungry? Aren't you tired of being on the run? This is a safe place to live. They offer their hospitality and you spit in their eye!"

"What's the price of that hospitality? Living in an apartheid like South Africa? Watching them exploit those helots?"

"It's the price of staying alive!" I shouted, my face twisted. "Of having a future!"

"I don't want that future," Lucia shouted back. Tears shone in her eyes.

"We don't have a choice." I stood up and stretched out my arms. "Look around! We've got squat! Even your clothes were a gift, for God's sake!"

"We have the three of us: Prit, you, and me."

"Apparently you have someone else," I said, jealousy gnawing at me. "A certain Carlos Mendoza said hello. You just got to Gulfport, and already you've got an admirer."

Lucia turned pale; her eyes glowed like embers. I instantly regretted what I'd said. It was unfair and mean, but I was tired and angry. The trouble with words is you can never take them back.

"At least Carlos Mendoza has the self-respect to despise Greene to his face," she said slowly.

"That's because he doesn't have to worry about keeping a woman, a cat, and a crazy Russian safe."

"Don't worry about the woman. I'll take care of myself from now on." She stood up, picked up the cat, planted a big kiss on his forehead, and then plopped him on my lap. Without a backward glance, she walked out of the room and slammed the door.

Lucullus looked surprised—his face was wet with Lucia's tears. And I was miserable.

1 8

Colonel Hong stretched. He had a throbbing headache. The Ilyushin-62 was one of the most uncomfortable aircrafts ever made. The engine noise filtered through the fuselage. It was so loud, he had to wear headphones during the trip. The only way to have a conversation was to yell, and even then it was difficult.

After thirteen hours in the air, the colonel felt as if someone had stuffed his ears full of cotton. When he stood up to stretch and clear his head, a folder slipped off his knees and fell to the floor. Hong picked it up and locked it away in a steel case. Inside were an envelope with detailed instructions and cyanide pills to pass out to the men when they landed.

As Hong walked slowly down the center aisle of the plane to the flight deck, he thought about the report the commander had shown him. He hadn't been allowed to bring it along because they couldn't risk it falling into the wrong hands, especially the Yankee imperialist enemy's.

"The Undead are dying," the defense minister had said at the meeting. Hong thought he'd heard wrong. But the generals sitting around the table hadn't flinched when the minister repeated that statement, so it must be true.

When he asked if they'd found a way to kill them, the minister replied, "No, it's not that. You can't kill something when it's already dead. Every effort we've made to develop an antidote or vaccine for the TSJ virus has been a failure. The thing's a marvel of genetic engineering. However, the virus's success has become its downfall."

Then he placed the folder with the words "Top Secret" in front of Hong.

Over the next half hour, Hong learned more about the TSJ virus. TSJ was a laboratory mutation of the Ebola virus combined with elements of other viral strains. It spread very rapidly and was so highly contagious that there were documented cases of people infected just by coming into contact with the Undead's saliva. But TSJ had a weak spot. Simply put, it was too good at its job.

The researchers who wrote the report estimated that only about thirty million people had survived worldwide, twenty-three million of them within North Korea's borders. The TSJ virus had wiped out six billion human beings in less than thirty days. As viruses went, it was hugely successful.

The problem was that TSJ eventually colonized virtually all the available humans, its only carriers. Since it could only survive outside a human body for a few minutes before it turned into protein soup, the virus was effectively trapped inside the Undead.

The Undead's bodies had no blood circulation, no way to breathe, and very little electrical or neuronal activity. The clever TSJ virus inhibited the bacteria responsible for putrefaction, preserving dead bodies as if they were in a freezer. It could stay in those bodies for years or centuries, waiting to pounce on another host. But in a strange twist, nature complicated matters. Even though TSJ nullified the action of bacteria, it was defenseless against fungus, one of the oldest multicellular structures on earth. Those fungi found a perfect breeding ground in the billions of Undead roaming the world. The huge slabs of walking flesh became the fungi's new homes.

The secret report included dozens of photos of Undead in various stages of fungal invasion. Over seventy percent of TSJ infections occurred within the first four weeks of the pandemic, so most of the Undead were likely to deteriorate along the same time line. At first, the fungal colonies weren't visible, except for some small patches of yellow or green fuzz in the corner of an Undead's mouth or eyes sockets. As the months went by, though, those fungal colonies expanded. Hong saw images of Undead so covered in fungi they looked like something out of a horror movie.

The report estimated that, in two years, most of the Undead would be so consumed by the fungi they'd collapse under their own weight and rot where they fell, reduced to piles of yellow bones. In fewer than four years, the report said, there would be no Undead left on earth.

Then it will be our turn, Hong deduced. Without the Undead, the whole world would be at the mercy of the People's Republic of North Korea. The estimated six million survivors scattered across the globe outside of North Korea wouldn't pose a serious threat to the glorious North Korean army.

He and his countrymen just had to tough it out for another four years, but without oil, they'd never make it. How ironic to survive the Undead only to starve to death.

Hong walked past a dozing soldier whose protective headphones had slipped down around his neck. He carefully placed the headphones back over the man's ears and headed to the cockpit. His men were afraid, of course, but they knew that he was the best officer to serve under and that he'd zealously take care of them. The colonel had handpicked all three hundred soldiers in his company. They'd follow him to the gates of hell, if he ordered them to.

When he walked through the cockpit door, a peaceful silence engulfed him, isolating him from all the noise. The Soviets clearly had their priorities straight when they designed the Ilyushin-62 back in the seventies.

"Colonel." The pilot saluted as Hong lowered himself into the empty navigator's seat. Only one of the six Ilyushin-62 on that expedition had a navigator. The rest were following his lead to the west coast of the United States.

This was a one-way trip, no return planned. None of the Korean People's Air Force planes was authorized to fly back to North Korea, so additional navigators weren't necessary. Of course, there was the remote chance they'd locate enough fuel for a return trip. That option had been studied for weeks, but finally discarded. The available information was very sketchy, obtained months or years before the pandemic had begun. The commanders knew there were oil reserves near their objective, but they had no idea what condition they were in—if they even still existed. In the end, it was too risky and uncertain to count on refueling, so the colonel's orders outlined an even riskier alternate plan.

"How long till we get there?" Hong asked.

"We'll reach our first destination in less than an hour. Twenty minutes after that, we could make it to destinations two, three, and four. Destination five . . . well . . . " The pilot swallowed.

Hong nodded as he did some mental calculations. The Ilyushin-62 was the longest-range aircraft in the North Korean air force, but it could only make it as far as the West Coast. The plan was to land at any airport where the runway wasn't obstructed or occupied by Undead. From there, he and his men were on their own.

When Hong heard all this for the first time, he protested loudly. They were asking him and his men to cross the United States with no backup plan. "That's madness! We don't even know what condition the roads are in. We'll be driving blind for thousands of miles through an infested country."

"We know, Colonel," one of the generals responded patiently.

"I think we can be more practical," Hong proposed. "Let's load extra fuel into a couple of the aircrafts' holds. Then, once we land, we can transfer it to the fuel tanks and fly to Gulfport without risking our lives. Plus it would be much faster."

"That's impossible, Colonel," replied the minister. "I already told you that our reserves are critically low, but I don't think you grasp how desperate the situation is. We only have two percent of the fuel our Air Force needs under normal conditions. We've already diverted most of the fuel from industry and the civilian population, but our reserves have almost dried up. We can provide you with enough fuel to fly to the West Coast, not one liter more."

"But we're only talking about a few thousand liters!" Hong implored.

"There's nothing we can do." The minister stood firm. "Our Dear Leader Kim Jong-Un, in his eternal wisdom, has ordered us to reserve enough fuel to keep our fighter planes in the air for at least two consecutive days, in case of attack. We need every last drop of fuel, Colonel. Do not insist."

Hong shook his head. Had he heard correctly? *Keep our fighter planes in the air? Who would they be fighting? That's the stupidest thing I've ever heard.* His mind was racing, but he kept his mouth shut. A direct order from Kim Jong-Un, no matter how absurd, could not be debated under any circumstances.

He made one last stab. "It will take weeks to reach Gulfport on the ground, and the journey will be exceedingly difficult."

"That's why we chose you, Colonel. Complete your mission successfully and, upon your return, you will be rewarded in ways you can't even imagine."

Now Colonel Hong and his elite soldiers were flying over the US in six Ilyushin-62s, their fuel tanks nearly empty.

"Red light!" exclaimed the pilot. "We now have a range of only thirty minutes."

"How far to the first destination?" Hong asked anxiously.

"We should see it in . . . There it is!" the pilot shouted in excitement.

The backwater airport had just one runway. Sprawled across it was the charred skeleton of a large commercial jet, making it impossible to land. The six aircraft circled around, then continued to the next airport on the list.

They couldn't land at destinations two, three, or four. The runways were blocked either by the remains of crashed planes or dozens of Undead.

"Land in the middle of them," Hong ordered.

"Impossible, sir," said the pilot. "If one of the Undead got sucked into the turbines, the engine could explode and we'd go up in flames.

Anxiety and fear of failure gripped Hong as they headed for runway number five.

1 9

The airport a few miles outside of Titusville, California, had never been a major hub. Its runway was one of the longest in the state, but few travelers wanted to land in a small town at the edge of the desert. The army built it during the Cold War, but for years it had only been used for local flights and the occasional drag race.

It hadn't changed much since the Apocalypse. On one side of the runway sat half a dozen wingless DC-7s propped up on cinder blocks, surrounded by piles of junk that were once bolted to them. On the other side of the runway, a dilapidated control tower, under a thick layer of sand, teetered dangerously in the wind.

The Titusville runway was about to have its busiest day—and its last. First came the rumble of far-off engines. As the noise grew, the dirty glass in the tower's windows rattled like decayed teeth in diseased gums. Then a huge transport plane with a red star painted on its belly appeared on the horizon. Five more followed, each staggered by five miles.

The North Korean pilots faced a difficult challenge. They had to land just a couple of minutes apart, with no ground control to guide them, on an unfamiliar runway covered in sand. The entire operation had to be synchronized like a ballet.

The first Ilyushin-62 skidded as it landed, but the highly trained pilot managed to bring the plane to a stop. He rolled to the far end of the runway as the next plane began its approach. Following his lead, the next four aircraft landed without a hitch. However, each time one of them landed, it kicked up a huge cloud of dust and desert sand. Under normal circumstances, the next plane would have overflown the airport for a few minutes to let the cloud settle, but the sixth plane didn't have enough fuel to wait, so the pilot took a chance and came in for his landing.

The big plane hit the runway at the wrong angle, at least sixty miles an hour too fast. The landing gear snapped like a twig and the nose of the plane dragged along the pavement, sending up a shower of sparks. One wing caught the base of the tower and upended the rotting structure. Then the plane cartwheeled three times and exploded in a fireball.

From the cockpit of his plane, Hong looked on helplessly, cursing a blue streak. The generals hadn't had enough jet fuel for their return flight, but they'd supplied diesel fuel for the tanks and trucks. Now, some of that precious fuel was burning in huge, hot waves.

This complicates things. We'll have to find fuel along the way. No use dwelling on that now. "Kim!" he bellowed.

Lieutenant Kim Tae-Pak was one of Hong's most trusted men, a veteran of many missions into South Korea.

"Unload the tanks as fast as you can. You could hear that damn explosion for fifty miles. I want to be far away from here if anyone—alive or dead—comes snooping around."

The lieutenant saluted and rushed off. As he walked down the runway, Hong studied the surroundings. He picked up a handful of sand, then let it sift through his fingers.

American sand. We've invaded our country's most hated enemy—what's left of it—and no one can stop us. A shiver ran down his spine. He didn't know how this mission would end, but they were making history. For the first time in two hundred years, soldiers from an enemy country had set foot on American soil.

Twenty minutes later, a convoy of fifteen tanks and two bulldozers headed east out of the Titusville airport. Behind them, flames engulfed their planes. Hong had burned his ships. The ruins of the United States were all that lay between him and Gulfport. That and millions of Undead.

2 0

GULFPORT

|||||||||||||||||||||||||||||||||||||||||||||||||

The next day I woke up with cotton mouth and a nagging headache. I'd stayed up late, drowning myself in a bottle of whiskey
and self-pity. Prit had joined me but hadn't offered any advice.
Just having him there eased my anxiety. He knew all too well
that sometimes there's nothing you can say.

I was caught in a dilemma. On one hand, the clean, germfree
world of Gulfport disgusted me as much as it did Lucia. On the
other hand, it seemed like our only option. Wandering around
in the Undead wasteland the United States had become, we
wouldn't stand a fucking chance.

"What do you think, Prit?"

My old friend stirred his coffee and collected his thoughts,
choosing his words carefully. "When I was very young, I lived on
a collective farm on the steppes in Central Asia. Our school was
a beautiful wooden building that had been painted red. We were
taught that our way of life was the pinnacle of human endeavor
and that the Soviet spirit was at the heart of a worker's paradise.

We knew nothing of the West, except that it was the Motherland's enemy. One day, when I was eight, I was on my way to school when I saw a policeman arrest a man. At first I thought he must be a thief or something like that." Pritchenko smiled sadly as the childhood memory came alive. "What did I know? I was only eight. Later I learned that the man was arrested because his son, who was a soldier stationed in Berlin, had defected to the West."

Prit paused for a moment, his mind far from Gulfport. "I always wondered what motivated the man's son to desert, knowing the price his family would pay. What drove a man to make a decision with such painful consequences? How much did he suffer when he made that decision?"

The Ukrainian looked me in the eye. "I know more about suffering now than I did back then. I also know that, to make a drastic decision, a person must feel he has no alternative, no matter the consequences. I don't think you've reached that point yet. Plus you let the responsibility you feel for us weigh you down too much." Pritchenko shook his head. "I'm your friend and I'd die for you if I had to. I see your point of view and Lucia's too. But I'll stand by you, whatever you decide."

"Thanks, Prit." I choked up as I looked into Prit's eyes. He'd hardly aged in the two years since we met. Except for those missing fingers on his right hand and a few wrinkles around his eyes, he was the same short-tempered, half-crazy guy who'd stuck by me in the ruins of Vigo. And one of the best people I'd ever known.

We had spent half the night talking and laughing about all the times we'd cheated death and all the things we'd do if the Undead ever disappeared for good. We had finally dozed off in front of the crackling fireplace.

When I got up, Pritchenko was lying on the couch, snoring like a freight train; Lucullus was curled up on his lap. I dragged myself to the bathroom, took a long, hot shower, shaved, and put on one of the suits hanging in a closet. It was a size too big, but I looked pretty good. It felt strange to be in a suit and tie after so long.

I went to Lucia's room. Her door was locked. I knocked softly, but she didn't answer.

"Lucia," I said to the closed door. "I'm sorry for what I said last night. I didn't mean to hurt you. Everything I do is to make sure we have a future." I wasn't sure what to say next. "Let's talk when I get home tonight. We'll straighten everything out. I love you."

I left the house feeling empty inside. A beautiful Lexus sat in the driveway with keys in the ignition. I assumed it came with the house. Since the town was too far away to walk to, I got in and started the engine.

As I drove through the empty streets, I realized that, for the first time in years, I wasn't trying to outrun anyone or anything. And yet, I kept catching myself looking around in a panic or accelerating through tight spots, as if a mob of Undead were after me.

The Apocalypse had changed me. Were those changes for the better? Would they last forever?

When I arrived at city hall, Mrs. Compton was waiting for me amid a sea of staff scurrying to their offices.

"Good morning," she said. "Hope you slept well. There's a ton of work waiting for you. Mr. Wilcox, who used to run the Office of Hispanic Helots, died on the golf course three months ago of an aneurysm. Mr. Talbot, head of the Office of Black Helots, has overseen the two departments since then, but he doesn't know a word of Spanish and has made a huge mess of everything. Hope you can make sense of all that paperwork."

"Paperwork?"

"You'll see. Follow me."

Mrs. Compton led me to a large office in the northwest corner of the building. When she opened the door, my heart sank. Mountains of folders were stacked on top of every surface and sticking out of overflowing filing cabinets. Some of the stacks were on the verge of falling over.

"Sue Anne will be your personal assistant." Mrs. Compton pointed to a blond girl in her early twenties sitting at a nearby desk. She was smiling nervously and chewing gum. She reminded me of a cow chewing its cud. "Ask her anything. She's here to serve you."

After talking to Sue Anne for a few minutes, I realized I couldn't entrust the girl with anything more complicated than making photocopies or bringing me coffee. She looked very Aryan, so she fit right in, but the Creator had apparently forgotten to give her a brain.

"Well, let's sort through this mountain of paperwork and determine what's a priority and what can wait. Write down the titles of the folders, then create an index, OK?"

Sue Anne looked at me dumbfounded, as if I'd asked her to piss into a glass and give it to Mrs. Compton to drink. She even stopped chewing her gum.

"You know what an index is, don't you, Sue Anne?"

"It's a type of music, right?" she said and nodded, feeling more confident. "The Music Index. My cousin Norma loves them."

"Forget it, dear," I sighed. "I have a better idea. Find me some coffee that's better than this swill."

As soon as Sue Anne left (*oh, God, let that coffee be very, very hard to find*), I sat down in the middle of my office and started to divide up the folders. After a while, I worked out a system. An hour later, I'd made three piles. One group of files contained the expenditures of the Hispanic helots. Another group referred to supplies and living conditions in the Bluefont ghetto. The third group of files pertained to the regular supply of Cladoxpan.

As I sorted through those folders, I got a clearer picture of how Gulfport was run. Twenty-three thousand white people lived in Gulfport. Seven thousand people lived in the helot ghetto of Bluefont, about twenty-five people in each of the three hundred houses. That was too many, even for those spacious houses. Bluefont was inside the Wall, but was separated from the rest of the city by a fence and a river they'd channeled alongside it like a moat. The bridge where I'd negotiated with Carlos Mendoza connected Bluefont to the rest of Gulfport.

Every week, helots gathered at the south end of the bridge, and Green Guards gave them the weapons they needed. Then they headed out on expeditions to towns within a hundred-mile radius. Sometimes they were gone for several days. When they came to a town, they loaded their trucks with any supplies they could find for insatiable, affluent Gulfport. When they returned, they parked the loaded trucks in the town's warehouse and turned in their guns. As payment, they received Cladoxpan, which kept them from changing into Undead.

On those expeditions, there were inevitable casualties, not from TSJ—nearly a hundred percent of the helots were already infected—but from the terrible wounds the Undead inflicted.

Due to these losses, the population of helots remained more or less stable. Every so often, like a steady drip, individuals or groups of people showed up at Gulfport or crossed paths with the supply expeditions. If they were black, Native American, Latino, or Asian, they were offered shelter and companionship in Bluefont, where they were compelled to live a life of semislavery. The few who were white, like Lucia, Prit, and me, joined the population on the other side of the fence.

The helots outnumbered the Green Guard, which comprised just forty Aryan Nations ex-cons and a militia of a hundred and fifty soldiers. Charged with maintaining the safety of Gulfport, the guards and militia would have been powerless to control the crowd of infected helots. So, from time to time, they carried out a Nazi-style "cleansing" in the ghetto. As I read, my palms grew clammy and I broke out in a cold sweat. I found numerous folders with "EXPELLED" written in big red letters across them, but no explanation inside. I hesitated, then picked up the phone and called Mrs. Compton.

"Oh, those are the helots who break the rules. Murderers, drunks, thieves, and rapists, the scum of the earth," she replied cheerfully to my questions. "The Office of Justice processes those files."

"I'd like to see those files." The lawyer in me had awakened and was trying to figure out what sort of twisted justice the Reverend Greene applied.

"I'm afraid that's not possible," Mrs. Compton said primly. "That department answers directly to the reverend and those reports are confidential."

I hung up, intrigued. After making sure Sue Anne hadn't returned, I prowled the halls until I found the Office of Justice. The door was locked. A number of people milled around in the hall. If I lingered too long or tried to force the door open, they would get suspicious. I'd have to find another way to get my hands on those files.

I returned to my office, brooding. One of the file cabinets was labeled "Certificates of Residency." I opened it and skimmed through folder after folder. After a while I stopped, gasping in horror. The papers told of a monstrous crime.

Greene and his thugs realized they couldn't rule over the helots by force. Controlling the Cladoxpan ensured some degree of submission, but it wasn't enough. And it didn't solve the problem of what to do with the thousands of helots, especially women, children, and the elderly, who were useless on those supply expeditions. So they hatched a diabolical plan to quash any chance of a rebellion.

At first, the Green Guard conducted random raids. The helots watched helplessly as dozens of Bluefont residents were arrested for no reason and put on trial. All of them disappeared and "EXPELLED" was written on their files. When the tension in the ghetto reached explosive levels, Greene's advisors took the next step. Half of the helots received certificates of residency and half didn't.

From then on raids affected only those without a certificate. So there were two groups in Bluefont: those who slept peacefully at night and those who feared there'd be a knock at their door and the Green Guard would drag them off to the unknown. When there was a raid, the privileged simply showed their certificate, thus ending their solidarity with the undocumented helots.

But that was not enough. One day, the guards started handing out two different types of certificates: with a photo and without. The helots could choose which they wanted. Many thought that a certificate with a photo seemed more official. The next raid rounded up the helots without a photo certificate. Those who had photo certificates breathed easier, thinking it had saved them, but a week later, the photo certificates were replaced by red certificates. Many were suspicious of the new document, so they declined it. Then, two weeks later, there was another big raid and everyone without a red certificate was dragged off.

That plunged the ghetto into despair and distrust. Soon, red certificates were replaced by two kinds of blue ones: "soldiers" or "no qualification." Since each helot could choose his or her classification and would then receive the corresponding document, doubts about which were better gripped Bluefont again.

Many smelled a trap and declared "no qualification." Others chose "soldier," thinking it was better to be seen as useful— Gulfport couldn't do without them. Three days later, anyone who had chosen "no qualification" stopped receiving Cladoxpan. Just hours later, fifteen hundred people changed into Undead. The remaining helots had to fight off the Undead and clean up the ghetto themselves, even as they became increasingly distrustful of one other.

Finally, the Office of Justice voided all existing certificates, declaring that many helots had fraudulently registered as "soldiers," and a new raid swept Bluefont. The outcry was terrible from the many helots who'd been duped into signing up in the wrong category.

A new type of certificate was followed by another and another in a variety of colors. Weakened and submissive, the ghetto accepted the situation, praying they'd have the right document at the next raid. Although they were infected, their will to live was strong, and they clung to any hope, no matter how small.

This cruel, merciless method gave Greene absolute control over Bluefont. The helots were firmly under his boot.

I leaned back in my chair, too sick to keep reading. The Nazis used almost the same system in the Jewish ghettos in Poland. It was cruel but terribly effective.

My God, what kind of shit am I mixed up in? Lucia was right. Taking a chance out in the unknown would be better than staying here another day.

We had to get out of there as soon as possible. That very night, if we could. When I got up to leave the office, I heard Sue Anne's voice on the other side of the door.

"Hey, you can't go in there without an appointment!"

The door burst open. There stood Viktor Pritchenko, gasping for breath, drenched in sweat. He must've run all the way from home. I could tell he had bad news.

"Lucia's gone," he said, panting. "She escaped to Bluefont!"

2 2

Lucia tossed and turned all night, too hurt and angry to sleep. She knew her boyfriend had good intentions, but this appalling place was too much to bear. Just thinking about the arrogant Reverend Greene gave her chills. There was something deeply disturbing in his eyes, something thick and dark like burned motor oil that enveloped her every time he directed his gaze at her. And those Green Guards were repulsive.

But she wasn't just upset about the town's shocking racism or the way women were reduced to window dressing. She was sick of the way her boyfriend and Prit made all the decisions. They never listened to her opinion.

When she replayed their argument, Lucia kicked herself for letting her damn temper get the best of her. *I should've listened patiently, reasoned with him, made him see that this place is cursed. Instead I acted like an ice queen. I wouldn't even look him in the eye.* As she listened to her friends' conversation down-stairs, she nearly jumped out of bed, ran down the stairs, and hugged her boyfriend till he couldn't breathe.

I forgive you, he'd say. *I love you so much. I'll go anywhere if you're there.*

Instead she lay there in bed, stewing; her wounded pride wouldn't budge.

She suddenly had a scary thought. What would happen the next day? How could they patch things up after everything they'd said? She wished she had a stronger argument to prove her point. Then an idea as bright as a neon light lit up her thoughts. A helot! If he just talked to one of them, if he saw first-hand the pain and sadness they felt, he'd understand.

Carlos Mendoza's smiling face floated before her eyes. A handsome, determined man who stared down those sailors when they threatened him. Suddenly she couldn't breathe, and she felt like she was burning up. She had to find that man and talk to him.

Before she knew what she was doing, she jumped out of bed and threw on some clothes. Her room was on the second floor, above the porch, so she wouldn't have any problem sneaking out her window. A voice in her head screamed, *This is a crazy idea. You're acting like a child.* Then she heard Prit's deep laugh coming from the living room, laughing at something *he'd* said.

They're having a good laugh at my expense. That gave her the impetus she needed. She screwed up her courage and started out the window. Then it dawned on her they'd be worried sick if she disappeared without a trace. They didn't deserve that, even if they were acting like assholes. So she went back inside and picked up a notebook lying on the dresser.

I'm going to Bluefont. Hope to be back soon. Don't worry about me. L.

She left the note on the bed and slipped out the window. She tiptoed across the porch roof to the corner of the house, where trumpet flowers grew up a trellis. She carefully placed her feet in the trellis holes and climbed down.

The fine mist had turned into a gentle downpour. As she looked in the brightly lit windows, a voice in her head cried out, *Don't go!* But it was too late. Shrinking from the rain, Lucia set off for Bluefont. Her tears and the raindrops flooded her face.

Her house was on the far side of town and she got lost a few times, so it took almost forty minutes to reach the border. As she turned a corner, her mission almost ended before it began. A Humvee with four soldiers from the Gulfport Militia was slowly patrolling down the middle of the road, lazily passing a spotlight over the houses. Lucia threw herself behind some dumpsters. She held her breath as the light shone on her hideout. For a moment she thought they'd spotted her, but then the light moved on as the Humvee drove off in the rain.

Lucia waited to make sure they were gone before she came out of her hiding place. Ten minutes later, she reached the channel that separated Bluefont from the rest of Gulfport. She stared into the rain-swelled river that roared through the channel, black foam curling on its surface.

She walked along the embankment, looking for a place to cross, but got discouraged when she realized that the channel ran the entire length of the perimeter. When it reached the Wall, it emptied into a long spillway. When Lucia rested her hand on the Wall's cold, rough surface, she heard a moan coming from the other side; a half dozen other voices joined in. Her hair stood on end. The Undead lurked just outside of town. They couldn't scale the barricade, but still they waited.

She retraced her steps and ruled out the bridge. The Green Guards in the tower would never let her cross. She looked over at the ghetto. In contrast to Gulfport's brightly lit streets, it was deep in shadows. Just a few dim lights flickered in the distance.

Just when she was about to give up, she spotted a pretty, petite brunette Mexican woman in her late twenties, wearing an army uniform two sizes too big for her. Her long black hair was pulled back in a ponytail that cascaded down her back. She was sitting under a metal awning pulling blood-caked clothes out of a bag, and then poking them with a stick into a kettle of boiling water that hung over a campfire.

"Hello!" cried Lucia.

The young woman was so absorbed in her work she didn't hear Lucia. When she called out again, the woman jumped up and looked around in alarm, holding the stick like a club.

"Over here! On the other bank!" Lucia cried, waving her arms.

When the woman saw her, she looked relieved. She walked to the edge of the channel, which was cordoned off with barbed wire on her side.

"Whaddaya want?" she yelled over the roaring water. "You selling or buying?"

"Neither. I want to come over to that side of the river. Where can I cross?"

At first the woman was shocked by what Lucia said. Then she let out a bitter laugh. "You crazy? Whaddaya want to do that for?"

"I need to talk to someone in Blucfont."

"Talk to your reverend or those Nazi assholes on the bridge. I can't help you." She turned and went back into the shed.

"Don't go, please! *¿Cómo te llamas?*" Lucia blurted out.

The woman turned, surprised. "Alejandra, but call me Ale. You speak Spanish!"

"I'm from Spain. Just got here."

"You're a long way from home, *gachupina*," she said, using the unflattering term Mexicans called anyone from Spain. "What the fuck do you want to come over here for? You're better off where you are, believe me."

"I have to talk to a man named Carlos Mendoza. You know him?"

"What do you want with Gato Mendoza?"

"I met him on the *Ithaca*."

Alejandra stared into the darkness for a few seconds. "How do I know this isn't a trap?" she demanded, looking around for Green Guards.

Lucia thought fast. She remembered her conversation with Mendoza on board the oil tanker. "He said if I ever needed him, to say I was one of the Just."

The woman's expression changed. "That sounds like Gato," she said, shaking her head. "OK. Follow me."

The Mexican woman and Lucia walked along opposite banks. Alejandra stopped next to the twisted remains of a bicycle, slowly rusting against the fence.

"Cross here," she said.

Lucia looked around. She'd passed by that spot twice but hadn't seen a way to cross. The deserted rocky bank sloped gently down to the swirling water.

"What do I do?" she asked, confused.

"Look closely and just walk," Alejandra replied, patiently.

Lucia walked to the edge of the channel where the water lapped at the toe of her shoes. She spotted several boards just below the surface.

"It's called a Vietnamese bridge." Alejandra sat on the embankment and pointed. "It's a normal bridge, just two feet below the surface of the water. Better take off your shoes."

Lucia took off her shoes and waded into the water. It was cold and the current was very strong, but walking over the submerged bridge was surprisingly easy. She realized she could never have swum across.

Suddenly a branch racing along in the current struck Lucia's ankle. She stumbled and stretched her arms, trying to keep her balance, but with no success. With a loud splash, she fell into the water headfirst.

The current drove her against the bridge and one of the pilings dug into her ribs. Lucia gasped and choked as she swallowed a lot of water. In the darkness, she lost her sense of direction; for a few long seconds, she didn't know where the surface was. She panicked. *I don't want to drown in a dirty river in the middle of the night.*

She kicked her way to the surface, where she gasped for breath and coughed up dirty water. She grabbed on to the bridge, wiped the wet hair out of her face, and peered over at the shore. The Mexican woman had disappeared, as if the earth had swallowed her up.

Before she could wonder where the other woman had gone, she heard the roar of an engine approaching along the bank behind her. Terrified, she saw a police car patrolling the embankment, sweeping its spotlight along the fence and both shores, about two hundred feet away. She didn't have time to climb back on the bridge, much less make it to the other bank.

Lucia only had one choice. She took several deep breaths; when the light was just a few feet away, she plunged back under the water. The first ten seconds passed slowly. The water was so cold she could feel her veins contracting. All sorts of debris hit her as it was swept along. She nearly panicked when something slimy grazed her face. When she couldn't take it anymore, she resurfaced, trying not to make any noise.

The patrol car was slowly moving downstream. She'd narrowly escaped. Physically and emotionally drained, she tried to climb back onto the bridge. Her wet clothes felt like they weighed a ton. It took her three tries to kneel back up on the submerged surface.

"*Gachupina!* Get a move on! They'll be back in a couple minutes!" Alejandra had materialized out of the shadows and beckoned her.

Placing her feet carefully, Lucia made it the rest of the way. On the other side, she climbed the embankment to the fence. Alejandra pulled back a cleverly hidden gap in the barbed wire, big enough for Lucia to drag herself through. Then she released the wire and resealed the gap.

The petite Mexican woman looked Lucia up and down, her hands on her waist. Despite her short stature, determination and character oozed out of every pore.

"Welcome to hell, *gachupina*. I don't know what the devil brings you to this side, but I hope it's worth it. I don't think you'll ever cross back over that river again."

2 3

"There's one over there! Shoot him! Shoot him, you idiot!"

Carlos Mendoza whipped around to see where Chino Cevallos was pointing. An Undead, about forty, wearing ragged jeans and a ripped T-shirt, was staggering down the sidewalk across the street. The guy had a severe bite wound at the base of his neck, but he was covered with so much furry orange fungus you couldn't see his much of his skin. The fungi had branched off and climbed up the guy's neck and into his nose. The image was repulsive and hypnotic at the same time. Mendoza and his buddy were seeing more and more fungus-covered Undead, but they didn't know why.

Carlos raised his Mossberg rifle. As always, he licked his thumb, wiped it across the sight, and took aim. When the Undead filled the sight, he pulled the trigger. An instant later, the guy's head sprayed like a fountain and he collapsed to the ground.

"That's fifteen," murmured Chino Cevallos.

For two hours they'd wandered around that backwater town looking for supplies, but it had already been ransacked by other looters. All they'd found were some cans of soup past their expiration date. They decided to eat the soup anyway, despite the risk of botulism. They'd seen several men die from eating bad food, but hunger got the better of them. They hadn't eaten for six days and were getting weaker and weaker.

Two cans of soup, Mendoza thought, *and only half of our ammo. A few more days like this and we'll be as good as dead.*

Then the Undead cornered them in the grocery store where they'd holed up. Up until the last ten minutes, they'd held their own. Now their luck was running out.

He and Fernando "Chino" Cevallos had spent over a year together. They weren't sure when they'd crossed the US border, but they were sure this was the farthest they'd ventured into gringo territory. Borders meant nothing when food was so scarce.

When the pandemic broke out, Carlos Mendoza joined one of the armed groups that went *"güero* hunting" along the US-Mexico border. For three weeks, volunteers patrolled the border, intercepting Americans who were fleeing south, hoping to evade the TSJ virus. Shoot first and ask questions later was the motto.

But the TSJ virus prevailed. Mexico, like the rest of the world, went to hell a few weeks later. Mendoza, Chino Cevallos, and a hundred other armed men found themselves cut off from their command center. Half the group deserted and rushed home to protect their families, even though deep down they knew it was too late. Others thought it was suicide to leave. Some, like Carlos Mendoza, had no place else to go.

For the next several months, the fifty *güero* hunters traveled along the border, fighting to survive. Hordes of Undead hounded them at every turn. They ran low on food and ammunition, and their vehicles broke down. Now there were just the two of them left.

"This soup isn't so bad," Chino said, taking a big gulp. "I think I'll—What the fuck!"

Mendoza jumped back as the window above his head exploded, raining down glass and wood chips. A huge man, covered with blood clots, was trying to get through the hole. At the same time, two women and a girl appeared at the back door. Footfalls on the front porch alerted them that at least one Undead was coming in that way too.

We're trapped. Mendoza cursed himself for being so careless. They'd let their guard down as they warmed up that damn soup. Now Undead surrounded the store.

Chino drew his gun and blew away the man in the window with the cold eye of a professional killer; before the Apocalypse, he'd been a hit man for the Tijuana Cartel. Then he turned to face the women staggering around in the middle of the room. When one of them stepped into their campfire, flames engulfed her fungus-covered leg, but she didn't seem to notice. Chino fired off three rounds before his Beretta jammed.

"*¡Chinga tu madre!*" he yelled as he cocked the hammer. Those were his last words.

A couple of Undead reached through the shattered window and grabbed Chino from behind. Before Mendoza could react, his *compañero* was dragged halfway through the window. There was a muffled scream, then a thud like a wet rag hitting the floor. Chino's legs stopped moving as a dark spot spread across his crotch.

Mendoza didn't have time to dwell on the gunman's fate; he had problems of his own. He fired his last two rounds at an Undead who'd stuck his head through the window. Meanwhile, that female Undead was practically on top of him, her leg ablaze.

Mendoza swung his rifle like a club and split the woman's head open. He squeezed his eyes shut a second before impact to keep her brains and blood from getting in his eyes. One of his buddies got infected that way, and they'd had to finish him off, on the spot, despite his pleas.

A jet of cold, sticky blood splashed on his face; a couple of clots slid down his nose. Carlos closed his mouth and exhaled, trying to keep his nose clear. A cold panic washed over him and his balls shrank to the size of marbles. He didn't want to die in the middle of that carnival of death in some no-name town.

Son of a bitch, Carlitos, you're done for if that rotten blood comes in contact with your eyes or nose. Keep your eyes closed tight till you wash off all that infected shit. You're fighting those fucking monsters blind. You can't even breathe. Could you be any more fucked, compadre?

Carlos threw himself on the ground and slithered blindly over Undead legs. Clumsy hands grabbed at his back, trying to get ahold of his clothes. Mendoza shook them off like a rabid dog. His hands swept the floor, feeling for the canteen he'd left with his backpack.

Gotta wash my face, gotta wash my face, gotta—FUCK!

Carlos screamed as he set his hand on a hot ember from the fire that had spread across the floor. Then his fingers found the soup. He didn't think twice; he threw it on his face.

The thick soup seared his skin, but it cut through the muck that had spewed out of the woman's brain. Mendoza howled in pain as he furiously rubbed off every bit of gray matter. He opened his eyes and immediately wished he hadn't. Burning

Woman was now a pyre; the fire had spread across half the room. Embers floated onto a stack of old newspapers that went up like kindling. Smoke filled the room as flames licked the ceiling.

This place is going to burn to the ground.

His charred face throbbed. Out of his mind with pain, he retreated to the door. In the smoke, Mendoza ran into another monster. He shoved the thing and it stumbled backward with a grunt. The flickering fire lit up the door.

I'm gonna make it.

That hope vanished in a second. If he'd started out the door an instant later, the Undead standing there (a charming old guy named Charles Richmond, beloved by the children in town, a Korean War veteran and Bronze Star recipient) would've been outside, running from the flames. But when Carlos Mendoza poked his head out of the building, he was still within arms' reach of the former Mr. Richmond, who bit down hard on Mendoza's shoulder with his few remaining teeth.

Carlos shouted in pain, fear, and anger. He grabbed the old codger by the shoulders, lifted him up, and heaved him into the burning store with ease. Carlos was tall, muscular, and pumped full of adrenalin; even when Mr. Richmond was still human, he weighed barely a hundred pounds.

The Mexican examined his wound. It was small but deep. One of Mr. Richmond's rotten teeth was lodged in Mendoza's skin. He pulled it out and threw it on the ground.

I'm done for. This is the end.

Carlos Mendoza collapsed on the dusty street. He'd outlived his buddies, but now he was exhausted—and doomed. He hoped they'd finish him off ASAP. Better that than changing into one of them.

The burning building crackled as flames devoured it. Small explosions punctuated Carlos's dream as he lost consciousness. They sounded like gunshots.

Carlos Mendoza tried to sit up, but he was too weak. A shadow fell across his face. An Undead, backlit by the fire, studied him, about to pounce.

Alright. This is the end.

But the Undead leaned over, felt his body all over, and clucked his tongue. To Mendoza's surprise, the Undead shouted, "We got a live one over here!"

"Damn! He ran out of that burning store!" said another voice.

The first guy brought a canteen filled with a thick liquid to Mendoza's mouth. "Yeah, and the street's full of Undead he blew away. This bastard put up a helluva fight."

The other guy laughed. "If he can survive all that, he's got more lives than a cat."

Mendoza bolted upright in his rickety cot, drenched in sweat. For a second, as the cobwebs of sleep cleared, he didn't know where he was. *I was dreaming about that place again.* He got to his feet and made his way to a washbasin, careful not to step on anyone. He plunged his head into the water, then straightened up, tossing his hair back.

Night after night, he dreamed about the helot patrol that had found him in agony and brought him to Bluefont. The memory of that night never left him. It was his private monster, his shadow of sin. *It's just a dream, but the memory'll be with me as long as I live. Got to get used to it.*

Carlos Mendoza's hatred for Gulfport and everything it represented burned in him like a flame. That anger kept him alive. He'd been addicted to Cladoxpan since the day that old Undead man bit him. He wasn't alone. Almost everyone in Bluefont needed that strange drink to survive. Carlos couldn't live without it, but he hated living like a slave almost as much as he hated the raids on the ghetto.

He put on a flak jacket, laced up his boots, and braided his long wet hair. He eased out of the room he shared with seven other people, all of them asleep on mattresses on the floor. As a group leader, he was entitled to the only real bed in the room, but that night he'd given it to a Brazilian guy and his pregnant wife. He didn't even know their names. How the hell did those two end up so far from home? Any Brazilian beach, even one packed with Undead, had to be better than this godforsaken hole.

He ran down the stairs and across the street. The rain was coming down hard, washing over the pavement. Bluefont had once been a high-end neighborhood, but no longer. The huge potholes became small lakes when it rained. Mendoza carefully sidestepped them to get to the Red Rooster, one of the ghetto's secret bars.

Inside, the smell of damp clothes, sweat, tobacco, and whiskey assaulted him like a slap in the face. Although the ghetto lacked almost everything else, alcohol and tobacco circulated freely. After the supply runs they made for Gulfport, several boxes regularly got "lost" before they reached the warehouse. Since Reverend Greene didn't look kindly on "the smoke of Satan and the blood of Beelzebub," Bluefont served as a black market for buyers on the other side of the fence.

"Hello, Gato," the waitress greeted him affectionately. She was a stocky woman with big breasts that stretched the neckline of her dress to the limit. "Rough night, huh?"

"Tell me about it, Morena," Mendoza replied as he brushed the rain off his clothes. Several customers greeted him and made a place at the bar. "Give me a bottle of tequila and something to eat, honey."

The woman set out a bottle of Jose Cuervo and a plate of beans that had seen better days.

"Come on. Is that the best you can do?"

"That's all there is, Carlitos," said the woman, patting his hand. "I got all the liquor, women, and tobacco you could want, but that's it for food."

The Mexican shrugged and knocked back his first shot of tequila. Fifteen minutes later, with the beans in his stomach and a quarter bottle of tequila warming his body, he began to feel good for the first time that night.

But then his life got really complicated.

The bar door swung open and the wind and rain blew in, making the oil lamps flicker. People grumbled or shouted complaints as two figures hesitated in the doorway. The shorter of the pair finally stepped inside, pulling the other person along.

Mendoza froze in his chair, wondering if the tequila was making him hallucinate. Next to Alejandra stood Lucia, her soaked clothes stuck to her skin, her arms folded across her chest, looking like a frightened doe.

"Gato! There you are, you asshole! Got a surprise for you, dude," Alejandra said proudly.

Mendoza slid off the stool, not taking his eyes off Lucia. "Please, have a seat, señorita."

He turned to the waitress. "Morena! Bring my friend something hot to drink and a towel. *¡Órale!*"

"I found you," Lucia muttered, slowly drying her face with the towel. She could feel all eyes in the bar staring at her back. Most looked astonished, but a few glared at her. She was painfully aware that she was the whitest person in the room.

"I'm glad you decided to pay me a visit," Mendoza said, flashing his best smile.

"This isn't a social call. At least, not the kind you think."

The Mexican sipped his drink and studied the girl over his glass. It was true. He'd hoped the girl had been drawn to Bluefont by the prospect of an affair with a handsome helot. Finding out that wasn't the case wounded his macho pride.

What the hell does she want? Drugs? Booze? She doesn't look the type.

"So tell me, what can I do for you, señorita?"

"I need you to talk to someone."

"Talk to someone," he repeated, as if he hadn't heard right.

"Yes, talk to my . . . to someone very special to me."

"What do you want me to say to this special person?" His ears buzzed from all the tequila.

"You have to explain how wrong all this is. That what they're doing here in Gulfport is horrible, that Greene's an immoral pig and—"

Mendoza burst out laughing. He tried to catch his breath, but when he saw the offended look on Lucia's face, he laughed so hard tears filled his eyes. When he finally collected himself, he slapped the bar.

"Hear that, friends? The señorita wants me to cross the channel, sneak into Gulfport, and enlighten some poor lost soul." He imitated Lucia's voice. "Mr. Greene's bad, very bad, he should treat us poor helots better . . ."

Lucia flushed with anger and threw the wet towel in his face. "Enough of this shit! I've had enough fights for one night, dammit! I'm trying to help you. The person you need to convince is in a position to help you. He's—"

Mendoza cut her off with a slap in the face that spun her like a top. Lucia stared at him in disbelief. She put her hand on her cheek, which was starting to swell.

"No one yells at me," Mendoza said in a velvety voice as he grabbed her by the arm. "Least of all a *gachupina* from across the channel who doesn't have a clue what the hell she's getting into."

"Gato, wait," Alejandra intervened. "The girl nearly drowned crossing the river. At least listen to what she has to say."

"You, shut up," Mendoza hissed. "She could be one of the reverend's spies. Now that I think of it, Ale, you got a free ride in the last raid and you didn't have any papers."

"I'm not a spy!" Lucia cried indignantly.

"Are you calling me a traitor, you fucking *pendejo*?" Alejandra was spitting mad.

Carlos Mendoza raised his hands, stepping back. "One at a time, señoritas, one at a time." A chorus of boozy laughter punctuated Mendoza's words as the small woman balled up her fists helplessly. "Fellas, take this *gachupina* to the cellar while we discuss what to do with her. And you, go wash rags—that's your job. Get a move on!"

Two men grabbed Lucia and dragged her to a trapdoor hidden under a dirty rug. As they shoved her into the cellar, she saw a couple guys rush Alejandra. The woman cursed and aimed kicks left and right, but a muscle-bound guy sent her flying out of the bar.

The trapdoor slammed over Lucia's head and darkness enveloped her. She heard someone drag something heavy across the rug. After a while the bar settled back down amid clinking glasses, shouts, and laughter.

Lucia curled up in a ball between two stacks of boxes and cried, cursing herself for being so stupid and blindly trusting a guy she barely knew. Most of all, she was terrified.

The next morning, the sky over Gulfport was lead gray. In the daylight, the squalid living conditions and mountains of trash in the ghetto underscored the true nature of the place. At least there weren't many rats. They'd been hunted down by bands of starving children or had fallen prey to the many dogs wandering among the houses, begging for a handout.

Carlos Mendoza woke up feeling like a psychopathic dwarf was inside his head, beating his brain to a pulp with a hammer. He'd fallen asleep on a table in the bar. The floor was littered with regulars snoring away or stretching as Morena, the bartender (whose hangover was as bad as his), woke them with a kick.

"What time is it?" he muttered in a raspy voice. He lit a crumpled cigarette.

Morena kicked a bearded, tattooed guy. "It's morning, Carlitos. Not that it matters."

Mendoza grunted and suddenly remembered the girl locked in the hidden cellar.

"Tomás, Adrian, bring me that *gachupina*."

The two men pushed aside a table (and the guy sleeping on it) and opened the trapdoor. One guy started down the stairs while the other waited above. A sudden howl of pain woke up anyone who was still asleep. "Fucking bitch sliced me!"

A noisy battle raged in the hole. When the guy reappeared, he had a deep cut on his left arm, and he was dragging Lucia up the stairs, his right arm tight around her neck. Nearly unconscious for lack of oxygen, the girl still waved around a broken bottle.

"*Órale*, Tomás, let the girl go. You'll kill her!" Mendoza muttered as he gargled a shot of tequila. Tomás tossed her to the floor with a menacing scowl. Looking at the girl's pale face, he got angry all over again.

Lucia tried to crawl to the door, but someone grabbed her by the hair and yanked her to her feet. Tears of pain filled her eyes.

"Where're you going, slut?" Tomás demanded. "We still need to talk to you."

"Turn her loose, Tomás," Mendoza barked. "You're bleeding. You might splash her."

The man glared at Lucia for a few long seconds but did as he was told. As an afterthought, he ripped off a long strip of the girl's shirt, exposing her breasts.

"I'll wrap my cut with this," he said, clutching the piece of shirt.

Lucia quickly crossed her arms over her breasts before Mendoza grabbed her again.

"Tell me what the hell you're doing here. And I better like your answer."

The door burst open in a whirlwind of rain and wind. A dripping figure stood in the shadows and surveyed the scene. He was short and stocky—that was all they could make out from the bar.

"Back away from her if you value your balls, amigo." The shadowy figure's voice was soft but menacing, like a voltage generator about to explode.

"Prit!" Lucia cried out in relief.

"Lucia, honey, come to me." The Ukrainian stood firm in the doorway, looking like an angry bull terrier, never taking his eyes off Mendoza and the other men in the room. Rainwater dripped off his clothes, forming a puddle at his feet, but no one seemed to notice.

"Bullshit," said Gato, gripping Lucia tighter. "The girl doesn't leave until I say so."

"Bad idea," Pritchenko replied, scratching his ear with the tip of his huge knife.

"Oh yeah? Why's that?" Not waiting for an answer, Mendoza kept talking as he secretly signaled to the men at the tables. "Gotta hand it to you, you've got balls. You're the first Aryan to come to the ghetto alone."

"I'm not one of those brainless Aryan Nations assholes," Prit replied, suspiciously calm. "For the last time, let the girl go."

"Tell that to them," Mendoza shouted.

Two men in the doorway jumped on Prit. In that split second, he blinked twice, spread his feet, and, unfazed, turned his right arm slightly and stuck his knife in the chest of the guy on one side. He let out a gurgling sound, and then fell into the Ukrainian's arms with a look of disbelief. Prit shielded himself with the first guy's body as he swung around to the second guy. As the goon stared down at the knife sticking out his buddy's back, Prit punched his chin with a sharp crack, sending the guy's head flying backward. Eyes dilated, the guy took a step back, and then collapsed like a heap of rags.

Prit threw the body of the first guy into the next two coming at him, then kicked hard at the crotch of a giant tattooed black guy stalking him. The guy let out a muffled scream and dropped to the floor, clutching his balls.

The Ukrainian had time to hit two other guys—and break the arm of one of them with a chilling crunch—before someone punched him in the temple.

Prit staggered and saw double. He got off two more kicks, but then felt a sharp pain in his side, like someone'd hit him with a baseball bat. He took a deep breath, gasping at the sharp pain. *Broken ribs*, he thought before a brutal kick to his back knocked him to his knees. He grabbed a bottle that had fallen on the floor during the brawl and smashed it in the face of a guy standing over him with a knife. The man writhed in pain as he pulled a sliver of glass out of his eye. As the blinded guy backed away, Prit tried to stand.

Although his rivals only knew how to fight in barroom brawls, Prit was outnumbered. It dawned on the Ukrainian that he was going to die there.

With one last effort, he roared and lunged at the three guys closest to him, who stepped back in surprise. Pritchenko took advantage of that hesitation to strike the neck of the one of them with the side of a hand, leaving him gasping for breath through his broken trachea. Suddenly, something hit him in the face so hard he felt his septum crack. He fell back and then they all jumped him, savagely kicking his curled-up body.

"Lucia! Run!" was all he could scream, frothy blood spilling from his lips, before a kick to his neck made him collapse in a ball.

Mendoza watched the fight, astonished. The little guy had seemed so low-key, but he'd killed two men and knocked out three others in less than a minute.

Suddenly, a shot rang out in the bar. They all looked up, startled. All but Pritchenko, who lay unconscious on the floor. Alejandra was standing in the doorway, an AK-47 in her hands. Although she was aiming at the ceiling, she could've lowered the rifle in a second and cut down everyone in the place. Morena let out a frightened squeak and ducked behind the bar.

"Everybody, back off!" the woman shouted, her voice shaking. "Get away from him! Careful, Gato! I know you've got a gun in your boot, so no tricks, got it?"

The guys who had been kicking Pritchenko backed away, not taking their eyes off Alejandra's gun. Lucia ran to her side.

"Are you crazy?" Mendoza hissed. "There aren't supposed to be any guns in the ghetto, you stupid shit. They could hear that shot all the way on the other side of Gulfport. In ten minutes, the whole fucking Green Guard'll be here."

"You're the crazy one, Mendoza," Alejandra shot back. "You lock up a girl and strip her, and then you nearly beat this man to death. That's the kind of thing Greene and his Aryan pigs do, not us. You're acting like your brain's rotten like those Undead out there. And you say we're the righteous ones? What the fuck's wrong with you?"

Most of the people in the bar looked down, confused or embarrassed, but Mendoza kept his eyes on Alejandra, furious. "They could be spies," he blurted out.

"She's here because *you* invited her. Admit it. Your fucking macho pride's hurt because she's here to talk, not spread her legs. As for him"—Alejandra pointed to Prit with her chin—"if he were a spy, Greene's men would be all over you by now."

Mendoza grunted, not budging, but he sat back down on the barstool. The atmosphere in the room ratcheted down a few notches.

"OK," he said and turned to Lucia. "Someone give the girls a hand with the Russian. Morena, find some clothes for the girl. I guess I owe her an apology."

Lucia knelt beside Pritchenko, not looking at Mendoza. When she saw her friend's face, she couldn't hold back the tears. His nose was smashed to one side and blood streamed out his mouth. Without acknowledging that she was bare-chested, she tore off a scrap of her tattered shirt and wiped the blood from the Ukrainian's face.

"Prit, please don't die." Her voice quavered. "Please."

The Ukrainian groaned and coughed several times. Propping himself up on one elbow, he spit out a broken tooth and bloody phlegm, groaning as he felt his ribs.

"I'm not going to die," he growled. "Not from this. Those guys fight like sissies."

"Oh, Prit!" Lucia grabbed the Ukrainian in a hug that made him grunt in pain. "Sorry . . . How'd you know I was here?"

"I read the note this morning." The Ukrainian glanced sideways before continuing, lowering his voice. "I warned you-know-who and then headed here. It wasn't hard to find the bridge. Last night you left tracks in the mud even a blind man could find. Your friend with the rifle"—he pointed to Alejandra, who knelt beside him—"showed me the way, after she made me cover my tracks."

The little Mexican woman grinned as she stanched the wounds on Prit's face.

"What do we do now?" Lucia wiped away her tears and put on a faded shirt Morena handed her. "I'm so sorry for everything."

A siren wailed in the distance, rising and falling in a strange cadence. Everyone jumped up and ran out of the bar, scattering in every direction in panic.

"What's that?" Lucia asked.

"Bad news," Alejandra said. "We gotta hide."

"Why?" Prit muttered as he tried to sit up.

"It's a raid," Alejandra replied. "And they're gonna be really mad."

2 6

GULFPORT CITY HALL
FIVE HOURS EARLIER

The day was one big nightmare. Discovering I was unwittingly contributing to a planned mass murder was horrible enough, but finding out my girlfriend had run off to the ghetto was a thousand times worse. The world stopped spinning for a moment as Prit leaned against the office door, panting, dripping with sweat, a helpless look on his face.

"What do you mean gone to Bluefont? When? How do you know?" I strafed poor Pritchenko with questions before he could catch his breath.

Prit dropped into a chair and told me about the note he found in Lucia's room. I was only half listening. My mind was racing as I tried to come up with a plan. My plan later turned out to be complete bullshit, to put it mildly.

"Prit, we gotta get out of here. Now!" I said, frantically shuffling the papers on my desk. "We'll have to split up. You go to the ghetto and bring Lucia back. I'll get transportation, supplies, and weapons. Shouldn't be too hard since I'm on the town council."

"Leave this place?" The Ukrainian arched his eyebrows.

"I'll explain later. Let's just say Lucia was right. This place is rotten to the core and we can't stay here any longer." I furiously looked through folders, then tossed them on the floor. "I know I saw some kind of a pass in all this, dammit!"

Pritchenko put his hand on my arm and I stopped, panting. I was losing it. If anything happened to Lucia, I'd never forgive myself. On top of that, the warning bells that had kept me alive were going off. Something bad was about to happen.

"Forget the pass," he said, quietly. "Our girl's smart, but if she found a way to the other side of the fence, I can too. It can't be worse than Chechnya."

"It's worse, Prit, believe me," I replied grimly.

Prit looked surprised, but didn't say another word. My old friend trusted me and knew there'd be time for explanations later. We threw our arms around each other in a bear hug. We were both downhearted. This was the first time we'd split up since we met.

"Be careful," I said. "Picture me by your side, covering your ass when you screw up."

"You be careful," he said with a confident smile. "Don't know what I'm worried about. All you gotta do is steal a damn boat. My Aunt Lyudmila could've done that, and she was blind in one eye and could only hear in the morning."

I flashed a tight smile, knowing Prit was trying to reassure me. The desk phone rang, breaking the spell.

I lifted up the receiver, then hung it up without answering. As the Ukrainian headed for the door, he turned and looked back at me. In that moment, I felt a dark shadow looming over me, but I didn't want to worry my friend.

As soon as Prit left, I put on my jacket and started to rush past my secretary, who waved a stack of papers in one hand and a cup of coffee in the other. If all went well, Prit would be back with Lucia by nightfall, and I'd have found a boat. I ruled out ground transportation—too dangerous. Air transportation was also out—I didn't know where the airport was, and helicopters would be closely monitored. I had a lot to do in just twelve hours.

Before I dashed off, I stopped and took a sip of the lukewarm coffee Sue Anne held out to me. To cover my tracks in case anyone came looking for me, I told her I was feeling sick and needed to go home to rest. It was a lame excuse, but I just had to buy a few hours.

I headed down the crowded halls, reading the signs on the doors till I came to one that said "Transportation Services."

I knocked, but no one answered. I cautiously turned the knob and poked my head inside. The office was empty. It was lunchtime, so most people were away from their desks. Perfect.

I slid behind the largest desk like a thief. I was relieved when the computer screen lit up. The system was password protected, but the user of this computer had left without shutting it down. I searched the Gulfport database for a boat that would solve our transportation problem. A wolfish grin spread over my face.

There it is. Just what we need.

As I suspected, a wealthy town like Gulfport had a lot of sailboats anchored in a marina. On screen was a list of half a dozen boats classified as "auxiliary surveillance sailboats." They were tied up in dock twelve, close to where the *Ithaca* had dropped anchor.

One of them, the *White Swan*, was a yacht of over sixty feet. It was larger than any boat I'd ever sailed, but it was just what we needed to navigate the treacherous waters of the Caribbean. The sailboat's record included a ten-digit code that matched its authorization documents. "Documents must accompany per-mit," read the warning on screen.

I cursed under my breath. Without those documents, the guards at the port wouldn't let us near the boat. We always had the option of using force to board, but that would call attention to what we were doing. That option also assumed we could get our hands on weapons. I had to find those documents.

Sweat poured down my back as I rummaged through the desk drawers. I glanced at the door from time to time, fearful that someone would come in and catch me red-handed. I'd have a helluva time explaining what I was doing there.

After a while I sighed in frustration. I'd gone through all the cabinets and drawers. I'd found permits and the permission stamp, but not the boat's authorization documents. I was afraid they were locked up somewhere, maybe even Greene's office. But that made no sense. There were too many vehicles in Gulfport for the reverend to oversee all of them personally. Then I spotted the wall safe. *Of course, you horse's ass.*

It was a modern safe, not very big, but sturdy. I grabbed the handle of the safe and tried to turn it. Of course, it was locked.

My stomach clenched in an icy knot. I knew how to pick simple locks, but this one was beyond my ability. Then a crazy thought occurred to me. I went back to the desk and rummaged through drawers and papers some more. When I lifted up the keyboard and turned it over, I stifled a shout of joy. Taped to the bottom was a slip of paper with a combination, a common trick of office workers with no time to memorize it.

Tucking the keyboard under my arm, I went back to the safe and entered the combination. A clank sounded on the other side of the door as the electronic circuit unlocked the bars and the safe opened.

Inside was a neat stack of carefully laminated papers. I quickly located the *White Swan*'s documents and put them in my pocket. Just as I was closing the safe, the doorknob turned and someone entered the office.

I dashed into the small office bathroom just as a bald man in his fifties walked in. The guy talked nonstop on a cell phone while gripping a greasy hamburger in his other hand.

"I know, I know. Listen, honey, when I get home, I'll take you out to dinner. I promise. It's just that—yes, I'm listening."

He chattered away as he sat down at one of the stations and looked for something on his desk. I realized that the keyboard from the neighboring desk was still under my arm. If the guy looked around, he'd wonder what had become of his coworker's keyboard.

Fortunately, the man was more engrossed in what the person on the other end of the line was saying than in his surroundings. With the door open a crack, I watched for a chance to get the hell out of there. The air in the bathroom was thick with dust from the files stored there. I struggled to contain a sneeze. Just when I thought I'd have to force my way out of there and take down that guy before anyone else came in (no small feat, since he was a mountain of flesh and fat), he said good-bye, blew the other person a kiss, picked up his hamburger and a folder, and left the room.

Before I ventured out of the bathroom, I waited a few seconds for my racing heart to slow down and to be sure he wouldn't come back for something he'd forgotten. I put the keyboard back in its place, took one last look around, checked that the coast was clear, and headed out.

My legs were trembling as I walked down the hall. The first part was done. Now I just had to get weapons and supplies.

I came around a corner and ran right into Mrs. Compton. The reverend's rotund secretary looked at me suspiciously.

"Oh, señor, I just spoke with Sue Anne. She said you weren't feeling well and you're going to home. You don't look so good."

I smiled faintly. My face was covered in sweat, and I guessed that dust from the bathroom had stuck to my skin, giving me an eerie gray appearance.

"Be sure to stop by the hospital on your way home. You might be coming down with the flu."

"Oh, I don't think that's necessary," I babbled. "It'll run its course. Plus the hospital's on the other side of town. I'd waste more time driving there and waiting—"

"I insist you see a doctor," interrupted Mrs. Compton. Suddenly the secretary's face brightened. "Wait a minute! You don't have to go to the hospital."

"Oh? Why not?" I mumbled hopefully. Time was running out and I had to get rid of that annoying woman, fast, without raising any suspicions.

"I've got a great idea," Mrs. Compton said as she grabbed my arm and practically dragged me down the hall. "Dr. Ballarini's team of physicians is in the health wing. He's a papist Italian, but he's a nice person and a great doctor. I'm sure he's not too busy to check you over. The reverend holds him in high esteem."

"Why's that?" I asked.

"Dr. Ballarini and his staff are from the CDC in Atlanta. They arrived two weeks after the Wall went up around Gulfport, praise the Lord. Fortunately one of our patrols found them. Satan's creatures, those Undead, would've reduced them to pieces of meat in a few days. Scientists are always thinking about their projects, not about survival." The secretary frowned. "I'm sure they don't pray enough."

"Scientists?" The missing piece of the puzzle was falling into place. "Why're they so important?"

Mrs. Compton looked at me wide-eyed. "You don't know? Cladoxpan is their main project. Dr. Ballarini and his team developed it."

I was speechless. Cladoxpan, the mysterious drug that slowed TSJ down. I'd been racking my brain, trying to figure out how a fanatical preacher had gotten ahold of such a drug. Now I understood. Before the Apocalypse, the CDC in Atlanta was the most important center for viral research in the world. A lab somewhere in the former Soviet Union was the only other place thought to have facilities and experts to equal the CDC. If anyone could find a cure for TSJ, it was the CDC.

But what were the odds that a team from the CDC would end up in Gulfport? That Greene was one lucky son of a bitch. He'd won the world's biggest lottery.

As all that ran through my mind, we came to a door blocked by two Green Guards slumped behind a desk. One of them looked bored as he leafed through an old copy of *Playboy*; the other one was cleaning his nails with a toothpick. I suspected this was one of the worst duties an Aryan could be assigned. Even so, they were armed with M16s and had big pistols hanging from their belts.

"Mrs. Compton, good morning, ma'am." The Aryan tossed the magazine under the desk so fast it seemed to vanish into thin air. The other guy threw the toothpick on the floor and jumped to his feet.

"Good morning, boys. How are you?" Compton said, giving them the once-over, her hands on her hips. "You haven't gotten in any trouble lately, have you?"

"No, Mrs. Compton," they answered in unison. It was comical to see those tattooed brutes act like scolded children in front of short, stout Susan Compton.

"Oh, no?" she answered, in a withering tone. "Then why has Mr. Grapes stuck you with this post? I know it's not because of your good looks."

The Aryans muttered an answer and hung their heads. I realized they were more afraid of what Mrs. Compton might tell Reverend Greene or Malachi Grapes than they were of her.

"I need to see Dr. Ballarini and his staff. Open the door, please."

"Of course, Mrs. Compton. We can let you pass, but not this man. He isn't authorized." The guard pointed at me, as if he needed to clarify who he meant.

"Nonsense." Mrs. Compton waved her hand as if she were shooing away a fly. "This gentleman works at the Office of Hispanic Helots. And he's my niece Sue Anne's boss. I'll vouch for him."

The Aryans looked at her for a few seconds. Finally, the guy with the clean nails, who seemed to be in charge, shrugged.

"Alright. If you say so." He pulled out a heavy ring of keys and opened the three locks on the door. "But you both have to sign the register."

I scrawled my signature below Greene's secretary's and we walked through the door. What the hell I was going to find in there?

As we walked down the hall, the first thing I noticed was a sweet, acidic smell. Not unpleasant. Just the opposite. It also smelled vaguely familiar.

Radiating authority, Mrs. Compton led me down several empty corridors. "We're now in an annex of city hall. This used to be a bank. Since there's no banking system or money anymore, there was no need for it. It's one of the safest buildings in Gulfport."

I nodded politely, taking everything in. I cast a worried glance at my watch. Time was running out and I hadn't gotten weapons or supplies. If I knew my friend, he'd already snuck into the ghetto, tracked down Lucia, and brought her back. Here I was, walking alongside a talkative old woman to see a doctor I didn't need.

Mrs. Compton stopped and turned, giving me a very serious look. "What we're doing is highly irregular. Dr. Ballarini's team doesn't see any patients except the reverend. I'm only doing this because I want us to have a good working relationship. On top of that, I hope you treat my niece well. I know the girl doesn't come off as terribly bright, but she is hardworking and comes from a good family. She'll be a great secretary if you give her a chance."

I put a hand over my heart and told a monstrous lie in my best lawyer voice. "I give you my word that I'll be the most caring and honest boss Sue Anne could hope for."

"I knew we'd understand each other." The woman gave a satisfied grunt and opened the door to what was once a boardroom.

The managers of the bank would've been very surprised to see what had become of their beautiful room. The huge walnut conference table had been shoved against a wall; lined up along it were three large electron microscopes, a centrifuge, an autoclave, and other equipment I couldn't identify. Through the door at the far end, I spotted another room just like this one. Half a dozen grave men and women in white lab coats moved among the instruments, engrossed in their work.

"Signore Ballarini." Mrs. Compton walked over to a tall man who was peering into a microscope. "I need your assistance."

Dr. Ballarini turned toward us. He was a handsome man, about fifty, with expressive eyes. White hair and a salt-and-pepper goatee framed his face. He blinked a few times, clearly annoyed by the interruption, and set down a notebook in which he'd scribbled a jumble of numbers and chemical signs.

"What I can do for you, Mrs. Compton?" he replied politely, his very proper English filled with the music of Italian.

"Can you spare five minutes to give this gentleman a checkup? I think he's coming down with the flu."

"That shouldn't be a problem," said the doctor. He studied me for a moment with a blank expression on his face. "We had better go to—"

He was interrupted by wailing sirens. I felt the blood drain from my face. I was terrified that someone had discovered I'd stolen the sailboat's documents. I was sure that, at any moment,

Green Guards would race in and arrest me. Instead, Mrs. Compton's cell phone rang. The secretary answered it, listened for a few seconds, and replied tersely, "I'm on my way."

"What is it?" I managed to ask, feigning calm.

"A riot in Bluefont. The guards heard a gunshot even though firearms are strictly prohibited there. I have to go." She wavered for a moment. She knew she shouldn't leave me there alone, but Greene had called and she had to go.

"Don't worry, ma'am. I'll leave as soon as my checkup is over. I can find my way out."

"Great, great! Go home and get some rest. See you back at the office tomorrow." Mrs. Compton waved and scurried out as fast as her little legs could carry her. "Take care of my Sue Anne!"

Once she'd disappeared through the door, I turned to Dr. Ballarini. The doctor looked me straight in the eye. "You're not sick. At least not with the flu."

"No," I confessed.

"Do you want to tell me what you are doing here? I have a lot of work, you know."

I could've apologized for the interruption and left immediately. I could've walked back down the hall past the guard post and blended into the crowd. If I had, I might've had time to get guns and provisions. We might've been spared all the horrors that came later. But Dr. Ballarini had developed the only treatment for the virus that had destroyed humanity. I needed to know more and to get my hands on some of that liquid. One bottle could be worth more to us than all the weapons and food we could carry.

"I'm the head of the Office of Hispanic Helots. Are you familiar with it?" I was making things up as I went along. "We need to know what the . . . uh . . . acceptance rate of Cladoxpan is among the patients. The reverend asked me to do this discreetly, thus the flu excuse. No one can know I'm here."

"Helots? What are you talking about?" Dr. Ballarini looked confused.

The good doctor didn't have a clue what I was talking about. How much did the creator of Cladoxpan know about life outside his lab?

"Dr. Ballarini, do you know how Cladoxpan is used?"

"Of course I do." His expression said, *Don't yank my chain.* "Strain 15b, or Cladoxpan, as it is commonly called, is a palliative retardant of the TSJ virus. It is a mixture of a viral suppressor and an immunoenhancer through a variation of enzymes that—"

"I know what it is, Doctor," I said, holding up my hands. But do you know who they're giving it to?"

"The newly infected, of course. It has absolutely no beneficial effect on other subjects. It is even toxic. Where are you going with this?"

I was about to explain the genocidal cesspool Gulfport had become, but I didn't have time. Any moment someone might read the register and discover I was there. Without Greene's secretary, I'd have a hard time sneaking out. That Italian doctor and his team would have to learn the truth on their own, the way I did.

"Never mind, Doctor. To carry out my research, I need you to provide me with a few gallons of Cladoxpan. To assess its effectiveness."

"This is outrageous!" Dr. Ballarini exploded. "I will not allow another laboratory to conduct a study when we have not fully developed the strain! I have told Greene that several times! Not a single fungus cultivar leaves here without our supervision!"

Fungus? Cultivar? What the hell was he talking about?

"Why don't you explain it to me, Dr. Ballarini?" I used my best lawyer voice and pretended to take notes. As long as Dr. Ballarini thought I was there on official business, everything was OK.

"The 15b strain is the first strain we were investigating in Atlanta." Glad to have a new audience, the doctor sat down and plunged into a story he was clearly proud of.

"When the pandemic broke out, I was in Atlanta, on a research exchange from the University of Bologna, to study a mutation of the Asian flu virus. They ordered all personnel in the laboratories, residents and guests alike, to research TSJ full time. No one refused, of course. It was a new disease and, therefore, intriguing. The ramifications were huge."

His academic viewpoint didn't surprise me. A new virus could lead to an award, an endowed chair, and prestigious publications. But TSJ put an end to all that in its first week.

"At first I could not believe what I saw. It was so . . . perfect." Dr. Ballarini's eyes sparkled with excitement. "I do not know who created it. I do not think we will ever know. The TSJ virus is a marvel. It combines the best of Ebola, the flu virus, and strains of three other unrelated viruses. Not only did they not reject each other, they fit together with unprecedented precision. *È un lavoro dell'arte magnifica.* Understand?"

"I understand, but what about Cladoxpan?" I said impatiently.

"All in good time, all in good time." Dr. Ballarini's mind was somewhere else. "When they gave us the first samples, we did not know what their effect was. Only when they brought in infected soldiers from Ramstein, Germany, did we understand that it was bigger than we had ever dreamed."

"So much bigger," I said under my breath.

"You do not understand!" The doctor's voice rose two octaves. "In that laboratory were the sixty top virologists in the world! For nearly a month, we were shooting in the dark. TSJ was so perfect that nothing we tried worked. Nothing! It was like trying to solve a jigsaw puzzle, blindfolded, without all the pieces. It was so frustrating." Dr. Ballarini pounded on the table.

"Fine, but in the end, the Cladoxpan . . ."

"It pains me to say we discovered Cladoxpan almost by accident." The doctor pushed his glasses up. "Do you know what *Cladosporium* mold is?"

"Honestly, Doctor, I have no idea."

"It is the most common fungus you can imagine. Laboratories are routinely contaminated by *Cladosporium*. That was precisely what happened. Some muscle tissue in a petri dish was contaminated with the fungus and nobody noticed. During a test of some potential vaccines, we inoculated TSJ in one hundred fifty petri dishes, but in one petri dish, the virus did not multiply. Guess which one it was?"

"The one with the fungus?" I said, sure I already knew the answer.

"Indeed. For some reason, *Cladosporium* combined with strain 7n of the vaccine, slowed TSJ infection almost to a halt . . . but didn't eliminate it. We were working on that when the Atlanta Safe Zone collapsed and they evacuated the CDC."

"How did you end up here?"

"In the chaos, our van and six others got separated from the rest of the convoy that was headed for Austin, Texas. I do not know what happened to the others, but I have heard that recent satellite images confirmed Austin is gone. We drove around aimlessly until we heard the broadcast from the Gulfport Christian Radio Station. It was the only signal on the air, so we

decided to take a chance. And here we are," the doctor concluded, with a theatrical wave of his hand.

"And ever since, you've been producing strain 15b."

"Cladoxpan, yes. It is the most stable strain we have developed so far."

"And it's a liquid," I ventured.

"Not exactly. Cladoxpan is simply the by-product of a genetically modified fungus grown in a water base." Dr. Ballarini's
voice swelled with pride. "That is my contribution. I devised a
way to produce that by-product cheaply and easily by means of a
protein modification. It used to take five days to make fifty mil-
liliters of Cladoxpan. Now we can make fifty liters in an hour."

"How did you manage that?" I asked, amazed.

"Follow me." He hurried out of the laboratory. I looked at my
watch. Time was flying by, but I was so close to getting some
Cladoxpan that it was worth the risk.

The doctor led me to the basement, where the bank vault had
once been. The armored doors had been removed. Stainless steel
vats lined the huge room like giant sarcophagi.

"They rescued those vats from a bourbon distillery. Not very
orthodox, of course, but they work like a charm."

"How does your method work?"

"The truth is, with the right conditions of humidity and temperature, you could make Cladoxpan in a plastic bucket. At 37
degrees Celsius, the strain produces Cladoxpan."

I looked into one of the vats and nearly shouted in surprise.
At the bottom, submerged in hundreds of gallons of water, was a
white bulbous thing the size of a brain, covered with nodules
and branches. It looked extraterrestrial. From time to time, it
secreted a whitish liquid. When the liquid came into contact
with water, it transformed into a dense, milky substance that
rose to the surface.

"That's a strain of 15b submerged in a solution of water and glucose," Dr. Ballarini boasted. "A vat that size can generate enough Cladoxpan to treat fifty people for decades. Best of all, if you break off a piece and place it into another vat, it will grow to the same size in just three months. It is self-replicating like the bacilli in buttermilk or kefir."

"So, you could manufacture it anywhere." The implications of this discovery were huge. With Cladoxpan, TSJ was a non-threatening infection, like a chronic cold. Of course, if you stopped taking it, you were toast.

"That's right," Dr. Ballarini conceded.

"It should be distributed worldwide immediately, Doctor."

"No! Not till we've developed a final version and have a patent. I will not allow anyone else to get credit for my research."

"Doctor, that world no longer exists!" I pleaded. But nothing I said over the next ten minutes changed Ballarini's mind. He was a genius, but he'd turned his back on reality. For him, the world began and ended with the four walls of his lab.

"Well, at least let me take a few liters of Cladoxpan." I had to get out of there. I heard an explosion in the distance. Something told me trouble was brewing.

"What do you want it for?" Dr. Ballarini asked. "You are not infected with TSJ."

I groaned. It was like talking to a wall. Just then someone entered the lab.

"Freeze, scumbag. Move an inch and I'll pump you full of lead." The voice was right behind me. I was fucked, really fucked. I turned around slowly.

"Hello, Grapes," I replied, courteously, not taking my eyes off the Aryan leader and the two Green Guards, all armed with M16s.

"Porca putanna, figlio di troia, ma che cazzo vuoi?" Dr. Ballarini sputtered. Gone was the congenial scientist. He changed so fast, he must've been mentally unstable. The idea that someone else might take credit for his work had sent him over the edge.

"You dumb shit. You shouldn't have come here, especially after security cameras recorded you breaking into a safe in an office you had no business being in." Malachi Grapes flashed a sinister smile.

He was enjoying himself. He reminded me of a school bully who had cornered his victim and was deciding how to make him suffer. He'd probably played that part many times in his life.

"I'm no fool." Grapes slurred his words as if he was high. "I knew there was something fishy about you. The ship captain reported that you questioned his methods. We've had you under surveillance the whole time, you idiot."

"Look, Grapes, this isn't what it looks like. It's all a misunderstanding. You're right. We don't fit in here. So why don't you let us go?" I edged toward the door, but two Aryans blocked the way. Unless I could distract them, I didn't stand a chance.

Dr. Ballarini looked at me, dumbfounded. A minute before, the scientist was convinced I was one of Greene's employees. Then, Grapes showed up, claiming I was a spy and a traitor. His face turned several shades of purple when he realized he'd been tricked. With a roar, Dr. Ballarini pounced on me, his fists flying. The doctor may have been a scientific genius, but he had no idea how to fight. I easily deflected his blow and shoved him into Grapes. They fell in a jumble of arms and legs, amid grunts of pain.

That was the moment I'd been waiting for. While all eyes were focused on Grapes, I feinted to the right to dodge the nearest Green Guard. The Aryan flung out his arm to intercept me, but I dove for a hole in the wall.

If I'd been a superhero, the guard would've missed me by a hair. An ingenious plan perfectly executed. But in real life, there are no superheroes.

The other guard tackled me like a pro football player. At one hundred seventy-five pounds, I was no match for that three-hundred-pound pissed-off Aryan who grabbed me around the knees and dragged me five feet till we crashed into one of the vats. When my head hit the vat, a white light and a searing pain blotted everything out for a moment.

I tried to stand up, but Malachi Grapes walked over with a perverse look of satisfaction on his face and kicked me in the head. He growled, "I've wanted to do that ever since we met, smart-ass. I never liked lawyers." I saw swirling colors for a few seconds, then darkness swallowed the light and I passed out.

2 8

What could be worse than being immortal?
and still having to behave by the rules?

—Rameau, *Platée*

When I came to, I felt a sticky substance on my face. I thought for a moment they'd poured Cladoxpan on my head, but when a drop fell in my mouth, I detected the coppery taste of blood. My blood.

I had a good-sized gash on my head, one of my teeth was loose, and I could barely open my right eye. They'd worked me over good.

I was sitting in a chair in Greene's office, all alone. Judging by the light coming in the window, the sun was setting. I had to get out of this mess or I wouldn't make it home in time. An air conditioner hummed nearby. My hands were cuffed behind my back, so I couldn't stand up without dragging the chair. I moved my wrists and heard the clink of a chain. Shackles. I'm sure I had the Aryans to thank for that.

I sat there for a while, struggling to think of something positive. At least someone had taken off my tie. My new suit was ruined, blood soaked, and ripped in several places. As if that mattered.

The door flew open and Reverend Greene strode into the room, followed by Malachi Grapes and a deeply worried Mrs. Compton. The Aryan seemed very pleased with himself and shot me a mocking look. The reverend's face was more gaunt than usual. His cheeks were a flurry of tics. The broken veins covering his nose made him look like a drunk, and his eyes had an opaque veil over them, as though he had cataracts.

"Hello, Reverend," I greeted him, trying to sound mocking. "What's the matter? You look horrible. You should take better care of yourself—like me."

"Shut up, asshole!" Grapes backhanded me and then pulled up a chair.

"Reverend, I swear I didn't know. I thought . . ." Mrs. Compton wrung her hands.

"Calm down, Mrs. Compton," said the reverend in a kindly voice. "You did what you thought best. Fortunately, the Lord is always watching over us and we apprehended this servant of Satan in time. Now, please take down what I say."

With a sigh of relief, Mrs. Compton stationed herself behind a stenographic machine in the corner to take notes. Greene sat down and let out a cavernous cough.

He leaned across the table. On one side was a bottle filled with a milky fluid; on the other was his Bible. "Know what this is?" he asked, pointing to the bottle.

"I'm guessing it's your piss," I replied. "Or maybe the Green Guard took up a collection. Maybe they got together and—"

Grapes's punch took me by surprise and hurt like hell, but I flashed a bloody smile, as if it were the most normal thing in the world.

"This is a bottle of Cladoxpan," Greene said, quietly. "What you tried to steal."

I didn't answer and just looked at him in silence. I had no idea where this was going.

"It is a blessing from the Lord. If you get infected with the poison of the Undead, it keeps you from losing your life. If you're healthy and drink even just a little, it's extremely toxic and you die in terrible pain. Two sides of the same coin."

That bottle made me very uncomfortable. You think you're ready to face death, but when the grim reaper comes, your whole being screams to live, if only for five more minutes.

"I wish I could redeem your soul, but you're beyond salvation. So, first things first."

With a trembling hand, Reverend Greene opened the bottle and poured a generous amount in a plastic cup. He placed it in the middle of the table, clasped his hands, and whispered a prayer. I clenched my jaws. My entire body tensed. If they tried to make me drink that toxic stuff, they'd have to break all my teeth.

The reverend ended his prayer with a loud "Amen," rose from his chair, glass in hand, stared into my eyes, and then drank the serum down in one gulp.

I was stunned. I thought that crazy old man had decided to speed up his meeting with his Maker, but then, in a flash, I understood everything. The tremors in the reverend's hands quieted. He recovered his natural skin tone and his veins shrank. The malevolent, mad fire in his eyes, veiled by a white film moments before, flared up.

I gasped. "You're . . . infected! You have TSJ!"

"The lawyer's no dummy, Reverend." Grapes seemed to find it all very entertaining.

"Dr. Ballarini is a genius and a good person, but he goes absolutely crazy when he moves beyond the realm of science." The reverend mopped his forehead. "He's so obsessed with his work on Cladoxpan, he's not aware of its interesting side effect."

"Side effect?" I asked in a shaky voice.

"Cladoxpan slows down not only TSJ, but all the degeneration in the human body. Only our Lord knows why. Your hair doesn't fall out, your skin doesn't age, you don't get wrinkles . . ."

"It makes you immortal?" I asked, shocked.

"Of course not, you stupid fool!" the reverend sputtered. "Only our Lord Jesus Christ can grant us eternal life. Even if you take Cladoxpan, you die a natural death." He paused, overcome with emotion. "You just age slower. Tests on rats and humans prove that." He leaned forward, his face glowing. "For the first time since the Flood, God has given us a way to achieve the longevity of the patriarchs! To live as long as Enoch, Lamech, and Methuselah! For a thousand years, if need be! It's a gift from God to me, His Prophet! I willingly accepted getting infected! I take Cladoxpan so I can preach His word for centuries and lead humanity in the Second Renaissance!"

"You're out of your mind, Greene." I shook my head in disgust. "Completely out of your mind. Wait till the helots find out you're just like them, except for the color of your skin. The faithful of Gulfport will turn their backs on you in disgust."

"No helot lives more than two years," the reverend said in a fever pitch. "The young and old are eliminated quickly, out of Christian charity. The rest don't last long out on reconnaissance. If they do, they're exterminated, like the wicked of Sodom. We save only those who have the mark of the Lamb, the Elohim: the pure, white Angels of God!"

I stared at Greene. His eyes were ablaze, the flame sweeping away his sanity and his soul. A powerful, dark force boiled inside him.

In the corner of the room, Mrs. Compton gasped, and then covered her mouth. Her face was deathly pale. She struggled to her feet and gazed wide-eyed at the Reverend. "Oh, God. This can't be true. Reverend, tell me it isn't true. You can't be—"

Greene waved a tired hand at Grapes. He'd forgotten she was there. The Aryan calmly stood, drew his gun, and shot Mrs. Compton three times. The first bullet pierced her lung and propelled the woman's bulk against the wall. The second and third shots entered her heart and eye. Mrs. Compton fell in a heap on the Persian rug. Blood streamed out of her wounds, staining the carpet with strange designs.

"That foolish woman should've known I don't tolerate people making their own decisions," Greene muttered. "I've put up with her for too long. Reverend this, Reverend that. She took her role too seriously. The Lord speaks through my mouth and His word is law. Everyone else is expendable."

I was paralyzed with terror. My whole cocky demeanor evaporated with the first bullet out of Grapes's gun.

"Mrs. Compton was beloved in Gulfport." Grapes took the spent shells out of his gun and loaded them in a beat-up revolver he'd taken from a bag. He tossed the old gun on the floor next to the secretary's body. "When people see the tape of you stealing the documents, they'll think the old lady found out and tried to stop you. You stupid fuck, you shot her as you tried to escape. They'll be screaming for your balls, my friend."

Shit. I'm going to die. I was surprised at how clearly I was thinking in the last moments of my life. I felt intense longing for Prit, Lucia, and Lucullus. Suddenly I wished I'd spent more time with my little furry friend that morning. *At least I won't die as one of those shitty monsters. It'll be fast. I wonder if it'll hurt.*

"OK, let's dispense justice on this sinful rat." Greene raised his Bible and read from a page he'd bookmarked. "'Thus saith the Lord God; I will leave thee upon the land, I will cast thee forth upon the open field and will cause all the fowls of the heaven to remain upon thee and I will fill all the beasts of the whole earth with thee. And I will lay thy flesh upon the mountains.' Ezekiel 32, 4–5." He closed the Bible with a thud. "God has spoken through me."

"What should I do, Reverend?" Grapes asked, obsequious.

"Expel him from Gulfport, as God expelled Adam from Paradise. Abandon him in the middle of the wasteland, with no water, no food, no weapons. Let the Undead, wild animals, and thirst finish him off. Let his death be long, slow, and painful, as penance."

"Greene, you bastard. You can fuck me over, but I'm glad I'm not one of your kind." My voice trembled with rage and relief, knowing I wouldn't die of a gunshot.

"Even in this you're wrong, you fool." The reverend came just inches from my face, made a noise in his throat, took aim, and spat a wad of yellow mucus into the wound on my forehead. I felt an overpowering sting as the reverend's saliva flooded my wound.

"You are now one of those marked by the fire of the Lord." He brushed my hair from my forehead almost tenderly. "Your death will take longer than you thought."

He turned away and left the room as Grapes shouted for a couple of Aryan guards.

I was too shocked to resist. A single tear rolled down my cheek. Two years. I'd survived for two years. But TSJ had finally caught up with me. I was infected.

When Lucia thought back, she could only recall bits and pieces of what happened, a broken mosaic of details, like a movie missing some reels.

When the siren went off, the helots scattered. Only Alejandra stayed behind, holding Prit's hand, staring down at him with concern.

"Where's everyone going?" Prit asked through bruised lips.

"It's a raid! And you don't want to get in the Green Guards' way. Especially if you don't have any papers."

"I don't have papers," Lucia replied. "Neither does Prit."

"Me neither," Alejandra added. "Half these people don't. Even if we did, that's no guarantee."

"What do we do?" Lucia asked, wide-eyed with panic.

"What everyone else is doing. Hide!" The petite girl struggled to hoist Prit to his feet.

There was chaos out on the street. Groups of people were running off, dashing into houses, trying to become invisible. A few stayed put with a stony look on their face. They had their papers in order (that week, a pink-and-purple striped certificate with a photo). In theory, they had nothing to fear. But only in theory. Things changed from one day to the next in Bluefont. Even some of those people joined the fleeing crowd.

"Where're we going?" Prit said, gasping. With each breath, he winced in pain. His broken ribs were sapping his strength.

"Don't know." Alejandra's voice trembled. "I've got a shelter near the fence, but it's only big enough for one person."

"Let's stick Prit there and we'll find another place to hide!" Lucia proposed.

Alejandra shook her head. "The shape he's in, it'd take ten minutes to get there. This place is gonna be crawling with Green Guards any minute. We gotta find Gato."

"That asshole?" Lucia's face twisted in disbelief. "No way! He almost killed us."

"Don't give me any shit, girlfriend. If anyone can help us, it's Mendoza." Alejandra swung her AK-47 across her back. The weapon dwarfed her and drew spiteful looks from the people who crossed their path. "Grab your friend's other arm and let's go."

Mendoza was still sitting in the bar, calmly finishing the bottle of tequila, as if all the excitement had nothing to do with him. But, deep down, he was seething. That raid could derail his plans. Then again, if he played his cards right, it could advance his cause.

"Gato, we need a place to hide," Alejandra pleaded. "Please."

"I don't give a shit what you do, Ale. This is all your fault."

The little Mexican woman flushed to the roots of her hair, but fought to control her anger. "It's as much your fault as it is mine. You provoked the fight and stripped this girl nearly naked. So, come on, help us."

Mendoza took a drag on his cigarette, his expression unreadable. Then he threw the butt on the ground, sighed, and stood up.

"Follow me. I don't know why the hell I'm doing this. I hope I don't regret it."

Mendoza strode out the door, not helping the women drag the half-conscious Pritchenko. They finally came to what had once been a beautiful Tudor-style home, but neglect and over-crowding had taken a toll. All the windows were broken. The once-manicured lawn was planted with spindly tomatoes.

The Mexican headed into the house and down some stairs to a damp basement that smelled like oil and mold. From a corner, the skeleton of a rat flashed a sardonic grin.

Mendoza slid his hand along the brick wall. With a satisfied grunt, he pulled a hidden lever and stepped back. A section of the wall moved a few inches, revealing a hidden room. He waved them in. Once inside, Lucia gasped. A huge bed took up one side of the room; hanging over it was a large mirror. Leather hand-cuffs and harnesses lined the walls. Vibrators, whips, and sex toys lay next to the bed.

"The previous owner hid his dirty little secret in here," Mendoza chuckled. "He didn't want his neighbors to find out what he was into. If we had time, I'd show you some very inter-esting videos he made. But you'd have to like really dirty sex."

"Some other time," Alejandra growled, exhausted from car-rying Prit. "Help me get him on the bed."

They settled the Ukrainian on the stained satin sheets and then sat on the floor to wait.

Nothing happened right away. They heard a Humvee roar through the streets and a garbled voice shouting something through a bullhorn. Then everything went quiet again. The plop-plop of a leaky faucet was getting on Lucia's already frayed nerves.

Several shots rang out close by. Silence again. Then a Humvee raced by.

"They're on this street," Mendoza whispered. He turned off the light and they sat in total darkness. "Now shut up, everyone. One word and we're dead."

They heard wood splintering on the floor above them, as if someone had flung furniture onto the floor. Then punching, yelling, and several shots. A woman screamed, but her cry was abruptly suffocated.

Their shelter was filled with a deathly silence and the sharp smell of sweat and fear. Even Mendoza abandoned his macho pose and sat in silence, his lips pursed, hands clasped in prayer.

One of the basement steps creaked, then the next. Someone was coming down the stairs, whistling "Hey Jude" off-key, under his breath. He paused in the middle of a verse, dragged furniture around, then started whistling again. It made their hair stand on end.

Lucia brushed sweat-soaked hair off Prit's face. The Ukrainian made a superhuman effort to control his breathing. He looked pretty bad but gave her a weak thumbs-up.

Starting at the other end of the room, the guy pounded the walls with something hard, listening for the hollow sound of a hidden room. Mendoza grabbed Alejandra's AK-47 with a grim look on his face. No was one going to take him—or anyone else in that hideout—alive.

Thump, thump, thump.

The pounding was getting closer. Lucia bit her hand to keep from screaming.

Thump, thump, thump.

The guy stopped whistling. He focused all his attention on the sound.

Thump, thump, *thump*!

Just then someone upstairs shouted. The pounding stopped and the guy stomped up the stairs. An engine started up and roared away.

They waited in silence in the dark for hours.

Alejandra whispered, "Sometimes Green Guards pretend they're leaving. They wait for helots to come out of their shelters, then shoot them down like dogs."

Lucia didn't hear a word the girl said. She was exhausted, emotionally drained, and about to crack.

The hours passed in a blur. Alejandra pulled out a bottle of water and a sandwich, but no one felt like eating or drinking. Lucia laid her head on Prit's legs and let her mind wander to someplace nicer than that grimy basement.

Six hours later, Mendoza decided it was safe to leave their hideout. He eased the door open and silently peered out. After all that time, it was unlikely Greene's men were still upstairs. But if they were, he didn't want to be picked off like rabbits poking their heads out of their den. He waved the others out once he was sure the coast was clear.

The house looked like a hurricane had hit it. Broken furniture, smashed dishes, and scraps of clothing blanketed the floor. Green Guards had dumped all the drawers out the window, sending their contents flying down the street. They'd torn away floorboards and ceiling tiles looking for hiding places. The worst part was the blood.

"What'll happen to all those people?" Pritchenko asked between bloody coughs.

"They'll put them on the train," Mendoza muttered. "Those assholes've gone too far. It's time for the Wrath of the Just."

3 0

At first I felt hot, very hot. Two Green Guards had dragged me out of Greene's office and thrown me in a cell in the basement of the Gulfport police station. The cells lined a narrow hallway and were painted puke green. Each had a toilet bolted down in the middle. I was the only occupant. Outside, an angry mob had gathered.

I was locked in a cell way in the back. The guards gave me a couple of kicks, and then, in one last evil act, they set a jug of water and a piece of moldy bread outside my cell, just out of reach.

"Thirsty, motherfucker? You'll be thirstier in hell," one of them taunted me.

"You shouldn't've bumped off old lady Compton," muttered the other guard. "She was a bitchy old bag, but she was the old man's secretary." He shook his head, as if he knew something I didn't. "Those people out there are gonna burn you alive."

The first guard spat green phlegm on the bread. "There's a little more to eat." The guy smiled, but had a pitying look in his eyes. "Don't turn your nose up at that. It's the best you'll get. They're sending you to the Wasteland with all those fucking helots. Nothing but scorpions and Undead out there. I'd hate to be in your shoes, asshole."

"Don't worry. I can take care of myself," I muttered, not looking up. It wasn't a threat. I just wanted the two idiots to go away and leave me alone.

The Aryan looked at me for a moment, trying to decide if that was an insult, kicked the bread out of reach, and headed down the hall with his buddy, leaving me alone.

How did everything go to hell so fast? That morning, I'd had a boat, a plan, and I was about to get my hands on a drug worth its weight in gold. Twelve hours later, I was rotting in jail, about to be put to death.

So much for your fucking plan, wise guy. What's next?

I was dripping with sweat. It must've been ninety degrees in there. I felt dangerously dehydrated. I looped my shirt over the water jug and tried to drag it, but I only managed to knock it over. *You idiot!* I watched helplessly as the last drop of water disappeared down a drain in the center of the aisle.

I dropped to my knees and leaned against the bars. My mouth felt like it was full of straw. I was so thirsty I couldn't think straight. After half an hour, I realized there was water in the toilet bowl. It tasted salty and was a weird color. I couldn't ignore the fact that I was drinking out of a toilet, but at least it was liquid.

I took small sips to make the water last longer. The small amount didn't quench my thirst, but it revived me a little. Then I started thinking about how to get out of this mess.

Breaking out of jail was out of the question. The locks were too complicated for me to pick. Plus the police station was surrounded by guards and that angry mob. They'd tear me apart like a pack of dogs for a crime I didn't commit. Greene's strategy was twisted and evil but shrewd. By killing Mrs. Compton, he eliminated a witness and made me the most hated person in Gulfport. No one would believe a word I said. I'd sound like a desperate murderer making up a crazy excuse. My only friends outside those walls were Lucia and Prit . . . if they were still alive and hadn't been jailed as accomplices.

I ached all over from the beating. My suit was in tatters and covered with stiff, dried blood. My infected blood. That thought made my head spin. I leaned into the bowl and threw up over and over until I'd emptied out what little I had in my stomach. I hugged the toilet, shaking.

Someone'll have to disinfect all this when I go, I thought as I looked at my saliva on the toilet bowl. I didn't feel anything yet, but I knew TSJ was rushing through my veins. In a few hours, I'd show the first signs of the virus. I wondered what it'll be like to change into an Undead. Would I realize what was happening? My curiosity surprised me. Picturing myself becoming one of those creatures, burst veins covering my skin, was too much. I clung to the toilet shaking and gagging, but nothing else came up.

The easiest thing would be to get it over with. Spare myself the terrible indignity of becoming a being with no control over itself.

What're you thinking? That's suicide.

So what? It'd be best way out.

You can't. Life means too much to you. Don't do it.

It'd be better than . . . that.

You don't know that.

Shut up, dammit. Shut up, shut up, shut up!

I cradled my head in my hands as I lay on the floor, moaning. I had to do something or I'd go crazy. But what? I had nothing I could use to end my suffering. When they threw me in jail, they took my watch, my shoelaces, and my belt. Those

Aryans had spent too much time behind bars to overlook a single detail.

Losing my watch hurt the most. It was an old, beaten-up Festina, but it was all I had left from my old life. Adding to my agony, I had no way to gauge time, since the light was always on in my cell.

After a couple of hours, I felt the first muscle cramps and a tingling in both arms, like when you fall asleep with your hand pinned under your body. The pain was mild at first, but unsettling. I knew what it meant—the change had begun.

I wiped my sweaty forehead with my shirttail. The stifling heat must be the first sign of the infection. Greene was sweating profusely before he took Cladoxpan.

A horrible thought crossed my mind. They were going to leave me here, locked up like a rabid animal, until the infection transformed me into an Undead. Then I'd be a carnival sideshow, a monster. Dads in Gulfport would bring their kids to see me, to teach them about the monsters outside the Wall. They'd throw popcorn and rotten vegetables at me.

I was going crazy. I furiously scratched my arm. Was that itch the next stage in my transformation, or was it just anxiety?

Suddenly I heard a bolt pulled back on the upper floor. Footsteps started down the stairs. Like a cornered animal, I looked around for something to defend myself with, but everything was either bolted down or welded to the walls. It dawned on me that my infection could be my weapon, so I tore at the scab on my forehead. It hurt like hell, but hot blood started flowing down my face. I soaked my fingers in that blood and waited. I'd flick my infected blood on the first person who showed up. If I was going to die, I'd take someone with me.

The footsteps came closer. I knelt down, hiding my hands behind my back, ready to pounce. Then I saw Malachi Grapes backlit by the fluorescent light.

"Hello, lawyer." Grapes's voice mocked me. The evil fuck knew I was trapped. In his arms was a frightened, squirming, wild-eyed Lucullus, horrified by the defeated, bloody figure eyeing him from the other side of the bars.

I froze. That was the last thing I expected. Lucullus yowled when he recognized me and tried to get free of Grapes's iron grip.

"Let my cat go, asshole!" I shouted. "Drop him *now* or . . . !"

"Or what? What're you gonna do? I could break his neck while you watch—"

"No! No, don't do that, please!"

"Then sit at the back of the cell. Keep your hands where I can see them. No surprises." The bastard was one step ahead of me. He had on safety glasses in case he got splashed.

I did as I was told and sat on the cot, looking from Grapes to Lucullus. When my little buddy heard my voice, he tried even harder to escape. The Aryan had two deep scratches on his arm. Lucullus had put up a good fight.

"Y'know, in prison, my attorney was always on this side of the bars," Grapes said with a wicked smile. "This is a nice change."

"I'm surprised you had any visitors. Even your lawyer."

Grapes laughed smugly. "I wish I could've brought your slut or that Commie dwarf to say good-bye. But they're smarter than

you. Can't find them anywhere. The only one at home was this
flea-bitten cat. Figured you'd like to see him."

"Don't hurt him, please."

"That depends on you. Tomorrow morning, we'll put you on
the deportation train," he said slowly, as if he were explaining
something to a child. "You need to behave yourself until then. If
it was up to me, I'd've put a couple of slugs in you by now, but the
reverend has a different punishment in mind. He decided you
should die alone, slowly. Give you time to think about the deep
shit you're in."

"Tell me something I don't know," I said sourly.

"No, you tell me. Why'd you do it? You had a fucking good
life. Nice house, steady job, a chick to warm your bed, even this
shitty cat. Don't get me wrong, I'm glad you fucked up. You
pissed me off from the start, but I never thought you'd make it so
easy for me. So, why'd you do it?"

"Because I'm not an animal like you. Because this place is
immoral and sick. It's all gonna blow up in your face one day. I
don't want to live in a place that saves my body but destroys my
soul. That's why I did it. I'm just sorry I won't be there when the
helots rise up and a couple of those guys fuck you till you can't
stand up. Considering all the time you spent in prison, you might
enjoy it."

Grapes's face turned bright red and I thought I'd gone too
far. His hand squeezed my poor cat's neck and he shook him like
a rag doll. Lucullus struggled, weakly meowing in pain, nearly
suffocating.

"Tomorrow I'll make sure to lock up a few helot crackheads
in your train car," he growled. "Then we'll see who gets fucked
up the ass."

There was nothing I could say to that. Grapes held all the
cards.

"This isn't a courtesy call. Here. This'll last you till morning."
The Aryan dug something out of his pocket and tossed it to me.

I snatched it out of the air and stared at it. It was a clear plastic bottle about the size of a soda can. Inside was a white liquid.

"It's Cladoxpan. You've been infected for eight hours, so you're showing the first symptoms. You're sweating like a pig even though it's freezing down here."

His words confirmed my worst fears. The extreme heat I'd been feeling indicated that TSJ was overwhelming my immune system.

"What do I have to do?" I asked in a hushed voice.

"You have two choices. Give me back that bottle and when I come for you in the morning, you'll be just another rotten Undead. We'll shoot you in the head, burn your body in the town dump, and that's that. Or you can drink the Cladoxpan slowly. The longer it lasts, the longer you'll last. You'll eventually die in the Wasteland. You decide." Grapes shrugged.

"I choose to live," I said faintly, looking at the floor. My whole life was ruined.

"What? I can't hear you."

"I choose to live," I said, a bit louder.

"Thought you'd say that. But I want an additional guarantee you'll behave yourself." The Aryan pulled a knife out of his boot, and before I had time to blink, stretched Lucullus across his knees and pressed the knife blade against my cat's tail.

"No!"

Everything happened in slow motion. Grapes's wrist arcing upward as he sliced Lucullus's tail in half. The knife covered in blood. Blood spurting from the stump of Lucullus's tail. My cat's eyes wide with pain and panic as he let out a long meow. Grapes's sadistic, satisfied expression.

My knuckles were white as chalk as I shook the bar. "*You fucking son of a bitch*! I'll kill you! Hear me? I swear I'll kill you, you asshole!"

"Tell that to someone else." Grapes calmly stood up and put the knife back in his boot. "Don't worry about your cat. One of the guys'll bandage what's left of his tail." His tone became menacing. "Control yourself till tomorrow if you don't want me betting with pieces of Persian cat at our poker game tonight. Got it?"

Lucullus's blood dripped onto the dirty tile floor, leaving huge, flower-shaped drops. I couldn't look away from those spots. I'd never hated anyone so much.

"I'll leave you alone to think. Have a good night."

That evil fuck Grapes walked down the corridor, a steel grip on Lucullus, whistling as my cat's cries of pain got weaker and weaker.

And then I was alone, the bottle of Cladoxpan in one hand and the piece of Lucullus's tail in the other. My heart was racing, but I couldn't cry. All I wanted was revenge.

3 2

BLUEFONT
THE DAY AFTER THE RAID

The first two hours of the morning were hectic. Mendoza set up headquarters at the Red Rooster and sent messages to the four corners of the ghetto via wily young kids. With fast legs and a hungry look in their eye, they slipped past the militia and the Green Guards. The kids memorized the messages so that if they were caught, they wouldn't be carrying any evidence.

Lucia and Prit crouched in a corner and watched. Alejandra found a first-aid kit and gently tended the Ukrainian's cuts and bruises. He'd recovered pretty well except for his broken ribs, but the former soldier could tolerate that. As he wolfed down a stew of mystery meat, his gaze flitted around that crowd, trying to decipher the group's plans.

"What's going on, Prit?" Lucia murmured uneasily.

"Not sure. But it has all the signs of an uprising."

"An uprising?" Lucia shrieked in alarm. "When?"

"In a few hours, I think," Prit said. "My guess, they've been planning it for a while. Today's raid just moved up their plans."

The Ukrainian was right. The plan had been brewing for months. The majority of the helots were far from defeated by the reverend's tactics. Greene and his men always kept in mind the possibility of an uprising—and feared it. At least four times, the helots had been about to revolt but had called it off at the last minute. Greene always got wind of their plans through a network of snitches that he'd bribed or blackmailed to work for him. Mendoza suspected that the Green Guards bugged the houses during raids. Mendoza and his men had checked every inch of the Red Rooster, but still he knew there was a chance the Aryans were on to his plans.

The morning's unforeseen raid had derailed all their planning. They had to act. Now.

Forty minutes later, thirty men and women crowded into the bar, trying to make themselves heard over the growing din. They all told an unsettling story. The Greens had taken over six hundred people from the ghetto.

"This raid was the worst yet!" roared a tall, leathery Latino. "They didn't just take the weak! They took adult men and women!"

"It was random," complained another. "They even took those with proper ID."

"When did ID ever stop them?" a voice in the back replied bitterly. "They're exterminating us little by little, like in those fucking Nazi ghettos."

"But we had a deal!" the first guy replied stubbornly. "We just needed to have ID!"

"You're a real idiot if you believe that bullshit. And a fucking sellout. You busted your balls to get that worthless piece of paper. Stop your whining."

"Who you calling a sellout, you son of a bitch?" The man reached for his knife.

Everyone was shouting at once, so Mendoza got up on the table and yelled himself hoarse, trying in vain to get control of the crowd. Finally, he picked up a broken computer and tossed it through the building's last window. When the crowd heard the breaking glass, they stopped midsentence and looked up at Mendoza, whose eyes were shooting sparks.

"You're a bunch of idiots! We don't have to wait for Greene's men to kill us. We can do it ourselves. Now shut up and listen if you want to keep living."

The crowd whispered and coughed. The two guys shot angry looks at each other. Clearly, their argument wasn't over, but everyone obeyed Gato Mendoza.

Mendoza cleared his throat. "The moment we feared—and hoped for—has come. The raids are getting worse. The Green Guards treat us like sacrificial lambs. We can't put up with this any longer. We have to act now."

"I don't think that's the wisest course of action." Out of the crowd stepped an old black man wearing a moth-eaten tweed jacket and thick glasses. Before the pandemic, he'd been a respected professor of philosophy at a university in the Midwest; he was used to being heard and respected. "Violence only begets violence. Chaos leads to chaos. Only with harmony and understanding can we find long-term solutions. I'm sure if we take this matter up with the reverend and explain the situation, he'll punish the guilty and make sure this doesn't happen again. Or we can apply passive resistance, Gandhi-style. But armed resistance won't solve the problem."

There was a flurry of reactions for and against. Everyone talked at once.

Mendoza quieted everyone down and continued. "Professor Bansted, you're one of the most levelheaded people in the ghetto, but this isn't that college where you taught. This isn't a student demonstration demanding better food in the cafeteria. It's not even the same fucking world. We're talking about saving our lives."

"Our lives are valuable to the people on the other side of the Wall," Bansted said, undeterred. "They need us to forage food, fuel, clothing, and medicine. They can't survive without us!" The ancient professor crossed his arms.

A murmur of approval followed the old man's words.

"That's only half true, Professor," Mendoza said. "First of all, not everyone in the ghetto goes out on reconnaissance. Children, the sick and the elderly—like you—are expendable in Greene's eyes." Bansted flinched. "Have you ever gone on a raid outside the walls? No. To them, you're one more useless mouth to feed, like a lot of us. At any one time, Gulfport only needs about five hundred of us for the raids. A couple of thousand would be plenty. And more manageable."

More arguments broke out.

"That's just your opinion," Bansted answered, stubbornly. "I lived through race riots in the sixties. If we'd taken up arms back then, the consequences would've been dire."

"In those race riots, did they take hundreds of black people on a train somewhere and they never came back ever?" Mendoza asked bitterly.

The old professor paused, looked down, and then answered with a nearly inaudible "No."

"We're being exterminated, like the Jews during the Holocaust. That's a fact, whether you like it or not." There was dead silence. "We can do one of two things: go meekly to the slaughter or stand up and fight for our lives. The worst that can happen is we get killed. Either way, we'll die."

Many people nodded gloomily as their doubts evaporated.

"The Hour of the Just has come!" Mendoza thundered. "It's time for justice and freedom to triumph over tyranny and oppression! It's time to take control of our lives! It's now or never, friends. Grab your weapons and let's take the damn wall! Let's burn Gulfport down! Let's teach those fat, lazy white people a lesson they'll never forget! Let's fight for our freedom! Together!"

The people cheered and raised their fists in a wild, mad fever. Even the college professor was swept up in the excitement. Some jabbed the air with their knives, picturing the Green Guards they'd kill.

Over the cheers, a slow, mocking applause rang out. Every head turned toward the sound and fell silent. Standing next to the wall, Viktor Pritchenko clapped and smiled bitterly.

"Bravo!" he said, his voice dripping with irony, as he kept clapping. "That was one helluva speech. You surprised me. I didn't think a two-bit thug like you had what it takes to lead a revolt. If you hadn't nearly killed me a few hours ago, I'd even respect you. I'm impressed."

"Got something to say, *güero*?" Mendoza replied, visibly upset.

"A couple of things." Prit climbed up on the table with Mendoza. "First, you're one hundred percent correct. Those racist pigs on the other side of the Wall want to kill you. And they'll do it too. Second, your little revolution is doomed before it begins."

"Whaddaya mean?" a woman demanded in a thick Southern accent. "We outnumber 'em, and we're not afraid to die."

"Actually, you don't outnumber them," the Ukrainian replied slowly. "There's a lot more people on the other side of the

Wall. They're better fed, healthier, and, above all, better armed. Are you gonna attack the Green Guards and the militia with knives?"

"We've got guns." Mendoza stuck out his chin, challenging Prit. "And there're only about three hundred militiamen and Green Guards."

"True," said Prit, "but I'll bet Greene could arm a couple thousand men the minute you attack. I was on the other side. I know what I'm talking about."

An uncomfortable murmur spread through the room as the Ukrainian continued. "What weapons do you have? The Green Guards take your guns after a raid, right?"

"We've stolen some weapons," said the tall Latino. "We find guns out on raids and sneak them back in the ghetto hidden among the supplies. I got a list." He handed Prit a few handwritten pages.

Pritchenko flipped through the papers and let out a sarcastic laugh. "Just what I thought. You have a couple dozen assault rifles, some hunting rifles, even some antiques." He stopped at one of the lines on the paper and looked in disbelief. "A tommy gun? Really? That's what gangsters used back in the Roaring Twenties. Where the hell'd you get that? I gotta see it."

"They kill, same as modern guns." The man stood his ground.

"They don't kill the same. Take my word for it." He handed back the list, shaking his head. "On top of that, you don't have enough ammunition for this hodgepodge. Ten minutes into the battle, you'll be out." He smiled wryly. "You gonna spit on them? Throw rocks? Very few of you have military training, including your leaders." He turned to Mendoza, who was red with anger. "No offense, Gato."

"We have the element of surprise," Mendoza muttered angrily, ignoring Pritchenko's taunts. "And we can seize ammunition from the Greens we kill."

"Helluva plan," Prit replied. "Now tell me how you plan to attack that concrete wall and the machine guns in those towers. You're forgetting one important thing: Greene has control of the Cladoxpan. If your plan doesn't work, he'll cut off your supply and, in a couple of days, you'll all turn into Undead. Truth is, he's got you by the balls."

"Not quite," said a deep voice from the back of the room in very proper English.

Viktor Pritchenko stared, speechless, as Gunnar Strangärd walked through the crowd, waterlogged and frowning.

Cowards die many times before their deaths.
The valiant never taste of death but once.
—William Shakespeare, *Julius Caesar*

"What the hell . . . ?" the Ukrainian stammered. "What're you doing here?"

"I could ask you the same thing," said the Swede and nodded politely to Lucia. "I'm glad to see you're in one piece, my friend."

"Not exactly in one piece," Prit growled, pointing to his black eye and broken nose.

"A lot of people are worse off, believe me." The Swede made his way through the crowd, waving to friends. He was clearly a familiar presence.

"Hello, Gunnar." Alejandra planted a kiss on his cheek. "How're you?"

"Hello, Ale. I'm glad to see you." Strangärd sounded relieved. "What a nightmare!"

"Tell me about it," the woman replied. "What's happening on the other side of the Wall?"

"They're getting ready to ship them off. We don't have much time." The Swede turned to Lucia and Prit with a grim look on his face. "I'm afraid I have very bad news. They've got your friend."

Lucia froze. The blood drained from her face and her voice shook. "What do you mean they've got him?"

"They threw him in jail. They claim he killed someone when he was trying to steal some Cladoxpan. He'll be on the train that leaves in two hours, along with everyone they arrested in the raid."

Lucia turned to Prit in panic. "We gotta get him out of there!"

"That's not possible." Strangärd shook his head. "The train is heavily guarded and the crowd at the station wants to lynch him. There's a price on your heads too. If you show up, they'll shoot you, no questions asked."

Prit looked like he'd been gut-punched. Lucia slumped against a wall and slid to the floor, nearly choking on her tears.

They're going to kill him. First the slaughter in the ghetto and now him. Oh, God, it's all my fault. How could I have been so stupid?

Alejandra put her arm around Lucia's shoulders and tried to comfort her, but she couldn't stop sobbing.

"Whadda we do now?" Alejandra cast a lost look around the room.

Mendoza was red-faced with anger. "It's time, Gunnar," he said, quietly. "We need the help of the Just."

"You'll have our help; don't worry," Strangärd replied calmly. "We'll get the stash when I get back to the other side."

"Wait a minute," said Prit, shaking off his gloom. "What're you talking about? What stash? Who're the Just?"

"Not everyone on the other side backs Greene," Strangärd replied. "There aren't many of us, but we see how corrupt

Gulfport is. We've organized an underground movement. If Greene found out, we'd be on that train."

"The Just have helped us from the start," Alejandra added. "They've let us know about changes in documents and given us fake IDs, medicine, food, and even weapons. We built that submerged bridge with their help."

"We have to be very cautious," Strangärd said. "Greene has eyes and ears everywhere. The minute I saw you three, I knew you weren't like those people. I wanted to explain the situation to you on the ship, but I never got the chance. Captain Birley and his crew kept a close eye on you."

"How many of you are there?" Prit asked.

"I can't say for sure. We're organized in independent cells. If they capture one, the rest of the organization isn't affected. But we have people in most sectors."

"The uprising doesn't sound so ridiculous now, does it?" Mendoza broke in.

"It still sounds ridiculous . . . and suicidal," Prit replied. "But there's no other option."

"I'm afraid not," Strangärd said. "We've heard rumors of a huge raid on the ghetto in a couple of weeks. Only two thousand helots will be left alive. We have to act now."

"The Cladoxpan . . ." Pritchenko said.

"That's no problem," said the Swede. "We've hidden nearly four thousand liters of Cladoxpan in a secret warehouse. Our people in the lab have risked their lives to stockpile it little by little. Greene will cut your supply, but you'll be able to survive for a few days. Long enough for the uprising to succeed, God willing."

"What if it fails?" asked the old professor. "And what happens when that Cladoxpan runs out?"

"If the uprising fails, that'll be the least of our problems. We'll all be dead," Mendoza said coolly. "How do you plan to get it to us, Gunnar?"

"Getting it past the Wall is impossible. There's too much to transport at one time. Making several trips would take too long and would be too risky."

Mendoza blurted out, "What if you left it someplace where we could pick it up later?"

"Good idea," Strangärd said. "But where?"

Silence filled the room. They'd reached a dead end.

"Outside," said Pritchenko, suddenly. "On the other side of the Wall."

"Not a bad idea." Strangärd smiled for the first time. "We could disguise the drums as garbage bins . . ."

"Our people can pick them up when they take the trash to the dump." Mendoza finished the Swede's sentence. "We'll hide those drums on the garbage trucks. The Greens never search them."

"Perfect." Strangärd turned to Pritchenko and smiled. "Brilliant idea, my friend."

"I have my moments," Prit replied uncomfortably. "When can we start?"

"The next trash dump is a week from now," said the Swede. "That'll give us time to transport the drums of Cladoxpan to the dump."

"A week?" Prit stirred uneasily. "That's too long! You just said the deportation train leaves in two hours!"

"We can't do a thing for those people." Strangärd shook his head. "But we can save the lives of those still here."

"You heard him!" Mendoza shouted to the crowd. "We've got seven days. Get your groups together, round up your weapons, and wait for my signal. In a week, the Wrath of the Just will fall on those sons of bitches in Gulfport!"

A cheer filled the room. Everyone felt strangely calm, as if they'd crossed a bridge and burned it behind them. Everything was riding on this one plan now, but at least fear wasn't eating away at them.

As people filed out of the room, someone grabbed Strangärd's arm. He turned to see Lucia's tear-ravaged face.

"Please," she sobbed, "please, you've got to help him. I love him more than anything in the world. If he dies, nothing matters to me. Nothing! Help me, please!"

Strangärd studied her for a moment. "I can't do anything for him. I can't get him out of jail or off that train. It's too dangerous."

"Listen to me." Lucia squared her shoulders, gathering every ounce of energy she had left, trying to control the tremor in her voice. "I know what I'm asking is really hard, but the man I love is on that train. If you can't help me, I'll cross that damn bridge, walk to that station, and get on the train with him. If he dies, I'll die with him. If he lives . . ."

Strangärd swallowed hard. What the girl was asking was far too risky, but the gleam in her eyes told him she was serious.

"'Cowards die many times before their deaths. The valiant never taste of death but once,'" the Swede recited quietly, staring off into space.

"What does that mean?" Lucia asked weakly.

"It means I'll help you," Strangärd sighed. "I'll help your man."

"Thank you." Lucia's eyes flooded with tears. "Thank you."

"That doesn't mean he'll get out of the huge mess he's in," Strangärd added. "I can get some supplies to him. The rest is up to him."

"Don't worry," said Lucia with a shaky smile. "He's a born survivor. He's gotten out of worst situations. I know he can do it."

3 4

MILE 110,
LOUISIANA INTERSTATE 190
HEADED EAST TO MISSISSIPPI

Colonel Hong was furious. The convoy had stopped for the third time that day, and the current delay was lasting longer than the other two combined. A very long bridge over a swampy ravine was blocked by two eighteen-wheelers, which were sprawled across it. The driver of the first truck must have abandoned it when it ran out of gas. Then the second truck crashed into the first, resulting in a pile of twisted metal stretching across the bridge. The back end of the second truck's trailer teetered over the edge.

After two weeks of traveling through the remains of the southern United States, even Hong's steely nerves were frayed. They'd made pretty good time, but not without problems. Their strategy was to find fuel and keep moving. Unfortunately, most of the derelict cars littering the roads didn't have a drop of gas in their tanks and were slowly falling apart. Their owners probably drove until the tanks ran dry, then got out and walked. At this point, many cars were just heaps of metal and broken glass.

Hong suspected the cars' owners had fled their homes as the virus rapidly spread. He speculated that they were already infected. People contracted TSJ many ways, not just through a bite. Sex, the carrier's mucus from a sneeze, or just a kiss could infect an entire family in a matter of hours. Most of the Undead were exposed in the early days of the pandemic. Every time Hong saw one of those wrecked cars, he pictured a guy speeding out of town with his family, his car loaded down, in a panic. As the hours went by, he felt worse and worse, until . . . Even the hard-hearted colonel found that image disturbing. The charred human remains with their grinning skulls lying by the side of the road proved his theory.

Hong and his men's search for fuel had become a nightmare. To run on regular gasoline, the engines of their Soviet-era BTR-60 tanks needed filters, which eventually got clogged. Even filtered, the fuel took a toll on the engines. They'd had to abandon two tanks along the way. Their crew had to squeeze into the remaining tanks, which caused the army's first casualties as they drove cross-country. Two soldiers had sat too close to the engine and died from breathing carbon monoxide.

Hong lit another cigarette and watched as the bulldozer rumbled over the bridge toward the wreckage. A soldier walked in front guiding it. They'd had to go through this maneuver at least twice a day.

How many cars were there in the US before the pandemic? Hong wondered. Judging by the number of cars on the roads, every American must've had at least three.

The colonel took a drag on his cigarette. One of the few good things about their mission was the American tobacco they'd found. It was so much better than the Chinese crap they were used to. Who knew what that stuff was cut with? Like most North Koreans, his men were heavy smokers. The smoke trail they left behind could have led a tracker right to them.

The bulldozer drove alongside the wrecked truck, raised its giant fork-like shovel, and started to push. At first there was just the roar of the dozer's engine, but little by little, the truck slid along the bridge, amid a chorus of shrieks, scrapes, and the biting smell of burning plastic. The driver of the bulldozer lifted the cab of the first truck and pushed it over the edge of the bridge. The trailer dangled halfway over, swaying dangerously, but the cabin was caught on a steel pole connected to the railing and wouldn't budge. The driver backed up and charged the twisted chassis, like a thirty-ton metal ram.

When the shovel struck the truck, it set off a chain reaction. The pole was torn loose, freeing the cab of the truck. As it started to fall into the void, its trailer spun around and hit the charred remains of the other eighteen-wheeler. That truck then shot forward and plowed into the bulldozer. Before the driver of the dozer could react, it skidded a foot and slowly tilted over the other side of the bridge.

"*No!*" Hong roared, flicking his cigarette on the ground and watching helplessly.

The bulldozer teetered on the edge, as if fate had reconsidered at the last moment. But the driver panicked, pushed open the heavy door, and climbed over the chassis, trying to escape what seemed like certain death. Had he stayed put, the bulldozer's momentum would have righted it, but that sudden movement disrupted the fragile balance. With a screech of metal scraping on cement, the bulldozer dragged down its driver and the mangled wreckage of those two trucks, abandoned so long ago.

The tangled mass of bulldozer and truck crashed into the ravine with a roar that must have carried for miles. A huge plume of smoke rose from below. For a moment, all the soldiers froze and stared in disbelief.

"Sir." Lieutenant Kim cautiously approached Colonel Hong. He knew that his superior was very dangerous when he was angry, and it didn't take a genius to see that Hong was seething. "Although we lost a bulldozer, the road is clear."

Hong took some deep breaths, his jaw tense. Losing a tank was bad, but losing one of their two bulldozers was a tragedy. They were specially designed to break through clogged roads. Their cabs sat up higher than normal and had reinforced glass to protect the driver from the Undead. They were invaluable to the operation.

Obsessing over it won't do any good, thought Hong. *Plus, we've got a deadline.*

"We're done here," he said to Kim. "The person to blame is dead." He waved his arm over his head, signaling to the drivers to start their engines. "Move out!"

The column thundered across the bridge single file, leaving behind a burning pyre in the ravine, consuming the bulldozer and its driver.

An hour later, Hong sighed and slumped in his seat. The trip was turning into a tactical nightmare. He'd decided to use secondary roads to bypass major population centers where he assumed there would be higher concentrations of Undead. Those alternative routes were also less likely to be blocked by wrecked cars. Satellite images had detected several spots where the main highways were completely impassable. In some places, the local authorities had blown up bridges and tunnels in a desperate attempt to stop the spread of the disease, just as they did in the Middle Ages to stop the bubonic plague. In other places, massive traffic jams of abandoned cars stretched for several miles. Some major highways crossed areas so populous that Hong and his men would have faced a battle just to gain a couple of miles.

So they drove on state or local roads. They even drove across fields. South Texas was flat and open, so they traveled quickly. Once they crossed into Louisiana, the trip got a lot more complicated and their progress slowed.

The most chilling part was the towns. The back roads passed through dozens of small towns. There was no way to skirt them. When they came to one, Hong gave the order to seal up the tanks and drive through the streets at top speed. The scene was always the same: tanks speeding down the deserted main street in tight formation, dodging cars, fallen trees, and trash. When the Undead in those towns sensed the presence of humans, they awoke from their stupor and blocked the tanks' path. But since the towns' populations were usually under a thousand, they didn't pose a big problem. The convoy drove through the streets so fast there wasn't time for more than a couple hundred Undead to gather. Only once did they have serious trouble, in the remote town of Livingston, Texas, near the Louisiana border.

Livingston, population five thousand, had been the county seat and the largest town in Polk County. Hong knew that but decided to drive through it anyway. Detouring would've taken them seventy miles out of their way. That was his first mistake.

His second mistake was to divide the group into two to search for fuel. That doubled the risk, but it also doubled the chances of finding fuel. Since the side streets were narrower than the main street, Colonel decided to send the bulldozers with that group in case they got stuck. Hong knew he was taking a huge risk, but he had no choice. After speeding across Texas in just two weeks, their fuel tanks were very low, and they'd run out of diesel thirty miles back. Livingston was the only town for miles. If they were going to find fuel anywhere, it would be in Livingston.

The third mistake was not anticipating the large number of Undead they would find in the town. The colonel wasn't to blame for that one. He couldn't have known that most of the people in the area distrusted outsiders and the federal government, and had ignored the order to evacuate to the Safe Zones. Instead, they'd congregated where they felt safest: the county seat in Livingston.

When the North Korean convoy entered the town and separated into two groups, they had no idea they were driving straight into a hornets' nest, where fifteen thousand Undead had been waiting for human victims for nearly two years.

The Undead fell on them from all sides. The first sign of trouble was a crowd of nearly a thousand Undead gathered at one end of the main street, blocking the path of the group without the bulldozers. The tanks charged the crowd, but the lead vehicle had to stop when a mutilated torso got stuck between the front axle and the chassis. The street was too narrow to go around the vehicle, so the whole convoy was stuck.

The terrified soldiers, locked in their tanks, heard the huge crowd moaning and beating their fists on the sides of the tanks. Even more frightening were the cries of the poor guys in the first tank who'd disobeyed orders and abandoned their BTR-60. At first they fired wildly and pounded on the other tanks for help. Hong kept a tight leash on his men so they wouldn't help their comrades. If they opened the hatch, the Undead would swarm the vehicles in seconds. The men's cries grew weaker, then stopped altogether.

Hong ordered the tanks to push each other, like a huge, armored caterpillar. With the combined strength of their engines, they pushed the first tank to one side and made their way slowly through the crowd, crushing the creatures under their wheels. Once they were out of town, they waited half an hour for the other group, who made it out unscathed but hadn't found a drop of fuel.

Late that afternoon, they finally found a gas station on a deserted stretch of highway. There they encountered just four Undead, the station owner and his family, who didn't pose a problem for Hong's men. The owner must have been a member of the National Rifle Association and a gun fanatic; they found an impressive arsenal in his house. He'd also been very cautious and had installed a complicated locking system on his gas tanks. For the average traveler, that system would've been insurmountable, but Hong's men got it open with a combination of ingenuity and brute force. Within half an hour, they were able to refuel and load several barrels of extra gas on top of their BTR-60s.

As the trip continued, the Koreans began to notice changes in the Undead. They saw fungus slowly eating away those creatures, although not always in the same way. Crossing dry and dusty Texas, the Undead had looked fairly normal, or as normal as a resurrected person can look. In wetland areas, the fungal growth was much more pronounced on the Undeads' open wounds.

As they got closer to Mississippi with its extreme humidity, the creatures' appearance changed drastically. Every Undead they saw was infested with fungus. Nearer the Mississippi River, the infestations got worse. Their condition was horrifying: human bodies so covered by green, blue, or orange fuzz—or all three—that they looked like they were wrapped in colorful chiffon scarves. Some had a layer so thick their bodies were barely recognizable as human. A growing number of fungus-covered Undead lay rotting in piles and would never rise again.

Looking at those decaying mounds, Hong understood, with a chill, that their trip would have been impossible just a year earlier.

One small town was entirely deserted. No humans or Undead. Not even any animals. As the convoy crept through it, the fearful soldiers looked all around and whispered among themselves. They felt like the last men alive on earth.

When they came across a group of living people five days later, they were shocked.

The convoy had stopped to refuel under the shade of some massive trees. They parked in a circle, the way settlers in the Old West had circled their wagons. Inside the circle, the men built a bonfire and boiled rice. Half the soldiers tried to sleep; the other half stood watch. Hong was sitting at his table under a tree filling out the daily report when he heard the shots.

At first he thought they were under attack. Hong dropped his pen, grabbed the Makarov pistol holstered at his waist, and jumped to his feet. More shots rang out.

"Kim! Kim!" he bellowed as he buttoned his tunic and raced across the camp. His assistant appeared beside him as if he'd popped out of a magician's hat, silent as ever.

"The shots seem to be coming from southwest of our position, about four miles away, Colonel," he said quietly as he checked his rifle's magazine. "But it's hard to pinpoint. Sound travels really far in this silence."

"Send two tanks to check it out." Hong was not going risk his entire column by rushing blindly into the unknown. But then he snatched the rifle out of Kim's hands. "No, I'll go. You stay here in radio contact."

"Colonel, I don't think that's wise," Lieutenant Kim dared to interject, but Hong's poisonous look stopped him. "Yes, sir."

When Hong climbed up on one of the tanks, its engine was already running and his men were at their posts, weapons drawn. The colonel's men were battle hardened and didn't need to be told what to do in combat.

Adrenaline roared in Hong's veins. "Men, feel Our Beloved Leader breathing courage into you. Now charge!"

The two tanks pulled out of the circle and rushed down an idyllic, tree-lined road that ran along a brook toward the source of the shots. The trees' red leaves formed a pleasant canopy, but to Hong it was like they were driving into battle through a blanket of blood. There must be humans nearby, and humans were a more interesting foe than rotting corpses. Plus humans had information—exactly what Hong needed.

As they approached, the gunfire grew louder. There were a few explosions, which Hong's trained ear identified as hand grenades. He was reassured by that. If they'd come up against a heavily armed platoon, they would've had problems since his tanks had no heavy weapons.

The small convoy stopped at the top of a hill. Hong eased the hatch open, peered through his binoculars, and spotted the place where the shots were coming from—a town with about forty houses a couple of miles away at the bottom of a valley.

The colonel carefully scanned the streets. He could make out about two dozen figures, dressed in camouflage, swarming among the houses. At one end of the main street, half a dozen vehicles, including trucks and tanks, formed an impassable barrier. Some of the figures entered homes and came out carrying supplies, which they loaded into the trucks. Another group walked slowly through the town, killing the clumsy, fungus-ridden Undead.

Hong lowered his binoculars and thought for a moment. It was a raiding party. And what few Undead there were posed no challenge. The colonel wondered whether it was an isolated group or a detachment from a larger base. Gulfport, for example.

That made sense. They were only about a hundred and twenty-five miles from their objective. If Gulfport's population was as large as they suspected, raiding parties would have to go farther and farther to get supplies. There was just one way to find out.

"Sergeant, roll your tank to about a mile from the east side of town and wait for my signal. We'll enter on foot at the same time. Those imperialists are in for a big surprise." He smiled, savoring the thrill of the hunt.

"Should we call for backup, sir?" the tall, gaunt sergeant asked cautiously.

"No time for that." Hong dismissed him with a wave of his hand. "They're loading their trucks and could leave any minute. If we bring more men, they'll spot us. We have to seize the opportunity now."

The sergeant saluted and drove off with his five men. Hong ordered his tank with the other five soldiers to roll slowly down the hill. About half a mile from the town, they parked in a weed-choked cornfield, climbed out, and approached on foot.

The raiding party's idling engines and the shots they fired covered up any noise the Koreans made. The colonel stealthily led his men to the first house. He split his team into two squads, then entered the empty house through the back door. The looters outnumbered them, but Hong had the element of surprise on his side. On top of that, his soldiers were very disciplined—and very brave. Their unit's motto was: No risk, no victory.

The colonel crawled up to a window for a direct view of the street. His shoulder bumped a table next to an armchair. He grabbed the framed pictures on the table before they crashed to the floor. A wry smile came over his face. In one photograph, a stern-faced Marine from the '50s looked straight into the camera. He and three of his buddies were posed next to a milepost that read "Pyongyang, 115."

The Colonel was struck by the irony of the situation. A Korean War vet. *As a young man, that bastard traveled*

*thousands of miles to kill my countrymen. Fifty years later, I'm
here in his house to kill Americans on their home turf.*

He looked up and saw a group of the looters headed for the
house where Hong and his men were hiding. Hong noticed that
they were all black, Latino, and Asian. The colonel didn't care
about their skin color. They were all his enemies.

One of the men pointed to the house and shouted, "Hey,
Luis, go to the house on the corner with Randy and Joseph.
Charlie, Fernando, and I'll take care of this one. Everyone else
can go to—"

A hail of bullets from Hong's AK-74 hit the guy squarely in
the sternum and sent him flying backward as if he'd been
punched by a giant fist. The guy next to him opened his eyes
wide in disbelief. Another burst of fire blew away his head.
Splinters of bone and blood splattered in every direction.

The rest of the men became frightened. Some raised their
weapons, looking around for the shooters. Others fired blindly,
and a few turned and ran.

Nothing they did made any difference. The North Koreans
were excellent shots and they had formed a perfect enfilade.
Shots from every direction mowed down the entire looting party.
The shooting lasted only a few seconds. When it was over, the
smell of gunpowder and blood hung in the air. Ten bodies in
camouflage fatigues lay sprawled on the dusty road.

Hong leapt through the window, barking orders. He knew
his men would stick as close as his shadow anywhere he went. At
the other end of town, the sergeant's group had sprung into
action. Their automatic rifles sounded like a giant typewriter.

Hong ran down the sidewalk, blood pounding in his tem-
ples. "Get to the trucks!" he barked to the other squad as his
group ran toward the boarded-up grocery store. He knew there
were seven or eight looters still in there.

When Hong was about a hundred feet from the store, three figures appeared in the doorway. Two of them had their rifles slung across their backs and were loaded down with large cardboard boxes of food. The third guy, a bald tattooed giant, held his M16 loosely in one hand and a bag of food in the other.

"What's all the damn racket?" the bald man shouted. "You trying to attract all the damn Undead? What the fuck!"

Hong let out a war cry and started running, firing from the hip. Bullets pierced the bald guy's chest and he spun around like a top. The other men dropped their boxes and grabbed their weapons, but they died before they got off a single shot.

Not breaking stride, Hong and two of his men leapt over the bodies and stationed themselves on either side of the door. At Hong's signal, they tossed three grenades into the room and took cover.

The explosion blew out the glass and ripped the boards off the store's windows. A man missing a hand and screaming in pain, his bloody uniform in tatters, stumbled out the door. He tripped over the bald guy's body, tumbled down the stairs, and lay motionless.

Gunshots rang out all over town. Hong's second group had gotten the jump on the men loading the trucks, and had taken them out. The helots had finally realized living beings were attacking them, and were trying to get organized to return fire.

Two Undead—an old woman and a woman of indeterminate age—stumbled out of one of the houses into the middle of the fray. Fungus had completely eaten off their faces, reducing them to macabre skulls. And judging from the way they lurched around, their brains were probably being eaten away too.

Bullets from one side stopped the younger woman in her tracks, but by some miracle, the old woman reached the middle of the road intact. Oblivious to the shoot-out, she focused her attention on a helot too busy reloading his M16 to notice her.

The Undead lunged at the soldier with a roar. The man had just enough time to raise the butt of his gun and smash the monster's face. Blood and broken teeth flew out of the old woman's mouth and she staggered back. The helot fired two shots at her head. He jumped to his feet, but even before the Undead's body stopped twitching, a half a dozen bullets tore into his chest.

A huge explosion echoed through the streets. Hong's men had thrown explosives into the helots' tanks and blown them up. They were now a smoldering heap.

"No!" Hong yelled. "Don't blow them up! We need them!"

In the heat of the moment, Hong stood up. A couple of bullets drove into the wooden wall above his head, raining splinters down on him. Cursing under his breath, Hong ducked behind a Ford pickup with flat tires. Another explosion shook the ground, sending a truck flying.

"Do not throw grenades. I repeat: do not throw grenades!" Hong shouted into his walkie-talkie, hoping the other group could hear him over the shooting. The explosions suddenly stopped. Either someone had heard his order or they'd run out of grenades.

The surviving helots kept shooting as they slowly retreated into a house at the end of the street and tried to mount a resistance. They outnumbered the Koreans, but they didn't pose a serious threat. These men and women had no military training. Battling small groups of Undead was one thing. Facing elite soldiers was a different story, as the bodies littering the street proved. Outgunned and outwitted, their resistance crumbled by the minute.

A white sheet appeared through one of the shattered windows in the house where the helots had taken refuge. Hong ordered his men to stop shooting.

"We're coming out!" shouted a hoarse voice. "Don't shoot, damn it! We surrender!"

Two men and three women filed through the door. One of the men was wincing in pain and holding his bloodied right arm. A bullet had shattered his right shoulder. *He'll never use that arm again,* Hong thought.

"Drop your weapons!" shouted the colonel in his careful English. "Hands on your head!"

The frightened helots obeyed immediately. A couple of Hong's men frisked them for concealed weapons, then forced them to kneel against a wall. The attack had been a complete success. Forty bodies were starting to draw flies. Only one of Hong's men had been injured when a bullet grazed his leg.

The colonel observed that one of the women prisoners had pissed herself. She must've been terrified that they were going to rape her. In other circumstances, Hong would have allowed that. He'd done that himself on more than one occasion. Rape was a very powerful psychological weapon. He could make even the most tight-lipped woman sing like a bird. It all depended on how brutally and how frequently they raped her.

Unfortunately there was no time for that, though their captives didn't know that. They'd apply the exact dose of terror they needed and not one drop less. Hong was a master at that.

At the end of the row were the two surviving men, the one with the useless arm and a black guy with huge, tattooed arms. Hong noticed that the man had a bandage around his bicep and one on his calf. Fresh wounds. Interesting.

"What's your name?" Hong asked.

MANEL LOUREIRO

"I'll be damned! You're Chinese soldiers! Or Vietnamese or somethin'. What the hell're you doing in our country, man?"

Hong stared at him with dead eyes. The soldier bravely tried to meet the colonel's eyes, but he had to look away.

"Go to hell," the tattooed soldier said haughtily, his head bowed.

The guy with the injured shoulder smiled—even on his knees, his buddy still maintained his dignity. Hong turned his head and studied the man for a few seconds. Then without a word, he drew his pistol and shot him in the head.

The man collapsed like a bag of sand as blood pulsed out of the hole in his forehead. The woman next to him screamed hysterically, her eyes glued to the pool of blood slowly approaching her knees.

Hong grabbed the hysterical woman by the hair and brutally beat her with the butt of his gun. Thump. Thump. Thump. With each crunch, the woman's nose and teeth turned to grit. Then he pressed the hot barrel of his gun to the woman's neck and looked down at the black soldier, whose eyes were shooting sparks of anger.

"Let's start over," Hong said, as the woman sobbed through bubbles of blood, tears, and snot. "What's your name? *What's your name?*"

"Darnell, Darnell Holmes," the man replied after a very long second, chewing each word with a deep hatred.

"Where are you from, Darnell?"

"Gulfport. If you do anything to Chantelle, I swear I'm gonna—"

Hong smiled at that. "You'll speak when I tell you to, Darnell Holmes from Gulfport. Tell me, how did you get those wounds?"

The soldier looked from Hong to his bandages. "What the hell difference does that make?"

"I'll decide that, Darnell Holmes. Now, answer my question."

"Look, I don't want any trouble. We're just looking for supplies—"

Hong cocked his gun and pressed it into the woman's neck. She shrieked in horror.

"I'm losing my patience, Darnell."

"OK, OK, dammit! We were in Africa a few weeks ago. Looking for oil. Some Undead cornered me on the dock and bit me."

Shocked by what he'd heard, Hong staggered back a couple of inches, and his hand wavered. He'd expected the man to say he'd gotten his injuries in a previous shoot-out. That would've suggested there were other armed groups he'd have to deal with. The last thing he expected to hear was that an Undead had caused that injury.

"How's that possible? Explain!"

Darnell smiled knowingly. "I'll tell you on one condition." He licked his dry lips as he thought at full speed. "You let the girls and me go, unharmed. Are we clear?"

Hong stared at the group for a few long seconds, then leaned forward, holstered his pistol, and placed his right hand over his heart. "You have my word as an officer that I will let you go on your way. Now explain how an Undead attacked you and you're still alive."

Darnell looked at him suspiciously. He didn't trust the bastard, but he had no choice. In his hometown of New Orleans, when someone points a gun at your head, you don't have many options. So he started talking.

The expression on Colonel Hong's face changed from amazement to deep reflection, then to determination. Darnell wondered if he'd made a big mistake.

An hour later, that determined look was still on Hong's face. The Korean convoy rumbled through the town, taking the soldiers' surviving tanks and trucks. The bodies of Darnell and the four others lay rotting by the side of the road. Coyotes would feast on them that night.

With a satisfied smile, Hong leaned back into the tank's hard seat. He peered into a bottle filled with a milky fluid that he'd pulled from Darnell's pack. He'd take back something even better than the location of an oil well: the key to his country's victory over the entire world.

3 5

GULFPORT, SHERIFF'S OFFICE

The next morning, a surprisingly large group of Green Guards and militiamen came to escort me from the police station. I guess they didn't want any trouble. They had me stick my hands through the bars to handcuff me, then they marched me out of the cell, three men in front, and three behind. They evacuated me through a side door to a van waiting in the alley. That way, they avoided any witnesses and the protesters throwing rocks in the front of the building. I was almost grateful.

The ride was mercifully short. The minute I climbed in the van, they pulled a sack down over my head. It must've contained onions once and the smell was sickening. I made a superhuman effort not to throw up. I wasn't worried about getting that ratty van dirty, but vomiting could cost me my life. I needed to retain as much liquid as I could and not waste a single drop of Cladoxpan.

After Grapes left the night before, I swallowed a little of the drug. With the first sip, my anger immediately ratcheted down a few notches. I'd never smelled anything so repulsive, a cross between spoiled milk and orange juice past its expiration date, with a touch of acidity that stung my nose. But its taste was the complete opposite . . . and absolutely wonderful. Although the liquid was at room temperature, it felt cool, as if I'd drunk a pitcher of ice water. Every pore in my skin seemed to open up and breathe again. My fever and tremors stopped abruptly; my hands stopped shaking too. I didn't need a mirror to know that the broken veins on my skin had disappeared.

It took all my willpower to stop drinking. Every cell in my body screamed for more of that sweet, creamy liquid. If I'd had a keg of it, I'd've kept drinking till I was full, then thrown up so I could drink some more. With that one sip, I was addicted.

I felt better than I'd felt in a long time—elated, even. It was as if a handful of amphetamines had kicked in. I was energized and eager to get a move on.

That feeling must give helot troops a boost when they went on raids outside the Wall. It reminded me of my grandfather's stories about how officers passed around bottles of brandy to the troops before an attack on the enemy's trenches. You wouldn't need that with Cladoxpan. I felt like I could wring a buffalo's neck. That must be why they'd sent so many men to escort me. How ironic . . . I was a junkie, but my jailers were the ones who'd gotten me hooked on this powerful drug.

The van rattled when we crossed over something rough. Train tracks, I guessed. Someone's hand whipped the sack off my head, and I squinted in the dazzlingly bright light. After the silent tomb of my cell, the sounds of hundreds of people were hard on my ears. I must've looked pretty scary. My hair was matted; there was dried blood on my face and a huge welt on my forehead.

"Careful, Sal," another guard told the man who'd taken off my hood. "This animal's got blood all over his face."

"That's why I'm wearing gloves and goggles. Let's go, pal." The first guard gave me a shove with the butt of his M16. "Outta the van."

I stumbled down. We were parked at what had once been a freight terminal. I could make out the passenger terminal off in the distance, far enough away that none of the fine citizens in that idyllic paradise could see how Greene's men disposed of the riffraff.

There was a huge concrete parking lot next to a long bank of portable toilets. On the tracks in front of me were a half a dozen train cars and a gleaming Amtrak locomotive engine. The front of the engine was outfitted with an inverted blade at least six feet long, like the cowcatchers that steam engines in the Old West used to push dead animals off the tracks. I figured the attachment now pushed aside the Undead that got in the train's way. The rumbling of the two idling diesel engines echoed across the parking lot.

I was shocked to see boxcars with a sliding door that locked from the outside. In front of each of the doors was a ramp. Heavily armed militants stood beside each car, laughing and passing around bottles of whiskey. In each group, one of the men gripped the leash of a vicious German shepherd, which was barking its head off. If it weren't so awful, I'd have laughed. It was a backwoods version of the trains to Auschwitz. All those assholes needed were SS uniforms. I bet none of them were aware of the parallels.

A huge group of helots, mostly women, elderly, and children, was being loaded onto one of the cars. The elderly men were covered in blood, cuts, and bruises and looked as pitiful as I did. The guards stood way back while the dogs rounded up stragglers, like border collies with a flock of sheep. My heart sank even more as I studied the scene.

Once the cars at the front of the train were full, the guards slammed the doors shut. From inside came the muffled groans of a crowd squeezed into a small space, desperate for air. Faces peered anxiously out the tiny windows as they took turns breathing the fresh air. I was terrified to see that the rest of the cars were like huge coffins on wheels, without even the meager luxury of windows. This trip was going to be a nightmare.

"Let's go, pal." The guard gave me a shove. "You're with this group."

I looked around, disoriented. An Aryan took my cuffs off and quickly herded me to a group of crying, frightened people crowded together in front of one of the cars.

"Wait!" a familiar voice boomed out. "Bring that prisoner over here."

The guards reluctantly separated me from the group. They wanted to get their job over with, and any delay pissed them off. Flanked by two guards with assault rifles, I obediently left the group and came face to face with First Officer Strangärd.

The clean-cut sailor looked totally out of place in that parking lot with the sun beating down. His navy blue uniform was impeccable and his stony face didn't betray the slightest emotion. I barely remembered the smiling officer who'd rescued us in the middle of the ocean. That seemed like a million years ago.

"As executive officer of the Gulfport Christian Militia, I am required by law to provide this man with a copy of his expulsion papers." Strangärd stiffly handed me a few sheets of pages stapled together.

"You shouldn't have gone to the trouble," I said sarcastically. I'd never expected to see him again.

"The reverend himself gave me this task. As I was the one who brought you into our community, he decided I should be the one to send you away."

"I respectfully invite you and the reverend to stick that document up your pious, lily-white asses."

"I insist." Strangärd's voice was a bit on edge as he thrust the papers at me again. For a moment, I detected a light in his eyes. He was trying to tell me something. I grabbed the documents, my eyes glued to his, but he was stone-faced.

"I have something else to give you." An aide handed him a wicker basket with a lid. Something inside the basket stirred and let out a weak meow. *Lucullus!*

I practically tore the basket out of Strangärd's hands. I opened the lid and sighed with relief. At the bottom of the basket, curled up on a dirty blanket, was my little friend, the stump of his tail wrapped in some gauze. My cat looked weak and his lustrous coat was bloodstained. But when he saw me, his eyes brightened.

"I found him at the police station. I felt it was my duty to bring him to you." The Swede stiffened as if he'd said too much. He clicked his heels, saluted, and said good-bye.

The guards shoved me through the crowd toward another boxcar that, mercifully, had a couple of small windows on each side. At least we wouldn't asphyxiate. Not all of us anyway. Fifty people were already standing in the car. The guards tripled that number.

"We aren't going to fit in here!" someone in the group shouted.

The guards paid no attention and kept pushing till they got everyone in. I was the last to climb in; they slammed the door behind me and bolted it shut.

At first I couldn't see anything. I heard coughs, moans, and whispered conversations all around me. Gradually my eyes grew accustomed to the dim light. I was shocked at what I saw. There must've been a hundred and fifty people squeezed into that small space with no room to sit down. We stood shoulder to shoulder, like a crowd at a concert. Shorter people, especially children, had trouble breathing. The temperature in the car rose steadily from the heat rising off our bodies.

That was the least of our problems. Where I was standing, half a dozen people were sweating profusely, scratching, or shaking. An old man leaning against a wall was shivering violently. Ugly, burst veins spread across his nose.

Horrified, I realized that all or nearly all the people in that car—in all the cars—were infected with TSJ. In a few hours, our car would be a rolling hell—a small space crowded with all those people turning into Undead. What would happen when the first transformations were complete? We had nowhere to run. It was a death trap and no one would get out alive.

With a jolt that would have thrown us to the ground if we weren't wedged in so tight, the car began to move as the engines dragged their load, heading who-knew-where. The destination really didn't matter. By the time we got there, we'd all be mindless monsters.

In every face, I read the same fear. Everyone saw a monster in the person standing next to him, parents and children alike. The good-natured Jamaican guy with dreadlocks, the pretty young mother cradling her newborn, singing a lullaby . . . In a few hours they'd be something far worse than the Green Guards who'd forced us in there.

A number of people pulled out containers filled with Cladoxpan. The fortunate ones had large bottles; others had a tiny amount or, worse, none at all, depending on what they'd been able to grab when they were arrested. If we'd been smart, we would've gathered up all that precious liquid and rationed it equally, but that wasn't going to happen. Everyone clutched their bottle like a sullen dog with a bone. Shouts and threats came from the back of the car. Before the end of that trip, I was sure there'd be more than one murder.

I only had half of what Grapes gave me the night before. Distraught, I took out the bottle and shook it with the stupid hope that it would've magically filled up. My heart sank when I saw that I had only about five ounces left. I could hold out for three or four hours, no more. I was fucked.

Lucullus shifted in his basket, uncomfortable and sore. I had no room to set the basket on the floor, so I hung it over one arm and took him out of his prison. His wound didn't look too bad, since someone had gone to the trouble of disinfecting it, but he'd lost a lot of blood. He must've been dying of thirst.

When I put him back in the basket, I realized it weighed too much for a basket with just an old blanket in it. Making sure no one saw me, I set Lucullus back in the basket as I rummaged around at the bottom. My hand found something round and cool. Pushing the blanket aside, I spotted a gallon-sized thermos. I cautiously unscrewed the cap and sniffed the contents. The familiar sweet, acid smell of Cladoxpan hit my nose.

I pawed deeper in the basket and found a compass, a combat knife like Prit's, and best of all, a loaded 9mm Beretta. It wasn't enough to hold off a boxcar filled with Undead, but it would give me a shot at survival if I made it to the train's destination alive.

Who'd put all that in there and why? It must've been Strangärd, but why would the Swede risk his neck for me? Then I remembered the documents he'd insisted I take.

I elbowed my way to one of the little windows, where there was enough light to read. On one side of the page was a lot of legal mumbo jumbo accusing me of the murder of Mrs. Compton and sentencing me to expulsion. The interesting part was on the back.

The first sheet contained a very detailed map of the train route, pinpointing train stations, towns, distances, and main roads. The second had a short message; when I read it, my heart leapt for joy.

"We're both fine. Survive and come back to us. I love you. L"

I looked up and smiled for the first time. The next few days were going to be hell. I'd have to find a way to survive, but at least I had a chance. And a goal: return to Gulfport and my friends. But one thought burned bright as a flame: *Kill Grapes and Reverend Greene.*

3 6

DEPORTATION CONVOY
300 MILES FROM GULFPORT

The train from hell just kept going. I thought it would never stop. The situation in the boxcar went from bad to worse. I didn't see how I could make it.

After nearly five hours, the air inside the boxcar was an almost unbreathable soup of the body odor of a hundred and fifty sweaty people, sour vomit, and the sulfurous sticky smell of the shit scattered around the car. At the start of the trip, a few voices sensibly proposed converting one corner into a latrine. Everyone thought that was a good idea, except for one detail: nobody wanted it to be the corner closest to them.

After some tense arguments, we still hadn't chosen a corner, so people were relieving themselves anywhere they could. The car became a shit pile on wheels. A layer of stinking slime spread over the floor and flowed from side to side as the train rocked along.

I was relatively lucky. I'd staked out a spot against a wall, so I had a place to lean. I set Lucullus's basket on the floor in front of me, blocking off about a foot of space that allowed me to turn around. The nearest window was about fifteen feet away, so most of the time, I was in the dark. When someone lit a cigarette or switched on a flashlight, I got a brief glimpse of my surroundings.

I used those moments to look at my cat. Lucullus was curled up tight at the bottom of the basket, in a restless half-sleep. Occasionally he stirred with a faint, pained meow that broke my heart. He must've felt sick from losing all that blood. I suspected his wound was infected.

My bigger problem was my unrelenting thirst. The Green Guards had loaded a couple of plastic drums of water into the car before they sealed the door. One of them disappeared into a corner and was jealously guarded by some grim-faced Latin Kings brandishing knives. The other drum was empty. I got chills thinking back on what happened to that drum. Any semblance of order evaporated as soon as someone opened it up. In the dim light, I heard screams and punches as the drum passed from hand to hand, spilling most of its contents. When it came to me, I only got a few sips before someone slugged me in the back, and then six people snatched it out of my hands.

I sat down in my little space and licked my moistened lips. I started to lick my fingers, which had gotten splashed when I grabbed the drum. I gasped when I realized my hands were dripping with blood, not water. As the fucking drum was passed around, it'd gotten drenched in some poor devil's blood. It took every ounce of willpower I had not to throw up.

Thirst and hunger weren't our only problems. We all knew we faced something worse, something that lived inside each of us and could show up anytime. Fear and anxiety plagued us as we jealously guarded our dwindling supply of Cladoxpan, our last defense against madness. After an hour, TSJ reared its ugly head in that dark boxcar.

The first to go was a heavyset woman in her fifties. She looked Caribbean. She'd probably already started transforming when they loaded her on the train, but in the chaos, no one noticed. She was on the other side of the car, so it was hard for me to see what was going on.

I peered over the crowd and got a glimpse of a girl in the back as she shouted in alarm and backed away in horror when she noticed that the woman's skin was cold as ice and that the whites of her eyes were laced with broken, red veins. Panic spread through the crowd as the people next to her tried to back away. That triggered a disastrous human wave that spread in every direction. In an uncontrollable, blind panic, people fell over each other and got trampled. An old man landed hard on top of me as that giant wave plowed into us.

People shouted and screamed as they tried to break free of the mountain of bodies, but no one could move more than a few inches. People were smashed together and crushed in the stampede. Above the noise came that monotonous, raspy sound I'd heard so many times. A cross between a moan and a groan punctuated by rapid, labored breathing, like a person who'd just run a marathon. Every hair on my head stood on end and my stomach clenched in an icy ball.

"Mwaaaaaeeergh . . . Mwaaaaaaeeeeeeerghhh . . ."

After a couple of minutes, there was a louder moan, almost a scream, poisonous and deathly, announcing that evil had awakened in that woman. Another woman in the same part of the boxcar cried out in pain. Then a man screamed.

Chaos broke out in the car. The crowd, blind and terrified, tried to flee in every direction, not caring what or who they crashed into. I had just enough time to crouch down and prop the basket between the wall and the crowd, forming a flimsy barricade. But my legs got trapped under someone and I couldn't move. My head was pinned against the wall by the back of a man howling in pain, his right arm twisted unnaturally between two people grappling for their lives. I tried to pull away, but bodies were stacked up all around me. A skinny guy with a scraggly beard lay on the floor, his head almost touching mine. I could feel his hot, sharp breath on my face. His eyes were nearly popping out, and the veins in his neck bulged like thick cables as he made a superhuman effort, in vain, to break free. He shot me a crazed look and whispered "Help me," barely audible in all this madness.

I wanted to help him, but one of my arms was pinned under my body. On top of that, if I pulled him free, I wouldn't have any room to breathe. All I could do was stare in horror as the man's face went from bright red to a terrible blue. Finally he fell over dead, his tongue hanging out of his mouth.

After the longest, scariest five minutes of my life, the panic began to fade. The cries grew muted. People sobbed everywhere, calling to each other. Someone pulled one of the people off me so I could sit up. My right arm was still asleep, but I managed to stand up and lean against the wall. Wood splinters dug into my skin, but I ignored them.

Someone in that car was no longer human, and I couldn't tell if the dark shapes walking toward me were human or Undead.

My hand trembled as I cocked the Beretta and rested it against my hip. Suddenly, a short, compact woman stumbled toward me. She was breathing rapidly and had her arms stretched out in front of her, like a drunken Frankenstein. I aimed the gun at her face. At that moment, the car rocked violently, shaking us like jelly beans in a jar, as the train crossed a section of broken track. I spread my legs to steady myself and grabbed some metal rivets in the wall to keep from falling.

When I looked up again, I couldn't see her anywhere. *Where are you, bitch? Where the fuck are you?*

A man's hand closed around my arm. I howled in terror and kneed the guy in the crotch. I slammed the butt of my gun against his temple, and he let out a strangled shriek and fell like a sack of laundry at my feet. I crouched down, pointing my gun in every direction, trying to spot any other threat. I noticed that my victim, lying unconscious with an ugly bruise on his temple, was a man in his late sixties. Not an Undead.

My panic subsided, but I didn't feel ashamed of beating up an old man. That car was hell and I was fighting to save my soul.

Someone fired two shots and flashes lit up the car. The shots reverberated in that tight space so loudly that, for a moment, all I heard was an annoying, persistent hum.

Careful, cowboy. You're not the only one with a gun.

Another wave of hysteria swept over the car. When the shooter fired his gun again, I caught a glimpse of the grim scene. The floor was piled high with bodies. Some were still moving amid moans; most were motionless. Everywhere groups of two or three people were fighting in a homicidal rage either because they thought the other person was an Undead or because they were trying to steal each other's Cladoxpan.

Some guy yelled, "He's got a gun! Get him!"

For one terrifying second, I thought he meant me, but the throng rushed in the direction of a kid who looked to be one of the Latin Kings. The shooter only had time to fire once more before the crazed mob fell on him, and kicked and punched him to death.

His death was a kind of turning point. Anger slowly subsided like water flowing down a drain. People who'd had each other in a death grip a moment before looked confused, as if they'd awakened from a bad dream. Their panic evaporated, and a mixture of fear, shame, and horror silently replaced it.

I surreptitiously tucked my Beretta back in the basket and made sure Lucullus was still alive in his feverish sleep. I helped a few people up and stepped to one side. The Caribbean woman lay dead in the middle of the car, her head split open. Beside her, a man with a torn neck was convulsing in a way we knew all too well.

"He's changing," someone in the shadows murmured. "We gotta do something."

A pretty young woman, her face smeared with blood, tangled hair covering her shoulders, stepped forward. With a cold, unforgiving look on her face, she took the gun out of the dead shooter's hand. Not missing a beat, she raised the gun, aimed at the convulsing man's head, and pulled the trigger.

The shot opened a huge hole in the man's face, and he stopped moving. The girl studied the guy for a while, then tossed the gun on the corpse.

"That was the last bullet," she said in a flat voice.

Suddenly a cramp shook my body so hard I had to bend over. I straightened up, panting. My clothes were soaked in sweat. I must've been feverish for quite a while, but with all the chaos, I hadn't realized it. I doubled over as an even stronger cramp washed over me and cried out in pain. A guy standing next to me shot me a suspicious look and backed away. I saw fear and disgust in his eyes. He looked at me like I was no longer a person; I was one of them.

Oh, no, no no, please. Not now, please.

"Everything's under control," I gasped, waving my hand like a drunk. "Be cool, pal."

I kneeled down next the basket and took out the thermos of Cladoxpan. My hands were shaking so hard that I could barely unscrew the lid. The first wonderful drink transported me out of that train car for a moment. The liquid flowed down my throat, shutting out the hell around me, and opening all my thirsty cells.

I screwed the lid back on and closed my eyes, savoring that glorious sensation. A part of my mind screamed, *This is what heroin addicts must feel like when they shoot up. Hello, addiction. I'm your willing slave.* I'd have to deal with my addiction later.

"So now whadda we do?" someone asked in a slightly guilty voice.

"Help the wounded," someone else replied.

"First we'd better bash in the heads of the dead," said the girl who'd done the shooting. She said it matter-of-factly, like she was talking about going shopping.

Honey, while you're out, would you stop by the grocery store and pick up a dozen oranges? Oh, and while you're at it, bash in the head of that dead child next to you.

"How do we do that?" murmured a frightened woman whose little girl pressed against her skirt, her eyes flooded with terror. "We don't have any weapons."

One of the surviving Latin Kings came forward, rummaged through his dead *compañero*'s clothes, and pulled out a hammer with a razor-sharp claw. Without a word, he walked over to the body of a twelve-year-old boy and brought the hammer down on his head with a loud chop. His eyes dark and vacant like a shark's, he kept pounding steadily until he was satisfied the job was done. The back of the boy's head looked like strawberry jam, with pieces of bone sticking out.

"That's how you do it." He handed the hammer to the man next to him, who held it away from himself as if it were a live snake. "Any blunt object will do. Just make sure the person's dead."

The other passengers looked at him for a moment, horrified. "You can't be serious," muttered the man to my right.

Suddenly, one of the bodies lying on the floor shook.

"There's your answer, jackass," said the kid with a shrug.

The man holding the hammer hesitated, swallowed hard, then stepped forward and struck the convulsing corpse in the head. As if someone had fired a starter's pistol, nearly all the living passengers began to stalk the glut of dead bodies lying on the floor, hitting their heads with a variety of objects.

The scene looked like something out of a Hieronymus Bosch painting. We were covered with bits of blood and brains. The boxcar's walls were painted with grotesque blood spatters that dripped slowly onto the floor amid lumps of gray matter.

Someone vomited. I shrugged and took another sip of Cladoxpan. Nothing disgusted me now. I'd long since passed my threshold for horror. Besides, there was nothing solid in my stomach.

The next few hours seemed endless. The train rolled along with a monotonous rhythm, punctuated by brief stops. I couldn't figure out why. Once, for no apparent reason, we even backed up for a couple of miles.

Occasionally there was a thud and the entire train shook. We assumed the train had collided with objects on the track. We could guess what those objects were. I slowly and tortuously wrestled my way to one of the windows. I climbed up a mountain of corpses piled there and peeked out the window.

At first I felt relief. The outside air was fresh and invigorating compared to the stench inside the car. Then when I figured out where we were and how far we'd traveled, my soul fell to my feet. The train was rolling across a parched plain. Groves of twisted trees dotted the landscape. We must be somewhere in south Texas, near the Mexican border. The map that Strangärd gave me showed distances and directions, but not the names of states.

The atmosphere inside the car was gloomy. Talk was at a minimum. We were all lost in our thoughts. Even the cries and groans had stopped, replaced by deep resignation and a fear of the unknown. No one knew where we were headed, but we all wanted the trip to end soon. Nothing could be worse than being locked in that train car of death.

Of the original hundred and fifty exiles in the car, fewer than half were still alive. The rest had been crushed to death or had their heads bashed in. We survivors now had more room to move around. Any Cladoxpan on the corpses had been looted. I'd shamelessly rummaged through the clothes of the skinny guy who died by my side and found a small flask. I topped off the contents of my thermos, which I hid at the bottom of the basket under Lucullus. I didn't want it to get around that I had such a big stash of Cladoxpan. I kept the gun hidden too. The Latin King's death proved that a gun was no guarantee of survival. People were desperate and had nothing to lose.

About two hours later, another case arose. This time, we were better prepared. He was a young guy of about twenty, tall and burly with a broken leg. His face was beaten to a pulp. Someone whispered that the Green Guards had beaten him up during the raid when he'd tried to stop them from seizing his sister and mother. Not only did he fail to save them (they were in another car), he'd nearly died. Maybe he'd given his Cladoxpan to his family or he'd been too weak to stop someone from stealing it. Either way, the kid was the next to transform.

First, he begged. He stood in the middle of the car, leaning on a makeshift crutch, and summoned all the dignity he could. Like a beggar in the subway, he pleaded for someone to give him a drink of Cladoxpan. Everyone—including me—either glared at him or looked away, tightening their grip on their own stash.

I was briefly tempted to share with him, but self-preservation kept me from opening my mouth. If my calculations were correct, I had enough Cladoxpan to survive for about five days—if I rationed myself severely. That would have to last till I got back to Gulfport or at least found a helot patrol. Sharing with this guy would cut that time in half, and along with it, my chances of survival. With a broken leg, the guy was doomed anyway. Even he knew it. Any Cladoxpan he drank would be wasted.

When he saw that his pleas weren't getting him anywhere, he tried to steal it. The kid had once been brawny; under normal conditions, he wouldn't have had any problem. But given the condition he was in, even an old man could've taken him. The most brutal sort of Darwinism was in force: only the healthiest, youngest, and strongest survived. After a few sad attempts and a few punches, the poor guy gave up.

Defeated, he slumped on the floor in agony. With a rosary in his hand, he prayed quietly as tiny veins burst all over his skin. From time to time, he writhed in pain from a cramp. His tremors became so severe he could no longer hold his rosary. After forty minutes, the string of wooden beads slipped through his fingers, and his hand contracted into a claw. His eyes were completely bloodshot. The kid raised his head and, with every ounce of control he had left, shouted, *"Please!"* His heart-wrenching cry stirred my soul.

Without stopping to think, I stood up and grabbed the hammer someone had hung on a nail by the door. Before anyone could stop me, I walked up to the kid. He sensed my presence at his side; his now-sightless eyes pointed in my direction.

"You sure?" I asked quietly.

The kid nodded and grabbed my pant leg. Maybe he was afraid I'd change my mind. His lips had nearly stopped obeying him, but he managed to whisper an almost unintelligible "Thank you."

I picked up the hammer, took a deep breath, and brought it down hard on the kid's occipital bone. He went limp, like a cow on the slaughterhouse floor. I hit him three more times to be sure he wouldn't rise from the dead.

Covered with blood, I slumped back to my corner. Everyone in the car stared at the corpse in silence. No one would meet my eyes, but they didn't reproach me.

As the train rattled on, I furtively wiped my eyes. The blood on my face mixed with my tears, forming ornate ribbons down my cheeks. I looked like a psychotic clown, but I couldn't stop crying.

I'd killed a man. A living man. The fact that he was about to become an Undead didn't mitigate my pain. I was a murderer. As the train rolled on, I realized that even if I survived that hellish journey, part of me had died in that boxcar.

3 7

THE WASTELAND, SOUTHERN TEXAS
DAY 1. 17:50 HOURS

We were the only ones left.

The train stopped five times; at each stop, they unhooked a car. Ours was the last car, so I suspected we wouldn't be traveling much longer.

I rummaged through the belongings of fellow passengers who'd died near me. In one woman's purse, I found a blank notebook and a lot of useless stuff, including a tube of pink lipstick. Pink lipstick? On a deportation train? Then I remembered that Jews had taken the most startling things with them, such as violins and lamps, en route to Nazi concentration camps. I don't know why, but I put the lipstick in my pocket.

I guess the will to survive, to see another dawn, is the trait we humans value most. The lipstick must have been a symbol for that woman, the way Lucullus was for me. She'd told herself that this nightmare would end someday and she'd want to look beautiful again. She'd be someplace safe and happy, where her biggest concern was having pretty lips. Just then the woman's body started wobbling on the floor, bumping against my shoes, in time with the train rumbling down the tracks. What good was her symbol now?

Only twenty people remained out of the original one hundred and fifty. Over half were crushed to death, died of thirst, or were killed when someone tried to rob them. The rest had succumbed to TSJ when they ran out of Cladoxpan. Most people's reserves had only lasted six hours, and we'd been traveling for nearly twelve.

I was in pretty good shape. With the Cladoxpan hidden in Lucullus's basket, I could hold out for several days. I didn't know how much the other survivors had left. Enough for a few hours? A month? It was like a poker game; you kept your cards close to your vest. You didn't know if the guy in the corner was glaring at you because he was terrified you were turning into an Undead or because he was turning into one. If it weren't for the basket, I'd have been dead hours ago, lying in the middle of the car.

I didn't understand why they dropped off each group so far apart. At first I assumed it was to keep us from ganging up on the guards and taking control of the train. That may have been partly true. Most likely, they didn't want us to transform into Undead all at once. It was easier to deal with one or two Undead, even a dozen, instead of hundreds all at once. We weren't people to them, just monsters. Maybe they were right.

I wasn't proud of the things I'd seen and done in that train car, but if I hadn't done them, I'd be dead. I was determined to fight to the end.

The train slowed down. The click-clack of the wheels finally stopped. The sixth stop for the sixth car. Our turn.

Its brakes screeching, the train came to a complete stop. Our journey of hundreds of miles was over. Inside the car, the silence was absolute, except for the flies buzzing around the swollen bodies and the hollow cough of a very sick man. They kept us waiting in there for five long minutes. The tension was unbearable.

"Why don't they open the fucking door?" a guy sitting near me muttered.

"Maybe they don't open the door," murmured a guy in his fifties, the oldest survivor. "Maybe they park the train car and leave, then collect our bones on their next trip."

"Shut the fuck up, goddammit," snapped the first guy. "They gotta open the door."

I hoped with all my heart he was right. I figured the Green Guards were scouting the area for any Undead. Finally, with a screech, the door opened for the first time since we'd gotten on. But the Green Guards didn't look inside.

"Everybody out, goddammit!" cried a distorted voice. "Man, what a stench!"

"Don't get too close to the door, Tim," said another voice. "There may not be anyone alive in there."

"Should we toss in a grenade?" Tim sounded unsure.

That comment spurred us survivors to move toward the door. Nobody wanted to die like that.

I squinted and shaded my eyes. The light was glaringly bright, even though the sun was setting. After twelve hours in darkness, my eyes were very sensitive. I took several deep breaths to clear my lungs of the stench inside the boxcar.

Then I saw why the Green Guards' voices were distorted. They were wearing gas masks. I understood why. The smell of the overheated car full of dead bodies, vomit, and shit was overpowering.

"Hey! You have to unload that car!" one of the guards said, pointing his assault rifle.

"Whaddaya mean?" asked the guy next to me. "It's full of corpses. There's just a few of us left. That'll take all day."

"You have one hour, you sons of bitches," said the guard, cocking his rifle. "Move your ass if you wanna live. Let's go!"

Like automatons, we organized into pairs and started clearing the bodies out of the boxcar. As I held the feet of a pregnant woman and dragged her off the train, I wondered why we were doing it. Why didn't we jump the guards and grab their weapons? Why didn't we fight? The answer was obvious—we wanted to live a little longer, even ten minutes more. Breathe that wonderful, clean air. Survive.

We piled all the bodies by the side of the road. We were at a crossroads in the middle of nowhere. A single train track stretched out of sight in either direction. There was also a double track for about a half a mile to let two trains pass each other. Our captors had chosen a very desolate place to get rid of the last car.

One look around told me we weren't the first group they'd unloaded there. The ground was littered with sun-bleached bones and scraps of clothing and shoes. A mountain of mummified bodies watched us with grinning skulls. I felt their empty eyes follow me, accusing me of being a coward, of wanting to stay alive.

Bones were scattered a long way across the plains. I suspected that, when the train left, coyotes and other scavengers would feast on the new corpses, dragging the bones in all directions. The TSJ virus didn't affect them. It provided them with food in abundance.

After we'd dragged off the last body, we collapsed against the charred remains of a van. One of the Greens Guards tossed us a few boxes of army rations.

"There's fifteen gallons of water in that drum," he said, pointing his rifle at a metal barrel some other guards were rolling off the train. "And here're some army rations. After that, you're on your own. Don't ever come near Gulfport again. Is that clear?"

"This is murder," murmured one of the three surviving women. "We're in the middle of a fucking desert. In a few hours, TSJ will transform us into Undead, and all you can do is give us a few gallons of water and some snacks to tide us over till then. How can you live with yourself? I hope you burn in hell!"

"Shut up!" shouted the guard. "Be glad I don't put a bullet in your head. You've been exiled. If it were up to me, I'd kill every one of ya. I'm just following orders."

"How kind of you," I muttered. I was starting to sweat again. I didn't know if it was from the stress or the virus attacking me, but I didn't want anyone to see my stash of Cladoxpan. I'd have to wait to take a drink.

"Let's get 'em," the Latino guy next to me said under his breath. "On my signal."

"What'd you say?" I asked, barely moving my mouth. I didn't know what he was planning.

The man at the end of the row, closest to a Green Guard, sprang to his feet and ran at the guard, who barely had time to raise his gun. The guy plowed into the guard, and they fell to the ground in a tangle of arms and legs. The guard's gun went off and one of them was hit, but I couldn't tell which. Then all hell broke loose.

Half of the deportees threw themselves on the guards, trying to grab their weapons. The surviving Latin Kings must've hatched some plan in the dark train car, and they were trying to carry it out. But they hadn't shared their plans with the rest of the survivors. Like me, half a dozen other deportees were confused and frightened. Some hid behind the wrecked van while others joined the surprise attack. Some just stood there, not knowing how to react. When the first burst of fire from an M4 cut one of that group in half, the rest scattered. I had to think fast.

The guys' plan was brave, but stupid. Instead of focusing on the train engines, they'd gotten in an unequal fight with the Green Guards, who'd had time to bolt the engine doors and take their positions. On the roofs of the locomotive, a Green Guard was quickly setting up a massive machine gun. I could guess what would happen in a matter of seconds.

"Take cover!" I yelled and threw myself into a ditch full of rotting corpses.

The machine gun opened fire, filling the air with heavy lead hornets. The helots out in the open twisted around in a dance of death as the bullets ripped through them. A Green Guard was also hit by friendly fire. After a minute, the failed revolt ended as quickly as it had begun.

"Damn! Those motherfuckers gave us a scare!" said a voice from behind a gas mask.

"You alright?" someone called down from the train.

"McCurry and Wyatt are screwed! Carlyle, you asshole. You shot Wyatt!"

"He stepped into my line of fire!" replied the guy on the roof of the locomotive. "It wasn't my fucking fault!"

"We'll discuss that later," the first voice said with authority. He must've been the boss. "Make sure they're dead, then let's get out of here. This place gives me willies."

From where I lay at the bottom of the ditch, I heard the Greens checking the bodies one by one. A couple of times they fired their rifles at close range to finish off the wounded. I grabbed a corpse and dragged it on top of me, then buried my legs in a pile of bodies. All I could do was lie still and pray.

The gravel alongside the ditch crunched under someone's feet. I held my breath, overcome by the stench of those corpses.

After a few long seconds, the guy walked away. I exhaled in relief. Then I realized I'd left Lucullus's basket next to the shot-up van. My heart stopped. If they found it, they'd kill my cat and take my medicine.

The minutes passed slowly, very slowly, as the men climbed back on the train. Finally the engines roared to life, then the train lurched forward and chugged away at a snail's pace.

I lay among the bodies for another five minutes, until the sound of the train faded in the distance. When I didn't hear anything, I pushed the bodies off me in disgust and crawled out of the ditch.

The train was just a black spot receding on the horizon. The sun was setting, casting a spectral, bloodred light across the landscape. There was no one in sight. If anyone else had survived the massacre, they didn't want to be seen.

I stumbled up the path, stepping over still-warm bleeding bodies. A couple of the dead didn't have any serious head injuries and were starting to shake in spasms. I'd have company soon. I had to get out of there.

Lucullus's basket was right where I'd left it. I picked it up, said a silent prayer, and opened it. At the bottom, Lucullus was still curled up; under him was all my stuff. I took a small sip of Cladoxpan and dug around for the compass. I knew which direction to head in, but could I last long enough to get where I needed to go?

I fashioned a backpack out of a dead guy's coat and packed it full of rations and the contents of the basket, all but Lucullus. The water drum was too heavy to carry. I searched the bodies and collected half a dozen bottles and canteens. One of the bottles even had a little Cladoxpan left in it, which I poured into my thermos. I filled the other bottles and canteens with all the water I could carry.

I drank my fill of water and washed up. I was still wearing the elegant Italian suit I'd worn to work two days before, but now it was torn and covered in blood, dirt, and all kinds of bodily fluids. I threw off the ripped sports coat and grabbed the army jacket off a corpse to ward off the cold night air.

As night fell, I headed southeast, following the railroad tracks. I was weak and wrung out with a long road ahead of me. On top of that, I was racing against the clock.

38

THE WASTELAND
DAY 2

I woke up with the afternoon sun hitting me squarely in the face. Every muscle in my body ached. I knew I had to keep moving, so I walked all night, until exhaustion and the cold finally got the better of me. With no moon to light the way, I nearly broke my leg.

After that, I decided to sleep through the hottest hours of the day and climbed into the skeleton of a bus. I hesitated at first. What if rattlesnakes, scorpions, or a dozen other critters, real or imagined, were hiding in that bus? Common sense prevailed when I heard coyotes howling close by—they were the real threat. I didn't know if coyotes attacked humans, but I didn't want to chance it.

I drank some water mixed with Cladoxpan and pried open an MRE ration. I tried to get Lucullus to eat something, but he was too weak to chew. I was sure his tail was infected. I was worried that if I didn't find some antibiotics soon, he would die. Even more pressing was transportation. When I took stock of how much Cladoxpan I'd consumed in twenty-four hours, I realized my reserve would only last five days. Six, if I stretched it. It would take at least three weeks to walk to Gulfport.

I climbed out of the wrecked bus and started walking. I felt strangely elated and free, the way I did at the start of the Apocalypse when I had only myself to rely on. Lucia's face rose up before me. I loved her with all my soul, but at that moment, she and I were on different paths. I prayed she was OK and that I'd find her again.

After two hours of walking, I stopped suddenly. In the distance, surrounded by a dense grove of leafless, dwarf trees, was a one-horse town next to the train tracks. My heart raced. I took the gun out of my bag and checked the magazine. I took out two bullets and put them in my pocket, with a shudder. If things went wrong, one of the bullets was for Lucullus. The other was for me.

I approached the town very cautiously. The station platform was littered with bodies, skeletons, and cast-off clothes. It must've been one of the stops where the Green Guards dumped their miserable human cargo. My senses on high alert, I plastered myself against a wall and picked my way through the wreckage.

The scene was very similar to the place where the guards had left us. Not a living soul in sight. I took a chance and walked down the deserted main street, which was lined with about twenty houses. From inside every window, dark, threatening shadows watched me. The only sound was my shoes crunching on the gravel-covered pavement.

When I heard a groan behind me, I whipped around like a snake, Berretta in hand. It was just an old Coca-Cola sign creaking in the wind. I lowered my gun, shaking.

I slipped into the town's only cafe. Shattered window glass crunched under my feet. The interior was dark and empty. Never taking my eye off the door, I skirted around broken chairs and overturned tables and inched over to the counter. In a fury, I yanked open drawers and cabinets. After five minutes I slumped, discouraged. There wasn't a thing to eat or drink. Survivors from previous trains must've looted every scrap of food in the place. Anything of use was long gone. I didn't need to check the rest of the town. I knew it would be the same in every house.

My eyes fell on a pile of bills and papers under the sink. Out of curiosity, I picked them up and read them over. Mixed in with the usual receipts and bills was a small treasure. It was a cheaply printed flyer advertising The Double J Ranch.

Want to feel like a real cowboy?
Experience the REAL Texas at The Double J Ranch
RIDE HORSES! BRAND CATTLE!
Enjoy the best Tex-Mex cuisine around!
THE DOUBLE J RANCH! You'll never forget it!

At the bottom were a phone number and a very simple map from Sheertown (the ghost town I was in) to the ranch. A photo showed galloping horses and smiling cowboys leaning on a fence in the background.

What the hell was the rancher thinking? Did he think any-one would come to that remote corner of the world to experience the "real Texas"? Even before the Apocalypse, Sheertown mustn't have been a thriving place. I figured you wouldn't need a reserva-tion at the Double J's restaurant. Visitors were probably few and far between.

A crazy idea popped into my head. The ranch was about four miles from town, in the opposite direction from the train

station. Maybe no one had noticed it before. Maybe I'd find vet-
erinary supplies and food there, or even a car that still ran. At
least I'd have a place to spend the night. I wouldn't sleep in
Sheertown for all the money in the world. It was an open-air
cemetery. Evil lurked around every corner there. And a lot of
misery and pain. I could feel it in my bones.

Without a backward glance, I started walking. After ten
minutes, I came to an unmarked dirt road that branched off to
the west. I checked the map; I was on the right track. The road
was covered with dead branches and leaves; in some places,
weeds almost entirely blocked it. Besides the coyotes' tracks,
there were no footprints. No one had passed that way for a long
time.

I walked for an hour down that dusty road, cursing in
Russian (thanks to Prit) every time I got caught on a thorn bush.
Once I had to fight my way through some weeds so thick I
couldn't see the other side. That gave me hope. With the road in
such a sorry state, it was unlikely anyone had visited the ranch in
a long while.

Finally at the crest of a small hill, I spotted the Double J
Ranch.

The ranch house was really run-down; a wooden fence surrounded it. Near the house was a huge red barn and a long, low
building I assumed was the stable. The place probably was never
very prosperous, but now it looked really spooky. In a corral next
to the house were the bleached skeletons of fifty head of cattle.
With no one to take care of them, those poor cows had slowly
died of hunger and thirst in the burning sun.

Then it hit me. The owners had to be around somewhere.

Gripping the Beretta, I eased down the road. At the arch
over the entrance, I set down my backpack and Lucullus's basket.
Better to be unencumbered.

First I inspected the stable. Its long central corridor was flanked by two dozen stalls. Half were empty; the other half contained the bones of a dozen horses. The metal doors were beaten in; some had bloodstains. Mad with hunger and thirst, the noble beasts had tried to break out of their stalls. Otherwise, the place was empty.

On my way out, I spotted a small refrigerator against a wall. I opened it with no expectations. I almost fell back on my ass when a wave of cold air hit me and soft white light bathed my face. The refrigerator still worked. The ranch still had power.

I just stood there for a moment, enjoying the cool air. Then I searched the stable, inside and out, before figuring out what the hell made that small miracle possible. Solar panels covered the roof and powered a generator somewhere. Either the owner didn't like to pay electric bills or couldn't afford a power outage in such a remote place. A stroke of luck either way.

Inside the refrigerator were several small bottles lined up in an orderly row. I rummaged around a shelf and found antibiotics for horses and cows. I hesitated. They might not be suitable for a cat, and too strong a dose might kill Lucullus. I didn't have many options, so I stuck some bottles in my pocket along with half a dozen hypodermic needles I found in a drawer.

I looked around one more time, then headed out of the barn. That's when I saw the first Undead. He was in his midtwenties, dressed in denim overalls and a red-and-black plaid shirt with a faded handkerchief tied around his neck. He staggered around the corner of the house in my direction.

At that distance, I couldn't see any injury. He hadn't been attacked by another Undead; the treacherous virus had hijacked him when he shared a bottle or a kiss. That was the good news.

The bad news was, when the Undead saw me, he groaned and made a beeline in my direction. I waited until he got closer, not wanting to miss the shot. Then I spotted an ax leaning against the door. I pocketed the Beretta and grabbed that ax with both hands. It was heavy and long, and its blade was dull, but still looked dangerous. And it was a lot quieter than the gun.

When the Undead was about six feet from me, I raised the ax over my head. I realized that, if I missed, I wouldn't get a second chance. Shooting might've been a better bet, but I didn't have time to ponder that. The Undead came at me with a roar. When his outstretched fingers had almost reached me, I brought the ax down on his head with all my might.

The blade struck the middle of his face with a crack, and he stopped in his tracks. I braced my foot against his chest and pulled the blade out with a watery *chuuup* that made my hair stand on end. The Undead fell backward into the dirt and lay there like a turtle on its back. I hit him a second time. The blade penetrated deep into his skull and destroyed his brain. The Undead kicked a couple of times and finally lay still.

I gasped, trying to catch my breath. It took me three tries to get the blade out of his head. Holding the bloody ax out in front of me, I headed for the house. I must've looked like a crazed psychopath.

I crossed the porch, eased open the front door, and peered inside. Two years' worth of dust covered the furniture. Outlined in the dust on the floor were halting footprints. My heart racing, I followed those tracks to the kitchen.

The trail led to an Undead woman standing beside a fireplace. When she saw me, she rushed forward but tripped over a stool and fell in a heap. Not hesitating for a second, I hit her with the ax over and over till her head was a mass of bone and brains.

I plopped down on a couch, sending up a cloud of dust. I calmly picked up a crumpled pack of Marlboros lying on the coffee table and lit a cigarette. I amazed myself. I'd taken out two monsters in five minutes, and my pulse was pretty steady. Strange . . . a while back, I couldn't have imagined doing something like that.

The Undead's blood meandered through the grit on the floor. When it reached my shoe, it branched off and disappeared under the couch. I threw the cigarette on the floor after just two puffs. I'd suddenly lost interest in smoking.

I walked around the house but didn't find anyone else. In the basement, I got a wonderful surprise: a freezer filled with huge cuts of beef. My mouth watered. That night I'd have a first-class dinner.

I still had to check out the barn. I went back outside and crossed the yard to the large red wood building. Two vultures were gorging on the scattered brains of the cowboy I'd just killed. The birds studied me, but made no move to fly away. They'd lost their fear of humans. I noticed how fat and shiny they were. No wonder—there was no shortage of food.

The barn door was locked with a heavy padlock. I cursed under my breath. The key had to be around somewhere, but I didn't have the time or inclination to search. I drew the Beretta and fired at the padlock. The frightened vultures flew off, squawking indignantly. The shot sounded like thunder and probably echoed for miles, but I didn't care. There wasn't anyone—or anything—around.

The interior of the barn was dark and very cool, but I was surprised at how humid the air was. I looked around and discovered why. A water pump at the back of the building had burst; water was spurting out of a well. A small lake had formed in the back of the barn and was disappearing under the wall, into the parched dirt.

Grain stored in the barn had sprouted in that damp air; the grain sacks had burst, filling the barn with a strange, vegetal smell. In the middle of the lake, a huge John Deere tractor sat dormant, waiting for a harvest that was years overdue.

I cautiously circled the tractor and spotted something large covered with a white sheet, wedged between a workbench and a rolled-up, moth-eaten orange rug. I walked around the table and the rug and pulled off the sheet.

"Thank you, God! Thank you!"

Under that sheet were two shiny motorcycles.

An hour later, the sun was setting and night was falling on the Double J Ranch. I was back in the barn, sitting in front of a fire, grilling some fantastic steaks.

Lucullus was sleeping peacefully, softly snoring, as near the fire as he could get without singeing his fur. I'd cleaned his wound, changed the dressing, and injected him with a tiny bit of the antibiotic I'd found. I'd tried to calculate the amount according to his weight, and prayed that it didn't kill him. The antibiotic seemed to be working. My little friend looked much better than he had in days. His tail was still a bit infected, but he was going to pull through, even if he'd left one of his nine lives on the road.

I was ecstatic as I gazed upon my new acquisitions: a huge, heavy Honda Goldwing and a small, ugly 125cc Korean dirt bike.

The Goldwing gleamed in the firelight. It was one of those sturdy touring bikes with a wide seat and a handlebar covered in dials. It was built for riding thousands of miles and was in superb condition. Of course the Goldwing was my first choice, but it had two problems. First, the battery was completely dead, and its fuel-injection engine would never start without a battery. Second, it was big and unwieldy. It'd be perfect on the open road, but I needed something more nimble to speed away from the traffic jams I knew I'd encounter along the way.

So I turned to the Korean Daystar dirt bike with its cheap finish. I'd never heard of that brand, but it was small, light, and rugged looking. Best of all, it had an engine I could kick-start.

I flipped the steaks and went over to the motorcycle. I rolled it to the center of the barn and got on. I gave it a shake and found that the tank was full. Perfect. I put it in neutral and tried to kick-start it. After being parked for two years, the engine sputtered and coughed and wouldn't start. I pulled out the spark plug, cleaned it, and put it back in. I got back on the bike and stomped hard on the kick-starter. The engine sprang to life with a raspy sound; black smoke blew out the exhaust pipe. I smiled, relieved, and revved the engine a couple of times. The bike gave a somewhat muted roar, but it was still a roar. I roared, too! I had transportation out of there!

I jumped off the bike and did a silly Irish jig around the barn, too ecstatic to stand still.

Suddenly, the orange rug groaned. I let out a startled yelp and collapsed next to the fire, my heart pounding. Surely I hadn't heard right.

The rug groaned again. I tore through my pack searching for the gun, knocking the steaks into the coals. The smell of burning flesh filled the air as I held the Beretta with trembling hands.

The rug growled again and, this time, moved a little. I approached cautiously, not taking my eyes off that mound of rotting fabric. When I looked closer, every hair on my head stood on end.

It was no rug. It was a damned Undead. What I'd thought was fabric was actually a huge colony of orange fungus that had quickly spread over the thing's entire body in that damp, dark barn.

I recalled that the barn had been locked from the outside. This person must've been the first to be transformed. The other two people on the ranch didn't have the guts to kill him. *Were they his parents? His brother and sister?* So they locked him in the barn, not knowing that TSJ was coursing through their veins too. And there the creature stayed, slowly rotting, till I arrived.

I wondered why the thing didn't move. I approached cautiously, bracing myself for any sudden movement. I could see that the fungus had eaten away most of the person's muscles. *Man? Woman? Impossible to tell.* It couldn't stand up or move what was left of its muscles. It was just a skeleton, wrapped in a thick orange down, barely covered by what flesh the fungus hadn't eaten yet. Protected inside the skull, the Undead's brain would last to the end. That couldn't be much longer.

It was a horrible sight. I couldn't imagine a worse agony.

I couldn't take my eyes off that wreck of a person. Where its head should've been was a lump that followed my movements. Its eyes were long gone and probably its inner ear, too, but somehow it sensed I was there. It was fascinating and repulsive at the same time.

I pondered what this development meant for all the Undead. I doubted it was a special case. If the fungus had swallowed up and nearly destroyed that Undead, why wouldn't all the others suffer the same fate sooner or later? At least the ones in humid, warm climates where fungus grew easily.

With its proximity to the ocean, the area around Gulfport would be ideal. I wished I'd asked a helot what they'd encountered on the outside. I'd bet all the Cladoxpan I had left that the Undead around Gulfport were starting to look the same way.

I thought back to my home in Galicia, a damp, rainy place on the Atlantic coast. It was as green as Ireland and damp three days out of four. It'd been two years since I left. Were the Undead there in the same condition? Tears welled up as nostalgia washed over me. I felt very alone, far from any place I could call home. The euphoria that filled me a minute before evaporated.

I heard a faint meow. Lucullus poked his head up and managed to crawl out of the basket. It was sad to see my frisky cat staggering around like an old man. He hobbled over to me and climbed into my lap, purring. Somehow that goofy cat sensed I needed him. Anytime I wondered why I'd dragged him halfway around the world, I recalled that moment.

Before I settled down to sleep, I bashed in the head of the fuzz-covered Undead with my ax. It wasn't a danger to anyone, but I didn't feel right leaving it that way.

Next to the embers, I burrowed into some horse blankets and tried to sleep, but I only managed to doze. The next day was going to be long and hard, but it would bring me a whole lot closer to my friends waiting for me in Gulfport. And closer to my revenge.

3 9

WASTELAND
DAY 3

I set out early the next morning. The roads were in such bad shape that I couldn't risk driving at night. I planned to ride until the hottest hours of the afternoon, take a break, then go on till nightfall.

For such a small bike, the Daystar weighed a lot. After a few miles, it proved to be an excellent choice. It handled well and had enough oomph to get me out of a tight spot. Plus its simple but rugged engine was less likely to stall. The bike puttered along cheerfully as I picked up speed, headed for the main road.

I had two choices: drive along the railroad tracks or take the secondary roads. Up till that point, I'd followed the tracks, but the map showed that they veered to the north before heading back southeast into Gulfport. They also ran dangerously close to some large towns and even cut through some of them. That wasn't a problem for an armored several-hundred-ton locomotive, but it spelled death for a guy on a motorcycle. Only a fool would drive through those towns. On the bike, I could dodge a lone Undead, even a small group, but in a crowd, I'd be dead in ten minutes. One of those monsters would block my path, and I'd go down. So I stayed on the secondary roads that passed through just a couple of smaller towns where I hoped I wouldn't find too many Undead.

But I had bigger problems. I needed to find gas. And my supply of Cladoxpan was dwindling at an alarming rate.

Lucullus was alert and feeling much better after the antibiotic injections. He wriggled around restlessly in one of the saddlebags, chewing on a leather strap. Beside him was the thermos with half of the Cladoxpan I had left. In the other saddlebag, I'd stashed water, supplies, and the rest of the drug, which I'd poured into an empty whiskey bottle. I'd divided the drug into two containers so that if I lost one, I'd have a backup.

That morning I drove on a deserted dirt road overgrown with weeds. Occasionally I passed a car in a ditch or a lone figure staggering around in the distance. When those creatures heard the motorcycle, they turned and headed for me, but by the time they'd reached the road, I was already gone. If I had to stop or slow down, an Undead might ambush me. But I didn't dwell on that. I just wanted to eat up the miles. Gulfport was drawing me like a magnet.

The first night, I slept out in the open on a treeless hill. Despite howling coyotes, I didn't dare light a fire; it would've attracted far worse creatures—and not just Undead. Along the way I'd seen signs of human travel. Fresh tire tracks, campfires, and lots of gleaming copper bullet casings. At one crossroads, I spotted the tracks of a convoy of heavy vehicles. I assumed no one out there was friendly and tried not to leave any evidence I'd been there.

To be safe, I tied Lucullus to my wrist with a cord and went to sleep. If someone or something approached the camp, the cat's keen senses would detect it long before I did, and he'd wake me up when he moved.

Two hours later, my safety precautions paid off. A pack of feral dogs came sniffing around at the bottom of the hill. They were a motley mixture of mutts, a golden retriever, and a huge pit bull. When Lucullus starting hissing, I jumped up, gun in hand. I shouted and threw rocks at them, but they just stared at me. They seemed shocked to find a lone human in the middle of nowhere. They must've decided I was too dangerous, because they finally turned and walked away, the pit bull in the lead. I breathed a sigh of relief, but didn't sleep the rest of the night. I'd pay dearly for that the next morning.

40

JUST OVER THE
MISSISSIPPI STATE LINE
DAY 4

||||||||||||||||||||||||||

I was going to make it. I was less than fifty miles from Gulfport. The sun was setting, but I was elated. That morning I passed a sign telling me I was entering "The Great State of Mississippi." I'd traveled two hundred and fifty miles in two days. I was making great time. But as I got closer, I came across more and more towns that were hard to skirt. In some cases I had to race through them at breakneck speed, ducking between houses, not knowing if I'd come to a dead end.

At the same time, it was getting easier to make it through even the bigger towns. Too easy. In towns that should've been overrun by Undead, I only saw a couple dozen. I easily dodged them on the bike as I snaked among the ruined buildings and cars. Nearer the coast, where the humidity was higher, every creature I saw was infested with that fungus. On some, it covered just their face or wounds. Others looked like Persian rugs with legs. Many were so consumed that they just slithered along, unable to use their legs. The worst were those whose brains had been colonized by the fungus. They moved erratically, like robots whose programming was failing. And thousands of mounds of bones, each covered by a layer of orange, green, or violet fuzz, marked the spots where Undead had fallen, unable to lift their own weight.

I realized with a shudder that this trip would've been impossible just a few months before. The plague was slowly being devoured by one of the oldest, most primitive forms of life on the planet. In a few years, the world would be habitable for humans again. Thinking about that made me angry. I didn't want to die now. Not so close to the end.

Occasionally I came across towns that were burned to the ground. I passed through one abandoned town that looked like the set of a movie someone had forgotten to film. But I only stopped for ten minutes to fill the tank with gas from an overturned minivan.

Up until then I'd kept TSJ at bay by taking a swallow of Cladoxpan every two hours. The moment I started sweating, I stopped, took another drink, and drove on.

That drug didn't just keep me in the world of the living. My craving for it got stronger and stronger. I didn't know if I was physically or psychologically hooked on the stuff, but the craving was as real as the back pain I felt after long hours on a bike with bad shocks.

Still, I was close. Very close. And that made me feel happy and relaxed. Combined with fatigue, that proved to be a lethal cocktail.

I was on a stretch of winding road in southern Mississippi, a region full of swamps, lagoons, and dikes. The Mississippi River spreads out in all directions as it nears the ocean, which made it harder for the Undead to move around. I pictured thousands of them trapped in the muddy waters. I hadn't seen a single Undead for an hour, and I was starting to feel sleepy. Time to stop and find a place to sleep.

When I came around a bend, I was stunned by what I saw: a white ice cream truck with a giant ice cream cone on the top. Its side doors were flung open. Dead leaves covered the speakers that had once blared out little tunes to attract customers. I'd only seen ice cream trucks in American movies. It was so out of place in the swamp that I looked away from the road for a second.

That was enough. In the middle of the road was a pile of decomposing bones (the driver of the ice cream truck?) covered with blue mold. I didn't see it until I was nearly on top of it. I swerved, but it was too late. A femur bone caught on one of the footrests, causing the bike to fishtail. I cut the handlebars in the opposite direction, but the rear wheel skidded on the rotting leaves that covered the pavement.

I hit the ground to the sound of twisting metal and snapping plastic. The bike slid sideways for about sixty feet, my right leg caught under it. Fortunately, the side defense rod didn't bend. If it had, my entire leg would've been reduced to a bloody pulp mixed with gravel as the bike dragged me along the asphalt. I felt a lash of pain in my ankle before I was thrown into some under-brush.

I rolled several times before landing in some bushes. For a moment I just lay there, blinking and glad to be in one piece. I gingerly felt my body. I couldn't believe it. At the speed I was going, I should've died on the spot.

I lay there on my back in silence, listening to birds chirping as the sun filtered through the trees and cast strange shapes on my face. Suddenly I remembered Lucullus. I jumped up, but when I put my weight on my right foot, I let out a scream of pain and fell back down. My ankle was broken. And it hurt like hell.

I straightened up again, careful not to put much weight on my injured ankle, and limped to the middle of the road, fearing the worst.

A ball of orange fur burst out of the brush, chasing a lizard. The lizard darted into a crack in the pavement. My cat clawed furiously at the crack, meowing in frustration.

"I'm fine, Lucullus, thanks for asking. By the way, I think I broke my ankle, you little shit."

Lucullus looked at me, hesitated for a moment, and then went back to his game. To him, it was just another adventure he'd survived without a scratch.

With a jabbing pain in my ankle, I hobbled over to the bike, which had come to rest against an oak tree. I realized I had a very serious problem. *No! Hell, no! I'm so close! This can't happen!*

The front wheel had smashed into the tree and the bike's fork was bent at an impossible angle. A dark pool of oil was spreading under the Daystar. It had gone its last mile.

On top of that, it had fallen on its right side, crushing the saddlebag. That was where I kept my supplies. And half my supply of Cladoxpan. With a heavy heart, I tried to lift the bike. That was difficult under normal conditions, but even harder when I couldn't stand on one of my feet. Using a tree branch as a lever, I finally raised the bike enough to drag out the battered saddlebag.

When I opened it, I detected a familiar, sweet smell. The glass bottle with half the Cladoxpan was broken and the medicine had spilled on the ground.

I slumped against the tree in despair. The situation couldn't get much worse. It was getting dark, I was in the middle of a swamp full of dangerous creatures, and I had no transportation.

I couldn't walk because of my broken ankle. The worst part was that I'd lost half the medicine that kept me from becoming an Undead. Just when I was almost to my destination. I wanted to shoot myself.

An hour passed and night fell. I wallowed in self-pity for a while, then struggled to my feet. I had to go on as best I could. No one was going to rescue me. I got out my knife, cut a low tree branch, and fashioned a crutch as Lucullus darted around after the flying wood chips. When I was finished, I studied it with a critical eye. It was the ugliest crutch in history, but it would have to do.

I couldn't carry much weight, so I decided to leave all my water behind. I was surrounded by streams and ponds, so I wouldn't need it. I packed the army rations, pistol, compass, and the remaining bottle of Cladoxpan. I draped the saddlebag around my neck and tied Lucullus's leash around my waist. My little pal would have to walk the rest of the way.

After two hours, I stopped, exhausted. I'd only gone about a mile and I was still surrounded by deep swamp. At that rate, it'd take a month to get to Gulfport. But I wouldn't be alive in twenty-four hours, given the amount of Cladoxpan I had left.

Disheartened, I collapsed in a clearing by the side of the road. I struggled to light a small fire and ate the last army ration. The fire would keep any creatures away. If it attracted a human being, so be it. No matter how hostile that person was, it'd be better than dying there alone. The thought of dying made the rest of the night seem even longer and more hopeless. Demoralized and weak, I fell asleep next to the fire. Game over.

4 1

OLD BOUIE SWAMP, MISSISSIPPI
DAY 5

IIIIIIIIIIIIIIIIIIIIIIIIIIIII

The next morning I was awakened by Lucullus licking my face. I grumbled and turned over, eyes shut tight. I didn't want to wake up. I didn't want to get up. I just wanted to lie there and transform alone. When the time came, I'd put a bullet in my head and end it all.

Lucullus kept licking me. His huge tongue covered one whole side of my face, from my chin to my eyebrows, soaking me with drool. With another lick, drool ran into my nose and down my entire face. Puffs of his hot breath rifled my hair. When he didn't get any attention, he let out a loud bray. *A bray?*

I opened my eyes and bolted upright. A dappled mule gazed at me with interest, waggling its ears. When it saw me react, it licked me again. Until you've been licked by a mule, you don't know how disgusting its breath is, but I didn't care. I rubbed my eyes and pinched myself to make sure I was awake.

"Hello, sweetie," I whispered soothingly. I didn't want to scare the animal.

It was a young female, medium height, in pretty good shape. She stood there, caked in mud to the tip of her muzzle. She was very docile and gazed intently at me. She seemed very happy to find me.

"Where on earth did you come from?" I ran my hand down her back and scratched behind her ears. There was no one in sight. I called out a few times, in case someone was watching from the bushes, but nobody answered. She must be alone.

She looked like she'd been living in the swamp for quite some time. Her shoes had fallen off and the nail holes in her hooves were almost closed up. Her brand was barely visible. Maybe she'd been abandoned at the start of the pandemic and hadn't seen a human since. So when she found me in that clearing, she approached me. I couldn't be sure, but she seemed to be as glad to see me as I was to see her. Lucullus watched us, his eyes wide as saucers.

She didn't have a saddle, but that wasn't going to stop me. Fate had given me another chance, and I wasn't going to waste it. I fashioned a halter out of a strap from the saddlebag and tied it around her neck. I settled the saddlebags over her back and tied them below her belly with the last strap. The mule stood quietly, as if she were used to this ritual. I stuck Lucullus in one of the saddlebags and climbed on.

I hadn't ridden a horse in a long time—and I'd never ridden a mule—but riding a horse is like riding a bike. You never forget how. I clucked softly and kicked her sides. As if that were what she was expecting, the mule started walking briskly down the road.

I ran my hand over my face in disbelief. One minute I was thinking about the best way to end it all, and the next minute I was headed for Gulfport on a mule. My guardian angel was definitely working overtime.

The road widened slowly and the vegetation became less dense. The sooner we left that swamp behind, the better.

"Just thirty miles, sweetheart," I whispered in her ear. "Think you can do it?"

The mule pricked up her ears and trotted faster, as if she understood. She seemed glad to hear a human voice. Maybe she thought we were headed to a nice, warm barn.

"You need a name. How about Hope?"

The mule trotted along, oblivious to my ramblings. I was so happy to be alive that anything put me in a good mood. Then suddenly I realized my Cladoxpan supply would only last another day. I figured we were only about thirty miles from Gulfport, but in my condition, Hope would never get me there in time.

Stay calm. Cut your dosage in half. That'll make it last twice as long.

Great idea. But what if the fucking TSJ isn't satisfied with half a dose?

What choice did I have?

I bellowed, helpless. The mule pricked up her ears, alarmed. I had only one card to play, so I cut my ration in half.

Just then, on cue, my whole body started to sweat. That was the first warning. My transformation had begun.

Two hours later, the cramps started. I drank only a tiny sip; the cramps lessened but didn't go away. I was sweating so hard I had to take a drink more often.

By noon, the cramps were unbearable. My hands shook so violently I nearly spilled my dwindling reserves. The temptation to take a long drink was very strong, almost unbearable, but I controlled myself.

By the afternoon I had a burning thirst. I stopped Hope next to a stream so I could get some water. As I climbed down, one of my feet got tangled in the saddlebag. I waved my arms, but couldn't keep my balance and fell face first on the ground, hitting my head and reopening the gash on my forehead. A few drops of my blood fell into the stream, and the current slowly carried them away in lazy spirals. I stared blankly at the bloody water. What would happen if someone drank that water downstream? He'd probably contract TSJ. How many liters of water would those drops contaminate? For how long? That damned Italian doctor could've answered those questions if he weren't such a lunatic.

After several failed, tortured attempts, I finally got back on the mule but only by walking her over to a crumbling wall and climbing on that way. She looked surprised, as if she wondered how anyone could be so uncoordinated. The shooting pains I felt weren't just from my broken ankle. My legs were starting to fail.

I rode for only fifteen minutes before I was dying of thirst again. The same gurgling stream ran alongside the road, so I stopped the mule again. This time, I plunged my face into the stream and gulped down a lot of water. As soon as I finished, I violently vomited all that water back up.

I put my head back in the stream and drank more sparingly, trying to rehydrate myself. But that didn't quench my thirst. At least not for water. I reached for the bottle of Cladoxpan and uncorked it. In a final act of self-control, just before it touched my lips, I stuck the cork back in. It was one of the hardest things I've ever done.

I don't know how much time passed. The mule walked at an easy pace down the road, sidestepping abandoned vehicles. Fortunately we were in an uninhabited area, so there were no

Undead. If we'd crossed paths with any, I know what would've happened. I could barely stay upright, let alone fight.

Hold on tight. Don't fall. Don't fall. You can't fall.

"Oh, go ahead and fall," Greene said cheerfully as he unwrapped an ice pop and eagerly sucked on it. "Just relax and let go. Everything will be much easier."

I turned my head, confused. The reverend was walking beside me, Bible under his arm. The crimson ice pop in his hand left a dark stain on his lips that looked like blood.

"What're you doing here?" I muttered between chapped lips.

"The question is, what are *you* doing here?" replied the reverend, lasciviously licking the ice pop. As he did, I caught a glimpse of his rotten gums, teeming with maggots. "You should be dead by now. You know that, don't you?"

"I think he wants revenge, Reverend," said a voice on the other side of the mule. I turned my head and blinked. To my left walked Grapes, pulling cats out of a backpack. He slit their bellies with his knife, ripped out their guts, and popped the entrails into his greedy mouth. "He wants to come to Gulfport to kill us, but he doesn't know he's already dead."

"I'm not deeeeaaaad," I protested weakly. I realized, scared, that I was slurring my words. "And you're not heeeerrre. This is a fucking hallucination."

"Oh, of course we are," said Greene. When I looked over, I saw that the reverend had turned into Ushakov, the Russian captain from the *Zaren Kibish*. "We're dead, too, you know. We're all dead because of you."

"And you'll join us very soon," said Grapes. He wasn't gutting cats anymore. Now he cut out bits of his own guts and popped them in his mouth. "Want some?"

My gut roared and my mouth filled with saliva. That hot, bloody human flesh looked so appetizing . . . I reached for it, but

Grapes pulled the piece back and gave me a sly look. He shook his index finger in front of my face, like a metronome.

"No, no, no. Get your own. Like the rest of us."

"Like the rest of us!" shouted Greene/Ushakov.

Beside them walked the sailor who'd tried to rape Lucia in the Canary Islands. He was so covered in that fungus, I could hardly make him out. It had grown over his tongue so he couldn't speak, but his gestures were unmistakable. The guy shook his pelvis lewdly. Then he put a piece of human flesh in his mouth and chewed furiously. Every time he bit down, a couple of teeth fell out and landed in the dust, like blood-soaked pearls.

"Gooo to heeellll," I cursed. My tongue was so thick I could barely form the words.

"Where do you think you are?" Greene whispered in my ear. Now he was riding behind me on the mule, clutching me around the waist as if we were lovers, holding his Bible open in front of me. "Look what it says in the book. Repent of your sins. You're dead."

"No!" I roared and gave him a shove. My arm flew through the air. Greene had disappeared, along with everyone else.

Trembling with panic, I uncorked the bottle of Cladoxpan and raised it over my mouth, but not a drop came out. The bottle was empty. I stared at it as if I were clutching an alien's arm.

I looked up at the deep-orange sun. It was starting to set. It was much later than I thought. I'd completely lost track of time.

This is the end. The fucking end.

With clumsy fingers, I struggled to get the gun out of the saddlebag. I had to do it now while I still had an ounce of control over myself. A growl came from inside the bag and I stopped. Lucullus was scared to death—of me. Or rather, of what I was becoming.

My hand was covered in spider veins. They hadn't burst yet, but very soon they would. Then I remembered I'd tucked the gun in my belt. I fumbled around and finally got it out of its holster. My eyes were blurry, so I couldn't see well. I raised the gun to eye level and checked the safety.

Two shots. First the cat, then me. Fast and clean.

Just then the mule hopped over a broken bicycle in the middle of the road, and the gun flew out of my hands.

"Nooooo!" I growled, twisting my lips, but I couldn't do anything else. The reins hung down from Hope's neck, so I couldn't stop her. My muscles contracted in a sort of macabre St. Vitus dance. I'd lost control of my body, so we just kept going, leaving the black Beretta lying in the road, the last rays of sunset glinting off it.

I'd failed. I'd failed everyone. I couldn't save myself or save them. I'd failed Lucullus, who struggled inside the saddlebag trying to escape. I'd failed Prit, who'd always been a faithful, true friend, even risking his life for me.

And Lucia. Lucia. Luuucíaaa. Luuucccíaaaa. Lcxciciiaia. Lucciihayayaa.

A huge black wave crashed over me. Then everything went dark.

4 2

TAUBEN
12 MILES OUTSIDE OF GULFPORT

"Virgin of Kazan! That's a horrible smell!" Prit groaned and covered his nose.

"You think that's bad," Mendoza replied cheerfully, "wait'll we get to the dump. It's about a mile from here, past that hill. Now *that's* a truly unbearable stench."

Gulfport dumped most of its trash into the ocean. Toxic waste and pollutants were thrown into a landfill a few miles from the city. That included the bodies of helots and the Undead that collapsed close to the Wall, overcome by fungus. No one wanted hundreds of putrefying corpses lying around causing an epidemic.

The convoy rolled slowly down a rough road that wound through abandoned buildings. One tank led the way and another one brought up the rear. Garbage trucks and a bulldozer—their cabs reinforced by iron bars—made up the rest of the convoy.

They left the city at dusk through the gates in the Wall. The bulldozer slowly pushed aside the crowd of Undead that surrounded the city, trying to find a way in. Then the convoy moved as fast as possible to outrun the Undead pursuing them. It was not difficult to leave the Undead behind. Previous expeditions had cleared the road of debris, and the creatures were in bad condition. Even those that were "fresher" couldn't keep up with the speeding vehicles.

When the helots first told Pritchenko that the Undead were being devoured by fungus, he hadn't bought it. Then the Ukrainian saw it with his own eyes. It boded well for the future. But first they had to gain control of Gulfport and the Cladoxpan reserves—or all the helots were doomed to suffer the next stage of Greene's plan.

"You sure we're carrying the cargo?" he asked Mendoza for the third time.

"Don't know, *güero*," snapped the Mexican. "And I won't know till we unload all the piles of garbage and bodies. But I'm sure of one thing. The Just have never failed us, and I don't think they'll start now."

Prit nodded and checked his weapon. Everyone in the convoy was wound tight. The assault on the city was planned for the next night. Everything was riding on the next twenty-four hours—the helots and their allies were nervous. Their plans had never progressed this far. Even Greene's snitches were in the dark. The reverend knew something was brewing in the ghetto, but he didn't know what it was or when it would take place. The missing piece of the puzzle was the Cladoxpan supply that they hoped was hidden in those trucks. As soon as they had their hands on it, the Wrath of the Just could be unleashed on that racist city.

The convoy labored up the hill and came to a halt at the top. At the bottom of a ravine was a mountain of charred debris being slowly consumed by a bonfire that had burned for months. A dozen Undead wandered here and there in the lunar landscape. The tank in the lead revved its engine and advanced through the fires. A pair of sharpshooters leaned out the hatch. They raced up to an Undead, opened fire, and moved on. Before Pit realized it, they'd secured the entire area.

"There aren't very many of them anymore, so it's easy," said the driver of the truck Prit rode in, a middle-aged man with an Indian accent. "Not that long ago, it took us several hours—and a lot of ammo—to get close enough to unload safely."

"Apu knows what he's talking about. He's one of the oldest residents of the ghetto. He's been making this trip for nearly two years," said Mendoza.

The man flashed a dazzlingly white smile and shrugged modestly. He raised his arm, revealing the scar of an old wound. "It happened about a year and a half ago. There were about two hundred of those creatures out there. One of them found a way inside the cab. But we got through, as always."

Prit studied him. People amazed him. Despite all the hardships, despite living a miserable, enslaved life, they still had the will to live.

"Is your name really Apu, like the convenience store owner on The Simpsons?" he asked with a sly smile.

"It's a long story," the man replied with a wave of his hand. "My real name has too many letters for anyone who wasn't born in Sri Lanka."

"I can imagine," Prit said, turning to Mendoza. "Now what?"

"Now, we take out the trash, bro," he replied, as Apu maneuvered the truck into position. "Time to get our hands dirty."

They positioned the dump trucks around a pit and started unloading their stinking cargo. Prit watched as arms, legs, and heads disappeared into the roaring bonfire along with medical waste and rotting garbage. The smell of burning flesh and hair filled the air.

"Hey! Be careful!" Mendoza shouted, waving his arms.

A few helots scrambled to the top of the trucks, ignoring the terrible smell. Armed with flashlights, they made their way to the back of the truck bed. After a while they came back out, flashing a thumbs-up.

"They're in the back, tied down with steel cables! A dozen barrels in each truck!" they shouted above the noise of the engines as they dragged one out.

"Perfect," murmured Mendoza. He opened the lid of a barrel with the tip of his knife. "Let's have a look."

When he uncovered the barrel, Cladoxpan's pungent aroma wafted into the air. The men smiled and walked closer to the barrel. A few were glassy-eyed and couldn't look away from the milky liquid.

"Gato . . ." The Hindu truck driver clucked his tongue and swallowed hard. His hands shook like an alcoholic's. "One sip. I think we've earned it."

The Mexican scowled, then nodded slightly. "One glass each. Not a drop more."

The helots cheered and gathered around the barrel. Prit stepped aside. He noticed that the men downed their glasses in great greedy gulps. The women sipped theirs. A few even saved some for later.

The Ukrainian smiled. He was sure his pal would've made some funny remark about that, and they'd have struggled not to burst out laughing. They'd have stood off to the side, pursing their lips, with tears in their eyes, choking back their laughter.

When he thought about his friend, he felt a deep pain. He hadn't accepted losing him. It would take a long time to come to terms with it. The Ukrainian was a hard man. He'd lost a lot of friends in Chechnya during the war. Then his wife and son had disappeared in the pandemic. He'd grown thick-skinned and hid his feelings. But feelings didn't go away. Prit knew they'd surface sooner or later. When they did, the pain would be huge and hard to deal with. For now he held it in and kept going. For Lucia's sake.

She was devastated. At first she'd had high hopes. Their wily friend was a man of many talents. They tried to convince themselves that his train car had unloaded close to town and that he'd find his way back to Gulfport. No deportee had ever done it, but if anyone could make it back, he could.

But it had been seven days and there was no sign of him. Even if he was still alive, he must have run out of Cladoxpan. When Strangärd told them the terrible news—that Greene had infected their friend with the virus as part of his banishment—they lost hope.

"OK, everyone's had a drink. Time to go!" Mendoza shouted.

The helots, visibly relaxed after their drinking, secured the barrels with their precious contents inside each truck, and climbed back into their vehicles. Mendoza gave the order to take off, and the dump trucks started back up the hill, away from the trash and the burned bodies.

A helot in the truck with Mendoza and Prit pointed at something in the distance. "What's that?" he asked, wide-eyed.

Prit let out a string of Russian curse words, and Mendoza crossed himself. The truck driver slammed on the brakes, terrified. The whole column screeched to a halt.

On the hill, a mule with a body slung on her back trotted happily toward the convoy.

Prit jumped out of the truck before it came to a stop and ran toward the mule. *It's gotta be him.*

When he reached the mule he stopped, panting. The rider lay facedown across the mule's neck. His legs were tangled in a torn saddlebag slung over the mule's back. If it hadn't been for that, he'd have fallen to the ground.

Something shifted inside one of the bags and uttered a meow that sounded very familiar. Pritchenko's face lit up as he reached into the saddlebag.

Suddenly the body slumped over the mule let out a horrifying groan.

Prit froze. The body on the mule rose up and looked at him with an all-too-familiar blank expression. His deathly pale skin was riddled with thousands of spidery veins.

Oh, hell, it can't be true!

"Get away from that thing!" Mendoza shouted as he ran up behind Prit, trying to catch his breath. When he saw what was on the mule, he drew his gun and cocked it loudly. "Let's get this over with," he murmured and took careful aim.

"No!" Prit shouted. "Don't shoot! Look at his veins!"

"They're swollen, like all the monsters," Mendoza insisted.

"Yes, but they haven't burst yet!" Pritchenko caught his sleeve, speaking quickly and urgently. "His transformation isn't complete yet! We can still help him!"

"He might not be completely transformed, but he doesn't have far to go," Mendoza replied caustically. "How do you plan to help him?"

"With Cladoxpan," said Prit, stern-faced. "With a massive dose. It might work."

"We're gonna need every drop of the stuff back in Bluefont," Mendoza snapped.

"Mendoza, don't fuck with me," said Prit with a snarl. "You've got thousands of gallons—I just need three or four. Do I have to break a couple of your ribs to change your mind?"

"OK, *güero*, take it easy." Mendoza raised his hands in surrender. "Take what you need. But you'll have to do it. I'm not getting anywhere near that rabid mouth."

As if he understood, the rider on the mule let out a threatening groan and stretched his hands toward Mendoza. Unfazed, Prit hurried to the first truck and grabbed two helots who were watching the scene from a few yards away. After a couple of minutes, the three of them came back up the hill, rolling one of the barrels of Cladoxpan.

"How're you gonna get him to drink it?" Mendoza asked. "He won't do it on his own."

"I'll do it the old Soviet army way," Prit replied as he stood the barrel on end and pried off the lid with his knife. "If you can't do something the polite way, you use brute force."

The Ukrainian came up behind the rider and, before he could react, grabbed him in a judo hold. At the same time, the two helots cut the straps that held the man to the mule. Then Prit shoved him headfirst into the barrel.

At first the thing fought back furiously, but the Ukrainian held his head under with one iron hand while the other gripped him in a rugby tackle. When the thing couldn't hold his breath any longer, he took a swallow. The Ukrainian pulled him out by his hair and then, after a few seconds, plunged him back into the barrel.

Pritchenko repeated this maneuver a dozen times with the coldhearted fury of a Soviet interrogator. Each time, the thing swallowed more and more Cladoxpan. Finally the seizures ceased and his body relaxed. Satisfied, Prit pulled him out of the barrel and gently laid him on the ground next to the mule, which watched, wide-eyed.

"Now what?" Mendoza asked.

"Now we wait," said Prit, trying to sound calmer than he felt. "And cross our fingers."

When I first opened my eyes, I was overcome by nausea. A foul stench hung in the air, and my lungs felt as if I were about to drown. I was lying on my back and someone had laid a blanket over me. It was dark and the stars twinkled in the sky. By the light of several huge bonfires, I could make out figures in the shadows.

I leaned to one side and vomited for what seemed like an eternity. My head pounded. I felt like I had the most monstrous hangover on record. But I was alive. I was alive!

That realization overwhelmed me. Somehow I'd escaped death, or rather nondeath. I was weak, bruised, and bone tired, but I hadn't become an Undead.

"Look who finally decided to wake up," said a familiar voice behind me.

"I would've laid here longer, but this place stinks. I'm sure you chose it," I said as I struggled to sit up.

Prit and I threw our arms around each other. My friend sighed with relief, and I shook uncontrollably as my body readjusted to being alive.

"I've told you hundreds of times, don't go anywhere without me," the Ukrainian scolded me with a smile. "See? You nearly got yourself killed."

"That was a close one. But you wouldn't have liked the trip. There wasn't a single bar anywhere."

A couple of helots walked up, whispering among themselves and pointing at me. Then a few more came over to get a look. A few crossed themselves and looked at me with a strange, reverent expression as they talked among themselves.

"What the hell're they saying?" Prit asked. He spoke pretty good Spanish, but couldn't follow their Puerto Rican accent.

"It's a passage from the Bible: He descended into hell and rose from the dead," I replied as fatigue washed over me again. "They think it's a sign. The mule too."

"They think you're the Messiah?" Prit asked, incredulous.

"That's stupid," I said sleepily. "I'm no Messiah. But if believing that helps them bring down that false Messiah in Gulfport, I'll be happy to put on a white robe."

"You won't have to," said Prit as he helped me to my feet. "In about twenty hours, the ghetto will rise up. We're going to take out Greene and his goons once and for all."

"What the hell're you talking about, Prit?"

"I'll explain on the way. Now we gotta get out of here."

I climbed into a truck as the rest of the convoy started their engines. Night was falling, and the helots were nervous about what they might run into out there in the dark. Prit climbed in next to me and the convoy started to roll.

"This is Carlos Mendoza," he said and pointed to the tall, stocky Mexican man who was glaring at me. "Don't pay attention to anything he says. He's got a bad temper. I've got a broken nose to prove it. But deep down, he's not a bad guy. He's the leader of all these people."

"We've met. The lawyer on the bridge in Gulfport, remember?" I stuck out my hand.

"Well, well. So you're the *gachupina*'s boyfriend," he replied, making no move to shake my hand. "I must admit, you're a tough nut to crack. You're the first guy to come back from the Wasteland, though you just barely made it."

"I got lucky," I said, lowering my hand. "If you hadn't been there, I wouldn't have lasted another half hour." I turned back to Prit, who beamed like a father watching his son learn to ride a bike. "What the hell're you all doing here, Prit?"

The Ukrainian explained everything that had happened. Mendoza joined the conversation, reluctantly at first, but got more and more animated as he reeled off his plans. The ghetto uprising was his obsession. The plan was all he thought about. And he was just a few hours from carrying it out.

When we were three miles from Gulfport, the truck driver slammed on the brakes. The lead tank had stopped, and the crew peered out the window. In the distance a red flare shot up in the sky, followed by two more.

"What is it?" I asked. "What does that mean?"

The Mexican looked at us, his face pale and drawn in rage. "It's the ghetto! That's the emergency signal for a raid. The Greens have attacked!"

"How bad is the situation?" Prit asked.

"Really bad. They must've uncovered our plans." Mendoza shouted into the walkie-talkie, ordering the convoy to proceed at full speed. Then he turned to us. "Get ready to fight. I just hope we get there in time. The 'cleansing of the ghetto' has begun."

4 4

"Ale, we need more rags," Lucia said. "And some bottles. We're nearly out."

Alejandra dashed to the back of the room where they were making Molotov cocktails with half a dozen other people. She grabbed a handful of cotton strips and a wheelbarrow full of empty glass bottles and rushed back to her post.

Workshops like theirs filled the ghetto. Some were making Molotov cocktails while others were making bullets, although they weren't sure that the ammunition would be reliable in battle.

Prit was right, thought Lucia. *Our supply of weapons is almost laughable. If we don't take the Wall in the first assault, they'll squash us like bugs.*

A lingering black cloud had replaced the girl's good mood. She'd been on an emotional roller coaster in the ghetto. From the top of the Wall, she scanned the horizon for her man all day every day, oblivious to the rain and the Undead roaring a few feet below. Alejandra and Pritchenko thought she was losing her mind. Finally Mendoza ordered her to get down. Her presence up there sent up a red flag for Greene's militia. Someone might ask some difficult questions no one wanted to answer just days before the ghetto rose up against its oppressors.

As the days passed, her hopes faded. She wouldn't admit it to herself, but she knew that with every passing hour, his chances of making it back diminished. She feared something far worse than all the dangers lurking on the outside or the infection running through his veins. What if they'd killed him when he got off the train? Night after night she woke from that nightmare screaming. All she could do then was curl up in bed, trembling and waiting for the weak morning light. Another day with no sign of him. Her face was puffy and she had dark circles under her eyes. She couldn't eat. All the life had gone out of her. She was going through hell, oblivious to everything and everyone.

One morning during their shift, Alejandra sat her down. "Keep your mind busy. If you don't, the pain'll drive you crazy. You're not the first to go through this and you won't be the last. There's two ways to handle that pain: turn it into something small and manageable, or let it grow till it crushes you and you can't breathe. Trust me, that second path leads to a gray, sad life with no future. You've gotta move on."

"I don't want to move on," Lucia said in a raspy whisper. "Not without him."

"You'll move on, of course you will." Alejandra gave Lucia's arm an affectionate squeeze, lifted her chin, and looked into her eyes. "You have to go on, for you and for everything you two stood for. For him, for his memory. Above all, you can't give up now. The future is so close. Sooner or later this nightmare'll end and then the world'll be a very big place for the few survivors. You have to tough it out somehow. So sit down and make those fucking Molotov cocktails as if your life depended on it. Clear your mind. Think about anything you like, but find a way to live!

If you don't, everything you've done, for yourself and for him, will be meaningless."

Lucia lowered her head and worked in silence, choking back tears, and burying her pain deep in her heart. The mindless work did help to keep her afloat. She didn't let herself forget, but at least she kept busy. And that was what she needed.

"How do they plan to break through the ghetto wall?" she asked Alejandra as she carefully filled half-liter bottles with gasoline and potassium soap shavings.

"No idea," said Alejandra. "Only a handful of people know that. Rumor has it that, in one of the basements, they've stockpiled huge amounts of fertilizer and God-knows-what-else to make a very powerful explosive." She looked all around. "The walls have ears."

"I hope it works, whatever it is—" Lucia stopped short when gunshots rang out.

Everyone in the workshop looked up, their eyes wide. Then there was a long burst of gunfire, and several assault rifles rattled in the distance.

"What the hell's that?" Lucia asked in alarm.

"Don't know, but it can't be good." Alejandra jumped up and eased over to the windows.

The windows had been covered so no one could get a look at what they were doing on the second story of the house. The petite woman struggled with the latches and finally managed to slide the window up. She stuck her head out to get a look from their second-story perch, then pulled it right back inside.

"The street's full of Green Guards and the militia! They've got dozens of trucks!"

"How many?" asked a tall, rail-thin Mexican man with a tangle of black curls. He tucked a couple of Molotov cocktails into his belt.

"More than normal. They must've enlisted more guards. They're all over the place!"

"Whadda we do?" murmured a very frightened woman. "Gato and most of the leaders are outside the Wall. Hardly anyone's left to coordinate the groups."

"We'll all have to step up." Lucia was surprised to hear those words come out of her mouth. She felt more centered than she had in days. She wanted to take the law into her own hands. Fuck everyone who'd destroyed her life. Let them share her pain.

"Is there any way to signal them?" she asked.

"Yeah, someone's got flares someplace," Alejandra replied. "I'm sure they'll shoot them off anytime now."

"Let's show them what we've got," said Lucia, dragging out a box of Molotov cocktails. "We'll blow the head off any asshole who comes snooping around here."

They loaded the cocktails into backpacks and headed for the street. Shots, screams, and the sound of breaking glass and wood came from everywhere. The Greens were clearing out the ghetto strongholds, showing no mercy to anyone who resisted. There was nowhere left to hide.

A couple of explosions rocked the street. The demonic rattle of machine guns grew with a crescendo and a huge fireball rose from the far side of the ghetto with a sickening roar.

"We're fighting back!" roared the tall guy, raising a fist. "Those are our AK-47s, not the Greens' M4s."

"We gotta hurry," Alejandra said. "They don't have enough ammunition to keep that up. They'll need all the help we can give them. Divvy up the bombs and split up."

The small groups scattered in all directions. Alejandra and Lucia went with the tall man, who seemed to have a plan. The shooting was widespread and the sky glowed with a dozen fires. People ran everywhere, screaming and looking scared out of their wits. A few clutched motley collections of weapons with a determined look in their eyes.

"Back a mouse into a corner and he'll attack a lion," Lucia muttered under her breath.

"What'd you say?" Alejandra asked.

Lucia felt an ice-cold fury rush through her veins. "It's something he used to say—"

"Explain it to me later." Alejandra tugged Lucia's arm. "Right now we have to hurry! Run!"

There was a screech of tires as a big army truck barreled around the corner with a group of militiamen perched in the truck bed. They'd painted Reverend Green's cross over the white US Army star. The driver smiled sadistically as he mowed down anyone who wasn't fast enough to get away.

"Run for it, girls!" cried the tall man. He grabbed a Molotov cocktail and planted himself in middle of the road. He lit the Molotov behind his back so the truck driver couldn't see what he was doing and stood in the middle of the street with suicidal bravery. When the truck driver saw him, he looked daggers at the man and speeded up. The man didn't flinch. He waited, lips pursed, eyes trained on the truck until it was ten feet from him. He darted aside as he tossed the Molotov cocktail through the open window of the truck that by then was less than five feet from him.

The bottle burst into a ball of fire that engulfed the driver and his passenger. The truck swerved, flames shooting out its windows. The guards in the truck bed held on tight to keep from being thrown out. Then the truck slammed into a house with the sounds of metal twisting and wood splintering. The soldiers in the back flew off in every direction like cannonballs. Most slammed into the house. Some soldiers broke their necks in the crash or were impaled on the house's broken wood frame. Others fell into the flames devouring the house. You could hear screams of agony over the roar of the fire.

"We're done here. Let's go," the tall man said matter-of-factly.

They shouldered their backpacks and continued to the next intersection. In a house on the corner, some helots were in a standoff with a group of militiamen who were trying to cross the intersection. The bodies of a dozen soldiers were sprawled on the ground. The surviving militiamen had taken cover behind their vehicles and were firing on the helots with assault rifles. Although the militia and the Green Guards' firepower was far superior, the helots were well protected in the house. Suddenly a Humvee equipped with a 50mm M2 machine gun raced into the intersection. From about a hundred feet away, it trained the M2 on the house.

The helots fired on the Humvee, but it was too late. The M2 roared with a lazy cadence and the front of the house collapsed in a cloud of pulverized wood, cement, and blood. After a few seconds, the firing stopped. There was nothing left of the top floor.

"Wait here," whispered the tall man as he lit two Molotov cocktails. "This'll be a piece of cake." With a bomb in each hand, he flattened himself against the building on the opposite sidewalk and edged toward the Humvee, out of its line of sight.

Just then a militiaman on the street spotted him and shouted an alarm. The tall guy let out a whoop and ran toward the Humvee, raising the Molotov cocktails over his head, but he was too late. The machine gun blasted away, nearly slicing the man's body in half. He collapsed like a rag doll. As he fell, the Molotov cocktails broke and the flaming liquid spilled all over his body, quickly reducing him to a pile of burning flesh in the middle of the road.

Alejandra and Lucia stared, terrified. Before they could react, another Humvee roared up behind them. The women were trapped. Lucia gritted her teeth. Just as she was about to light a Molotov cocktail, the second Humvee turned and headed straight for the soldiers, who cheered when they saw it. The first Humvee screeched to a halt and its crew peered out the hatch. The soldiers' faces froze in horror when the machine gun on the second vehicle took aim at them and opened fire.

The second Humvee mowed down the soldiers like a giant sickle cutting wheat, and kept firing until nothing moved on the street. Bullets penetrated the first Humvee's fuel tank and it exploded in a raging fireball. The burning house and Humvee cast a spectral glow on the dozens of bodies lying in the street.

The Humvee door opened and a soldier cautiously stuck out his head.

Alejandra cried out, "Strangärd!"

The Swede sprang out of the Humvee, aiming his rifle. When he saw Alejandra and Lucia crouched behind a hedge, he breathed a sigh of relief and lowered his rifle.

"What the hell are you two doing here? I almost shot you, for the love of God!"

"What're you doing here?" Lucia asked, incredulous.

"We came as soon as we could." Lucia noticed he was wearing a white armband on his right bicep. "We learned that the 'cleanup' had started. We knew we had to try to prevent a slaughter, but this is way worse than I imagined. There aren't many of us, but we're well armed. Where's Mendoza? I need to talk to him."

"Gato took the trash convoy and went to get the Cladoxpan," said Alejandra.

"Damn it!" the Swede snarled. "This is no time for him to disappear! What about the short, blond guy, the Russian soldier? Where's he?"

"He's with Gato," said Lucia. "And he's not Russian, he's—"

"Ukrainian. I know, I know. So who's in charge?"

"I have no idea," said Alejandra. "We're trying to get to the center of the ghetto to find out. And to get these to the fighters there." She pointed to the Molotov cocktails.

"You won't get very far on foot," Strangärd replied. "Most of the fighting is in the center. Grapes brought reinforcements. Nearly a thousand men. Get in the Humvee. We'll get as close as we can, and then, God help us."

Once the women were in the Humvee, the driver sped off past the burning remains of the tall helot, who looked like a charred mummy. Then the street fell silent. The fallen on both sides gazed at each other with the empty eyes of death.

4 5

Malachi Grapes was finally happy. His life had never been easy. When he was a little boy, everyone had called him white trash. The son of a single mother addicted to crack, little Malachi learned to defend himself early—first with his fists, then knives, and then guns. Transitioning from a street gang to the Aryan Nations had been a no-brainer.

Grapes's whole life had been violent, including his long prison term. He'd come to enjoy violence. Fuck it! He really liked it. The prison psychiatrist described Grapes's personality in detail, his severe schizophrenic fits and his above-average intelligence. But none of that mattered to him. He was motivated by other people's pain. That and power.

But nothing he'd experienced before compared to what he felt standing in the middle of a blazing street as his men hunted down all those losers in the Bluefont ghetto.

His boots splashed through a pool of helot blood as houses collapsed around him in an inferno of sparks and charred timbers. Grapes felt more alive than ever. He felt like a god. A violent, destructive god of war. He grew light-headed as the feeling of power swept over him.

He was going to kill every last one of those sons of bitches, including the two thousand helots Reverend Greene had told him to spare. He'd make up some excuse. *They fought back, Reverend. They wouldn't agree to your terms. They didn't let us take them alive.* He'd come up with something. He was so drunk on blood that only one refrain ran through his head: *Destroy. Kill. Maim. Inflict pain.*

"Hey, Malachi," said a voice behind him. It was Seth Fretzen, his right-hand man. "They radioed that the streets on the other side are under control, but they're having some problems in the center of the ghetto. Them assholes are fighting back."

Grapes looked down at the phrase tattooed across his knuckles: HATE JEWS. He flashed a big, satisfied smile. Those morons had just given him the excuse he needed.

"OK, Seth," he said amiably. "Let's go kick their brown asses. We'll teach 'em who's fucking boss."

Seth Fretzen smiled, flashing his broken, rotting teeth— what few were left. He was having a great time too. He signaled to the militiamen and Green Guards surrounding Grapes's tank, then got behind the wheel as the rest of the men climbed into their vehicles. They roared through the burning streets. Along the way, dozens of people ran for the shadows. Grapes sneered. *I'll take care of them later. First, I'm gonna take out the mother-fuckers who're fighting back. That'll break their resistance and the rest'll be gentle as lambs. Stupid shits.*

The Just, they called themselves. What did justice have to do with it? In Grapes's mind, justice died when the Apocalypse destroyed the old world. Now the only law was survival of the strong and the fit. With Greene behind him, he was the strongest of all.

As his convoy turned the corner, shots rang out from every direction. Grapes heard a howl of pain next to him as a soldier fell from the turret of a Humvee, half his head blown away. Bullets pinged against the side of Grapes's truck and cracked the reinforced glass, leaving bumps on the inside of the door. If the truck hadn't been reinforced, Grapes would've been toast.

The Aryan was stunned when one of the vehicles in his command flew into the air in a ball of fire. His men gunned down the helots who'd thrown the Molotov cocktails as they ran from the scene, but his convoy was suddenly in chaos. The veins in Grapes's neck swelled in rage.

"Seth, call in all the reinforcements now! Let's take out these fucking pussies! And get a heavy tank over here!"

The man nodded and barked the orders into his radio. Grapes jumped from his truck and organized his men into a firing line out of the snipers' range. He was too pissed off to duck as bullets pinged around him.

He finally got his men into a semicircle at one corner of the plaza. The helots were mainly concentrated on the opposite side. His men were firing blindly, wasting ammo as if this were a shooting contest. Of course, they had plenty to spare: the whole fucking Navy warehouse in Gulfport.

The helots' firepower had dwindled to a trickle compared to the torrent of fire Grapes's men unleashed. He grunted, satisfied. He suspected that the assholes were running out of ammo, but he didn't want to take a chance.

Suddenly a Humvee like his, but without the green cross on the side, appeared on a side street. The driver slammed on his brakes, as surprised to see Grapes as he was to see them, then revved his engine as his shooter opened fire on Grapes's line. Its huge machine gun pierced Grapes's armored shields as if they were soda cans, and half a dozen of men fell on the ground, writhing in pain. Then that Humvee drove off, disappearing into the shadows like an evil ghost.

Grapes scanned the night, frowning, trying to follow the roar of the Humvee's engine as it rushed from corner to corner, hiding in pools of darkness. When his men returned fire, the Humvee disappeared behind a row of houses. The helots howled with joy.

Grapes swore under his breath. How did those fuckers get ahold of one of his vehicles? Did they have allies on the other side of the Wall? That worried him more. Grapes tried to make out who was inside as the Humvee came back for another pass, but it was too far away and the flash of gunfire blinded him.

Stopped there in the middle of the street, Grapes's large convoy was an easy target. As the rogue Humvee made its second pass, nearly all its bullets hit their mark, forcing his men to take cover behind their vehicles. Grapes wished he had the night-vision goggles that were back at the military base. He never dreamed they would put up such a fight.

Just then he felt the ground shake. Coming around the corner, a heavily armored Bradley tank rolled over its chains, cracking the pavement.

"The tank's here, Malachi!" Seth cried, elated.

"Have them take out those lunatics once and for all," Grapes growled, pointing to the houses on the other side of the plaza.

The driver of the Bradley nodded. Unfamiliar with the vehicle, he ground the gears a few times before finally getting it in gear. The mammoth tank headed straight for the helots.

The Humvee crossed its path, desperately firing its machine gun at close range, but the big tank's armor was too thick. Then the Humvee's driver made a fatal mistake as he spun around too sharply in an attempt to avoid a blast from Grapes's men. The Humvee skidded and the driver had to slow down to regain control. That left it a sitting duck as the Bradley fired at it broadside.

The blast hit the engine and it exploded, sending shrapnel in all directions. The Humvee's crew ran off in the opposite direction in a hail of bullets. Two of them fell dead in the street. One screamed when a bullet struck his leg.

Grapes cursed at the top of his lungs. The men in the Humvee were white. Could there be more of them, even some of his own men? Suddenly, he didn't feel so safe and powerful. The silent fear of an ambush stealthily seeped into his mind, but he'd come too far to retreat.

The fire from the helots' houses had nearly burned out. From the windows, Molotov cocktails rained down on the Bradley, but the huge tank kept shooting, unfazed, and then launched a quick series of incendiary bombs into the houses. Flames peeked through the windows on the lower floor. Then something exploded in one of the houses. Its roof lifted into the air like a sailor's hat, then crashed to the ground a few feet away. The intersection was strewn with rubble and charred remains.

Helots threw themselves out the windows on the upper floors, their clothes in flames. Grapes's men fired at them as they fell. Their bodies continued to sizzle in the road.

A few ran out the door, wrapped in a thick cloud of smoke, coughing and stumbling.

Grapes spotted some familiar figures among the fugitives and raised his arm. "Hold your fire!" he growled. "Don't shoot, dammit! I want those fuckers alive!"

A group of soldiers surrounded the half-dozen battered survivors. Grapes shook his head incredulously when they were dragged before him and thrown to the ground. "Strangärd, you arrogant Swedish piece of shit. You're one of the fucking Just!"

The Swede raised his head and calmly looked up at Grapes. The gunshot wound on his right leg was bleeding heavily. "Grapes, this is a massacre. Don't do this. You don't have to obey

Greene. You're slaughtering innocent people just to please a crazy old man."

Grapes stared down at him as if he couldn't believe what he was hearing. Suddenly, he burst out laughing, slapping his leg.

"I always thought you were a scumbag, but this is too much!" He leaned down and grabbed Strangärd by the collar, pressing his mouth to the Swede's ear so no one would hear. "You idiot! You think I'm doing this for the Reverend? Don't you realize this is my first step to something bigger? This is my manifest destiny! I'll climb over the bodies of each and every one of those fucking bastards, if I have to. No one can stop me. No one! Hear me? I'm a god of war, you Swedish pussy. You made a big mistake crossing my path."

He cocked his gun and pressed it against the Swede's head. "Your uprising was over before it began." He pointed to the smoldering ruins of the houses. The shooting continued, but it was growing weaker. The better-armed Greens outnumbered the helots and were gaining control. "If it's any consolation, you never had a chance. Now, tell me who your pals are on the other side of the Wall. I want names, addresses, plans. Everything!"

"Eat shit, Grapes," Strangärd spat. "We both know you won't let me live. There's nothing you can threaten me with. So shove it up your ass."

The Aryan stared at the Swede sprawled on the ground. "Have it your way." He pointed his gun at Alejandra and Lucia, who cowered next to Strangärd, their clothes singed, eyes wide in horror. "Seth, take one of those sluts behind the tank."

Seth Fretzen flashed his rotten smile as if it were the happiest day of his life. Out of his jacket pocket, he pulled out some strips of paper. He swiped a strip across the scratches on Alejandra and Lucia's faces and waited a few seconds. His smile grew evil and filled the women with horror.

"They're clean, Malachi. Both of 'em. No sign of the fucking virus."

Grapes waved his gun, as if to say, *I don't give a shit.* He locked eyes with the Swede.

"Names, faggot. I want names."

"Go to hell," Strangärd growled, paler than usual but just as strong as Grapes.

"Suit yourself. Everything that happens from now on is your fault."

Two Greens grabbed Alejandra's arms and lifted her into the air. The Mexican woman kicked and cursed, but she was no match for the Aryans.

"What're you doing?" Lucia cried. "Let her go, you assholes!"

"Don't be in such a hurry, pretty lady," Seth laughed as he dragged Alejandra behind the tank, out of sight. "You'll get your turn. We've got enough for you both."

For a few seconds, Alejandra screamed, struggling with her captors. A punch rang out and her screams trailed off into tearful pleading. Clothing ripped. The sounds they heard next left no doubt about what was happening. The rhythmic beating against the side of the tank speeded up until it reached a climax. A man's voice bellowed and the pounding stopped. All they heard then were Alejandra's sobs.

Seth Fretzen appeared from behind the shield, hitching up his pants, a satisfied look on his face. On the other side of the tanker, the pounding and sobs began again as another Green took his place. Six others waited their turn, a greedy look on their faces.

"Names," Grapes repeated. "Give me what I want or she's next."

Strangärd spat on Grapes's boots. Enraged, the Aryan kicked the Swede in the chest so hard he doubled over.

Strangärd gasped and looked up at Lucia. "Sorry, but I can't do it. They're going to kill us anyway."

The second man was even noisier than the first. As the third guy was unzipping his pants, they heard heavy gunfire approaching fast. The radio in Grapes's Humvee suddenly came alive with excited chatter.

"A column of tanks is rushing through the ghetto—identification unknown!" Seth shouted in alarm.

"Stop them once and for all, for fuck's sake! They're running out of ammo," Grapes replied, annoyed at the interruption.

"The men say they can't," said Seth, suddenly frightened. "They're armed to the teeth and rolled right over our forces. They're headed straight for us."

Grapes raised his head and felt stymied for a second time that fateful night. *Was it an ambush? Did I underestimate those fuckers?* "Where'd they come from?"

"From . . . from . . ." Seth Fretzen hesitated, as if he didn't believe what he was hearing on the radio. ". . . from outside the Wall, Malachi."

The Aryan reeled from the news, but recovered right away. There were more of them than he'd thought. And apparently they had plenty of ammunition.

"OK. Let's give 'em a welcome they won't forget. Spread out around the plaza. None of those sons of bitches gets out of here alive. Seth, move the Bradley into position next to those—"

A huge explosion thundered through the night. Everyone looked toward the horizon in alarm. To the east, on the other side of Gulfport, a huge plume of fire rose in the air. Hot air that smelled of gasoline blasted through the ghetto. Embers flitted among the ruins.

"What the fuck was that?" Grapes's voice cracked. Greene's simple plan was turning into a nightmare full of surprises.

"No idea," Fretzen replied. "It came from the refinery, outside the ghetto—"

"Confirm that by radio, you worthless piece of shit!" Grapes yelled. He was suddenly nervous. He had amassed all the available troops for the final assault on the ghetto. Only about fifty inexperienced militiamen and six Aryan guards protected Reverend Greene. Now there was an explosion on the other side of town. That was not good. No, goddammit, that was not good at all.

From off in the distance came the faint but unmistakable sound of assault rifles. Grapes didn't hesitate. Something big was happening on the other side of the Wall—and protecting Gulfport was his first priority. These helot bastards would have to wait.

"Let's go," he ordered. "Seth, radio everyone to fall back behind the inner wall and get the fuck out. Turn the helots in the truck loose and head for the other side. On the double!"

"Whadda we do with them?" Seth stammered, pointing to Strangärd and Lucia.

Grapes dug his pistol into the Swede's neck. Without blinking, he coolly fired. Strangärd fell dead on Lucia's lap, blood spurting out of the hole in his neck. Lucia screamed as warm blood soaked her clothes.

"Shut the fuck up, bitch," Grapes muttered, pointing his gun at the girl. At that moment, the tank started up and began to move. Alejandra came into view.

She looked terrible. Her clothes were torn, her face was covered in bruises, and blood dripped down her bare thighs. Grapes saw her out of the corner of his eye a second before she threw herself on him, a homicidal rage burning bright in her eyes.

The Aryan jumped aside as he squeezed the trigger. The first bullet hit Alejandra in the shoulder and spun her around like a top. The second bullet went straight into her temple and blew off the top of her head like the lid of a pan. She crumpled to the ground. The whole grisly scene lasted fewer than ten seconds.

Panting, Grapes turned to take out the last survivor. The Aryan cursed at the top of his lungs. Lucia was gone. He looked around, trying to spot her in the darkness, but he couldn't see a thing. Lucia had slipped away when he shot Alejandra.

Grapes cursed himself for letting her get away. He gave the order to head back to Gulfport, and the rest of the soldiers rushed to their vehicles.

She could be hiding anywhere, but I don't have time to look for her.

"I'll take care of you later!" he shouted into the darkness. "You can't hide from me, I'll find you!'

He jumped into his Humvee and it roared to life. The convoy sped through the inner wall, out of the ghetto. Behind him, Bluefont was a sea of flames, death, and pain. Thousands of helots rushed around, frightened and confused. On the other side of town, Grapes and his men would face a very different battle.

4 6

For three hours the North Koreans hid in a dense swamp, half a mile from the Gulfport Wall. Hong's men maintained an iron-clad silence as mist rose off the swamp, enveloping them in lazy wisps of fog. Two squadrons had patrolled the perimeter and confirmed what they'd seen in satellite images. The town was fortified by a concrete wall, strong enough to keep out the Undead, but not Hong and his men.

Their first idea had been to demand the town's surrender. Capturing the town intact would be ideal. That way, they could use it as a starting point for other invasions. But Hong realized he didn't have enough men to defend it. And as he always said, only the weak surrender. Survivors in the new world must be the strongest of the strong.

As the colonel studied the refinery's tower, glowing in the distance, he thought about how his plans had changed. Discovering the town's source of oil was no longer his main objective. His gaze darted to the bottle of milky liquid tucked away in his kit bag. He'd hit the jackpot. With that miracle drug, his country could send an entire army to conquer the world without worrying about infection. Once Hong had the town's fuel supply under his control, the army could leave without delay. All the colonel had to do was find out how the thick, sweet-smelling liquid was concocted. He felt sure he'd solve that mystery soon.

"Is everything ready?" Hong asked Lieutenant Kim. The stern-faced soldier nodded as he climbed up the tree where the colonel was scanning the town through binoculars.

"At daybreak, we'll enter over there," Hong said, pointing to a section of the Wall near the refinery.

Fewer Undead were gathered at that section of the Wall due to the pools of water from the swamp and the refinery. Even so, a couple thousand monsters swarmed the area. Half were in such a pitiful state that the colonel doubted they could go more than fifty paces without falling on their faces. The rest, however, were still active and very dangerous.

"The explosive charges are in place, Comrade Colonel," Kim said quietly, pulling out a small pad to take notes. "The patrols reported very few guards on the Wall."

"Strange," Hong mused. He'd assumed they'd have to take out a lot of guards around the town, but so far they'd only seen a few.

Suddenly the staccato of gunfire sounded in the distance to the right of them. The sound of gunfire grew louder, and then an explosion shook the air, followed by three more in rapid succession. On the far side of town, several fires glowed on the horizon.

At first, Colonel Hong thought they'd been discovered. But the shots sounded far away. Nothing broke the silence of their damp, smelly corner of the swamp.

"What's happening, sir?" Kim looked confused.

"I have no idea, but I don't like it," Hong replied, startled. Fighting was going on inside the town, but he didn't know who was fighting or why.

A more powerful explosion lit up the sky in a giant flash.

"That explosion was inside the Wall, Colonel!" Kim whispered excitedly.

The Undead ambled off toward the shooting. Some took a couple of steps and collapsed, but those in better shape moved along at a steady pace.

"I saw it," said Hong. He had a terrible hunch that someone else was attacking the town. Someone was getting the jump on them. *Could it be the Russians? The Chinese? A European imperialist country? If we found Gulfport, so could they.*

Horrified, the colonel realized someone might cheat him out of his success when he was so close. He had to strike first.

"Kim! Get everyone ready. Rush to that section of the Wall. We're going in now."

"Now?" Kim asked. "But, sir, entering an unfamiliar town at night—"

"If we don't attack now, it'll be too late!" Hong yelled, and scurried down the tree. He knew the risks. *What else can I do? The Politburo might accept a failed mission, but they'd have my head if another power seized the town from right under my nose.*

As the colonel climbed into his tank, his troops fired bombs into a section of the Wall, sending up a muffled explosion. Chunks of concrete and twisted metal flew in every direction. Hundreds of pieces of red-hot iron shot at least fifteen hundred feet over the fence enclosing the refinery. One piece hit a huge storage tank that contained thousands of gallons of refined fuel, piercing the tank's steel and anodized aluminum lining as if it were butter. In a heartbeat, a second explosion rocked the air, engulfing everything within a five-hundred-foot radius in a gigantic fireball.

The fireball didn't reach the North Korean army, but the shock wave rocked the tanks and uprooted the trees they were hiding behind. The Undead twisted and turned in a macabre dance, wrapped in flames.

Now we've lost the element of surprise, Hong thought. *We'll have to rely on our combat skills.*

"Forward, comrades!" he yelled into the radio. "For our glorious country!"

Their tanks thundered across open ground toward the Wall and through the breach. Minutes later, the first Undead showed up. With no one to stop them, hundreds of Undead filtered into the compound in a relentless drip. The last inhabited city in the United States was about to fall.

4 7

It took us only ten minutes to make our way, unopposed, through the double gates in the Wall and into the city compound.

At the Wall, a couple of terrified militiamen ran off when they saw us. Two helots scaled the Wall from the roof of the truck and got the outer gate open in less than a minute. The tank at the rear of the convoy kept the Undead from gaining access to the town.

After closing the outer gate, the helots tried to open the inner gate.

"Open it, for fuck's sake!" Mendoza shouted. We heard shooting inside the ghetto. Every minute meant dozens of lives lost.

"We can't!" yelled one of the helots. "The guards destroyed the controls!"

Mendoza let fly a string of curses. He knew charging the gates wouldn't do any good. They were built to withstand a tremendous impact.

"We gotta blow it open," he said, resigned. "We've only got a few plastic explosives."

"If you're gonna do it, do it now!" Prit urged, visibly worried.

I was worried too. Lucia was somewhere in the middle of that inferno.

Mendoza barked orders, and two helots wedged a small package of C4 into the door's huge hinges. They ran back toward us, unwinding a thin wire behind them. Once they reached our position, they connected a detonator cord and let fly.

The bombs exploded with a dazzling flash, visible for miles. The hinges flew off in pieces. The shattered door staggered like a drunken giant, then fell inside the perimeter of the Wall with a deep groan, sending up a dense cloud of dust.

"How'd you know the door would fall in?" I asked the trigger-man, a kid way too young to be fighting.

"I didn't," he said with a shrug.

I sighed, discouraged. The helots had courage and determination, but their experience and training were nil. I hoped they wouldn't be put to too big a test.

Our convoy drove full speed into the city. The scene was devastating. Houses were burning and sidewalks were littered with dozens of bodies. In the shadows, we spotted groups of people fleeing from us, terrified we were Greene's men.

Mendoza muttered, "Look what those fucking *pendejos* did."

We drove on. A group of militiamen came around a corner. They stared at us for a moment, wondering who the hell we were and where we'd come from. We answered their questions with a hail of bullets. A few survivors fled, but we took out most of them.

"Prit! There!" I shouted as the truck lurched dangerously over a mound of blackened remains.

We entered what had been the central plaza in Bluefont. Flames consumed all the houses on the north side. On the south side, a sea of gleaming copper shells in the road marked the site of some horrific shooting. In the midst of those shells lay two

313

bodies. Someone was kneeling between them—someone I knew well.

I bolted out of the truck before it came to a complete stop and limped as fast as I could toward her. Lucia's expression changed the moment she saw me. She jumped up and ran toward me with the wildest joy I'd ever seen on a human face.

Suddenly I froze, then backed up what seemed like a thousand miles, even though it was just a few feet. "Honey, stay back!" I held up my hand to stop her.

Lucia stopped short, confused. "What's wrong?" She took a step toward me, her arms wide. "You're alive! Thank God!"

"Don't take another step, please." The words stuck in my throat. "I'm infected. I have TSJ. These open cuts could infect you too."

Lucia looked at me for what seemed like an eternity. Very slowly, she walked over and took my hand. The world disappeared. It was just the two of us. No flames or screams or gunfire.

"I can't touch you," I stammered. "I can't kiss you; I can't hold you. I'm alive only because of—"

Lucia pressed a finger to my lips. She looked at me with the tenderest expression I'd ever seen, a mixture of love and commitment. I got weak in the knees. She didn't say a word as she wrapped her arms around my neck and brought her face inches from mine.

"For days I thought you were dead," she said, very slowly. "Every second of every minute of every hour of those days was hell. Worse than hell. It was like being dead in life. I never want to go through that again."

Before I could stop her, she kissed me. The kiss was brief, gentle, and loving, but our saliva mixed.

"Now I'm infected too," she said, calmly. "I choose it voluntarily. If that's our destiny, so be it. I have to live the rest of my life with you, no matter how long or how short, until we draw our last breath. Now we're joined forever."

"Joined forever," I repeated, overwhelmed by her devotion.

We kissed again, longer and more passionately this time. Never, no matter how many years passed, would I taste another kiss like that, there in the desolate ruins of Bluefont.

4 8

Bathed in sweat, the Reverend Josiah Greene woke up and felt for the lamp. Then his hand slid past his Bible to a bottle of Cladoxpan. His nightmare faded as he took a long drink.

He'd dreamed about that damn lawyer. He was riding on a mule, dressed like Jesus Christ with a halo encircling his head. Greene and the rest of the apostles were walking beside him, gazing up at him, but not understanding what was going on. The lawyer suddenly turned and said, "You are the weed in my vineyard, Josiah. You're a snake in the nest. I must cut off your head."

Greene protested and tried to defend himself, but the apostles surrounded him, grim-faced. The Son of God slowly trotted away on his mule. Perched on the mule's withers was a huge orange cat that winked at Greene, smirking.

The apostles—all with Malachi Grapes's face—turned into Undead and devoured him. A black shadow, dark as the deepest night, floated overhead, relishing the scene.

It was just a crazy dream, Greene told himself. But he couldn't shake off the terror that had invaded his body. When he got up to take a piss, pain exploded in his right knee. The reverend screamed and grabbed his leg. It wasn't the familiar pain he felt when something was about to happen. No. This was infinitely worse. A million times stronger. If the usual pain was the flame of a cigarette lighter, this pain was a nuclear explosion.

He dragged himself, cursing, to the bathroom. He lived on the top floor of city hall, in a space renovated to his specifications. There weren't many luxuries: a twin bed, a wooden desk and chair, and a huge crucifix hanging on a wall. A safe was bolted to the floor in a corner of the room. That was all he needed. The Lord provided the rest.

He swallowed a handful of Vicodin to deaden the pain. Then he heard gunfire coming from the ghetto. He'd ordered the "cleansing of the ghetto" that afternoon. A voice told him it was the right time. Those who were not pleasing in the eyes of the Lord must die. Jesus Christ, in His infinite goodness, would allow him to save a couple thousand. They could atone for their sins by doing His work before they died. But that was all. The fire of the archangel Gabriel must lay waste to those sinners, and he was the archangel's instrument. He leaned on the windowsill in the bathroom and waited for the painkillers to take effect, still trembling from his nightmare. It had seemed so real.

A dark foreboding flooded over him. Something really terrible was about to happen. His knee was never wrong. He yelled, louder than he had ever yelled before.

As if fate heard his cries, explosions erupted in the ghetto. *Grapes must be having trouble taking out those helot bastards.*

Grapes. He was getting too hard to control. He was very smart and fanatically loyal, but a streak of madness made him unpredictable. He'd been an effective instrument for the Lord, but his time was coming. Greene told himself he had to get rid of that man. *Maybe an accident. Or poison.* The Lord would show him the way.

As Greene pondered this, a massive explosion shook the building. A huge fireball rose in the sky over the refinery, sending glowing chunks of steel into the air.

Reverend Greene's testicles shrunk into balls of ice. His knee throbbed with a steady beat he'd never felt before. Thump, thump, thump. Like drums at an execution.

Greene shook off those morbid thoughts and went back into his room. He threw on clothes and ordered the guards in the hall to be on alert.

Still half-dressed, he opened the safe. Inside, along with a file crammed with photos that were for the reverend's eyes only and a couple of sacks of precious stones, lay his Colt M1911 and two cartridges. Greene loaded the pistol and stuck it in his jacket pocket. Time to defend his kingdom. The moment had come to be the instrument of the Lord. The black shadow asleep inside of him stirred uneasily.

Hong's tanks made their way through the town like a hot knife cutting through butter. The convoy came up against just a few scattered groups of militiamen in the crossroads. They were no match for the colonel's disciplined troops, who decimated them with insulting ease. Defending themselves wasn't the problem. The damn problem was—they were lost.

In the dark, the city was a maze. They couldn't stop to get their bearings because civilian snipers were firing on them from every direction. Little did those civilians know, a few minutes later, they'd face a far worse threat—wave after wave of Undead.

When his convoy reached an intersection, Colonel Hong grunted in satisfaction. At the end of a long, deserted street flanked by houses, he spotted the ocean. Anchored in port like a sleeping giant floated a huge oil tanker. Its lights were on and sailors prowled the deck. He'd located his target. But that wasn't enough—not anymore.

"Kim, take half the men and attack the port. Seize that ship intact. Capture at least one crew member who can tell us where they got the oil. Start the engines and be ready to sail as soon as the rest of us are on board. We may have to fight our way there, so stay on high alert."

"Yes, sir," Colonel Kim mumbled, worried about the responsibility that suddenly fell on his shoulders. Avoiding the colonel's icy stare, he dared to ask a burning question. "Where are you going, sir?"

Hong held up the bottle of Cladoxpan as if it were a priceless jewel. "I'm going to find the source of this." The colonel could hardly contain his excitement. "When I find it, we'll be celebrated for all eternity."

The helots' convoy sped toward the inner wall. Prit and I were crammed into a garbage truck with Mendoza. At the south bridge into Gulfport, a powerful spotlight shone down on us from one of the massive towers. A figure stood up and shouted into a megaphone. We couldn't make out his words over the roar of engines and the explosions dotting the city, but you didn't have to be a genius to guess what he meant. From the other tower, bullets rattled down on our tanks.

"Let's get 'em!" Mendoza yelled into the radio.

The driver of the tank answered him by ramming the vehicle into the gate that separated Gulfport from the Bluefont ghetto. Unlike the outside gates, it wasn't reinforced. With the first blow, one of its hinges flew through the air, but the second one held fast. From the towers, frightened militiamen started lobbing grenades. One of their grenades slid through the air vent of the tank in the lead. The tank exploded like a piñata full of firecrackers, bringing down the gate. Flames shooting out from the tank sent up thick smoke that curled around the tower, blinding the guards.

That's when panic spread among the militiamen. Grapes's convoy had just whizzed past them in the opposite direction, and they could hear explosions and gunfire coming from the other end of town. On top of that, two hundred armed and angry helots had just blown up their gate. The militiamen took off, racing home to protect their families. Ignoring the four Green Guards in charge, they scattered in a disorderly mess.

In all the confusion, the rest of our convoy crossed into Gulfport. It was the helots' first time on that side. As for me, I was heading back into the lair of those Aryan cocksuckers.

For the hundredth time since the night began, Grapes asked himself, *Is this a nightmare?* What started as a simple operation had turned into a disaster. The "cleansing of the ghetto" was a fiasco, and now some unknown group was demolishing the eastern part of Gulfport. What else could go wrong? With a shudder, he realized he no longer had the upper hand.

He'd positioned a hundred men along the inner wall to monitor the helots' movements. He was sure that the towers on the bridge and the beating he'd given those fucking helots would keep the rest quiet and confined in the ghetto while he dealt with the intruders.

He was counting on one key element to work in his favor: he knew the city better than this new threat, whoever they were.

Redemption Avenue (named Fourth Avenue before Greene arrived) was one of the main roads into town. Grapes knew that the mystery army had blown up the refinery. From there it would have to travel down Redemption to reach the center of town. It was the perfect spot for an ambush.

He stationed four hundred men along both sides of the wide street, hidden behind hedges and on rooftops. Residents were scared shitless when the heavily armed men, covered in dirt and sweat, rushed in and transformed their living rooms into machine gun nests. Down the middle of the road, they placed antitank mines they'd taken from the Seabees' storehouse. And then they waited.

Hong's convoy sped through the streets of Gulfport, sweeping away the weak resistance in its path. It was a very risky blitz; their flanks were completely exposed. But Hong was heeding the call of battle. He'd bet everything on speed. Hit like lightning, destroy the enemy, and get out before the enemy could react. So far, that strategy was working.

A wide street stretched out before them. In the background, he could make out a large, brightly lit building with a giant white flag emblazoned with a green cross. Hong's smile grew wide. That had to be his goal.

A rumble alerted Grapes. He stood up and peered out the hatch of his Humvee, which was hidden behind some tall bushes, and spotted the source of the sound. At the end of the street was a column of heavy vehicles headed up by a tank with a bright red star painted on its side. In the flickering streetlights, the star looked like blood.

The convoy was advancing at full speed. One hundred feet, fifty, twenty, ten . . . Then the first tank ran over a mine in the street.

Hong's BTR-60 shook like a matchbox when the tank in the lead blew up in a blinding cloud of fire and dust.

"Mines!" the panicked driver shouted and swerved.

The BTR rocked violently as it sped around the burning wreck of the first tank. Then another tank ran over a mine and disappeared in a huge flash. Bodies and twisted metal leapt skyward in grotesque pirouettes, and a violent, mottled fire licked at the sides of the other tanks.

"It's an ambush!" Hong shouted. "Circle up and return fire!"

The colonel cursed himself. They couldn't keep going at full speed if they were in the middle of a minefield. They'd have to battle their way through.

The militiamen howled with excitement when the first tank flew through the air. They roared even louder when the second tank set off another mine.

"Kill 'em!" Grapes roared, feeling his confidence reborn. "Kill 'em all!"

Meanwhile, Lieutenant Kim's group made it to the port without a hitch. They entered through a single gate, which stood wide open. The militiamen who should have been guarding it had fled when they saw the convoy of tanks. The BTRs roared up to the ship. Meeting no resistance, Kim and half his soldiers jumped out in the harbor parking lot.

Kim studied the *Ithaca* for a few seconds, mesmerized by its size. He spotted three ramps leading up to the ship, so he divided his men into three squadrons. He led the first group as it stormed the tanker.

The moment he set foot on the deck, he came face-to-face with a very young, very confused red-haired officer.

"Hey! What the hell're you doing here? You can't—" The young officer didn't finish his sentence. A bullet from Kim's Makarov pierced his chest and he collapsed, dead before he hit the deck.

"Let's go! Let's go! Move it!" Kim urged his men.

Shots rang out throughout the ship as the Korean squadrons fought their way into the bowels of the *Ithaca*. The lieutenant had no choice but to divide his squadron into smaller groups. It was the only way to gain control of the entire ship and its miles-long corridors. He had more than one hundred men and the element of surprise in his favor. A handful of sailors were no match for them.

Something hot whizzed past his ear. Kim ducked as a second bullet struck the bulkhead behind his head. The Korean looked up and saw a stocky man with a thick white beard and a captain's uniform leaning over the gunwale on the bridge above him. The man was firing with homicidal rage.

"Look out!" the lieutenant yelled to his men, but the captain's next bullet pierced the head of the soldier next to him.

"Climb up, Lieutenant!" A sergeant pointed to a metal ladder bolted to the tanker's wall.

Kim raced up the ladder to the bridge, followed by a handful of soldiers. As they climbed, the captain picked them off, one by one, and they fell back on the deck.

The lieutenant's lungs felt like they were going to explode. Fear and anger propelled him around the limp bodies and up the last blood-soaked steps.

When Kim broke into the bridge, the captain turned, gripping his rifle. His weapon was unwieldy in such close quarters, but he still opened fire. A bullet hit Kim in the hip, throwing him against the gunwale. The lieutenant grabbed on to anything he could as the captain struggled to load the next bullet.

Kim raised his pistol and fired twice. The first bullet struck the captain in the stomach. The second entered his chest, right below his name tag. The man doubled over, let out a long moan, and collapsed on the deck.

Kim limped over to him. He realized he was the only survivor from his small squadron.

The captain looked up, anger glowing in his eyes. "You . . . yellow . . . bastard," he muttered, his lips stained with blood. Then his head dropped onto his chest and he stopped breathing.

Kim checked the captain's pulse to make sure he was dead, then looked around. He was standing in the doorway to the bridge. He wished he'd taken the captain alive, but he was sure that the ship's charts and a map of its last route were somewhere on the bridge.

The lieutenant was euphoric despite his wound. They were going to make it.

His gaze drifted to the ship's deck. Shooting was heavy at the back of the tanker, but the front of the ship was under their control. The lieutenant saw the soldiers on the bow advancing to the back to take out the sailors who still resisted.

They stopped at a fence that stretched from one side of the deck to the other. Even from atop the bridge, the lieutenant detected his soldiers' confusion.

The commanding officer rammed the fence several times, but it held tight. Then he made a decision. Kim watched helplessly as the officer placed an explosive charge at the base of the fence and ordered his men to back up.

"Noooooo!" Kim yelled, waving his arms in desperation. But it was too late.

About half of the thousands of tons of oil the *Ithaca* had transported to Gulfport were still in the bowels of the ship. Highly flammable petroleum gases took up the rest of the space in the hold. Normally, inert gas filled that space, but the ship's gas exchanger was damaged and there were no replacement parts for a thousand miles.

The charge ripped out a section of the fence. It also blew up a hose connected to a hold filled with petroleum gas. The fire reached that hold half a second after the explosion. The gases, concentrated under enormous pressure, flared like a match, generating a temperature of tens of thousands of degrees.

Before Kim's desperate cry had faded, the *Ithaca* flew through the air in the most gigantic explosion Gulfport had ever seen.

Grapes fired with maniacal fury. Although he and his men had the assholes in the convoy (*Were they Chinese? Japanese?*) pinned down behind their tanks, they couldn't get a clear shot at them.

Grapes had to admit that those yellow assholes were very good. They rebounded quickly from the mines, falling back in an orderly line, returning fire, never wavering, always hitting their target. A tall, gaunt officer moved behind them, shouting orders rapid-fire. Grapes tried to take him out several times, but he was too far away and didn't stay in one place for long.

Those Chink soldiers had tried to flank Grapes's men, but he'd outsmarted them by stationing his men on the side streets to ambush them. But both sides were equally matched at street fighting. They fought dirty, with knives, bayonets, even their fists. Nobody gave an inch.

A burst of bullets hit the Green Guard next to him in the back, and the Aryan fell dead without a word. Grapes's jaw dropped. *Where the hell did those shots come from?*

Grapes hit the ground when a second burst shattered the Humvee's windows and punctured its tires. He whipped around and spotted a group of men wearing white armbands making their way down a side street, firing on the confused militiamen caught in the crossfire. *White armbands. Like the one that fucking Swede had on.*

"Those are the Just!" he shouted. "They're fucking traitors! Shoot 'em!"

His soldiers turned and fired on the Just, who ducked behind a house. The Koreans, as surprised by the new onslaught as Greene, didn't hesitate and started to advance again, firing as they went.

Suddenly a ragtag convoy came roaring up from the far end of Redemption Avenue. It was a strange collection of tanks, garbage trucks, cars, and vans. Each one was spilling over with helots, shouting at the top of their lungs, shouldering their weapons.

The Koreans turned to face the new threat at their back. One soldier fired an RPG at one of the trucks. With a shrill whistle, the rocket raced toward its target and struck its radiator. The truck blew up and a fireball engulfed its crew. The other vehicles swerved around it. The helots jumped out, took cover, and started shooting.

The street was plunged into chaos. In the dark, the four groups attacked each other, not sure who was in their sights. Hong looked in amazement from the soldiers who'd ambushed them to the newcomers firing on that group, then to the scruffy group at other end of the street shooting at everyone. In the turmoil, with enemies running around everywhere, he couldn't tell who was who, so he ordered his men to fire on anything that moved.

"Kim! Kim!" he shouted. Then he remembered that the lieutenant was storming the tanker. Hong let out a string of curses. The situation was getting more complicated by the minute. He had to get his men out or they'd be lost.

How many sides are there? he asked himself as he ran along his thinning lines.

Seconds later, the *Ithaca* burst into a fireball that spread out over a thousand feet. Flames spilled onto the docks, incinerating everything in their path. A sea of fire crossed the road and swallowed up the houses along the dock as if they were made of paper. The monster fire kept advancing, followed by a gigantic tidal wave stirred up by the blast. A boiling, hurricane-strength wind raged ahead of the flames, tearing off roofs, blowing out every window in Gulfport, and overturning cars. The fireball peaked, then folded back on itself, leaving hundreds of burning houses in its wake. The shock wave continued to advance, demolishing everything in its path.

"Who the fuck're you shooting at?" I yelled in Mendoza's ear, but he ignored me. Clutching his M4, white-knuckled, he fired steadily, carefully selecting each target.

Prit crawled to my side, skirting a mountain of broken glass. Dozens of bullets whizzed over our heads and slammed into the truck. The damn thing looked like a sieve.

"This is crazy!" the Ukrainian yelled over the din of gunfire. "It's a free-for-all! If we stay here much longer, they'll kill us! Our flanks are exposed!"

"We have to take out Grapes! Without him, the militia will turn tail and run!"

"Those aren't militiamen out there!" Prit pointed to soldiers in strange uniforms who were attacking a house. "Judging by their uniforms, I'd say they're North Koreans!"

"North Koreans? You're shitting me! Where'd they come from?"

The Ukrainian shrugged and fired at some shapes approaching in the dark.

Suddenly, everything stopped.

First a flash of light blinded us for a moment. Then a volcano of fire shot up above the roofs. Next came the loudest roar I'd ever heard as a roiling windstorm flattened us. That blast of air hit with such force that the houses tilted and creaked. Except for the tanks, every vehicle was overturned. Splinters of wood and concrete rained down on us like shrapnel. I rocketed through the air, along with the hundreds of people around me who'd been swept up in the maelstrom.

I ended up fifteen feet away, my fall cushioned by a bed of flowers. I lay there on my back, trying to catch my breath, as colored lights circled overhead. My ears rang with a shrill whine.

I struggled to my feet, relieved to be in one piece. The only sounds were the crackling fire and houses collapsing after being thrown hundreds of feet in the air. Then I heard the groans of the wounded.

At least half of the men and women who'd been fighting a moment before lay on the ground, dead or so badly wounded they were beyond help. Not far from me, a helot stared in amazement at a piece of pipe protruding from his stomach. The fragment had skewered the guy like an arrow. Everywhere I turned, I saw bodies mangled by the explosion and shrapnel.

"Prit! Prit!"

"Over here," said the Ukrainian, dragging himself out from under a section of a roof. "What the fuck happened?"

"I have no idea, but this is hell!" All the houses were demolished. The surviving civilians who lived in those houses ran out of the ruins into the dark, desperate to reach safety. What none of them knew was that the outer wall had been breached, leaving nothing between them and the Undead.

In the distance, the sky was aglow with what was unmistakably a fire. A really big fire.

"That fire'll devour the town in a hurry," the Ukrainian muttered, brushing off his clothes.

I grabbed my friend by the shoulders. "We've got to get to city hall! That's where the supply of Cladoxpan is. If we don't get one of those fungal cultivars, Lucia and I are screwed! And all the helots, too!"

Prit looked at the distant flames with a pained expression. City hall was backlit by the flames of the approaching fire; the blast of wind had destroyed its roof and shattered all its windows. There was no trace of Greene's flag.

"It's gonna be the race of our lives," he said as he loaded his AK-47. "You ready?"

I nodded, scared shitless but determined.

"Let's go," Pritchenko said with a growl. "See you on the other side."

Grapes rose out of the rubble. All the skin on his forehead was scraped off. A piece of corkscrew-shaped metal had landed just inches from his head. Blood trickled out of his right ear from a ruptured eardrum. He staggered through the ruins to the spot where he'd been crouching until a minute ago.

At first he thought his Humvee was gone; then he spotted it, twenty feet away, embedded in the living room of a house. Most of his men had been holed up in houses, poised for the ambush. Now those houses were piles of burning rubble. Here and there, a dazed militiaman stumbled through the ruins.

Grapes's forces were shattered. His only consolation was that the other groups hadn't fared any better.

Then he detected movement out of the corner of his eye. Two figures were scrambling over upended vehicles. He rubbed his eyes. It couldn't be! But there they were: that goddamn lawyer and his Commie friend. Somehow the fucking lawyer had survived the Wasteland and made it back to Gulfport. There he was, limping along, not fifty feet away. Anger consumed Grapes, crushing the defeated feeling eating away at him. That asshole was not going to make a laughingstock out of him.

Grapes tripped over an assault rifle and picked it up. His eyes locked on the two men as they crossed the Chink soldiers' lines and ran toward city hall. Grapes fired, but the gun didn't go off. Grapes pulled the trigger again and again, until he realized that the blast had destroyed the M4. He threw the gun to the ground in disgust.

He spotted two Green Guards climbing out of the rubble. "Over there! Get 'em!"

The Green Guards looked around, then opened fire. Their delay gave the figure in front enough time to move out of the line of fire. The second figure, whose limp slowed him down, took cover behind an overturned car as bullets took chunks out of the concrete around him.

"Don't let that motherfucker get away!" Grapes roared at his men. "I'll get the other guy!"

He jumped over a pile of bodies and headed for the figure who was running full speed toward city hall.

5 1

Bullets whistled around my head as I curled up into a ball behind an overturned car. We'd almost made it to the far side of the bombed-out battlefield when a couple of militiamen opened fire. I threw myself to the ground as Prit vaulted over a low brick garden wall and out of the line of fire. My old pal looked at me, about to jump over to my position.

"Go on, damn it!" I shouted. "I'll catch up."

He hesitated.

"Prit, one of us has to stay behind and stop those guys, or else they'll nail our asses before we reach the end of the street!"

Pritchenko glanced around and shook his head. He knew I was right.

"Be careful!" he shouted and tossed me the magazine from his AK-47. "I'll be back soon! Hang in there!"

I nodded, wondering how the hell Prit thought I was going to hold out for even ten minutes. But I didn't say anything. Time was the enemy. Flames were leaping out the roofs of the houses next to city hall.

Pritchenko waved, as if to say, *Be cool. Everything'll be OK.* Then he took off running, and I lost sight of him.

5 2

The explosion threw Hong against the side of his tank so hard he cracked a rib. He stifled a howl of pain as he stood up. Out of the hundred and twenty men he'd led into battle, he saw only a handful, most too badly injured to be of any use.

The colonel guessed where that explosion came from, and he knew it meant he'd failed miserably. The mission was over. That defeat was hard for him to swallow.

As he leaned against the tank, staring off into space, he felt a hard lump in his jacket pocket where he had put the bottle of Cladoxpan for safekeeping. All was not lost.

The colonel took a deep breath, leapt to the other side of the tank, then ran in the direction of city hall. Hong was playing his last card.

Mendoza heard the shots and peered out cautiously. Flames lit the street, casting an otherworldly glow over the dozens of bodies strewn everywhere. The fighting had stopped, except for two Green Guards firing at an overturned car.

They were the last of the Greens. The rest were dead or had fled. Mendoza savored the victory. The whites-only city was on fire and he was still alive. The Wrath of the Just had triumphed. Their revenge was almost complete. There was just one small detail left. Screwing up his courage, he hurled himself toward those bastards. Then he'd take care of Greene.

Hong and Mendoza spotted each other at the same time. The Mexican was surprised to see the Korean's uniform, but he didn't miss a beat. He didn't know who the guy was, but he wasn't one of his men. He raised his gun and started firing as he sidestepped the fallen bodies.

Hong picked up his pace without firing. *Closer. I've got to get closer.*

When they were thirty feet from each other, Mendoza's bullet hit the colonel in the shoulder. Hong staggered, more surprised than hurt, but didn't slow down. He raised his Makarov and fired at the Mexican three times in quick succession.

The first bullet went high, but the other two drove into Mendoza's chest and he fell in a heap. His body convulsed a few times and then went limp.

Panting, the colonel stopped and looked at his shoulder. The wound wasn't deep, but he'd need to clean it out first chance he got. Still clutching his gun, he walked up to the Mexican's body and kicked him. *You son of a bitch! You nearly killed me.*

Hong looked away from the body toward city hall. A hundred feet from him, a soldier wearing a green armband was shooting at a wrecked car. The fallen body of the other soldier was proof that his target was a good shot. Hong decided not to bother with them. Let them kill each other. He had more important things to do.

He heard a jingle at his feet. He looked down and saw a couple of metal rings rolling on the ground. A bloody hand gripped his pants leg. *What the hell?*

Carlos "Gato" Mendoza looked up as his life ebbed out of the bullet holes. On his chest lay two deadly grenades with their pins pulled.

Hong paled and tried to take a step back, but Mendoza held tight to his leg.

"*Chinga tu madre*, you bastard," the Mexican mumbled, bloody spittle bubbling out of his mouth in his last act of defiance.

The grenades exploded simultaneously. Their flash was the last thing Colonel Hong saw. He died clutching the broken bottle of Cladoxpan.

Prit crunched through the broken glass that carpeted the lobby of Gulfport's city hall. The curtains fluttered through the broken windows. The fiery wind had blown burning embers through the cracks in the walls. Small fires burned here and there, threatening to come together into a monster fire. Sparks from a transformer lit up the room.

Prit tossed aside the AK-47. It was useless without ammunition. He crossed the lobby, clutching his old knife.

The Ukrainian had no idea where to start looking. The building was huge and time was short. He heard wood beams crash down in one of the offices. The whole building groaned and creaked as the fiery wind wafted inside, inundating everything with the smell of smoke. Just then Pritchenko heard footsteps behind him.

"Well, you finally got here. You almost beat me." He turned, smiling. "I told you to wait—" The words died in his mouth and his smile faded.

In the doorway, Grapes glared at him with a wild look in his eyes, his face covered in blood. He clutched an ax he'd taken off the wall.

"You piece of shit," Grapes growled and moved to the center of the room. "You dirty Soviet midget."

"Nice to see you, too, Grapes." Prit took a deep breath. "You look a little tired."

"The first time I saw you, I knew you had balls." Grapes let out a squeaky, tuneless giggle. "Dammit! We could've had it all. Women, power, wealth."

Prit shifted his knife to his other hand, concealing it as he leaned against the reception desk, never taking his eyes off the Aryan.

Grapes inched slowly, almost imperceptibly, around the seal in the center of the marble floor. "You didn't choose your friends wisely, Russian," he barked with a contemptuous laugh. "Your lawyer buddy is dead by now and you're trapped like a rat. You should've picked a better side to be on."

Prit yawned exaggeratedly. "Are you finished, or do I have to listen to more of your stupid babbling?" he said, feeling the heft of the knife in his hand.

With a roar, Grapes lunged at Prit. He'd tried to distract the Ukrainian and get as close as he could so he wouldn't miss, but Viktor Pritchenko was a sly old dog.

The ax sank into the wooden counter with a sharp crack, exactly where Prit had been standing. Grapes yanked out the blade and attacked again, brandishing the ax like a Viking.

Prit dodged a couple of times, steadily retreating toward the foot of the stairs. Grapes swung the ax in huge, deadly circles in front of him. Each time the blade cut the air with a sinister hum, the Aryan let out a roar. The giant thug came at Prit faster and faster. The little Ukrainian desperately feinted at the last minute. He was running out of room. Armed with only his knife, he couldn't get close to Grapes.

As Prit backed up, he stumbled on the bottom of the staircase that led to the second floor. The Ukrainian lost his balance and grabbed hold of the oak handrail. Grapes saw his chance and brought the ax down toward Pritchenko's arm. Prit threw himself flat on the ground, and a split second later the ax crashed into the railing and sent splinters flying.

Grapes growled as he tried to pull out the blade, but it was stuck deep in the wood. This was the chance Prit had been waiting for. Quick as a snake, he sprang up and drove his knife into Grapes's forearm. The big Aryan screamed and recoiled. There wasn't much room between them, but it was enough for a guy Pritchenko's size to maneuver. The Ukrainian's arm shot forward and buried the serrated blade in Grapes's groin.

The Aryan howled and staggered back, furious. Instead of continuing his attack, Prit crouched, waiting, his eyes fixed on the leader of the Green Guard.

"I'm gonna carve you up, you motherfucker," Grapes gasped. He ran his hand over his face. His vision was blurry and he was really cold. He felt something sticky on his pants. He looked down—they were soaked in blood.

"Your femoral artery is severed," Prit said, his voice ice cold. "You're bleeding out, Grapes. It's over."

No! Can't be! No, no, no, no! The Aryan took a couple of steps toward Prit, but his legs buckled and he fell to his knees. Pritchenko came over to him unhurriedly and grabbed him by the chin.

"Bleeding to death is a painless way to go," he said, squatting beside him. "You drift off to sleep and then it's over. A better death than the hundreds of victims on the trains got. So here's my parting gift to you."

Grapes opened his mouth, but before he could utter a word, Prit plunged his knife into the man's stomach. The Aryan howled in pain and his eyes teared up.

"You motherfucking psychopath," Pritchenko growled, his teeth clenched. He yanked out his knife and plunged it in again, this time skewering Grapes's genitals. "That's for Lucullus, you son of a bitch."

Grapes collapsed in a heap as the pool of blood around him spread. The Aryan stared into Pritchenko's face. The hate-filled gleam in his eyes faded and finally went out.

Prit looked at him for a moment. The Ukrainian rarely enjoyed killing anyone, but this was a special case. He bent over Grapes's body and wiped his knife on the man's shirt. Then he stood and started for the lab.

He didn't hear the shot. He felt like someone had punched him really hard in the back, and then he got hot, very hot. His arms weighed a ton and his legs were like melted sticks of butter. He tried to turn his head as he fell forward, but couldn't.

Pritchenko's body collapsed like a felled oak tree onto the lobby floor. His clenched hand scratched at the ruined parquet floor a couple of times, then stopped.

At the top of the stairs stood Reverend Greene, gripping his smoking Colt, his dark eyes glaring at Prit. A dense, black shadow behind him seemed to draw more life.

One down, one to go. But the second guy had me pinned down. He wasn't shooting wildly; he was saving ammo, waiting for me to pop up and fire.

The Green Guard turned in surprise when he heard the grenades explode. Acting on instinct, I stood up and fired. I emptied half a clip into his chest.

The Aryan spun around in a wild dance, then collapsed. Then everything was quiet on that wretched street. I looked around. No one was standing. The wounded moaned softly and crawled for cover. The ones in better shape crept away slowly. The most seriously injured watched helplessly from where they lay on the ground as the huge fire sped toward them, about to swallow them alive.

I couldn't hang around to help. They'd have to fend for themselves or die trying. I had one thing on my mind as I limped on my broken ankle toward city hall. We had to get out of there. Time was running out.

I finally staggered up the front steps of city hall. Leaning against a doorpost was the headless body of a man thrown there by the explosion. His clothes were so drenched in blood that I couldn't tell which side he was on. At that point, I didn't care.

When I entered the lobby, I froze, paralyzed with shock.

Grapes lay motionless in a huge pool of blood. Next to him another body lay facedown. His hair was unmistakable. *No. Oh, no, please, oh, no, it can't be . . .*

I fell to my knees next to Prit and turned him over. A high-caliber bullet had torn through his back between his shoulder blades and exited out the front. My old friend was covered in blood.

"Prit! Prit, say something! Come on, man, say something!" I was too distraught to think clearly. I whipped off my shirt and tore it into strips to plug up his wound. Those dressings were soaked the minute I laid them on the gaping bullet hole. No way was a shirt going to stop the bleeding. I didn't want to think about Prit's internal injuries.

Prit groaned and opened his eyes a slit. He swiveled his head around until he found me. His skin was freezing cold, but he wasn't even shivering.

"You . . . finally . . . made it . . ." Pritchenko whispered, his voice rising and falling, like a radio signal about to fade out. "You . . . took your . . . sweet time."

"Prit." I choked up as tears welled up in my eyes. "Prit, don't die. Please, don't die."

"Don't think I have a choice . . ." Deep coughs racked his body. Bloody saliva flowed from his mouth and tinted his mustache a sinister red. "You have to live . . . you and Lucia . . . Do it . . . for me." He gripped my hands and fixed his gaze on me. "Promise me you will!"

All I could do was nod. Tears streamed down my face as I gripped Prit's hands.

"Greene . . . is up there." Pritchenko raised a bloody hand. "He did this . . . Be careful . . . OK?" More deep coughs interrupted him. The Ukrainian said in a faint voice, trying to smile, "I . . . told you . . . we'd see each other . . . on the other side."

Pritchenko's face contorted in pain. His body tensed, then went limp, and a peaceful expression spread across his face. Then he was gone.

I don't know how long I knelt there, cradling my friend's body. I know I cried and cursed at the top of my lungs. I dragged his body into the street so his blood wouldn't mix with Grapes's, and propped him up against a car, his skin so pale, his hair falling in his eyes. I ran back into the burning building, muttering over and over, "Greene, you're a dead man."

5 5

City hall was now an inferno. Sparks blew in through gaping holes in the shattered windows and fell on papers strewn everywhere. Flames shot up from those papers almost instantly. Parts of the building were already ablaze. What had briefly been my office was a cauldron of fire.

I ran toward the passageway that led to the old bank building where the labs were. The smoke was getting thicker and I couldn't stop coughing. My throat was as dry as sandpaper, and it was getting harder and harder to breathe. But the flames hadn't reached the passageway, so fresh air still streamed in through broken windows there.

I reached the guard post where Green Guards had stood watch what seemed like a lifetime ago. Their girly magazine still lay on the floor. I trampled it as I eased inside the lab.

In the first room, I came upon the body of a middle-aged woman in a lab coat; she'd had the misfortune to be on the night shift. She'd been shot once in the heart and once in the forehead, mafia-style. *Whoever did that knew what he was doing.*

The next body was Dr. Ballarini's. The Italian wore a trench coat over his pajamas. When he heard the shooting and the explosion, he must've jumped out of bed and run in to protect his precious lab. Someone had stopped him along the way. The scientist's execution was messier, less professional. He had a huge hole in his stomach. His face was twisted in surprise, as if he couldn't believe he was dead. One of his slippers lay three feet away. There were drops of blood on the toe.

I heard metallic clangs coming from the floor below. I cocked the AK-47 and descended the stairs to the old bank vault. The overhead light blinked a few times, then dimmed. The backup generator automatically kicked in. I crept the last few feet in silence and looked around the door of the chamber.

There was Greene. With him was a beefy Aryan, his arms the size of hams. He was whacking away at the steel vats where they fermented the Cladoxpan.

He'd already broken all the vats except two; a small lake of medicine covered the floor and trickled down a drain. Greene watched with a fevered look on his face. His gun was in one hand and in the other was a metal bucket that held that white, knobby brain-sized thing that was the planet's salvation. The reverend planned to destroy all but that one fungal cultivar.

The guard finally managed to overturn the vat; it fell over with a big clang. The Cladoxpan spilled out in a huge wave that splashed almost to the men's waists, before rushing down the drain and out the door. I formed a bowl with my hands, plunged them in the little river as it passed by me, and took some greedy sips.

The liquid burned my throat. It was more concentrated than I'd ever tasted. The adrenaline rush was brutal and I felt dizzy. The cuts, bruises, and burns dotting my body stopped hurting as if by magic. When the effect passed, the pain would come back a hundredfold, but right then I felt great.

I planted myself in the doorway. At first, they were so busy attacking the last vat they didn't see me. Then Greene grabbed his right knee as if he'd been hammered by a horrible pain and turned, wide-eyed.

"You!" he shouted.

"Yeah, it's me . . ."

I shot the guard before he could grab the Beretta he'd set on a shelf. The first bullet hit him in the leg and he fell to the ground. The second tore through his heart.

I turned to Greene. The reverend was trembling in fear and anger as he relived his terrifying nightmare, unable to tear his gaze from me. He thought he was seeing a ghost. He aimed his huge Colt at me, his hands shaking.

"You're the spawn of Beelzebub," he said in a guttural whisper. His Stetson hat had fallen off and his hair was a tangled mess. "You're the Devil, the Antichrist, an abomination in the eyes of the Lord! It's time for you to join Satan forever!" Then he pulled the trigger.

At that moment, the generator flickered for the last time and the lights went out. I threw myself to the ground as a ghostly flash from Greene's gun lit up the room, and the bullet whizzed by like an angry wasp, just inches from my head. From the ground, I fired blindly, hitting the reverend in the arm. He screamed in pain and dropped the Colt. He bent to pick it up, but I was already on my feet.

In a homicidal rage, I jumped on Greene so hard he fell backward. The preacher's hands clawed at my face, his jaws snapping furiously as he tried to bite my neck.

"You can't kill me! I'm the Prophet! *I AM THE PROPHET!*"

The last vat of Cladoxpan was right next to us. I grabbed Greene by the lapels and lifted him up the way a cat shakes its kitten.

"You're not the Prophet," I hissed in his ear. "You never were, you crazy son of a bitch."

Greene looked at me with terror in his eyes. His right leg had not stopped shaking throughout the fight. Then suddenly it was still. "It stopped hurting," he murmured in disbelief. "That can't be . . ."

"Well, this'll really hurt, you bastard." And I plunged his head into the vat.

The reverend struggled wildly, trying to surface so he could breathe. I held him tight as the Cladoxpan spilled over the edge. After a while, his body stopped writhing.

I collapsed on the floor, panting. I should've felt good. I'd killed the man who infected me, who took Pritchenko's life, and who convinced thousands of people to follow him in that orgy of pain and destruction against their fellow human beings. But all I wanted to do was close my eyes and rest.

A loud boom sounded overhead. Something on the floor above had collapsed. The air was very hot and I smelled smoke. I struggled to my feet and picked up the ax the guard had used to destroy the vats. I went back to Greene, raised the ax over my head, and, with one blow, decapitated the old man.

"Let's see you come back from the dead now, asshole."

I slung my rifle across my back and darted out of the vault with the bucket in one hand and the reverend's head in the other. The corridor was pocked with small fires.

I climbed the stairs through the stifling heat and rushed from the burning lab back over the passageway and through the lobby of city hall. Blinded by the smoke, I felt my way down the front steps. When I finally got outside, I collapsed to my knees and threw up.

Flames were slowly engulfing Gulfport. Only the Bluefont ghetto was spared from the fire's fury, thanks to the channel that formed a natural barrier.

I raised the reverend's head to eye level. His face was frozen in anger and his mouth hung open, baring his old, worn teeth. I spat in his eyes, swung his head over my head, and cast it into the inferno that city hall had become. Moments later, Greene's head disappeared into that enormous pyre, black smoke rose above the flames, and I heard an inhuman howl. The smoke twisted and turned with a life of its own.

The roof came crashing down as a sea of fire washed over everything.

5 6

PONTEVEDRA, SPAIN
SIX YEARS LATER

I drove the Jeep SUV slowly through the bushes and weeds that had grown up through cracks in the pavement. Most of the houses were weather-beaten, and some were on their last legs. Aside from that, not much had changed. As we drove, crushing piles of rotting, bleached bones under our tires, I pointed out landmarks to Lucia, as excited as a child to be back.

We finally came to an intersection and turned left. I could barely make out the paint a long-dead soldier had sprayed there years before, during the evacuation.

I stopped the car and turned off the engine, but I couldn't get out. There were too many memories.

"Is this it?" Lucia asked softly, putting her hand on mine. She was very pregnant, so we'd need a place to settle down—soon. At least for a few months.

I nodded, choked up. My house. I was home.

"Are we there yet?" asked a high-pitched voice in the back-seat.

"Yes, Viktor, we're here." Lucia turned around. "But wait until Daddy opens the door before you get out." Little Viktor shot us a mischievous look and nodded. He was a calm, alert boy with his mother's vivid green eyes.

"Is that where we're going to live?" he asked, wrinkling his brow. "I don't like that house. It's old and dirty."

I laughed and tousled my son's hair. "Don't worry, there're plenty of empty houses. We can live anywhere in the city, I promise. But Daddy wants to pick up something."

I got out of the car as Lucia checked that our Cladoxpan starter had enough water. Caring for that strange fungus has been part of our daily routine for so many years now.

I walked up to my house with a heavy heart. How many years had it been? Eight? Nine? I still recognized every brush-stroke in the paint. Even the smell was familiar. We were back.

A ball of orange fur shot past me. Lucullus didn't move as fast as he used to, but he could still zip around when something interested him. He meowed, switching his stump of a tail, and looked at me questioningly.

"You remember this place, don't you, buddy?" I whispered as I petted him.

It was the end of a very long journey. It had been six years since we left the ruins of Gulfport. Six years of constant travel, meeting small groups all over a world that was slowly rising from the ashes.

But the world was still a dangerous place. No one had seen or heard of any Undead for over four years, but not all human groups were friendly or peaceful. Little by little a precarious new social order was falling into place, but it couldn't hold a candle to what the world was like before the Apocalypse. The Second Middle Ages, some called it.

On top of that, the TSJ virus still circulated through the veins of many survivors. For some mysterious reason, little Viktor was immune, even though Lucia and I were infected. When transmitted from mother to child, TSJ mutated and lost all its virulence. In a few generations, it would be just a bad memory.

The door was still open, the way I'd left it years ago. I carefully entered. Lucullus shot like a rocket to the backyard where he'd spent so many good times.

My house was a mess. A family of foxes had made its den in my living room. A water pipe had burst on the second floor, ruining the rugs. The furniture smelled musty and the paint was peeling off the walls, but I was happy to be home.

I went into the living room and opened the top drawer of the china cabinet. There, in a plastic sleeve, were my family's photo albums. My last link to the past.

Lucia and little Viktor came in behind me, holding hands. My son looked at everything with curiosity—and caution. He knew that a dilapidated house could be dangerous. Children of this new world knew things that generations of children before the Apocalypse hadn't.

"What next, Manel?" Lucia rested her head on my shoulder. "Where're we going next?"

"I honestly don't know. But it doesn't matter."

We were alive. We'd survived the toughest test of humanity. The world was ours.

ACKNOWLEDGMENTS

After a journey of three years and a thousand pages, it's hard to acknowledge all the people who made this adventure possible.

First, thanks to the hundreds of thousands of anonymous readers online and the tens of thousands who followed. Your word of mouth turned a little story of a frightened survivor into this trilogy. I'm lucky you gave me such a boost. Thanks for paving the way.

A big thank-you to everyone at Plaza & Janés Editores for your patience, understanding, and unflagging support. You've been a great team, from beginning to end, and have made this trip easier and more enjoyable. A special thanks goes to my editor, Emilia Lope. Thanks for having confidence in me, Emi.

To Sandra Bruna, my agent, and her fabulous team in Barcelona for putting up with my ramblings and getting this story read in so many countries and in so many languages.

To Juan Gómez-Jurado, outstanding bestselling author, but above all, my friend. You've been my guiding light. I always learn something new from you. And to his wife, Katuxa, for stoically putting up with two writers camped out in her living room.

To Freskor Itzhak in Berlin, and Manuel Soutiño in Santiago de Compostela, Spain, for showing up at the right time and solving problems with the power of a cyclone. To Aurora and Manolo, for giving up their home in that beautiful, remote corner of Galicia so I could finish this book.

To my family, for their patience and support. My parents—steady as a rock, an island in the middle of a storm—and my tenacious, smart sister, who continue to be the pillars of my life.

And of course, to Lucia, my wife, my first reader and harshest critic. Every time I look at her, I understand why men risk death for the sake of a woman with a smile on her lips.

Now brace yourself. The journey has just begun.

ABOUT THE AUTHOR

An international bestselling author, Manel Loureiro was born in Pontevedra, Spain, and studied law at the Universidad de Santiago de Compostela. After graduation, he worked in television, both on-screen (appearing on Televisión de Galicia) and behind the scenes as a writer. *Apocalypse Z: The Beginning of the End*, his first novel, began as a popular blog before its publication, eventually becoming a bestseller in several countries, including Spain, Italy, Brazil, and the United States. Called "the Spanish Stephen King" by *La Voz de Galicia*, Manel has written three novels in the Apocalypse Z series. He currently resides in Pontevedra, Spain, where, in addition to writing, he is still a practicing lawyer.

ABOUT THE TRANSLATOR

Pamela Carmell received a Translation Award from the National Endowment for the Arts to translate *Oppiano Licario* by José Lezama Lima. Her publications include Matilde Asensi's *The Last Cato*, Belkis Cuza Malé's *Woman on the Front Lines* (sponsored by the Witter Bynner Foundation for Poetry), Antonio Larreta's *The Last Portrait of the Duchess of Alba* (a Book-of-the-Month Club selection), and the short-story collection *Cuba on the Edge*. Her translation of poetry by Nancy Morejón is forthcoming. She is also published widely in literary magazines and anthologies. This is her third translation for Manel Loureiro's internationally bestselling Apocalypse Z series.